W9-CFY-254

Owen Brookes

INHERITANCE

PUBLISHED BY POCKET BOOKS NEW YORK

POCKET BOOKS, a Simon & Schuster division of
GULF & WESTERN CORPORATION
1230 Avenue of the Americas, New York, N.Y. 10020

ISBN: 0-671-41398-8

First Pocket Books printing February, 1981

10 9 8 7 6 5 4 3 2 1

POCKET and colophon are trademarks of Simon & Schuster.

Printed in the U.S.A.

This novel is dedicated to the memory of

JOHN KNOWLER

whom I valued as a friend, admired as a writer, and whose idiosyncratic editorial brilliance can never be replaced.

PART ONE

"WHAT GAME WOULD YOU LIKE TO PLAY TODAY, Peter?"

He had not heard them approach, but the soft, indulgent voice did not startle him. In a way that he did not understand, they were expected. When he was with them it was difficult to think, to question or recall. Had he planned to meet them, gone in search of them? His thoughts snapped against a mental wall. That is how he thought of it: an old, weathered wall. Yet there was another part of him that *had* to glance down at the lake, which appeared only as a shimmer of light through the densely packed trees.

"Ah," Carl said, and stepped softly toward him on the carpet of pine needles.

"The lake," Linda said, following Carl, her voice an echo of his.

It seemed that they both understood, and Peter, excited, turned his head to look at them. Tall and beautiful, they stood close behind him, staring over his head. Their vision was not fragmented by the trees. Twisting his head farther, Peter saw the others, standing a way off in the gloom. Grizzle, with her impassive face and lumpen body. Reggie's cold eyes, which

3

reminded Peter of the fish he pulled from the lake, were slightly hooded.

Linda put her pale hand lightly on his shoulder. Carl's grip was stronger, tighter. Obediently, Peter faced the lake again.

The ground sloped steeply to the black water's edge where he had moored the boat. He had climbed to this point with difficulty, his feet slithering among the dried needles so that he frequently had had to grasp a low, pliant branch, or haul himself along by the slim, rough-barked trunks of the trees. They stood on a sort of shelf or plateau. Behind them, the ground rose again and the trees darkened.

Peter looked down, down the slope which became precipitous, then sheer, then liquid. The air was clammy, like wet silk. The already dim light became complete darkness, a black mist, lapping. He floated free, his eyes adjusting to the murk. Unexpected shafts of light revealed darting, shadowed forms. He was gently descending and rising. Something swam past him, something monstrously large. A pike, disappearing into the darkness with a single flick of its long, sinuous body. He felt something pulling him, then something compelling his own, floating body forward. It seemed that he turned and somersaulted like a free-falling sky diver. He kicked out with his legs, pushed his arms forward, and drew them back. He was a strong swimmer and now the current aided him. He was propelled through the water at great speed, and yet there was time to absorb everything. It was, he thought—and thought that he should remember this— both fast and slow at the same time. Such attempts to rationalize, hang on to the sensations, were always dangerous: like the time they had shown him fire and he, marveling at the beauty of the flames, had dared to wonder why he was so cold, only to feel his skin scorching, blistering. Now he felt his lungs bursting. He threshed in panic, knowing that he had been underwater too long. The need for air was intolerable. He struggled to rise up, toward the light and air. Then he was distracted and the panic, the need, left him as swiftly as it had come.

The pull of the current was strong and almost hurled him against a half-clogged and rusted grille. Leaves, weeds, and silt blocked and adorned it. Beyond was blackness, a cold rushing blackness which filled him with fear. The weight of water pressed him against the grille. He knew, as his hands clasped the rough and rusted metal, that he had to open this underwater gate and that he was not strong enough. He pulled against the current, against the weight of entrenched metal.

Open it. You must open it. Pull hard. Now.

The voice was everywhere, in the water, in his head. It calmed him, for it was both confident and insistent. He pulled with all his might, throwing his body left, out of the main tug of the current. And the gate, like a gate in a dream, swung with him, slowly, soundlessly. Weed and silt rose up, clouding his vision, darkening everything. But the gate was open.

He was aware of the silence. There was no breath of wind that afternoon to make the trees all around him rattle and sigh. His hands hurt. Blinking, he held them out in front of him. They seemed huge against the unsettled perspective of the slope, which gradually altered, came once more into proper focus. There were red weals across his palms.

"Oh, your poor hands," Linda said, taking his left hand in both of hers and stooping to inspect the damage.

"That's nothing," Carl said, squeezing his shoulder. "We'll soon put that right. Okay, Peter?" Carl turned away, began to walk between the trees.

"Yes, we'll soon fix you up," Linda agreed. Her arm was light and bony on his shoulders. He wanted to be brave and not make a fuss.

5

"It's all right," he said. His head hurt slightly with the warning of a headache.

"Of course it is. Come on."

Guided and steadied by Linda, he trailed after Carl. Behind them, the others followed. Grizzle moved gracelessly. Reggie shoved her in the back and she protested. Their voices—Grizzle's gruff and petulant, Reggie's singsong teasing—made the most normal and reassuring sound in the world, that of children squabbling.

Pamela glanced up at the sound of their voices. It still surprised her how far and clearly sound carried here, as though the lake acted as an amplifier. It was particularly startling on such a calm and deeply silent afternoon. She smiled. A shout bursting into laughter allayed that lurking, irrational fear which always gripped her when Peter was out of sight, away from her. She stared across the water in the direction of the voices, but could not see the children. It surprised her, too, how quickly Peter had made friends with the youngsters from Home Farm. She felt, in spite of the many cuts and scratches and blisters he seemed to collect when he was with them, that he was in safe hands. Apart from anything else, they were older than Peter and therefore, she felt, more reliable. Indeed it was hardly accurate to call them children at all. Pamela was vague about their precise ages, but certainly Carl and Linda were virtually grown up, yet they seemed to feel none of that impatience with younger kids that she could remember so clearly from her own adolescence. She was grateful that Peter was not made to feel like a nuisance, was not shut out as she had often been. They were remarkably tolerant, especially if, as she privately suspected, Carl and Linda were in love.

The voices were silent now. Her eyes adjusted to the glare and made out the dim shape of the rowboat where Peter had left it. The lake was so still that the boat did not move at all. The tie rope dipped into the water, then reemerged to be swallowed in shadow. Pamela hoped that he had fastened it securely. She hoped that he would not go too far, get too tired and try to row back, exhausting himself. Her hands gripped the edge of the board on her knees so tightly that her fingers ached. She looked down at them and, taking a deep breath, extended each finger in turn. It was a trick, one of many she had begun to practice, to make her relax. It was for Peter's sake. And she thought again that she was glad he had made friends, glad that he was growing stronger and more independent. Scrapes and bruises were a necessary part of a boy's growing up. She must not smother him, cling to him. Looking at her hands, now limp and hanging loosely over the edge of the board, Pamela permitted herself a small, cautious pat on the back. She was getting better. She was keeping the promises she had made to herself.

A year ago she could not have considered renting a house by a lake, even though Peter had been taught to swim years ago and had, until recently, swum twice a week, summer and winter, in London. She *had* hesitated about the boat, but only for a moment. He was a strong swimmer. The lake was so placid that even her imagination could not turn it into a plausible danger. True, she had been alarmed when Peter first told her about his new friends, but instead of forbidding him to have anything to do with them, she had forced herself to walk to Home Farm, introduce herself, and look them over. That had cost her a considerable effort, for she was not comfortable with people and lacked social confidence. But she *had* done it. She had reported it all to Elsa in her weekly letter and had been grateful for her reply. "Progress," she had written, "is measured in these small steps, taken one at a time. To many they may seem trivial, but you and I know that they are triumphs."

It was to Elsa and to this place that she owe

7

"recovery." (Elsa said that was too strong a word since it implied illness, a breakdown. Pamela had simply been overanxious and confused.) Ian found the place gloomy and, objectively, Pamela could see what he meant. She could see how it might appear gloomy if you found the press of trees accentuated by the steepness of the hills surrounding the lake oppressive. To her this sense of being at once surrounded and cut off was comforting. It was a safe place. That, too, was a sign of progress. It was a long time since she had been able to appreciate spontaneously and without a sense of threat that there were two or more ways of "seeing" a place, interpreting a situation. Although it had been a gray, overcast day when she had first come here, she had been certain of it at once. Inwardly, she had perceived it as it was now, in high summer, with the impenetrable black-green veil of the trees spilling down to the water which, in these windless conditions, had the appearance of a tautly stretched sheet of oiled plastic. The far ends of the lake, the opposite bank where the boat was moored, were black and dull, but the greater, central part was a dazzling silver beneath the sun, a vast mirror. And beyond, only a short walk away, was the more familiarly English park with its squat oaks and the fallow, rather unkempt fields of Home Farm. A perfect place for a boy to grow, for Pamela to relax and grow confident again.

It hardly seemed possible now that she had panicked when Elsa had first suggested she take Peter away, out of London, for the whole of the summer holidays. She remembered a branch, laden with pink blossoms, rattling against the window in the spring breeze. The cold, ugly sweat on her hands. Elsa's large, immobile head dimly silhouetted against the light which suddenly pained Pamela's eyes. She could not manage without Elsa. Surely her greatest fear, the very reason she spent two hours a week sitting in that room, would be exacerbated if she was to be cut off somewhere, entirely alone with Peter. Besides—and she could remember how she had clutched at this thought with relief—Ian would never agree. What Elsa proposed was exactly the sort of holiday that Ian detested. And she couldn't possibly organize it all herself. She would not know how to begin.

"That is precisely why I suggested it," Elsa had replied in her slow, steady voice which bore now only the faintest trace of an accent. "This way you will learn many things, Pamela. That you are capable of making decisions and arrangements. That you do not need to use your husband as an excuse. Above all, to trust yourself to be with Peter and set him free."

At that moment Elsa had unclasped her hands, large, ugly hands which made an eloquent gesture, as though releasing a fragile bird.

"You must take it slowly," the reassuring voice had continued. "Step by step. I will help you. And I suggest that you start straightaway."

"But how . . . what will happen to my sessions?"

Pamela had heard the panic in her own voice, could still feel the dryness of her mouth, the wetness of her hands.

"You will write to me. It will be just like keeping the journal. Once a week you will write to me."

Swallowing painfully, she had whispered, "And you'll reply?"

"I shall reply, of course." She had folded her hands together again, indicating that the time was up.

Outside, in the gritty London wind, Pamela had cried. She was being forced out too soon. Too much was being demanded of her. She did not know where to begin, and even now she was uncertain where she had found the courage to make these plans.

Perhaps from Peter, to whom she had mentioned it casually that same afternoon when she fetched him from school. "Somewhere really in the country? For months and months? Oh, can we really, Mommy? *Please?"*

Or from Ian, who had said that it would suit him perfectly. But not too far away, so that he could come down for weekends, perhaps for a whole week if things slackened off. He wanted to be with them? He had not given up entirely? Pamela had clamped her mouth shut, did not ask the questions which would only make him irritable. And because she had not trusted herself to speak, she had simply shaken her head when he had casually offered to help with the arrangements.

Or from a naked, defenseless desire to please Elsa, on whom she had come to rely as totally as Peter once relied on her?

Probably a little bit of each, Pamela thought, and smiled because Elsa would say that it was all her doing, that the courage had always been there, in her. It had taken courage, amazing courage, to do the very things that had made Elsa's help necessary.

The smile faded. Pamela looked at her hands and at the forgotten drawing fixed to the board on her knees. It was a botanically precise, academic study of a field poppy, and she was pleased with the drawing. She had just begun to color it when she had been distracted by the children's voices floating across the lake. The bright orange had dried and in drying had faded. It was too pale. She looked from the drawing to the poppies she had gathered that morning and placed in an old preserve jar, which now stood on the table before her. Some of the largest petals had fallen, unnoticed. The others looked wilted and shriveled, yet their color was still more vibrant, more living than her faded copy of it. The brush she had been using lay on the table. She did not remember putting it down. The sun had dried the little puddle of orange she had mixed in the china palette of her watercolor box. She set the board aside. She could do no more today. Perhaps Peter would help her find more poppies in the morning. Pamela half closed her eyes, reducing the poppies to a blur of color, an abstract shape—that she could paint, free and splashy, but it was part of her therapy to learn to paint precisely, with complete fidelity. Part of her therapy, but of her own devising. Once she had taken that first step, Pamela had begun to impose her own rules, to embroider and flesh out the skeleton of this summer.

She had been afraid that Elsa would expose all her plans as mere attempts to provide herself with safe-guards, but Elsa had only nodded, made a gesture of releasing the bird again, and said, "You see?"

Dear Elsa. Pamela leaned back in her chair so that the sunlight penetrated beneath the brim of her hat, dazzling her with its glare and warmth. She concentrat-ed on her shoulders, willing the tension out of them. She pushed out her legs, brown from the sun, made to seem darker by her white cotton skirt. Through nar-rowed eyes she looked at the house. She still did not know how to describe it, what to call it. It was not a cottage, though part of it was built with old, weathered stone. The French windows and veranda gave it the look of a seaside chalet. Insofar as it consisted of only one floor, it *was* a bungalow, but the wooden roof and fancy timbering made it more like a log cabin, set into the hillside. The present owner of Halford Hall, which lay beyond, grand and emptily imposing in the park, had leveled the ground, created a terrace on the hill, and cleared a wide swath of trees right down to the lake. The felled wood had been used to build the house, the veranda, and the small landing stage which jutted into the lake. Shallow steps had been cut into the reddish earth and each one was shored up with more of the razed wood. The house had been built because of the view. The trees pressed close against the back of it, encroached right up to the far end of the veranda, and surrounded the ugly patch of tarmac which flanked this side of the house. Her car was parked there. A smooth, narrow driveway led between the trees and joined, eventually, the much older, grander drive of Halford Hall itself. Earlier, Pamela had carried the little white wicker table from the veranda and set it on the hard-baked earth that could have been, but was not, a garden. And that was where she sat, her mind drifting, her body growing limp with sunshine.

At night, when there was a wind, the trees, all conifers, sighed and sang, rattled against the wooden roof, the many windows. Pamela loved the sound they made. Lying in bed, hanging between sleep and wakefulness, she would imagine herself perched in their topmost branches, lulled by their strong swaying. Sometimes when there was a wind there were little waves on the surface of the lake, which then seemed more than ever protected by the hills and trees. Then, on other days, the wind would blow up suddenly, snatching at her hat and skirt, yet the lake would remain undisturbed. Only when the wind blew straight down the cleared slope was the lake affected. Pamela thought it was sad that the present owner, Mr. Appledore, had not been able to enjoy the house he had so carefully planned and built. It was her good fortune that he had been called back to America, and therefore was prepared to let the place. Not for the first time she wondered if he would be willing to sell it. Her hands tightly gripped the arms of the wicker chair. There was a precedent: he had sold off Home Farm. Could she ask Ian? Could they afford it? Would he even consider it? There was no point in approaching the estate agents, no matter how vaguely, if Ian was opposed to the idea. And he would never consider it. He had taken one look at the house and pronounced it an architectural monstrosity. Of course he was right. But he had also said, with a rare show of gruff, embarrassed kindness, "Still, if you like it . . ." Adding as an afterthought: "And Peter. That's all that matters."

So perhaps she would ask him this weekend, just mention it, casually. Slowly, she made her hands loosen their sharp grip. She *could* ask him. Now, here in the sun, it did not seem so very daunting. She closed her eyes completely.

"Honestly, you kids!"

The words were cross ones, but he knew from the way Regina said them that she was not angry. She held her fingers tightly, looking at his palm.

"And why is it always Peter, eh? You lot ought to take better care of him. He's younger than you."

She dabbed sticky pink, bad-smelling ointment on his newly washed hands. The pain grew sharper for a moment, like a nettle sting, then faded magically away.

"I don't know what your mother'll say," she continued, seizing his other hand and applying the ointment. "I wouldn't be surprised if she doesn't say you're too rough with him," she told the others.

Peter felt himself blush. It was true. It was the sort of thing his mother did say and it embarrassed him to hear it repeated by Regina.

Reggie snorted. Peter stared at Linda who was braiding her hair with thin, nimble fingers.

"Oh, don't go on, Ma," Carl said, putting an earthenware pitcher of homemade lemonade on the big, scrubbed pine table.

"You especially ought to know better," she retorted, pushing past Carl and taking glasses down from an old Welsh breakfront. "What's your excuse this time?" she asked wearily. She was looking at Peter and pushing her thick hair back from her face with an unexpectedly bony wrist. She was a big woman, not fat, but heavy. There was a roundness, a fullness about her which was accentuated by the long, foreign-looking dress she wore. In fact, her legs were surprisingly slim and shapely. When she wore short skirts Peter wondered how such elegant legs could carry the weight of her large torso and heavy head with its mane of dark, wiry hair. "I'm talking to you, young man," she said, leaning toward Peter. She smelled of spice and had very dark eyes, like Carl, though hers were far more glittering and sort of piercing. Staring into them, he could not remember the question, let alone the explanation.

"It wasn't our fault anyway," Reggie said, sulky.

"Oh?" She cocked her head inquisitively, transfixing Reggie with her look. Although Peter could not see the boy, who stood behind him, he could feel his embarrassment. Reggie shuffled his feet on the kitchen flagstones.

"That's right," Carl said smoothly. "He rowed across the lake, to the steep side. You can't walk up there. He had to pull himself up. You know how rough the bark of those trees is." He poured the lemonade. Even the sound of it was cool.

"Not to mention the pine needles," Linda added, twisting a small elastic band on the shiny end of her pigtail.

Peter remembered then.

"That's right," he said.

He remembered his feet slipping, then pulling himself up. And he remembered something else, but not quite. He could see them, standing on the plateaulike shelf, in shadow, waiting for him. But there was another thing he couldn't quite remember, that made his head hurt.

"I'm glad to hear it," Regina said, and he could feel the others relax, as if they were all joined together. She pushed a glass of lemonade toward him and he picked it up carefully, holding it with the pads of his fingers because of the ointment on his palms. "Even so, you lot, remember what I said."

Carl and Linda exchanged glances. Linda chewed the end of her braid to keep from giggling. Peter smiled at her. It was nice here, and yet he never felt quite comfortable. The uncomfortable part had to do with Regina. He couldn't, for example, get used to calling her by her name. She was older than his mother, and

14

yet they all called her Regina, except Carl, sometimes, when he wanted to butter her up. Also, she had a way of saying cross things without being cross, kind things without being kind. There was no doubting her authority—indeed Peter was a little bit afraid of her—yet he had never seen her exercise it. And then he didn't like the way she spoke about his mother, as though she knew all about her, when really she didn't know her at all. Most of all he didn't like the way she spoke differently to them. It was difficult to put a finger on, but when she spoke to his mother, she never said "my lot" or "the kids." She spoke of "the children" and what a nice boy he was and how he was always welcome. Only he didn't feel welcome, not really. She was always trying to be kind to him, but he felt awkward with her.

"What's the matter? Got a headache?"

She rested her warm palm on his forehead, brushed the blond hair back. He squirmed away from her touch. That was another thing. She was always touching and knowing things when he hadn't said them.

"Too much sun," she said, ruffling his hair. "You'll live."

"Stay to tea. Can he, Regina?" Reggie pressed down on the back of Peter's chair, lifting his feet off the floor.

"If he wants."

He didn't like the way she had of speaking about him as though he wasn't there, either.

"No. I'd better get back," he said, but he couldn't stand up because Reggie was still tilting the chair, pressing his legs against the edge of the table.

"It's gingerbread men," Reggie said. "Come on."

And the smell of ginger filled the kitchen as Regina opened the oven door of the big modern range and pulled out a black baking sheet.

"His mother'll worry," she said, slipping the sheet onto the table. Rows of little aromatic men peered at him with crinkled, dark eyes.

15

"She's asleep," Reggie said matter-of-factly, and let the chair go suddenly so that it banged down onto the floor. Lemonade slopped from Peter's glass.

"Reggie," Regina said threateningly, but it was impossible to tell whether she was reproving him for the business with the chair or for what he had said.

"Isn't she?" Reggie said, pushing Peter's shoulder.

And in among the gingerbread men, perhaps even in their dark, shining eyes, he saw his mother quite clearly, sleeping in a white wicker chair. A poppy petal fluttered to the table before her. Then he saw the neat rows of gingerbread men again, smelled them, and felt his stomach contract with hunger.

"Yes," he said and wondered if it was a lie. She had gotten into the habit of napping lately.

"All right then," Regina said flatly. Her hand flew out and slapped Reggie's reaching fingers, hard. "You'll burn yourself. They have to cool first."

The lemonade was tangy-bitter and very cold. Peter drained his glass.

"Give him some more," Regina said, "since you made him spill it." She mopped up the puddle on the table. But it was Linda, smiling gently, who refilled his glass. He liked Linda. He thought that she was very beautiful and probably the person he liked most in the whole world after his mother. Linda made everything lovely and all right. He liked Carl, too, and even though Reggie made him see things which sometimes startled him, he liked Reggie. It was difficult to like Grizzle. There was nothing about her to like. He looked at her. She sat apart from the others, staring at the floor. Nobody had bothered to give her any lemonade but somehow he knew that she didn't mind. It was very hard to tell whether Grizzle was just sulking or indifferent to everything that went on around her.

They were all silent now, doing nothing. He had never known a family to have such long yet safe

16

silences. Not that his experience of families was great. In fact, it was entirely confined to his own and this one. And this one was definitely different, which was not really surprising because they weren't a proper family at all. Only Carl was Regina's child, a fact that any fool could see because they looked so much alike and had a special way of being together. The others were foster children, homeless orphans like him, which was why they were his friends, Peter often thought. Because his mother was not his mother and Ian not his father. They had come and fetched him out of the home. They had done something complicated called adopting him, and that had made them his parents in a way that Regina was not Grizzle's mother, or Linda's, or Reggie's. Which was why, he supposed, they all called her Regina, except sometimes Carl.

And then there was no man, no father to make Regina tense and miserable, to make mysterious phone calls like the ones that upset his mother, to not come home until late. Regina was more like one of them and yet unquestionably in charge. And no matter how he puzzled about it he could not say why he did not like Regina.

"How are the hands?" she asked.

"Fine. Thank you."

"Come on then, eat up. These are cool enough now."

He had not noticed that someone—Linda probably—had placed plates on the table and that Regina had put one of the gingerbread men on his. They were all sitting at the table now, including Grizzle, and he was suddenly afraid to eat the gingerbread man, as though it was a real man. He watched Grizzle lift hers in both pudgy hands, open her mouth and smoothly, viciously bite off the staring head. Reggie laughed, a guffaw of cruel sound.

"I don't feel very hungry, thank you," he said,

pushing his plate away. Yet a moment ago his stomach
had churned at the thought of the sweet, spiced cake.
Reggie bit off an arm, Linda a leg, and they all laughed.

"Go on," said Carl. "They're smashing."

"If he doesn't want it, he doesn't want it," Regina
said and Peter felt a wave of coldness from her that
made him shiver. He stood up quickly and his chair
made a harsh, scraping noise on the uncovered floor.

"I think I'd better go. Thanks anyway."

They were all looking at him, chewing, and holding
incomplete, maimed gingerbread men in their hands.
For a moment he felt paralyzed by their stares. There
was a tightness in his chest, as though he couldn't
breathe. Reggie was the first to turn away.

"See you tomorrow, then," he said and the casual,
ordinary words released him.

"Yes," he said, and meant it.

"Peter?"

He stopped, turned toward Regina.

"Take this for your mother, with my compliments."

He took the package of warm waxed paper, and
mumbled his thanks. Regina seemed to have lost
interest in him and so he was able to go.

Outside, in the shambles of the yard, he felt stupid.
And because he felt stupid he became angry. It was all
Regina's fault. Only he didn't know why. He crossed
the yard quickly, let himself out through the old
five-barred gate and entered the woods. There was a
path here which wound quite clearly along the contour
of the hill and ended at their veranda. He had
completely forgotten the boat. He wanted to get home
quickly. He remembered that sudden tightness in his
chest and, thinking about it, the dim light under the
trees seemed to become aqueous and damp. He
clutched the parcel tighter, to reassure himself. Below,
for the trees grew less closely on this bank, he saw the
sheen of the lake and remembered. It was more like
seeing than remembering. The swift dart of the disap-

pearing pike. A gate. Pulling. His head hurt. He had difficulty breathing. What was it? If he forgot all about it, made himself push it out of his mind, he knew it would be all right. It always was. He made himself walk and concentrate on his feet, on placing them neatly one in front of the other, walking a pretended tightrope. Then there was birdsong, the sharp smell of pine resin, and shafts of dusty sunlight between the trees. The path was like a tunnel and, at the end of it, highlighted by the blazing sun, was the wooden veranda. He began to run, pumping his legs into the ground, then leaping the two wooden steps to the veranda. And there she was, waking, stretching in the sun.

"Oh, I fell asleep," she said, smiling her special smile at him. She raised her fingers to her face. "Am I very red, darling? I think I've gotten a sunburn." Her nose was red and there was a glossy flush on her cheeks. She laughed as he threw his arms around her. "Darling," she said. "Did you have a nice time?" Over her shoulder, he saw the waxed-paper package, still clutched in his hand. He pulled back.

"Regina sent you this."

"Oh? For me? How kind." She placed it gently on her lap. "But, darling, don't you think 'Mrs. Thomas' would be more polite?"

Yes, he did, but she insisted. "She likes to be called Regina."

"Oh well . . ." Pamela shrugged. "I suppose she is rather casual. And then fostering all those children, I suppose it wouldn't be fair to make them call her 'mother.' "

"You're my mother," Peter said firmly. It sounded like a demand. Pamela looked at him, the little package forgotten. He could not see her eyes under the brim of her hat. She reached out and grasped his hand.

"You know I am, darling. Don't you?"

She said it in such a funny way, sort of pleading, yet intensely, that he felt strange. He could only nod.

19

"What on earth's on your hand . . . ?" She pulled her hand away, stared at the translucent pink oil of the melted ointment.

"Peter, what have you done?"

"It's all right. I just scraped my hands a bit, that's all. Regina fixed it." She was so frightened that he wanted, desperately, to change the subject. He hated the fear in her voice, the pallor under her reddish skin.

"Let me see."

He snatched his hands back, clasped them behind him.

"Open your parcel first."

She began to protest and then remembered her vow, her promises to herself and to Elsa. Her fingers shook as she unfolded the paper.

"Oh, how lovely. How clever. Peter, look."

He stepped closer, peered down into her lap. Her hands shook, making the waxed paper rattle as she held it carefully free of the gingerbread lady who wore a big hat, edged in white icing, and a white icing skirt. It was horrible.

"It's you!" he said.

"Yes. Isn't it clever. How very kind of Mrs. . . . of Regina."

"Don't eat it," he said, too loudly, so loudly that he surprised himself as well as Pamela.

"Of course not, darling. I'm going to keep it." She folded the paper lightly over it and stood up. Making her voice calm but firm, she said, "But you've been out in the sun for too long, I think. We'd better go inside. And then I'm going to have a proper look at those hands."

He felt safe then, and followed her into the cool living room. His head was throbbing.

"Why do I love you?"

"At the very best that's an academic question."

"You're so bloody romantic."

20

She flopped down on the bed beside him. He lay on his belly, his arms hooked around the pillow. It was not that Ian objected to talk after sex, simply that he was apprehensive of the direction this particular conversation might take. Lately—by which he meant the last couple of weeks—Liz had talked a lot about love. Or was it simply that, since Pam and Peter went away, he had seen so much more of her that the word had begun to register?

"Well, I suppose the reasons don't matter. I mean, they won't help anything, will they?"

"Now who's being romantic?" he asked the wall across from the bed. He ought to get up, shower, dress.

Liz ignored the remark.

"No, seriously. I'm never sure about that, you know."

"About what?"

"Reasons. Whether it's better to understand something or just accept it and make the best of the consequences." She sighed, lifted her arms, and linked them behind her blond head. "I mean, I don't think *I* could ever go to a psychiatrist, like Pam. I can't see it *doing* anything for me."

Ian turned his head awkwardly and looked at her breasts, tautly lifted by her raised arms. Pam's name on Liz's lips always made him feel uncomfortable.

"That, my darling," he said, carefully casual, "is because you don't have Pam's sort of problems. And as a matter of fact, she's not going to a psychiatrist but to a psychotherapist. There's a difference."

"Well, whatever." She twisted her neck to look at him. Her very large, hazel eyes could only be described as frank. He tried to avoid them, knew it was cowardly, and looked back at her. "Are you one of Pam's problems? Is this?"

"Oh, for God's sake!" He rolled over, sat up.

"Don't be cross." Liz traced the line of his shoulder blade, the knobbed lumps of his upper vertebrae. "It's

21

just that I wondered. I like to know what I'm responsible for."

"And I wonder why you have this sudden obsession with my wife." He untangled his long legs from the sheet and sat on the edge of the bed. "It's not exactly sexy, Liz."

"You're not going?" She sounded more alarmed than disappointed.

"Even I have to work, sometimes," he said, standing up and stretching. The implication was unfair. She, too, had stolen time off from work, and it had been entirely at his suggestion. Naturally, she'd banked on spending the evening with him. But she let it go.

"Now that she's out of the way, now that I see more of you, I can't help wondering."

"That," Ian said, "was exactly what I thought." He walked, naked, out of the room and into the tiny shower stall which, like all the rooms in the flat, opened off the windowless, narrow rectangle of a hall.

"Hell," Liz muttered. She knew she was pushing and she didn't like it any more than he did. She didn't like that aspect of herself that became uncertain and demanded commitment. Liz tried to play by the book. She knew that Ian was married when she met him. She accepted the role of mistress. In many ways it suited her, but now, with the long stretch of the summer before them, with all the increased opportunities, she had begun to think of the future.

She got out of bed and pulled on a cotton housecoat. She raised the blind, letting in heavy, golden sunlight. Although the window was wide open, the room still felt airless. She leaned out, looking at the quiet street, but the only thing that interested her was his familiar car, parked a little way down.

Besides, she was in love with him. She had been in love before. But not like this. And if Pam really was so much better, able to stand on her own feet . . . These thoughts were dangerous. She moved away from the window and began to brush her hair.

In the shower, Ian realized that he had not answered her question about Pam because he did not know. He did not know because he did not like to think about it. Pam was Pam. She had problems he would never fathom. If he was, if his relationship with Liz was, a contributing factor, he would really prefer not to know about it. In any case, he thought, scrubbing hard at his armpits, the whole bloody thing was circular. There would have been no necessity for Liz if Pam hadn't had problems. You could go on parceling up blame in tidy little chunks until you were blue in the face. But cause and effect, he liked to believe, were rather more complicated than that.

"What work?" Liz stood, deliberately posed, in the doorway. The housecoat barely covered her breasts, fell away from one firm thigh.

"What?" He switched the shower off. "Can't hear."

"I asked what work you have to do tonight?" Automatically, she handed him a towel.

"Thanks. We tendered for an office building in Kilburn. Nothing spectacular, but they want to talk about the interior. I've done a few preliminary sketches."

For the first time ever, Liz wondered. You could never doubt a man who said he had to get home to his wife, or take his son to the cinema, but a man who worked evenings . . .

"But why tonight? Why not some civilized hour?"

"Because," he answered, "a great many people consider it more civilized to discuss business over dinner." He dropped the towel untidily on the floor. Liz moved against him, put her arms around his neck.

"I think it would be much more civilized to have dinner with me."

He held her buttocks, warm and exciting through the thin cotton.

"So do I," he admitted, "but . . ."

"No chance."

"None."

"Damn."

"You'll just have to accept that our idea of civilization and Mr. Grubb's are diametrically opposed." He patted her rump. "Now, if I may get dressed?"

She released him, stepped back out of the shower, and let him pass. It gratified and excited her that he was semiaroused.

"He can't be called Grubb. Not really," she said, following him.

"Afraid so. Where the hell are my pants? And there's a Mrs. Grubb. And lots of little Grubblets."

"Here." She found his underpants tangled in the sheet and handed them to him.

"Thanks."

She sat on the edge of the bed, watching him.

"I like your body."

"Good. I like yours."

"I've noticed."

"Meaning, too much and I don't pay enough attention to your mind and your emotional needs."

"If the cap fits . . ."

He looked at his crumpled shirt.

"I'll have to go home and change first."

"After all, you must admit that it does look a bit like a quick fuck before a dull evening. Sort of to bolster you up."

"Liz," he said warningly.

"Well, doesn't it?" She faced him squarely, demanding again.

"One of your best qualities is a placid temperament, an ability to accept the status quo. Speaking entirely personally, I regret its apparent passing."

"Sometimes you talk like a bloody textbook," she said angrily and stood up, walking to the window.

Ian dropped his trousers on the bed and followed

her, put his arms around her and cupped her breasts. She felt his hardness nuzzling her bottom.

"Don't pick a fight," he said, kissing her hair. Her nipples hardened at the slightest brush of his fingers.

"You want me." It was a statement of fact.

"You know I do. More and more."

"You're not just . . . aroused?"

"I am not *just* aroused. But I do want to fuck you."

She twisted around to face him.

"I'm not exactly famous for my powers of resistance."

"Now who's talking like a textbook?"

"Maybe it's catching."

"Like desire." He kissed her. "And seeing as how I want to fuck you and you can't resist me, why don't I come back here after grub at the Grubbs', possibly armed with a couple of bottles of wine, and do just that?"

Liz put her head on one side, considered the proposition and said, "Champagne?"

"Done."

He moved away and continued dressing. Watching him, Liz told herself that what she thought was ridiculous. She had not sold out.

"You won't be around during the weekend?" she asked.

"You know I won't." He sounded impatient.

"It's just that I might want to make some plans of my own."

Ian opened his mouth to speak, then closed it. If she was threatening him, there was nothing to be gained by acknowledging it. Besides, it was time for him to go.

Perhaps because she had napped that afternoon, Pamela could not sleep that night. It was hot and still. She missed the sound of the wind in the trees and even her thin nightdress seemed too heavy. The timbered roof creaked as the wood contracted, but apart from that there was only the whisper of her own shallow breathing. Only the familiar, dangerous track of her own thoughts. She had no sleeping pills. Elsa, like many psychotherapists, did not approve of drugs. Pamela knew, too, that they did not trust her with anything dangerous. Well, perhaps Elsa did, now. But not Ian, not their GP. Which was silly, because she had everything to live for. There was nothing further from her mind than suicide. To be fair, she had thought about it, in those first bleak years of marriage. Thought about it, but never tried. And it was a terrible thing to describe the first, in many ways the best, years of her marriage as bleak. Only her childlessness had made them bleak. Ian had been devoted, loving, kind. An exciting man. Pamela's heart thumped painfully and she placed her hot, trembling hand over it, as though by doing so she could calm it, as she could calm Peter when he was ill or troubled by a nightmare. In those days, Ian had not needed other women. Or if he did, he had been discreet about it or had controlled the desire.

Elsa had said, often, "Are you jealous? Do you mind?"

Pamela had never been able to give a satisfactory answer, satisfactory to herself, that is. By what did you measure loss, losing? Pamela only had one yardstick, her terrible, broken barrenness. Compared to that, nothing she dared to think or imagine could touch her. Except losing Peter, Peter dying.

She sat up in the bed, her legs already halfway to the floor. Every nerve in her body prompted her to go to him, check, make sure. There was a sound like a scream in the back of her head. Elsa's remembered voice penetrated the scream.

"You must not. You must put all such thoughts out of your mind. Examine them rationally. You will see that they have no basis in fact."

She had, at least, to get up, to walk around. There was a moon. Silver light flooded the room around which she padded with the dogged air of a person performing a necessary but uncongenial ritual. Her arms were clasped tightly across her breasts. She looked down at her feet as she walked, round and round.

She had not suspected for a year that she was barren. Another six tortured months passed before she consulted Dr. Collins and through him the first of three gynecologists, each more eminent, expensive, and highly recommended than the last.

"There is absolutely nothing wrong with you, Mrs. Woodford."

"I can find no physical cause, Mrs. Woodford."

"Under the circumstances, Mrs. Woodford, we can only wait and hope."

She had told no one. Ghosts haunted her womb every month. At first Ian had been delighted by what he called her "insatiable appetite" for sex. Twice, sometimes three times a night—the desperate search for a baby, life. In the morning, before he went to the office. Once in the car because she was slightly drunk from a dinner party where one of the guests had confessed that she was pregnant. Pamela had embarrassed the woman with questions, was barely able to suppress an almost obsessive desire to touch the woman's belly. Some of the magic might rub off. Then that terrible night, when Ian had cried out, "This is bloody useless. You're a machine, not a woman."

A machine that did not function. She had broken down. Weeping, she told him. She came so close to telling him everything, but fortunately he had soothed her before she had stumbled across the line she must never cross. He had been so concerned, so gentle. He insisted on having a sperm count taken.

"My poor love, you mustn't assume that it's your fault. All those doctors can't be wrong. It has to be my fault."

But it wasn't and the positive result of his test only

made her feel worse. They had tried for another eighteen months or so. Pamela could not remember the precise length of time. It had been a gentle agony for her. Then it was Ian who tried. He bought books. He placed pillows under her buttocks and she lay there, compliant and unresponsive, knowing it was no good. She understood more fully than any woman ever had the real meaning of the old expression: make the punishment fit the crime. She was properly, justly punished.

She waited, tensed and panicked, for the first mention of adoption. Ian had consulted Dr. Collins. He thought it was an excellent idea. Ian could not understand Pamela's reluctance. How could he?

"Won't you even consider it? For your own sake?"

Yes, she would consider it. On certain conditions.

"Anything, love. Anything at all."

He must be ten years old. A boy, ten years old, fair with blue eyes.

"Well, don't I get any say in the matter?"

"No, Ian. Forgive me. But I will know him when I see him."

He had agreed, but he had also been afraid, afraid that her obsessive certainty that there was a particular, special child, destined to be hers, would alarm the adoption authorities.

"Darling, if they think you're even slightly cranky . . ."

But she had been discreet, firm, careful. She exploited the fact that they were "tragically childless" and, from any agency's point of view, eminently suitable. She posed as a snob, declaring that a child's background was every bit as important as theirs. When necessary she did not hesitate to remind them that she, the eminently suitable Mrs. Pamela Woodford, was doing them a favor. Everybody wanted babies. Ten-year-old boys were not easily placed.

She despised herself, of course, and frequently felt

ashamed. Sometimes as she leafed her way through files and dossiers on every likely blond-haired boy of ten, she wept for rejecting them. But she could justify herself. Hers was an act of expiation, reparation. She was not thinking of herself. And when the time came she knew that the files would be redundant. She and the boy would know, would recognize each other.

It took months. Long months in which the Woodfords, though undeniably suitable, gained a reputation for being unusually hard to suit. Even Ian became impatient, pointing at some luckless child and saying, "Won't that one do?"

Perhaps he had sensed by then that there was no room in her heart for both of them. A few weeks before she had found Peter, he had said, "Let's call the whole thing off. After all, there are advantages to not having kids around the place."

"Such as?" she asked in a cold and certain voice.

"Well, you might notice my existence again, for a start."

She had tried to make it up to him, but once she had seen Peter . . . And she had seen him, staring at her, wordless, unblinking in a room full of noisy, playing, quarreling children.

"I've found him," she said, her eyes, even her skin, glowing with excitement. "Will you come and see him tomorrow, Ian?"

He had raised halfhearted objections. The child had been considered autistic. He was variously labeled "disturbed" and "emotionally maladjusted." He might turn out to be a handful. Even the matron of the children's home admitted that she had not thought Peter a suitable candidate for adoption.

"But that's all the more reason why we should love him. Don't you think we owe him something?"

Ian had agreed. She had her boy at last and there was never any possibility of regarding him as anything but her son.

Peter had clung to her, pathetically afraid. For a year she had scarcely left his side. She taught him all the conventional skills, including the more important ones like confidence and trust, to speak and to love. At last, even to laugh. It was during that year, the hardest and happiest of Pamela's life, that Ian had begun to sleep with other women. She knew and she dismissed it. She was too tired and too preoccupied to make love. Their social life withered. She told herself that she was glad Ian had found an outlet.

Peter was eleven, and at last she had been able to let him go to school. The only really bad row she and Ian had ever had was about his school. He wanted to send him away. She would not hear of it.

"Don't you see," he shouted, "if we're to have any sort of marriage at all, he's got to go away?"

"Then we will have no sort of marriage, Ian."

Oh, she had been brave then. She had meant it then, before the terror began. It began in the long, empty hours when Peter was at school. She saw him being set upon by bullies. She saw him falling from some dangerous piece of gymnastic equipment. She saw him tripping down stairs, being run over. She saw him lying with a broken leg on the soccer field. The day she read of an outbreak of ptomaine poisoning at a school in the north, she had rushed to his school and prevented him from eating his lunch. After that, she had collected him each lunchtime, fed him, drove him back to school. She began to invent illnesses for him. Every Wednesday and Thursday she wrote notes. "Please excuse Peter from gym." From soccer, cricket, even swimming. Twice, sitting in the gallery of the local pool, she had seen him drown, his face blue, his lungs swollen with bitter water. She believed that he would be kidnapped, assaulted, and murdered. She began to spend entire days watching the school, guarding him. She allowed every knife in the house to become blunt. When he cut himself on a screwdriver while playing with an Erector

30

set, she had become hysterical and thrown the whole kit in the wastebasket.

Ian had found her, shaking and in tears. Peter, red-faced with anger, had told the whole story with a string of accusations that had torn her heart. Oddly, it was the swimming he resented most. That and the fact that the boys called him names, said he was a Mommy's boy. He had no friends. But most of all, the swimming.

And so to Elsa and the long, slow process of recovery, of demolition and recovery.

She had stopped pacing. She could not remember when. She was facing the bed. Her heart still fluttered in the old way, and her body was cold with sweat. The alarm bell, the scream, was not sounding in her head. And she had not gone to Peter's room.

"Thank God," she whispered.

She pulled at the sheet and wiped her arms, her armpits, her face and hands. Only one-half of the window was open. She moved toward it, thinking that in any case the lake would look pretty in the moonlight. Her fingers fumbled with the catch, found it. She leaned from the hips, pushing the window wide open, and below her, at the edge of the lake, she saw that all her fears were not in her head. They had come true at last.

"And you really think Pam's all right now?"

Ian, almost asleep, could hardly believe his ears. It was sweltering in the room, despite the open window and the raised blind. He could see her, wide-eyed in the greenish light of the streetlamp. The light made her look sickly and pallid and for a moment he wondered if . . .

"What the hell is this? Why are you suddenly so obsessed with my wife?"

She turned away from his anger.

"At one time you were obsessed with her. You couldn't talk about anything else."

That was when they had first met, when she had made the big decision to buy a house, a dilapidated shell which she thought could be converted into three self-contained flats, two of which she would rent to cover the mortgage repayment. Her father helped, of course, but the house was also a gesture of independence. It was independence that had made her reject Daddy's architect, Daddy's builder. She simply could not afford them. And this time money *was* to be an object, as she firmly told her father. Woodford and Hasell had seemed a modest enough firm, were reasonably local, and proclaimed on their yard gates: CONVERSIONS A SPECIALITY. The foreman, looking over the house with her, scratched his head.

"For what you have in mind, you'll need an architect. You'd best see our Mr. Woodford. Shall I send him along?"

Not a very romantic beginning, they both agreed. And at first Liz had had him clearly labeled. A classic case of a man whose wife did not understand him. She did not think that he would be very good in bed and even if he was, she would give it a few months at best. There was a crisis. But wives, as experience had taught her, had a very healthy resilience. They tended to get over their "nerves" or their "postnatal blues" the moment they suspected that hubby was having an affair on the side. Liz couldn't blame them. She didn't really approve of poaching, although she poached. But at least she didn't have any expectations. Whatever else she was, she was a realist. But a lousy judge of character. He'd been bloody fantastic in bed, the best.

And she had misread the situation. It was more than two years since Pam's crisis and only in the last couple of weeks had there been talk of real improvement. More than two years in which to get accustomed to him, to fall in love with him. To wonder if, now that Pam could look after herself . . .

"I'm sorry about that. You didn't seem to mind at the

time." He sat up, clasping his knees. Liz continued to stare at the window, at the dark blue London sky.

"I didn't. That's why I don't see what's so wrong with wanting to know now."

"I'll tell you what's wrong. I don't come here to discuss my wife's mental health. I come here to forget it."

"That's rather what I thought."

Liz could have bitten off her tongue. Ian, who was good at avoiding issues, knew that this one had come home to stay.

"What exactly do you want, Liz?" He clutched his knees tighter. The arrangement suited him. Liz suited him. That didn't mean that he didn't love her. It was just that he was confused about Pam. Now wasn't the time to make decisions, plans. In the autumn, perhaps. Pam had improved, but it was still early. And Pam improved might be Pam desired, loved again. Not, he thought, that he had ever stopped loving her.

"A bit of consideration would do for a start."

He suppressed a sigh of relief.

"I am sorry I didn't make myself clear about this evening, that I had to go out. It won't happen again."

"Thank you."

"Now can we go to sleep?"

"Yes."

She hunched over, away from him. Ian did not try to kiss her. There was something sulky and forbidding about her shoulder. He lay down, looking at the ceiling and wondering how much time he had bought. For there was no point in pretending that they had even touched on the real subject. If Liz gave a damn about this evening, a small misunderstanding, it could only be because she wanted something more. Well, who could blame her? He wasn't even very surprised. She had been too good a mistress, too understanding, too accommodating for it to last. Liz should be married. To him? He tried to imagine being married to her and

33

could not. Marriage meant Pam, and it wasn't all it was cracked up to be. He wasn't sure he wanted to do it again even if he could. And he had no idea if he could. Pam had been a shock to him. Liz had cushioned him against that shock. Now his wife was a mystery, an unknown quantity, and Liz was becoming a nuisance. Unfair. But true?

"What about Peter?"

Peter.

Peter filled him with more confusion and guilt. There were times when he blamed Peter for all his problems. And that, too, was unfair. The boy had done nothing. He still felt a stab of fear and emotion when he recalled how the boy had turned to him that day Pam became hysterical. Until then, Ian had felt like a stranger in his own home, shut out and made redundant by the bond between Pam and Peter. Hence Liz. But the boy's angry, distressed appeal to him had made him feel dreadful. He should have been more vigilant, he should have seen the signs before they got so bad that evidence had to be placed before him, damning Pam. Damn Pam.

"He's fine," he said.

"So everything's fine," Liz said, meaning that she was unhappy.

Ian reached out and clutched her hip.

"I'm sorry, love."

She sighed, covered his hand with hers.

"So am I."

"It's just . . ."

They both waited for him to finish the sentence, but he could not. Even after he had persuaded Pam to see a psychotherapist he had not been able to get close to the boy. He had been unable to capitalize on that appeal, his own very strong response. There had been gruff, mutually awkward chats about Mommy's nerves and how patient and helpful they had to be. Peter knew that Ian wasn't being very helpful. His eyes said it. He had

34

made sporadic efforts to get to-know the boy, talk to him, but Pam hung like a ghost between them when they were alone and separated them by her concerns when they were all together. He did not feel, as Pamela did, that Peter was his child. He could not dismiss the facts so easily. And Pam had never really allowed them to get close to each other. Ian knew that he had not tried hard enough. He accepted that he was not very paternal, but he was capable of making an effort. Only it had been easier to turn to Liz.

Her hand slipped from his and he realized that she was asleep. This weekend, he would try. He would really try to talk to Pam and spend some time with the boy. Maybe he and Liz had come to the end of the road. It seemed like it. That road had never led anywhere, anyway. He turned over quietly, so as not to disturb her. Closing his eyes, he saw it as a literal road, narrow and tree-confined. At its end was a great metal gate. It swung open. He realized that Liz was offering him a way out. What he didn't know was whether he wanted to take it.

Peter had gone to bed and, in the moments before sleep, had indulged in his favorite fantasy. The funny, creaking house became theirs. His mother was always happy and peaceful. The summer went on forever and Linda came to live with them. She was his sister. He was never quite sure how this relationship was discovered, but it seemed possible because they were both blond. His mother loved Linda and they lived happily ever after by the lake.

Slipping into sleep was like lowering himself into the soothing waters of the lake. His body became weightless, floating. He saw clouds of fish, brown against gray, the preying mottled shadow of a pike. Voices called to him. Faraway voices. He could not be bothered to answer them. He was too content just to float, his body revolving. The voices, though, persisted, edged into his mind, insidious and demanding. He had to obey them and then he could float peacefully in the waters.

He was standing, looking down at the little parcel in the tin where she had packed it. The paper was gray in the light. When he folded it back, it looked like a ghostly paper coffin. The sugary skirt and outlined hat had a sheen, like some costly material. Carefully he lifted it out, held it flat in the palm of his right hand.

Then he was standing at the very end of the jetty, the boards still warm but rough beneath his bare feet. He was frightened for a moment, not knowing how or why he had gotten there. His pale arm and hand were silhouetted against the black waters of the lake. The moonlight made the gingerbread lady a uniform gray. He forgot everything else and even before it happened, he saw the iced white skirt wavering, sinking into the water. He tilted his hand. It fell, turning, catching the light. If it made any noise entering the water, he did not hear it. To his surprise it did not sink but hung just below the surface, the white skirt particularly visible.

Then she screamed at him, her hysterical voice shutting off all the other voices, and he thought the thing in the lake was screaming. He thought that she was drowning and a terrible empty fear gripped him.

"Peter. Oh my God! Peter. Peter!"

He stooped down guiltily, perilously, to snatch her from the waters. His fingers passed through the dissolving mush. Sodden and sticky, the thing broke up, became food for the fish.

"Peter!"

He stood up. She seemed to hang on the hillside, a gray blur. For a moment he saw her dissolving and was afraid of her cold ghostflesh. Then everything became quite clear. The sound of her troubled breathing was familiar. He walked quickly toward her.

"It's all right," he called. "I just remembered the boat. I wanted to make sure it was tied up safely."

She fell against him, her arms tight around his neck.

Her tears burned his bare chest. He felt awkward and embarrassed. She babbled about sleepwalking, frightening her. She talked of drowning.

"It's all right," he said again. "You're not drowning."

He put his arm around her waist, supporting her. Her vision was distorted by tears and the imperfect moonlight. For a moment he appeared older, stronger. It was a trick of the light. Her baby was safe, safe again. She clasped him but his body felt hard and seemed to pull against her. He was staring in such a strange way at her, with an expression that roused sharp, disturbing memories. He put out his hand and only then did Pamela realize that the thin shoulder strap of her nightgown had slipped. Quickly, backing away from him, she covered her breast.

"You'll catch cold," she said, her teech chattering, though it was not cold. "Go in at once and go to bed."

He lowered his head. He was only a little boy. She had spoken too sharply. Her heart thudded against her ribs, beneath the breast which she still held protectively. He walked back to the house and somehow Pamela managed to follow him.

After the fear, shame. Shame at her own thoughts, at the recession into panic. Pamela rewrote the scene over and over in her head until it became safe. Peter had woken, remembered the boat and, without disturbing her, had sensibly gone to check on it. She had been too preoccupied to hear him anyway. She pushed the guilt that came with this admission away from her. That argued for a confident, well-adjusted, and responsible child. She had not damaged him. And if he had put out his hand to her breast it was in wonder, to cover it, or with the instinctive yearning of a child who had never been suckled. Any other interpretation could be put down to her own morbidity, to a trick of the light, an errant memory.

At some point in the long night, Pamela went into the kitchen to make herself some tea. The tin in which she had placed the gingerbread was standing on the counter, the lid resting beside it. She saw that it was empty and smiled. The sight of the tin made her rationale perfect and complete. He had been hungry. That had woken him, and then he'd remembered the boat. He had never helped himself to food before and perhaps was a little apprehensive because he had eaten something intended for her without asking. She screwed up the paper in which Regina Thomas had wrapped the cake and dropped it in the wastebasket. This was just another sign of his growing up. The midnight hunger, the raid on the kitchen—all the more pleasurable because secret. She made the tea and thought that she would be able to sleep now.

First, though, she ought to write it all down for Elsa. She automatically reached for the pad and ball-point pen. It was her lifeline. But as soon as she held the pen poised between her fingers, Pamela did not want to write it down. With a shock, she considered the possibility of having secrets from Elsa. She became excited. If she wrote down all that had raced through her mind, she would have to relive it. Some things were best left unmentioned anyway. To keep something from Elsa would be a sign of independence, proof that she could cope by herself. She began to write, feeling slightly guilty, but elated.

Dear Elsa,

I had rather a shock tonight. It was so hot I couldn't sleep. I got up to open the window more widely and saw Peter standing at the edge of the lake, in full moonlight. You can imagine my reaction! But it turned out that he'd woken up hungry and then—after helping himself in the kitchen—had remembered that he'd left the boat on the other side of the lake and had gone to make sure it was safe. Of course I panicked, but only for a moment. The important thing is, I realized that he is growing up fast. Adolescence can be such a spurt. I'd forgotten. But I was glad at this new confidence and independence in him. He has grown so strong, so tall. . . .

She broke off, staring into space. So strong that his body had felt like a man's. His shoulders were broad from swimming and the moonlight had played tricks, putting shadows and lines on his unmarked face. A clear case of the eye seeing what it wanted to see. Only she did not want to see or think about it. An unwanted memory, that was all, which was best forgotten.

Pamela put down the pen and closed the pad. She felt sleepy, and doubted that she would send the letter to Elsa. The whole thing was far too trivial. She yawned and went to bed.

The boy looked like the perfect little Aryan, Regina thought as she watched him creep out of the house and hurry down to the lake. His body was golden in the morning light, his hair bleached by the sun. She moved to a better vantage point on the shadowed path and saw him slip quietly into the water as though reluctant to disturb its absolute stillness. He struck out for the opposite bank, leaving a silver wake, iridescent rainbow drops falling from his threshing arms. The sound of his swimming, trapped by the bowl of the hills, reached her. It reminded her of the splashing of many bodies in an enclosed pool, the damp chill of a tiled swimming pool that was also steamy and too humid, the sharp, ugly smell of chlorine, the sound of children's voices, their limbs splashing and beating the water, and the terrified face of a woman.

Regina shook her head. There were beads of sweat on her upper lip. She forgot the boy and the memory. It was easy, a trick. You just let it slide away, like a shadow thrown behind you. Always there, of course, but so easily put out of sight if you altered your relationship to the light. She continued along the path and, lifting her long skirt a little, climbed the veranda steps. The boy had left the glass door open. Inside it was dim and cool.

Regina tapped on the glass, called. "Mrs. Woodford? Mrs. Woodford? Are you there?"

A startled sound from the bedroom, as though something had been knocked over in haste. A muffled voice, indistinct. Regina stepped into the room, glancing around critically at Appledore's "modern rustic" furniture.

Pamela Woodford appeared, pulling on a robe. Her hair was tousled and she resembled, Regina thought, nothing so much as a startled roe deer. There were blue rings of exhaustion round her eyes.

"What is it? Has something happened to Peter?"

She began to hurry toward the door which Regina blocked. She revised her opinion. Like a frightened bird, trapped in this room, fluttering. If not consoled, reassured, she would beat herself to pieces. Pamela stopped, looked up at the taller woman who was solidly silhouetted against the light.

"No. He's fine. Down there. Look."

Regina stepped aside. Pamela leaned against the jamb of the door as though she might faint.

Peter was pulling hard on the right oar, turning the boat toward the far end of the lake. After a moment, Pamela went out onto the veranda, called his name, waved. He looked up at her and waved back.

Pamela came slowly back into the room, buttoning her robe.

"I'm sorry. You must think me very rude . . . and foolish."

Regina considered for a moment, and then said, "I brought your milk." She held out the old-fashioned milk can to Pamela. "When Peter didn't come, I guessed you'd slept in."

"Oh, how kind. I'm so sorry. You shouldn't have, really. I had no idea of the time." She took the can and looked at her left wrist. Her watch, of course, was beside the bed.

"It's about nine-thirty," Regina said. "But what are holidays for?"

"Yes. Quite." Pamela's cheeks burned. "Still, I hadn't meant—" She broke off, turning back to the door. "Peter's had no breakfast."

"Neither have you," said Regina sensibly. "When he gets hungry he'll come. Here, let me." She took the milk can from Pamela's hand and went into the kitchen. "If he makes his way to my place, they'll give him something. Tea or coffee?"

Pamela, who had followed her, feeling slightly bewildered and still heavy with sleep, stared at her speechlessly.

"You don't mind?" Regina asked, raising her thick eyebrows. "The truth is, I could use a cup of coffee and you look done in. Sorry. None of my business." She turned to the sink and filled the electric percolator.

"No, of course not," Pamela answered, singling out the one question. The woman made her feel weak and useless, and yet curiously comforted. She felt silly, standing in her own kitchen. She sat down. The pad and pen lay in front of her. She gathered them up quickly, embarrassed in case Regina might ask about them, and put them on a shelf behind her. "It's very kind of you," she said.

"I told you. I want a cup myself."

The coffee pot spluttered, gurgled, then settled into a regular rhythmic bubbling.

"You really don't look well," Regina said. She perched on a corner of the red Formica table, her arms folded across her breasts.

"I couldn't sleep," Pamela said.

41

"It was very hot."

"It was Peter, actually. Well, not entirely. He gave me quite a scare." Without meaning to, she heard herself telling Regina about Peter's midnight foray to the lake. She tried to make fun of her obvious anxiety, but she knew her voice sounded brittle. "I imagine you think I'm very stupid," she finished, clasping her hands together.

"It's not my business to think anything." Regina got off the table and took down two mugs. "Milk?"

"Please. No sugar."

"I like it black, myself."

"You shouldn't be doing that," Pamela said. "I should be entertaining you."

"Why? I invited myself. I woke you up, barging in here."

"Thank goodness you did, or . . ." Pamela hesitated, embarrassed by the familiar anxiety.

"Or what?" Regina placed a mug of coffee in front of her.

"Or I might have slept all morning."

"Would that have been so dreadful?"

"Well, no, I suppose not. It's just . . ."

"Peter."

Regina sat opposite her and sipped noisily at her too-hot coffee.

"You do think I'm a fool. I know I worry too much and by comparison you seem so—"

"I've had a lot more practice than you. But don't think I didn't go through it all with Carl. There was a time when I couldn't bear to let him out of my sight. That's one of the reasons I decided to foster other children. To take the pressure off Carl."

Pamela could have wept at this shred of comfort, but instead she asked shyly, "You didn't consider having more of your own?"

"I lacked one of the prerequisites—a man." Pamela

glanced at her with an expression that made Regina burst into laughter. "Don't look so shocked. I mean, my husband was dead and . . ." She shrugged.

"I'm terribly sorry. I didn't mean to pry."

"It was a long time ago. There were men, but I couldn't see myself married to any of them. And what could I do? I had no skills except that I can bandage knees and make gingerbread men."

"Oh!" Pamela sounded startled. For a moment Regina thought she was going to clap her hand over her mouth like a naughty little girl. "I never thanked you. I truly meant to."

"Don't be silly."

"It was very kind of you."

"As long as you enjoyed it."

"To tell you the truth, Peter ate it. When he got up in the middle of the night."

"And you're worried that you didn't make him breakfast!"

She sounded both amused and exasperated. Suddenly, Pamela saw the funny side of her own neurosis. She laughed. Regina, she thought, had a knack, not unlike Elsa's, though less considered, of putting everything into perspective.

"That's better," Regina said, settling back in the chair and watching her.

Elsa had said, early in their sessions, that Pamela lacked friends, that she should mix more with other women. Friendship with members of her own sex would give her a sense of proportion. She was no longer cut off from them by her barrenness. Pamela wondered if she could add this to her repertoire of therapeutic tasks. She felt, somehow, that Regina could be her friend.

"Your husband's coming down this weekend?"

"Oh yes. Yes. On Friday, I expect."

"Maybe that's the answer for you. Another child."

43

She saw Pamela's body stiffen as though anticipating a blow.

"Peter's adopted. I wouldn't want to go through all that red tape again." She stood up and carried her mug to the sink.

"Well, I have a prescription for you. Go back to bed. Have a really lazy day. I'll look after Peter. One more among my brood . . ." She too stood up and faced Pamela.

"Oh no. Thank you. But I couldn't possibly."

"You could," Regina said flatly, rinsing her own mug under the tap. "If you'd trust me."

"It's not that. You mustn't think that."

"I promise you he'll come to no harm. I won't let him out of my sight." She shook the mug and then wiped the moisture from her hand on the side of her long skirt.

Pamela was suddenly tempted. She felt that she could sleep. It was more than that, though. An act of faith on her part. A test. An opportunity to show that she was willing to meet this straightforward, competent woman halfway, in friendship.

"I did rather want to do some painting," she admitted.

"Painting? Oh, then you can do me a favor in return. Reggie's always drawing. Always wanting to know how to do this, how to do that. Me, I'm completely ignorant about art. So, let's make a bargain. I'll take Peter off your hands today, and tomorrow you can look at Reggie's drawings."

Pamela hesitated. She wanted to help. She wanted to be a good neighbor, to share things. She remembered the happy hours she had spent with Peter before he became bored with paints and paper.

"Is it a bargain?" Regina stuck out her hand in a curiously masculine gesture.

"Yes, all right. Of course."

They shook hands.

"Now I must be off. You rest."

"Peter's got no clothes with him," Pamela suddenly remembered. "Only his bathing trunks."

"You think he'll catch cold on a day like this? It's sweltering already."

"Well, I don't know. Sitting around in a wet bathing suit."

"It'll be dry in ten minutes. If not, I've got a house full of clothes he can borrow. Don't worry. Trust me."

"Yes, of course. I'm sorry."

"And don't keep apologizing." Regina went to the door. "He'll be back by six, in good time for supper."

Pamela could only nod and smile.

She *had* done the right thing. She would write and tell Elsa. She would go back to bed for a while, then have a bath. The hours suddenly stretched, blank and meaningless, before her. Perhaps he would come up from the lake first. She could tell him that Regina was expecting him and he would say no, say he wanted to stay with her. There was nothing to be afraid of in the empty hours. She could rest, bathe, paint. Later, she would go and look for more poppies. She lay down and made herself think only of the poppies, tried to discover and comprehend the essence of their color.

The sort of weather they were having was unbearable in London. In his brick-built, first-floor office set at the back of the yard, Ian perspired uncomfortably and thought of Italian hill towns, Spanish beaches. His cheesecloth shirt and denim trousers clung to him like a second, occlusive skin. He thought of water, of surf and breezes. The Serpentine would be tatty and crowded. Highgate Pond was too far away and the local swimming pool would be clogged with sharp-voiced children.

He and Jim Hasell, who had started the firm with his

father, had held an inconclusive meeting on the Grubb tender. Ernie Kent, who would be the foreman on the project if they got it, was unenthusiastic. The Grubb job, which had sounded like a nice little bonus when first discussed, had become a pain in the arse. Staring at the morning's still unanswered mail, Ian knew that he had hoped his report on the Grubb meeting would be well received. Jim's and Ernie's congratulations would, in part at least, have made up for the fiasco with Liz. But they were rightly skeptical, he thought. Grubb wanted to cut corners. He wanted flash without solidity and that was something the old guard resisted. Ian went to the long, metal-framed window which sloped outward, open, and looked down at the yard. Three youths, stripped to the waist, were lethargically unloading and stacking bricks. A pall of reddish dust hung around them. Not for the first time, Ian felt out of place, yet in sympathy with Jim and old Ernie. Woodford and Hasell were essentially jobbing builders. They could put on a new roof efficiently, build an undistinguished but functional back extension with the very best of them. They had a good team of brickers and plasterers and, as more and more of the new middle classes bought old terraced houses and decrepit Victorian dwellings, work had boomed. Sometimes Ian thought that he would be happier working with a plumb line and a trowel full of cement than designing a loft conversion to house the increasing hordes of little Samanthas and Simons. He was the icing on the workaday cake, the patcher-up of middle-class compromise. He was, he realized, sick to death of stripped pine louver doors concealing avocado bathroom suites. He never wanted to see another stainless steel sink or explain to some TV floor manager's pretty wife how to conceal her new automatic washing machine.

He turned away from the window and stared at his drawing board. The latest job was a game room, to be fitted on top of an existing two-car garage. With a pencil he tapped the paper clipped to the board and suppressed an angry impulse to scribble all over the neat, uninspired drawings.

He thought of the lake, black and placid, and longed to swim.

He was an architect who had never designed anything that a decent surveyor and an experienced builder couldn't have done just as well. The Grubb project would have extended his range, but he had no real enthusiasm for it. It would be all planning permission and olive green burlap. Damn it, it he was not an interior designer, yet that was all the Grubbs of this world cared about. Interiors of synthetic luxury on a strict budget. Half-price chic.

To Ian's father, architects were the apogee of glamour. They were the men with vision, the ideas merchants. When, as a muddled, directionless eighteen-year-old, with a respectable number of O and A grades, Ian had vaguely said he wouldn't mind being an architect, his father's eyes had brightened.

"D'you think you could make it, son? That'd really be something."

Ian had always regretted that he had not reminded his father that these glamorous, talented persons also gave him, in his own words, more bloody trouble than they were worth. He had grown up with this contradiction: glamour and the power of ideas versus a total inability—if his father was to be believed—to grasp the rudiments of plumbing or the basic laws of construction. It was only much later, when he had completed his course at a North London Polytechnic, that he realized his father had scotched two birds with one stone. Ian would obtain status, be a member of a respected profession and, perhaps even more important, be that rarest of all creatures, the architect who was on the builders' side. He had banked on Jim Hasell refusing to have him brought into the firm, but somehow the old man had talked him round.

Expansion was a magic word to Jim. But Ian had never intended to stay. It was partly in order to marshal his arguments so he could let his father down gently, and partly to please his mother, who hadn't had a decent holiday in twenty years, that he had persuaded the old man to slacken off and take a vacation abroad, a package tour to Spain where the beer was guaranteed English and paella optional.

Ian had never seen them again. It was one of those pointless, stupid accidents that could have happened anytime, anywhere. They had gone—Ian was certain at his mother's insistence—to a monastery in the hills and, on the way back, negotiating a hairpin bend, the bus had suffered a blowout. It hadn't even gone over the cliff. The driver had hauled the damn thing into the side of a mountain, killing only three passengers: Vera and Jack Woodford, and a spinster lady from Dumbarton.

Ian had buried his parents decently in a single grave and thought that now, at last, he could break away. He couldn't see Jim Hasell tolerating him now that Jack was gone, but there he had been mistaken. Firstly, as the only child, Ian inherited everything, and secondly, Jim came to look on him as the son and heir he did not have. None of his three daughters was interested in the firm, and even if one of them had been, Jim would never have accepted a woman in business, except to answer the phone and type the estimates.

"You owe it to me, son, and to old Jack. Anyway, I can't afford to buy you out. Oh, it's worth a tidy sum, but it's all on paper. And you wouldn't sell me out to some jumped-up property speculator, would you?"

Ian had hesitated, but finally agreed. He had stayed on for three reasons, the most influential of which now seemed to be lethargy. At the time though, he had discovered that his father had, over the years, bought a number of properties when they were cheap and that he

48

was, comparatively speaking, a rich man. By improving and selling off some of this real estate, he could amass enough to buy his freedom. Besides, by then he had met Pamela and wanted to marry her, and it didn't seem the right moment to make a radical career change, even if he could think what that should be. So he had stayed, and stayed. It was what his father would have called a cushy number, but he had long since ceased to feel guilty about that.

Such energies as he had, had been invested in Pam and, lately, Liz. Whom he had promised to telephone, with whom, for once, he had no definite date. That and the thought of the lake again decided him. He went out of his office and down the stairs. The lads had finished stacking the bricks and were smoking, sunning themselves against the neat piles. Jim's office was a tiny, cluttered room on the other side of the yard. He refused to move. It had been good enough for him when he first started, and it was good enough now. He was adding figures with a chewed stub of pencil when Ian came in.

"That bloody timber yard's fouled up again," he said, pushing the papers aside. "What's on your mind?"

"I was wondering if you'd mind if I sloped off. There's nothing much happening."

Jim's eyes narrowed. He leaned back in a creaking swivel chair, circa 1940, and studied his strong, calloused fingers. Ian suspected that he knew about Liz and was certain that if he did, he disapproved.

"I was going down to join Pam tomorrow anyway."

Jim's face lightened at once.

"You don't have to ask me, Ian. You're as much boss as I am. Yes. Push off. It's time you saw a bit more of Pam and the kid. How is he?"

"Oh, fine. Well, I'll just go and finish up a few things and then get going."

"Give Pam my best. And the lad." He reached for the papers again.

"Yes, I will. Thanks. See you Monday, then."

"Yes. Monday."

Recrossing the yard he knew he would have to ring Liz and for the first time felt dread rather than instant sexual anticipation. From his office, he put the call through and was told that she was with a client. There was nothing unusual about that since Liz worked for one of the pioneer Free Legal Advice Centers and was invariably busy.

"It's Mr. Woodford, isn't it?" said the girl on the switchboard. "Shall I get her to call you back?"

"Please. At the office."

Then he went to the door and shouted for Ros, his secretary, who sat sullen and showed a disconcerting amount of bare tanned leg, while he dealt with his mail.

"Are you out to lunch?" she asked.

"Yes. In fact, I shall be out until Monday."

"Oh! Have a nice time then."

Ian told himself that he only imagined the smirk in her voice. Ros also knew about Liz, or rather that he received regular phone calls from a woman who was not Mrs. Woodford. Ros no doubt envisaged a dirty weekend somewhere. Brighton probably. For a second, Ian considered it, too. It could be easily fixed. The phone shrilled.

"Hi. You rang."

"Yes. Look, love, I'm sorry but I've got to shoot down to Pam. Yes. Today."

"Oh."

"I'm sorry."

"Something's wrong?"

"I'm not quite sure but . . . well . . . yes. She wants me to go, anyway." It was the first time he had lied to Liz.

"Oh well, it can't be helped, I suppose." Her

disappointment and resentment made an eloquent silence.

"You did say you were making plans of your own."

"I said I might want to, and for the weekend. Not Thursday night."

"Look, Liz . . ."

"Sorry. I've got to rush. See you."

She hung up. Ian couldn't help wondering if his lie, his unthinking use of Pam as an excuse, was tempting providence.

He had been diving at the far end of the lake where a strip of grassy bank lay below the path to Home Farm. The water seemed much colder there and was opaque with silt. After several dives, he felt the strong pull of a current and thought that he heard a rushing noise. He could not stay down long enough to explore further, and when he broke the surface, Regina was calling him.

"Come on," she said. "I've just been to see your mother. She's not feeling too well. I said you could spend the day with us."

He did not answer but clambered out, getting his legs muddy on the bank. Regina had taken his towel from the moored boat and, unbidden, wrapped it around him.

"What's wrong with her?" he asked, his voice betraying the alarm of a child who is too accustomed to the ill health of others.

"She's just a bit tired," Regina said, casually. "She didn't sleep well last night."

Peter turned his back on her, dunked his legs in the water to wash off the mud. His memories of the night were hazy, confused, yet he felt vaguely guilty.

"Why? Is she often under the weather?" Regina inquired.

"No," Peter answered, quickly and definitely. He began to dry his legs and put on his old sneakers.

51

"Come on, then. I expect you're hungry. I thought we might have a picnic. Would you like that?"

He spread the towel to dry in the bottom of the boat.

"With the others? Reggie and Linda and the others?" he asked.

Regina regarded him with a quizzical half-smile.

"No," she teased. "I thought just you and me, all by ourselves." The boy's face clouded. His eyes shifted away from her. The resistance Regina always felt in him now seemed palpable, like something drawn taut and dangerous between them. It will have to be soon, she thought. Soon, or he will be too strong for me. Peter's head jerked toward her. His mouth prepared to form words, as though he had read her thoughts. Regina laughed, caught his pointed chin in her strong hand and said, "No, you chump. Of course all of us. And I've promised you'll be home by six," she added, releasing him.

"Thank you. That'll be nice," he said, formally.

She would not have been surprised if he had bowed from the waist. She turned away before her face could reveal anything.

"Come on, then," she said again, and began to climb back toward the path.

Peter looked back at the house but it was screened by trees from that bank. There was nothing to do but follow her.

They piled into Regina's beat-up old station wagon, clutching a collection of plastic bags. Grizzle carried a spade.

"What do you want a spade for?" Carl demanded, thrusting its handle out of the way.

"Digging," Grizzle said, and poked out her tongue.

"What for? Buried treasure?" Reggie chimed in.

"She's crazy enough," Carl murmured.

"That'll do, Carl. Leave her be." Regina eased

herself in behind the wheel. "Now, have we got everything?"

"Yes. Come on."

"Let's go."

It was quite unlike Peter's idea of a picnic. His parents had a big hamper with places for special plates and things. They had only used it once, though, in Kew Gardens, when the rhododendrons were out. Sometimes, if the weather was good, his mother took him to a little park near his school and fed him cold chicken and sausages wrapped in foil for his lunch. But this was much more fun. Linda put her arm around him, hugging him. She had helped him rummage for food at the Farm, since Regina had said that each could take what he or she wanted.

"Where are we going?" he asked.

"Down by the river. A place we know."

"What river?"

"You'll see."

"There's caves," Reggie promised.

"Yes," Regina chipped in, "and I don't want anyone getting lost in them, all right?"

"Yes, Regina," they chorused, and giggled.

"Carl?" Peter leaned forward, tapping him on the shoulder.

"Mm."

"If there's a river near here, do you think there's an underground stream draining the lake?"

Carl turned toward him, his dark eyes searching his face.

"What makes you ask that?"

"Nothing, only this morning I was diving at your end of the lake and found a really strong current there, so I wondered."

Carl turned away, shrugged.

"Well, if there is, there'd have to be another stream at the other end to feed it," he said.

"Given the way it lies, in all those hills, I wouldn't be surprised," Regina said. "It's very deep. Yes, I should say it's fed and drained like that. So you be careful when you're doing your deep-sea diving act, or you'll give your mother a heart attack."

Peter sat back wishing he had never mentioned it. Why did she have to reduce everything to his mother's health?

"Since when have you been such an expert?" Carl asked, teasing her.

"Since before you were born," she retorted and they laughed together as though they were completely alone.

Peter stared out of the window at the flashing summer hedgerows. Linda was humming quietly under her breath. Grizzle clutched the spade as though it was something precious. Kneeling in the back, Reggie was already eating his picnic. Peter wondered what his mother was doing. Suppose it was a trick? Suppose Regina had just said that he was to spend the day with them? His body stiffened.

"It's all right," Linda whispered, pulling his shoulders back against the car seat.

He looked at her, but she only smiled.

Regina parked the car on a wide embankment close to a gate. Reggie, Grizzle, and Carl scrambled out of the car. They were obviously familiar with the place. The two boys climbed the gate at once and ran, whooping, over the brow of the hill. Peter saw a strong padlock, almost new, fixed to a rusted hasp. He was about to climb over like the others when Linda pulled him back. Grizzle walked to the gate and stood quite still, the spade trailing from her hand. Regina slammed her door, locked it, and walked around the car. She stopped when she saw Grizzle, a smile playing about her lips.

The girl was staring at the padlock. Although her

54

back was to him, Peter felt the intensity of her stare. It puzzled him and he looked at Linda, as though for an explanation. She shook her head, forbidding him to speak. He turned back to the gate and Grizzle. A sharp click sounded and the padlock hung open. Peter caught his breath. The sound was unnaturally loud in the still, empty afternoon. Grizzle had not moved, had not touched the padlock, but even as he absorbed this fact, she had unhooked it and pushed the gate open. Regina passed through, into the field as though nothing at all had happened. Linda gave him a push.

"How . . . how did you do that?" he asked, pausing and trying to make Grizzle look at him.

"Come along, Peter," Regina called and, before the girl could answer, Linda grabbed his hand, was running, laughing, tugging him after her. He didn't think Grizzle was going to reply anyway.

The river lay like a smooth-rippling snake before them. It curved to the west, between trees. There was a rough, trodden path beside it, along which Reggie was already walking, whirling round, shouting to the others to hurry.

"The caves are along there," Linda told him.

"How did she do it, Linda? You saw."

She ran along the path, chasing Reggie. Her blonde hair flew about her head, like sunlight. Peter felt not frightened but excluded. He simply wanted to know how it was done, if he could learn the trick. He followed slowly, almost sulkily after the others. Probably the thing was open all the time. But he had heard the click.

Around the bend of the river, a sort of cliff extended close to the path. It was high, gray, streaked yellow, and eroded in such a way that it contained many ledges, foot- and toe-holds. Carl and Reggie were already climbing. Linda waved him on. He looked where they climbed, toward two black holes, like eyes.

"We'll have the picnic here," Regina said. He had not realized she was so close behind him. "Tell the others to be careful, Peter."

"I don't think I'll go. I'm not very keen on caves."

"Oh?"

She walked off the path, onto a semicircle of bright green grass that bit into the trees. She carried a rug, as well as her plastic bag. The rug blazed red against the green as she shook it out. Peter sat on the grass, staring at the river. Grizzle came slowly along the path, dragging the spade behind her, making an irritating, grating sound. Regina sighed, sat on the rug, and arranged her skirt.

"Why not?"

"Mm?"

"Why don't you like caves?"

Peter shrugged.

"I think somebody's sulking. What's up?"

"Nothing."

More to escape Regina than out of any real desire to be with Grizzle, Peter jumped up and followed her. Before reaching the picnic spot, she had veered off into the trees. They were old, thick-trunked, deciduous, with plenty of room to move between them. Peter walked parallel to Grizzle, watching her. She seemed indifferent to his presence. After a while she stopped and pushed her toe experimentally into the ground. Then she moved on, drawing closer to Peter. Again she tested the consistency of the earth and this time seemed satisfied. She dropped her plastic bag and began to dig. Peter leaned against a tree, picking at its bark, half watching her.

"How did you do it? Open the gate?"

Grizzle grunted as she pushed down hard on the spade. She pulled it free of the soil and made a second cut adjoining it.

"Thought," she said.

"Thought what?"

"Just thought."

She made a third plunge with the spade, a fourth with her back to Peter, then she began to remove the soil carefully, until she had made a neat rectangle.

"Can anyone do it?"

He thought she shrugged, but could not be sure. With a sort of dogged determination, she began to make a second, identical hole.

"I mean, could I? Could you teach me?"

For a moment she looked at him. Her eyes were very pale blue, almost milky, like a baby's. She so seldom looked straight at anyone that her eyes, their near-colorlessness, always surprised.

"No."

She made a third hole.

"Really just by thinking of it?"

"Pe-ter. Gri-zzle." Reggie's voice floated through the trees and a moment later they heard him crashing toward them. Grizzle took no notice.

"Why didn't you come to the caves?" he asked, swinging around a tree, panting.

Peter shrugged.

Grizzle was kneeling, her lumpy white knees sinking into the soft earth. The plastic bag rustled as she took something from it. Peter could not see what, for she carried it close to her body and kept her back toward him. Curious, Peter went forward and peered into the first hole. He started back in surprise, collided with Reggie, who grasped his upper arm.

There was a gingerbread man in the hole. He had no head.

Although he did not want to, Peter moved forward and looked into the other two miniature graves. Each contained a gingerbread man: the second lacked a leg; the third was whole. It was while staring at this one, protests and questions forming on his lips, that it happened.

The hole expanded. He felt his body become stiff and

dry. He was staring up, out of the hole. Perspective was exaggerated. Grizzle's legs like receding pillars of white rubber. The earth pressed cold and clammy against his back, through his borrowed shirt. The spade was enormous. It rose, receded, came down, blocking out light and sight. Clods of earth tumbled on him, pressing his body down. He tried to move but his limbs were stiff and clumsy. The earth rained down, damp, dank-smelling. His legs were covered, chilled. A great weight on his belly, his chest, made it difficult to breathe. He opened his mouth to scream and tasted earth, bitter and horrible. He could see nothing. There was only the cold press of the earth and, he thought, the awful slither of a worm across his neck.

"Whatever's the matter?"

He was pressed hard against Regina's body.

"What have you done to him?"

He fought her, not realizing for several seconds that the awful noise, part scream, part rattling struggle for oxygen, was coming from his own mouth. It seemed that Regina was trying to hit him as her arms flailed, trying to control his.

"Peter," she shouted. "It's all right. Stop it. There's nothing . . ."

He broke free from her, turned and ran, blundering among the trees. Voices called behind him, Regina's louder than the others. He skidded to a halt, dazzled by the sunshine. Linda, pale against the black river, held out her arms to him. He ran into them, sobbing with relief.

They were all there then, Regina talking about asthma attacks, shooting questions at him. Did he have hay fever, fits? He shook his head repeatedly. Linda led him away, soothing him. He felt, somehow, beneath the noise of Regina's questions, Reggie's explanations, that Linda spoke to him, but he could not quite make out the words. Finally, she drew him back to the red rug and made him sit beside her. They were all silent, self-absorbed. She offered him food from her own bag, his, but he could not eat.

"I think we'd better take him home," Regina said. "Some picnic this turned out to be."

Peter wanted to say that it was not his fault, but somehow he knew or Regina made him feel that it was.

They packed up in silence, and walked in single file back along the path to the field and the car. Peter felt that they all blamed him, even Linda. He had ruined everything.

Poppies grew in several fields around Home Farm, but Pamela could not go there. It would be a breach of trust. Regina would be bound to think her anxious, spying. There was a spot on the road to Halford village where she had noticed a clump of the flowers, but she did not want to go so far away. She could take the car, of course. She hesitated, looking at it. The sun burned on her back. The tarmac was hot through her shoes. The narrow, tree-lined drive looked cool and inviting. She would try the park. Although she could not remember having seen any poppies there, she had not consciously looked. Anyway, the park seemed a proper compromise.

She walked slowly along the drive, for even out of the direct sun it was too hot to hurry. The trees were still and silent. Even the birds seemed to be taking a siesta. Pamela paused only once, to pick a couple of fern fronds, one still not completely unfurled. Unconsciously she used them as a fan.

The main drive to Halford Hall looked white in the glare, although the gravel was made up of beige and orange-brown chips, with only a sprinkling of white. Pamela liked the crunch and slip of it beneath her feet. Trees grew on one side only. Within yards the parkland began, falling away to her left. A few sad-looking cows sought the shade of two oaks. They looked posed, as though waiting for a latter-day Constable to romanticize them.

About fifty yards from the Hall itself, the drive divided. The main artery continued straight ahead to form a sweeping half-circle in front of the Hall. A branch went to the right, following the line of the woods which here resembled a plantation. Pamela supposed that that was what the woods had been originally. This tangential track led to Home Farm. The gravel soon petered out, leaving only a rutted dirt road. She was facing the side of the Hall and, for the first time, appreciated that it was beautiful. A terrace flanked it on three sides. Balustrades, the sweep of two mirrored, symmetrical flights of steps, led down to the grass. The building had excited Ian and she tried to recall what he had said about it. Mid- to late-eighteenth century. Compromised Palladian, he had called it. A cube with restrained ornamentation and many small-paned windows. Pamela noticed how cunningly the balustrade was echoed along the edge of the flat roof, joining foundation and roof, earth and air in a simple harmony.

She was drawn to the house, curious about it. The steps to the terrace were cracked and moss-covered. She walked along, studying the windows which threw back her pale reflection, and pressed her face to one, cupping her hands on either side. Pamela could see only an impression of black space, as though the windows, the many windows, admitted no light. She walked right around the terrace. At what she supposed to be the back of the Hall, the facade which looked toward Home Farm, there was a door. Its brass handle was green from neglect. Out of an instinct she did not understand, Pamela grasped the handle and turned it. It was locked, of course, and she felt like an intruder. The house must have cost a fortune and yet Mr. Appledore had done nothing to it. Its emptiness seemed oppressive. She turned into the third segment of the terrace which lay in shadow, gray and cool. It was possible to make out the formal lines of a knot garden below the terrace. She smelled lavender and saw a small clump of invading poppies.

Pamela hurried to the steps and then followed the weedy paths, twisting and turning like the prescribed passage of some formal dance, until she reached the poppies. She selected carefully. Some full-blown, others with the crushed appearance of a thing newly born, just opened. She added several swollen green bud cases, just beginning to split and reveal the scarlet blaze within. They reminded her of the slashed sleeves of medieval gowns. She wound her way through the garden, regretting its neglect, pausing to add a few sprigs of lavender, among which bees were busy. Then she reached the last flourish of the drive. The double front door of solid oak was set between four pilasters which seemed to melt into the fabric of the house. They were purely ornamental. Pamela could not resist going up to the door. There was a large unpolished knocker, shaped like a howling gargoyle. She raised the knocker, which creaked a little, and let it fall against the wood. The sound surprised her, a hollow boom, trailed by after-echoes. She heard the sound traveling through the house, and it seemed the very embodiment of emptiness, desertion. Suddenly, the place seemed unbearably lonely to her and she jumped, almost dropping her improvised bouquet, when the sound of a motor horn cut across the silence. She turned toward the noise, which was immediately repeated. Three short blasts and a long one.

Ian was standing beside the car at the turnoff point for the cottage.

"Ian," she called, and waved. She felt relieved and elated. She began to hurry toward him and was even more pleased when he began to stroll easily toward her. Then a cloud tempered her happiness. He had come

61

unexpectedly to say that he could not make it this weekend. He would stay only one night, perhaps not so long. That woman . . .

"Hello. Sorry if I startled you. There was no one at home?"

Automatically Pamela lifted her cheek for his customary kiss. She was surprised when his arm went around her shoulders, hugging her against him.

"Of course not. I was just being silly. There's something irresistible about a knocker when you know there's no one to answer."

Ian laughed quietly.

"I'm sorry I didn't let you know I was coming. You don't mind?"

"You're staying?"

"Of course. If what's-he-called had thought to put a phone in the cottage . . ."

"Nothing's wrong?"

"Yes." He felt her body tense against him. "London was unbearable. Too hot. There's nothing much doing at the yard and I suddenly thought of the lake. I badly want a swim."

They reached the car and Ian released her. He stooped a little to open the door for her.

"That's wonderful," she said, smiling.

"I also wanted to see you. And Peter."

Pamela felt shy, like a girl being courted. His voice had not contained such warmth for longer than she dared to remember. She got into the car.

"So you'll stay until Monday?"

"Yes." He almost added, "Or until Sunday night anyway," but checked himself. "Where's Peter?"

"Up at Home Farm. Regina—Mrs. Thomas—invited him for the day." Impulsively, she touched his arm. "I am glad you came."

"Good."

He started the car, turned into the drive. He parked

beside her car, got out, and stood looking down at the lake.

"God, that looks good," he said when she joined him. "Would you mind if I had a swim straightaway?"

"Of course not."

They went into the house, Ian pulling his damp shirt from his trousers.

"Would you like some tea, afterward?" Pamela called, putting the poppies and the fern in water.

"No. There's some Soave in the car. Let's begin the weekend early and in style."

"It won't be cold," she said, pleased by the idea.

"Put some ice in the glasses. Vulgar, but effective." He came out of the bedroom, fastening the drawstring of his trunks.

"All right," Pamela said. "I'll see to it. Enjoy your swim."

She could not help wondering why London had suddenly become unbearable, what had happened to all the work that was supposed to keep him there all summer. It didn't matter, she lectured herself. She would not spoil it. When she went to the car to fetch the wine, Ian was already in the water.

It was deliciously, bracingly cold. After the first shock Ian felt his body relax. He swam a few yards, turned over onto his back, and floated, squinting at the cloudless sky. His mind emptied, as though sluiced clean by the water.

Pamela arranged the flowers on the white wicker table on the veranda and pulled up a second chair. In the bedroom, out of habit she gathered up Ian's clothes and brought out a towel for him. She had put the wine in the refrigerator, filled the ice bucket. Then she paused and gazed at herself in the mirror. Her hair was a neat dark cap, framing her pale face. On impulse, she added a smear of pink lipstick and smoothed her dress over her hips.

Ian clambered onto the jetty, shaking himself like a dog. Watching him, Pamela smiled. He looked relaxed and happy and, she realized, with an almost forgotten stirring, handsome. She went to fetch the wine.

Shivering a little, Ian toweled himself briskly and then flopped into one of the chairs, rubbing his legs.

"Here," Pamela said, putting the bottle on the table. "Good swim?"

"Marvelous. Bloody cold though."

"Can I fetch you something?"

"No. The sun's already warming me."

She dropped ice cubes into the glasses, poured the almost amber-colored wine over them.

"Cheers," Ian saluted her. "You look well. Good week?"

"Mm. Do you remember . . .?" Pamela stopped, afraid to presume on memories.

"Venice," he said at once. "That restaurant up behind the . . . where was it?"

"Our first meal there. I can't remember. By the first church past the Doge's Palace, off the Riva."

"That's right. The food was good, too."

"And this is delicious."

He leaned back in his chair, welcoming the sun.

"What's this woman like up at the Farm?"

"Nice. She's very competent." Pamela paused, searching for words. "There's something trustworthy about her, you know." She laughed a little. "I suppose I mean maternal." She looked almost shyly at Ian as though the word was dangerous, but he was impressed only by her unusual willingness to talk enthusiastically about a comparative stranger. "Peter's made such friends of the children. She fosters three, apart from her own boy."

"It's good that he's made friends."

"Yes. Regina insisted on having him for the day. I didn't sleep very well last night. She packed me back off to bed."

"That was very good of her. You're all right?"

"Yes. Fine." She laughed, nervously, and drank some more wine. "It was just too hot to sleep."

Ian leaned forward, refilled her glass and his own.

"What time will Peter be back, then?"

"Six."

"That gives us plenty of time." His voice was low, caressing.

Pamela looked down at her glass.

"Please," he said. "The sun always makes me excited."

"I don't know. I . . ."

She felt him retreat, saw him grip the glass more tightly.

"Peter might come back early," she said.

"And it would be really dreadful if he found us making love," Ian said caustically.

"No. Oh, please don't. I didn't mean to spoil it. If you must know, I just feel silly. I mean, in the middle of the afternoon."

A smile lightened Ian's face.

"Have another glass of this and you won't feel silly."

She nodded, held out her glass. The bottle was almost empty. Gathering her courage, she said, "Let's take it into the bedroom."

He stood up at once, still grinning, and held out his hand to her.

In the bedroom, he pulled her against him, kissing her throat, her lips. She protested about his damp bathing suit.

"That's easily settled," he said and wriggled out of it. Pamela turned away, but he caught hold of her, gently began to unzip her dress. She tried not to think of anything, least of all about what might have made him so eager for her. Then he touched her breasts, eased her body onto the bed, and began to stroke her insistently, demanding yet leading. Pamela clung to him, her body rocking to the rhythm of his fingers. His

65

breath brushed her ear as he entered her smoothly and strongly. She clasped his buttocks, holding him tightly inside her. This way, she thought, there would be no terrors, no ghosts or memories. A sound like a sob escaped her and she became liquid, melting. Ian buried his face in her throat, mouthing, murmuring. His body was slick with sweat. She melted into him.

They were sitting on the veranda, talking in lazy, relaxed voices when Linda brought Peter back. Ian watched Pamela carefully as she turned to greet the boy and was relieved to see no marked change in her mood.

"Hello, darling. Look who's here." She smiled at Ian.

"Hello," he said and reached to ruffle the boy's hair. Ian was aware of the girl behind Peter, standing in the shadows.

"Linda, you don't know my husband," Pamela said, drawing Peter against her.

"Come and have a drink," Ian invited.

"Thank you." She walked to the table and Ian thought that she had the sweetest smile that he had ever seen.

"Peter, fetch another chair for . . . Linda, is it?" He asked, only because he wanted to make her look at him.

"Yes, that's right," she said. Her eyes were large and soft.

"I'll go and get another glass," he said. Something about the girl made him feel awkward. Inside the house, he winked at Peter, who was carrying out a kitchen chair. "I like your girl friend."

"She's not my girl friend," Peter said, blushing, and stomped out.

"Did you have a nice time?" Pamela asked.

"Yes, thank you."

"We went on a picnic," Linda explained. "But Peter didn't feel very well."

"Not well?" Pamela reached for him. "What's wrong, Peter? What is it?"

"Nothing. I'm all right."

"Here we are." Ian sounded hearty and brash. He poured Linda's wine. "What's up?" he asked, becoming aware of the tension.

"Peter's not very well," Pamela said. Her mouth was drawn down at the corners in a way that was all too familiar.

"He looks all right to me. Very well, in fact." Ian felt the boy's forehead. "A touch of the sun, I expect."

"That's what I thought," Linda agreed. "Though Regina wondered if he might be asthmatic."

"I'm all right," Peter repeated belligerently.

"You see?" Ian said to Pamela.

"No. Not at all. Whatever made her . . .?"

"It was just a touch of the sun, Pam," Ian said, raising his voice. "There's nothing at all wrong with him. Right, Peter?" The boy nodded solemnly. "I could swear he's grown another two inches in the last week."

"You wouldn't like to lie down?" Pamela fussed, leaning toward Peter.

"Have a glass of wine, Peter. That'll set you right."

"Oh, Ian!"

"Watered down," he snapped. "French kids are brought up on it. Go and get yourself a glass, Peter."

Peter stood up obediently and went into the house.

"Well now, Linda. Tell us all about yourself." He turned toward the girl, aware of her small breasts, naked under a thin blouse.

"If you'll excuse me I'll just . . ." Pamela would not look at him. She hurried into the house, calling to Peter.

"My wife worries," Ian said flatly, looking into his glass.

"Yes. I know."

He was angry with Pam. She had spoiled their

newfound intimacy. He had been surprised and pleased that she had allowed Peter to go off for the day. Maybe he had expected too much.

"I'm sure you took very good care of him," he told Linda. "Not that he really needs it."

"I'd better be getting back," she said.

"But you haven't told me about yourself, and you've hardly touched your wine."

"There's really nothing to tell."

"Perhaps the wine will loosen your tongue." He picked up her glass and handed it to her. For a brief moment, her fingers lingered against his. They were surprisingly cool.

"I live at Home Farm and help out there."

"I'd like to see it sometime. Do you have much stock?"

"No. But we grow a lot of things. We try to be self-sufficient."

"A sort of commune," Ian suggested.

"Not really. We're more a sort of family."

"How nice."

"You don't sound as though you meant that."

He looked at her quickly, but she seemed quite unembarrassed.

"Sorry. I . . ."

"I really had better be going." She stood up before he could protest.

"I'll walk part of the way with you," he volunteered. "I'd like to stretch my legs."

"Hadn't you better tell Mrs. Woodford?"

Ian hesitated for a moment, then said, "No. She isn't likely to think that any harm will come to *me*."

Linda turned away, laughing softly. He put his hand under her elbow to help her down the steps and she smiled at him over her shoulder.

Peter sat at the kitchen table, a glass of apple juice untouched in front of him. Pamela had explained that she did not think wine a good idea when he had been feeling out of sorts. His head thumped dully.

"I expect you were overexcited, too. A picnic. That must have been fun." She began to prepare supper, making an effort to appear calm even though she knew that something was wrong. "Isn't it nice that Daddy was able to come down early?"

"Yes."

"We'll have a lovely long weekend. You can go swimming together. You do look odd in those clothes," she said suddenly. "Not like my boy at all. I'll wash them and tomorrow you can take them back to Regina."

"I don't think I want to go there again."

Pamela heard the scream of alarm in her head. It was not a light remark but had obviously cost him considerable effort. She put down the lettuce she was holding and, very slowly, as though afraid of startling him, sat down.

"Peter?" Her throat was dry. They had been rough with him. Boys could be cruel. She trembled with anger. Regina had *promised*. Pamela had trusted her. "What happened? What is it?" Her voice rose dangerously close to hysteria. He shook his head. "You must tell me. If they've done anything to you . . ."

"Most of the time it's all right," he said quickly, knowing that he must say something if he was to prevent her becoming tearful, frightening. "With Reggie and Linda and the others, I mean. Then I don't mind. It's very interesting. They make me see things."

"See things? Oh my God, Peter." Pamela did not understand. Her racing mind imagined indecent displays, horrible assaults.

"Fire, one time. Yes. Fire. And then water. A gate under the water. It's good fun. As long as I don't try to hang on to it, I know it'll be all right. And then I . . . come back. Only today . . ." He looked at Pamela, at her open mouth and wide eyes. Her hands

69

twisted in spasms on the table. She frightened him even more than the memory of the earth. "It was Regina," he said, fighting back tears. "I know it was. It's all right without her. Only it was like I was being buried alive. I was frightened and then they thought I'd ruined everything." He put his head down on the table. His shoulders shook.

"Ian!" Pamela shouted at the top of her voice. She jumped up, her chair falling with a crash on the floor. "Ian!" She ran out of the kitchen, onto the veranda, calling his name. She was stunned by the empty chairs. The wineglasses and the bottles looked unreal. She ran back, scooped Peter up, pressing his face into her shoulder.

"It's all right. We'll go away, tonight. I won't let anything . . . Oh, darling, it's all my fault. I should never have let you go. But you're safe now. I promise. We'll go right away. Tonight. Now."

He pulled away from her, his face red with anger and fear.

"No. I don't want to go away. You don't understand. Oh Mommy, Mommy, please don't cry."

Ian wasn't quite sure whether he or Linda had stopped at the bend in the path. She was leaning against a tree. Below her, the lake shimmered in a haze of light and heat. Ian could see the soft pale arc of one breast beneath her casually buttoned blouse. He rested his hand against the trunk, uncertain what they had been talking about. Linda turned her face toward him with an inquiring expression. Her bottom lip was moist and trembled a little.

"Ian!"

Pamela's voice sounded close, as though she was standing just behind him. He jumped back, turned toward the house. The empty path was crisscrossed with beams of light as the sun began to wane.

"I think you'd better go," Linda said. "Thank you for walking with me."

He turned back to her, trying to think of something to say. She laughed softly and walked away. Cursing, Ian went back to the house.

"What is it? Pam?" he called as he reached the veranda. He knew, as he went inside, that his anger was unfair, was caused by his reaction to the girl, not Pam's shout. Then his heart sank. She was slumped on the kitchen floor, her head buried in Peter's lap. For some reason he thought her legs looked ugly, splayed on the floor as though useless, but it was the stricken, broken expression on Peter's face that hurt him most, and forced him to be calm. He reached down and pulled Pam away from the boy. She moaned in protest. Grunting with the effort, he hauled her to her feet. She leaned against him.

"Go to your room for a bit, Peter. I'll see to Mommy."

He nodded once, and went straight to his room.

Gritting his teeth, Ian pushed Pam away from him, wedging her body between the table and himself. Then he hit her hard on the cheek. She let out a single wail, stared at him as though he were a stranger, and then flung her arms around him, sobbing pitifully.

He half dragged, half carried her into the living room and dumped her on the couch. He poured a shot of brandy, handed it to her, and stood over her while she sipped it, coughing and spluttering.

"You've got to take us away from here. Oh God, where were you? I'm so frightened. Peter . . ." She turned, panic-stricken, toward his room. Ian grabbed her shoulder and pulled her round. He sat beside her.

"He's okay. Now stop this and tell me what happened. But I warn you, Pam, if you upset that kid any more, I won't be responsible for myself."

She looked at him with naked, hysterical terror and

71

then slumped back on the couch. Tears trickled from beneath her closed bruised-looking lids. Ian got up and went quickly to Peter's room.

"You all right?"

The boy was curled on his bed, reading—or pretending to read, Ian thought.

"Yes. How's Mommy?"

"She'll be all right. Do you want to tell me what happened?"

He looked down at the book.

"I just said I didn't want to go to the Farm again. I don't know. She just went on at me about being ill." He looked straight at Ian. "You *know*." It was an accusation.

"All right," Ian sighed. "Look, this may take a while. You can amuse yourself?"

"Yes."

"Good. I'll see you later."

Pamela had not moved. Ian took the glass from her clenched fingers, drained it himself, and then dabbed at her cheeks with his handkerchief.

"Hadn't you better tell me about it?"

She swallowed, nodded, sat up.

"I'm sorry I hit you," he said.

She shook her head, dismissing it. He did not understand what she said. A babble about Peter seeing things, being buried alive. Fire and water. When he interrupted to ask questions, she could not explain but veered into rage and hysteria.

"Ian, he's in danger. We've got to get him away from here."

"Keep your voice down," he ordered. "Nothing you've said makes sense."

"Ask him," she screeched. "You think I'm mad. You think I'm making it up. You ask him yourself."

"That's exactly what I intend to do. Now listen to me." He took her roughly by the shoulders and only with the greatest difficulty prevented himself from

72

shaking her. "You've got to calm down. Go into the kitchen and get supper started. I'm going to talk to Peter." She opened her mouth to protest, but Ian went on, raising his voice. "I promise you, if there's anything in these stories or whatever they are, I'll deal with it. All right?"

After a long time, during which her moist, frightened eyes darted about his face as though searching every line and contour for evidence of a lie, she nodded.

"Go on then," he said in a more gentle voice. "I'm hungry."

She nodded again, sniffed. He watched her, deliberately waiting until she had crossed the room and gone into the kitchen. After a moment he heard a tap running. He felt completely exhausted, but he knew that he had to keep his side of the bargain.

He tapped lightly on Peter's door before going in. The child was fast asleep, lying on his side, the book forgotten. Ian walked quietly to the bed, squatted down.

"Peter?"

The boy did not stir. He touched his forehead. It felt hot but not alarmingly so. Ian envied his ability to cut out, to retreat into sleep. He was also glad that he could finally rest.

Pamela froze as he came into the kitchen.

"Well?"

"He's fast asleep."

"Are you sure? He's not . . .?"

"For Christ's sake, Pam, no," he shouted, smacking his hand down on the table. "I can tell the difference between a normal, healthy sleep and a coma, or whatever else you're imagining."

"But he hasn't had any supper."

"So what? He probably stuffed himself rotten at the picnic."

"He didn't have any breakfast either."

"So you want to go and wake him up and spoon-feed

73

him, I suppose? And then you'll find an excuse to sit up all night, fussing over him, making him feel . . . oh God, I don't know."

She walked stiffly to the sink.

"You always blame me," she said.

"You are always to blame," he retorted brutally. "I honestly thought you were getting over it and now . . ." He felt hopeless and it showed in his voice.

"I was. I *am*," Pamela insisted. "Really I am. Only I am not imagining this. He told me that they made him see things. He said he had been buried alive . . ."

"Pam, use your common sense. Kids get up to all sorts of things and tell tall stories too. There's not a scrap of dirt on his clothes. Even if they did do something that scared him, he's perfectly safe. He's lying in that room there, sleeping. Do you understand?"

"If you'd only ask him. You promised."

"I will," Ian said, tired. "In the morning. But it's quite simple. If he doesn't want to play with those kids anymore, he needn't."

"He said it was her, Regina. And I trusted her." New tears welled.

"Pam, there's nothing they could do to him, nothing at all that could be as bad for him as this. If he's in any danger, it's from you."

She fought to get her breathing under control. Ian watched, knowing that he had hurt her.

"All right," she said at last, as calmly as she could. "Then take us back to London. If I'm unfit I need to see Elsa. You'll be able to protect him from me. Please. I don't mind."

"I'm not going to promise anything until I've talked to the boy. Will you please get supper?"

Slowly, she began to make the salad. Ian went out onto the veranda, which was now entirely in shadow. The Soave was slightly warm, but he didn't care. He just wanted to get away from Pam, to avoid another scene. His head ached dismally. He thought of Liz and wished with all his heart that he had not left London. Then he remembered Peter's face, the child's struggle to comfort a grown, hysterical woman, and knew that he had to be here.

"Supper's ready. I'm going to lie down."

"You should eat."

"I can't."

She walked away from him into the bedroom where, he thought with a keen pang of sadness, the bed was still rumpled from their lovemaking. He had been so happy then. So hopeful. Only hours ago.

He ate the salad, the slightly sweaty ham, and opened another bottle of wine. Afterward he washed up, made coffee, and went to the bedroom to ask Pam if she wanted any.

"No."

He sat down beside her.

"I'm sorry. It's just that I . . . You seemed so relaxed when I arrived. It was good, wasn't it?" He touched her breast lightly, to remind her.

"It's spoiled now," she said, shifting away from his hand. "Now that I know what you really think of me."

"Pam."

"I know. You're sorry you came. I've ruined everything. Well, that's just too bad, Ian. This time I'm not imagining things. This time, I swear to you, he told me he was upset. I knew something . . ."

"We'll see in the morning," he said. He could not face another row. "Try to sleep. I'm going to sit outside for a while."

She huddled down in the bed, saying nothing.

He sat on the veranda, drinking coffee and thinking, not for the first time, that it was clearly his duty to separate Pam and Peter. He was certain there was nothing wrong with the boy, except the pressure she put him under. But—and he needed no experts to tell him this—if he did take Peter away, send him to boarding

75

school for instance, it would probably tip Pam over the edge. Maybe a complete breakdown was the only way out. He saw her, like a cartoon character, shattered into little, neat pieces which could, slowly, be fitted back together again. Perhaps Elsa Rath simply wasn't enough? Full analysis, hospitalization even? Could he do it? Could he actually commit her? She *had* improved. She was not lying. He had not been mistaken. He simply expected too much, too soon?

The arguments were old, familiar and worn. They went in circles. He was profoundly weary of them. He would talk to Peter. He would defer any decisions until then. He would talk to him man-to-man. Could he cope with Pam? Did he want to go back to London? And almost as an afterthought, he remembered that he must try to get to the bottom of this crazy story of Pam's. After all, the kid must have said something to set her off. She wasn't completely insane.

He stood up. The house oppressed him. It was not for this, this load of intolerable responsibilities, that he had come here, full of good intentions. Liz. Well, he could answer her question about Pam now all right. That is, if she was remotely interested in hearing the answer.

He pushed his hands into his jean pockets and stepped off the veranda. The moon had risen, pale and watery. It hung over the trees, blazing a silver path across the black water. He walked morosely down the long flight of shallow steps. It was a mess, all of it, a bloody mess. But he had to do something for the kid. He owed him that much. He reached the bottom of the hill and stepped onto the jetty. The boards creaked under his weight. There was the faintest lapping sound. He walked to the far end and sat down, staring along the insubstantial path of moonlight.

He stayed there for a long time, letting his thoughts turn aimlessly. The moon was higher, its light more diffusely spread across the lake. As it grew later, Ian began to feel cold. Sitting still, he felt the closeness of the water. He scrambled to his feet and began to walk back up to the house. He still was not tired. The house depressed him. The path beckoned invitingly. He strolled along it, listening to the mysterious but not alarming night noises. A breath of wind, a falling pinecone. The rustle of some foraging animal. Laughter, silver-light, becoming husky. At first it seemed just another of the night's sounds. Then he recognized it and realized that he was not alone. He went forward cautiously, his heart thumping pleasantly.

He stood where they had stood earlier. He put his hand against the same tree, looking for her. Slowly, as his eyes became used to the light, he saw her on the grassy bank at the far end of the lake. The light caught her hair as she bent, pushing down her jeans. She kicked them away, stretched her arms up, as though worshipping the moon. Ian held his breath. It was a deliberate display, a magnificent invitation. And then he realized that she could not possibly know that he was there, watching her. He drew back. He felt like a voyeur. She was only a child. An innocent girl. He knew, then, how much he had wanted her on the veranda, by this tree. He began to steal along the path, looking for a way down. After all there was no harm in . . . He stopped. She was sitting on the bank now, her legs dangling in the water. Her arms were raised, holding up her hair. Her breasts were quite visible in the moonlight. He forgot everything but the desire to go to her. He ran on, a few more yards, searching for a safe way down. Then he heard her laughter again. He was about to call her name when he saw the boy, tall and slim-bodied, step from the shadows. A young satyr, naked, bending toward her. The boy's hands covered her breasts. Their mouths joined wetly. A cold sweat prickled on Ian's back. Now he *was* a voyeur. He turned away, sharply, unable to bear the sinuous, beautiful yet appalling intertwining of their limbs. He walked on the balls of his feet, terrified of making a sound. A sigh pursued him, a sigh of gratification and sensuality. He stood on the veranda, trembling. He thanked God that they had not seen him. He collected the glasses and bottles, carried them indoors. He looked into Peter's room. He had turned over onto his other side, but still slept. Ian was very quiet in his own bedroom. It was not so much that he was afraid of disturbing Pam but that he felt embarrassed by the strength of his response to that girl. Linda. He cursed her. He slipped into bed, trying to keep his body away from Pam's. She stirred, turned over, touched him.

"Ian?"

"Yes?"

"I'm sorry."

"It's all right."

He thrust his hands down between his thighs and felt ashamed.

"Ian?"

"Mm?"

"Where were you, when I called?"

He felt as though his whole body must betray him.

"I walked that girl along the path. What's her name?"

"Linda." Pamela sighed, settled.

Linda. He closed his eyes and saw her, white in the moonlight. He opened them quickly, stared at nothing, at the darkness that was the wall. Her laughter trilled in his head, making his blood race.

Peter woke up. He was hungry, starving. The house creaked around him. He recognized the tapping of a branch on the roof, the sigh of the wind in the trees. He got off the bed, still wearing the borrowed clothes which felt slightly unfamiliar. He went into the kitchen and found some ham, salad, and bread. He made a thick wedge of a sandwich and, munching it, drifted out onto the veranda. The breeze felt good. He left the veranda, welcoming the breeze, turning his head to watch the dark trees swaying.

They were standing by the jetty, their hands linked. He tried to remember if there had been voices. A jumble of sounds came to him, raucous and incoherent. His mother's sobbing, his own screams when . . . Carl raised his arm, beckoning him. He went down the hill to them, eating his sandwich.

"Hello."

They had been swimming. Beads of water shone in Carl's hair. Linda's blouse was damp on the shoulders, above her breasts where water dripped from her hair.

"Your mother's upset."

"You shouldn't tell her things."

"Not because they are bad."

"No."

"Because she can't understand them."

"Some things have to be secret."

"You want to know, don't you?"

"You like our games."

"But you should be careful what you say."

"It's not nice to upset your mother."

"Not necessary."

"No."

"Your father will be worried, too."

"Might take you away."

"You ought to put his mind at rest."

"Peter."

"Peter?"

He opened his eyes to full daylight, to his father's face hanging over him.

"Come on, Peter. Let's go and fetch the boat."

The sky was full of scudding white clouds. The breeze had freshened. His father said it was too cold to swim. They would walk to the boat, then row it back, in time for breakfast. Peter preceded him along the path, showed him the best place to get down. Their feet slipped on pine needles, which gave off a resinous smell. Dust rose around them. They reached the bank where the boat was moored, where Regina had been waiting for him. He knew that his father was steeling himself to say something. He made no move toward the boat.

"You're old enough now, Peter, for me to be able to talk to you like a grown-up. If there's anything you don't understand, well, just speak up and I'll try to explain. Peter?"

"I'm listening."

"It's about your mother. You know, don't you, that she's been sick, ill, for a long time now?"

Peter began to chip away at a grassy clod of earth on the edge of the bank.

"She's getting better," he said.

"You think so?"

"Don't you?"

"Yes. I did. Until last night. Now I'm not so sure and I don't know if you can put up with it, cut off down here with just her."

"I've got Reggie and Linda and the others. I've got more people to play with here than at home."

"You really like them? Tell me about them."

The clod fell with a heavy plop into the water.

"They're nice."

"I liked Linda."

Peter said nothing.

"Only your mother seems to think . . . Well, to be honest with you, I'm not sure what she thinks."

"She worries," said Peter. "You *know*."

"Yes. But something you said made her worry."

"I didn't mean . . . She always says it's wrong to lie."

"Were you lying?"

"No."

"So what did you tell her?"

"Just things. Things we do. Games."

"Tell me?"

"Well, like we lit a fire once. And we went diving, down there, where it's deep and there's a current."

"Is that all?"

"Yes."

"She said something about being buried alive."

Peter laughed, loud and slightly scornful.

"Peter?"

"That was just something Reggie said. When we were in the caves yesterday. It was really creepy, good though. And Reggie said what about if the roof fell in and we got trapped. You know, like miners. Buried alive. That's what people say, isn't it?"

He turned to Ian, his face open and smiling. His eyes shone with the remembered excitement and slight terror of it. Ian wanted to hug him. The knot of tension in him unraveled.

"Well, far be it from me to encourage you to lie, but it's not really lying if you don't mention certain things. Do you understand?"

"Course."

"But you did feel poorly yesterday?"

"I didn't have any breakfast, and then I didn't like the food at the picnic. It was hot and I felt . . ." He shrugged. "I don't know. Everybody fusses," he complained.

"Not me. And not you anymore, if you're discreet." Ian reached for the prow of the boat and pulled it in slowly to the bank. "Do you know what 'discreet' means?"

"It means being careful, keeping your mouth shut."

"To put it crudely," Ian laughed. "In you go. And you can row."

He held the boat steady as Peter climbed aboard and settled himself.

"There's just one more thing. Promise you'll tell me honestly what you want?"

"What?" He fitted the oars into the rowlocks.

"Would you rather leave here, come back to London?"

Peter looked at him steadily, frowning.

"You mean because of her?"

"I mean, what do *you* want."

"I want to stay here of course—it's great."

"Okay." Ian got into the boat and cast off. Peter rowed with strong, steady strokes. His rapidly developing shoulders bulged beneath his shirt. Ian thought that, in spite of everything, this holiday had done him good. "I'll have to talk to your mother," he said casually. "Do you think you can make yourself scarce after breakfast?"

"We can stay?" It was a challenge. Ian nodded. "Sure."

Ian felt that he had struck a bargain with an equal, a bargain that even Pam's anxiously hovering figure, waiting for them, could not break.

It had taken Ian most of the morning to calm Pamela and convince her that she had misunderstood, misheard the boy's excited and garbled account of his games with the children from Home Farm. She had wept brokenly when he explained that Peter's distress had been induced by her.

"He's afraid of your reactions. He anticipates them. And you become so agitated you leap ahead, making it impossible for him to talk sensibly. You are beyond listening."

She had nodded, accepted her responsibility with an ease—he thought almost eagerly—that faintly disturbed him. And when at last she had flung her arms around him crying that she did not know what she would do without him, or how he could put up with her, he had wanted to shrink away. In place of yesterday's desire, there was only a sort of sad repugnance.

Throughout their talk, Peter had shown a tact beyond his years. He remained well out of earshot, but always in sight, playing in the rowboat, and when he came up to lunch, he behaved as though entirely ignorant of any tension. Ian had felt, as he had earlier in the day, a strength in the boy which seemed not just a bonus but a cause for hope.

He thought about this as, affecting aimlessness, he walked toward Home Farm that afternoon. He had not broached the idea of sending Peter away to school, although he still felt that this would be the wisest course—for the boy's sake. Before, Pam had recognized that he had been thinking of himself, their relationship. But could she accept that Peter needed to be separated from her? Any decision would have to be deferred, for he had promised Peter that they could spend the rest of the summer here, though Ian was still not happy about this. It was these doubts, he told himself, that led him to Home Farm and not, definitely not, the possibility of seeing Linda. The girl's smile, laugh, body had haunted his mind all morning, a sort of irrational, erotic background which had made concentration difficult. He just wanted to see the lie of the land, to explore the possibility of taking Regina Thomas into his confidence. Damn it, he needed a fail-safe mechanism of some kind, and yet the thought of enlisting the help of a stranger was against all his instincts. Apart from anything else, it made him feel like a traitor to Pam.

He barely glanced at Halford Hall as he passed it, mulling over these possibilities. His mind returned again and again to Linda, so that by the time he reached the gate to the Farm, he was accusing himself of being a lecher. He stopped at the gate, thinking that he could turn back. The yard was untidy with bits of machinery, weeds, a few scrabbling, unpenned hens. The farmhouse itself was an old brick building, with a fluted tile roof. It looked homely, comfortable. A large wooden barn stood on one side of the yard, to his left, and it was from this structure, carrying a pail, that

Regina emerged while he was still considering leaving. She caught sight of him at once, put down the pail, and looked directly at him. Her thick hair was tied back so that it resembled a black hood about her handsome face. She regarded him silently, but with open interest. Ian drew himself up, his hands resting on the top bar of the gate. He felt self-conscious, even challenged.

"Good afternoon," he called. "I'm afraid I'm trespassing."

"Not until you pass the gate you're not," she said, matter-of-factly, and picked up her pail again. She was wearing dark pants stuffed into an expensive but much-worn pair of knee-length boots, with a loose red shirt. "You must be Mr. Woodford."

"Ian," he said, reaching for the catch on the gate. "May I?"

"Sure. Peter's not here, though, if you're looking for him."

Ian opened the gate and went into the yard. Regina stood, the pail hanging from her hand, giving an impression not of hostility but of a woman who was determined to make no concessions. Ian walked toward her, knowing that she would make no move toward him.

"I know," he said. "I was just out for a stroll. You must be Mrs. Thomas."

"Regina," she said, and smiled. Ian had no idea if this was in conscious imitation of him. "Want a cup of tea?" She did not wait for an answer, but walked toward the house.

"Thank you, if it's no trouble."

"I was going to make one anyway."

The front door was open and Ian had to bend his head a little to avoid the lintel. There was a wide paved hall with passageways leading left and right. A carved oak staircase rose to a landing, turned and rose again. Regina went straight ahead, into the large kitchen. She set the bucket on the table and began immediately to transfer eggs from its straw-cushioned bottom to a series of boxes. She did not look at Ian.

"Put the kettle on, will you? It's full." She jerked her head at the range. Surprised, Ian went to it and lifted the kettle from the side to one of the burners. He looked around. The room was light and airy, functionally furnished with predominantly old wooden pieces. He could easily imagine it a warm haven on a winter's night, with the wind raging outside.

"You've lived here long?" he asked.

"No." She shook her head. "Only a few months."

He walked to the window. A large and flourishing vegetable garden stretched to an overgrown hedge. Beyond that, fields rose, forming a false horizon, shutting in the house. The bucket clattered behind him.

"There," she said. "Sit down."

"Thanks."

He sat at the table and watched, not knowing what to say, while Regina washed her hands at the sink and prepared the teapot.

"How's your wife today?"

The stock answers rose automatically to Ian's lips. Then he remembered that Regina knew Pamela had slept badly.

"She's better now, thank you."

"Linda said she was upset about Peter yesterday."

"Well . . ." It was the mention of Linda that made him feel tongue-tied, and he resented this since Regina had, unknowingly, given him the very opening he wanted. He cleared his throat.

"There was no need, you know. The boy's got an overactive imagination, that's all."

"You've probably noticed that my wife worries unnecessarily," he said stiffly.

"Since you mention it, yes." She lifted the kettle with a soiled potholder and poured hissing water into the teapot.

For a moment her brusqueness startled Ian, but then

85

he saw her expression. There was a softness, a sensible sympathy in her eyes, which regarded him steadily. He recalled what Pam had said, about her competence, her maternal quality, and found himself agreeing. But there was nothing sloppy or sentimental about her, he felt. She was probably a woman who kept her emotions on a tight rein, in their proper place. A balanced person, he thought. Just what Pam—and Peter—needed.

"We're both really glad that Peter has made friends with your children."

"He's quite safe with them, you know." She plonked the pot down on the table. "Milk? Sugar?"

"Just milk, thanks. I'm sure he is."

"But your wife . . ."

"Mrs. Thomas . . . Regina, I wondered if . . ."

She looked at him, her hand resting on the teapot. Her eyebrows were slightly raised, giving her face a half-questioning, half-surprised expression.

"No," Ian said, shaking his head. "It really doesn't matter." Suddenly it seemed that he was presuming. He might be mistaken in his assessment of her and that created the possibility of being unfair to Pam, of embarrassing them all.

Regina poured the tea into two thick mugs and, with a lack of ceremony, pushed one toward him.

"You want to ask me something but you feel you'd be imposing. And probably being disloyal to your wife."

She was so accurate that Ian could not prevent a burst of surprised laughter. She ignored it, dragged a chair from beneath the table, and sat down.

"You must please yourself, of course," she said, "but I can keep my own counsel."

"I'm sure . . ." Her directness now inhibited him. "It's true, I *don't* want to impose."

"I won't let you. I'm far too busy."

"I'm sorry."

"Oh come on. That's not what I meant. You want

86

something. If I can do it, fair enough. If not . . ." She shrugged.

Ian pulled his mug closer to him and watched the steam rise for a moment.

"You have a phone?" he asked.

"Yes."

"I wonder if I could take the number and leave you mine? Perhaps you'd ring me if there were any problems."

She thought about it, looking at her strong, capable hands. She picked dirt from under one fingernail.

"You want me to keep an eye on Peter?"

"Well, yes. And Pam."

"What exactly are you afraid of, Ian?"

"Oh not afraid. It's just that I . . ."

"What's wrong with Pamela?"

He sighed. His instincts again prompted him to trust Regina but the feeling of possible disloyalty still held him back.

"Nothing serious," he said at last. "Truly." He looked at her but could not be sure that she believed him.

"I'm not being nosy. I just like to know what I'm letting myself in for."

"That's only fair." Regina settled in her chair, waiting. "My wife, Pamela," he began awkwardly, "is unable to have children."

"Oh?" She sounded surprised.

"It's definite. We had all the necessary checks. Peter's adopted, and since he came to us, she's been, well, neurotically afraid of something happening to him. She's receiving help and I promise you she's much better than she was, but . . ." He did not know how to go on.

"You're apprehensive. Afraid of a relapse? Anyone can see she puts the kid under pressure."

Ian lifted his mug and drank, to cover his embarrassment.

"I think this holiday is doing them both a lot of good," he went on, putting his cards on the table, "but Pam's easily scared and then . . ."

"You want me to call you if I think things are getting to be too much for him, or her?" she interrupted.

"If you wouldn't mind."

"No. But I'm not making any promises, either. I can't watch them night and day. I'll do my best."

"Of course not. I wouldn't expect anything of the kind. But I would be grateful. I'd be easier in my own mind."

"Okay. And I take it this is strictly between ourselves?"

Ian felt his face redden.

"If you don't mind."

"There's no need to feel like a traitor. Frankly, I've been worried about Peter myself. I know it's none of my business, but I can't pretend to be blind."

"I've made it your business now," he said, "so please don't feel that you're intruding."

She did not answer. She stared at the window for a while, then put up her left hand and deftly untied her hair, shaking it loose. It had the effect of softening her face, making her look younger and gentler.

"What do you know about Peter's background?" she asked, twining the hair ribbon around her fingers.

"Next to nothing. He's had a hell of a life."

"It might help me to know. I foster children. I'm used to most of the problems."

"I know. That's one of the reasons I felt I *could* approach you. Well, he's spent his entire life in institutions. He was abandoned at birth. About twenty-four hours after, they think. In a rooming house. They never traced his mother or found out anything about him." Regina took this information as though it was an everyday occurrence which, Ian supposed, it probably was to her. "I think that may be partly why Pam's so concerned for him. She feels, I think, that she's got to make up to him for all those years of . . . neglect's too strong a word . . . but institutional care is no substitute for a family, a mother."

"Or a father," Regina said firmly. "That boy needs you every bit as much as he needs mothering."

"I know."

"Well, I'll do my best. I know how she feels. I told her the other day how I'd gone through it with my own son."

"That was kind of you."

"It's just common sense. It'll be easier for her to relax and let go if she realizes she's not the only one who feels like that."

"You could do her a lot of good," Ian said.

"You think so?" Regina laughed, a warm, husky sound.

"Yes, I do."

"Well . . ."

"You've been very kind. I do appreciate it." He stood up, feeling that it was time for him to go.

"The phone numbers," Regina reminded him. She went out into the hall and turned right. The telephone stood on a small table, below the staircase. She wrote her number on a pad, tore the sheet off, and handed it to Ian. "Help yourself," she said, indicating the pad and pen. Ian bent, wrote down his office and home numbers. For a moment, he wondered if he should add Liz's in case of emergency, but as quickly as the thought came, he dismissed it.

"Why don't you come and have a drink with us tomorrow night, if you're free that is."

"God, a civilized invitation! Thanks. I'd like to. I'm becoming a recluse down here."

"I can't believe that," he said, smiling.

"It's true."

"Well, come and be civilized, then. About eight-thirty?"

"Fine."

"And if you'd like to bring the children, I'd like to meet them."

She laughed again, warmly.

"Don't tell a soul, but I'd like to get away from them for an hour or so."

Ian laughed, too.

"Your secret's safe with me. I'll meet them some other time. And thanks again."

She looked at him for a moment, her eyes dark and slightly challenging.

"Tomorrow, then."

"Yes." He felt dismissed and, as he crossed the yard, he told himself that he had done the right thing. There was nothing to feel guilty about at all. Regina would be discreet and sensible. If she phoned him it would be out of genuine concern. He felt relieved and also curious. She was a remarkable woman. He wanted to know a lot more about Regina.

Pamela displayed little enthusiasm for Regina's visit, but Ian did not offer to cancel it as once he would have done, automatically. Saturday was overcast, with a threat of rain. Ian drove his wife and son to the nearest town to shop and felt throughout the expedition that they must look like an ordinary middle-class family on a routine outing. It was an unfamiliar sensation. He was both part of the group and outside, observing. The experience raised disturbing questions. Could they ever be a so-called normal family? Did he want them to be? Or, rather, did he want to be part of such a family? His feelings for Pam alternated between anger and pity. For Peter, he felt a sort of detached, fond guilt. He became silent, even morose, thinking that these ties were no basis on which to build anything. Yet he had loved Pamela—only a few hours ago. And it wasn't just desire or physical need. It had been spoiled, though whether by her hysteria or his involuntary attraction to Linda, he was unwilling to decide.

He was shocked to realize that Liz figured nowhere in these thoughts but there was no time, then, to face the implications of her absence from his mind. Pamela, intensely aware of his withdrawal, inevitably assumed that he was missing his other woman. She knew that she had blighted the weekend but could not believe that she was solely responsible. If Ian really loved her, he would not be so quickly bored. She did not doubt that he had come with the best of intentions, but she resented his inability to stick to them. When they passed the estate agents from whom she had rented the cottage, she remembered her vow to ask Ian about the possibility of buying the place, and knew that now it was impossible. Besides, she was no longer sure that she wanted to.

Peter was silently watching his parents. He did not understand the shifts of tension between them, but he felt them. They never quite seemed to synchronize. Pamela filled Ian's silences with chatter. When he made an effort to talk, she fell silent. They were like two armies staking out the territory of battle, but neither wanted to fire the first shot.

It was a relief to all of them to get back to the cottage. Ian and Peter unloaded the shopping. Pamela shut herself in the kitchen. Peter wandered down to the lake and skimmed pebbles across its flat surface. Ian dozed, thinking that he would leave on Sunday after all. He had done everything he could. They were all together again at dinner and the effort to make conversation became more and more strained. Afterward, Ian carried the portable television into Peter's room and began to prepare for Regina's visit. He plumped the cushions, prepared the bar, and was both surprised and pleased when Pamela changed into a plain lilac dress that made her look younger, even girlish. He gave her a drink and told her that she looked nice. She smiled, but it was wan and unconvincing. He noticed her left fist bunched tensely in her lap. Instead of asking her about it, he took her resisting arm in his hand and gently opened her fingers.

"That's better," he said. "Isn't it?"

Pulling her hand away, Pamela said, "You're not happy. There's no need to pretend."

"Why do you mind Regina coming? On Thursday you said you liked her."

"I do. It's just that I don't have very much confidence in her."

He knew why she had changed her mind and he faced a simple choice. He could go on, over the familiar ground of Pamela's irrational anxieties, or leave it be. He opted for the latter course and felt the silence stretch between them until it became unbridgeable. Regina's step on the veranda was a welcome relief. He rose at once to let her in. He had placed his trust in Regina and it still felt right. He could only hope that Pam would come back to her earlier enthusiasm for the woman.

Regina had a raincoat draped round her shoulders, over a long red caftan, embroidered with traditional Indian motifs in gold and blue. Her hair shone from brushing.

"Hello, Pamela," she said, as Ian took her coat.

"Regina."

"What will you have to drink?"

"Scotch?"

"Do sit down," Pamela said, too formally. Regina looked around, chose a corner of the settee, and sank into it with a sigh.

"Where's Peter?"

"Watching TV. *Starsky and Hutch* is indispensable," Ian laughed.

"I left mine playing cards. Is it that I'm getting old, or were card games really quiet when we were children? Thanks." She took the heavy tumbler Ian handed her. "Cheers." She sipped. "Oh, that's better."

She turned slightly toward Pamela. "I said to Ian that this is the first civilized invitation I've had for months."

Pamela smiled vaguely.

"You are rather cut off," Ian said. "No neighbors to speak of."

"Why did you come here?" Pamela asked sharply. "I mean, if you find it so . . ." She couldn't think of the word.

"It was the only place I could afford that was suitable. And it *is* suitable. I don't really regret it. It's just that I miss adult company sometimes."

"I can sympathize," Ian said.

"Whereas I, I think, would be quite happy with a house full of children," Pamela said, getting up and going to fill her glass.

Ian looked at Regina, seeking support, but her dark eyes remained pleasantly aloof, uncommitted.

"Surely Carl and Linda are old enough to be, well, companions for you," Pamela added.

"Yes, but they are also still children to me."

"But I thought you *liked* children." Pamela sat down again. Her tone was needling.

"All she said was that she liked to get away from them from time to time," Ian said.

"If you two are going to fight, will you please not do it over me?" Regina said, softening her bluntness with a laugh.

There was an awkward little silence. Pamela frowned at her glass, as though offended.

"Where were you before?" Ian said, quick to change the subject.

"London. America. Denmark originally. I was born there."

"But I thought you were English," Ian said at once.

"Most people do. My mother was English. I was brought up to be bilingual, and now I've lived so long in English-speaking countries."

93

"Even so, you're to be congratulated," Ian said. The warmth and studied gallantry in his voice stung Pamela.

"Are your parents still in Denmark?" she asked. It was a reflex question. She did not sound at all interested.

"No. They're both dead. In the war."

"Oh." Pamela drank quickly and looked vaguely round the room.

"And after the war you went to America?" Ian asked.

"Yes. Then, when my husband died, I traveled all over for a while and finally settled here."

"What an interesting life you've led," Pamela put in. She was slightly high and Ian wanted to stop her from pouring another drink but feared that to do so would only precipitate a scene.

"I suppose it must sound like that," Regina said. Her elbow rested on the arm of the settee. She held her glass up to the light, turning it, looking at it. "But when you've virtually grown up in a concentration camp, it seems more like a flight."

Muffled shots, the screech of car tires, sounded in the embarrassed silence. Regina slowly lowered her glass and drank, quite unruffled.

"Excuse me," Pamela said quickly, setting her glass down. The noise increased for a moment as she opened Peter's door, then became muffled again.

"I'm sorry," Ian said, aware that he was apologizing for Pamela as well as expressing sympathy. Regina drained her glass and held it, almost laconically, out to him.

"I'm quite used to the English embarrassment at the mere mention of the camps. I don't understand it, but I am used to it. After all, you fought against them."

"It must be very painful for you," Ian said, pouring her drink.

"In America now, people are interested. Sympathetic, certainly. They want to understand. Here, it's just a conversation stopper."

A little unsteady, Pamela came out of Peter's room. She had evidently persuaded him to lower the volume on the television set. She collected her drink, brushed against Ian, and went back to her chair.

"Your parents were Jewish?"

"My father."

"Which camp were you in?"

"Not one of the famous ones." She smiled reassuringly at Ian when he brought her freshened drink.

"I'm sure you don't want to talk about it," he said, looking directly at Pam.

"Not particularly. Though not, I think, for the reasons you imagine."

"Yes. I can understand that."

"Can you?" She stared at Ian, challenging him.

"You can only have been a child," Pamela cut in, in a slightly wondering tone.

To change the topic, Ian said, "Tell us about your children."

Regina sipped her drink and held the glass up again, as though admiring it.

"They're all casualties of one kind or another, but progressing, I think. You said you'd look at Reggie's drawings," she reminded Pamela.

"Yes. Of course."

There was another tense silence. Only Regina seemed unaffected by it. She continued to stare at her glass.

"How long will you foster them?"

"As long as is necessary," she replied simply. "Awhile, yet, I think."

"And then you'll have more?"

"I suppose."

"It's good work, worthwhile I mean." Ian was aware that he was floundering.

Pamela stood up. Her face was slightly puffy with alcohol.

"You have a remarkable effect on my husband, Regina. He's not very interested in children as a rule. Are you coming to say good-night to Peter?" she asked Ian.

"No. You do it for me."

She laughed, humorlessly.

"You see?" She threw the words at Regina, swaying toward Peter's door.

"I think I'd better finish this and go," Regina said, as soon as Pamela was out of hearing.

"I'm sorry. Please don't go. She doesn't—"

"Mean it? I know that. But she still feels I failed her, didn't look after Peter properly."

"That's no excuse," Ian said angrily. "Besides, he explained all that."

"Oh?"

"Yes. I know it was all a misunderstanding. Pam just got it all mixed up."

"Well, I must try harder, that's all." Regina drank. "I can't say how sorry I am."

"I'm fairly thick-skinned," Regina told him, holding up her glass again, revolving it against the light.

Pamela came back and, to Ian's relief, sat down without picking up her drink.

"Everything okay?" Regina asked her.

"Yes. Thank you."

"Well, I'd really better . . ."

There was a crack, like a pistol shot. Pamela started half out of her chair, her eyes swiveling wildly to Peter's door.

"Good God!" Ian exclaimed.

The room suddenly reeked of whisky. It was like a tableau, frozen, unbelievable. Regina's raised hand was open. She stared at it with a mixture of fascination and pain. A jagged triangle of glass stuck into her palm. Blood welled around it, trickled down her arm.

"How on earth did that happen?" He caught hold of Regina's wrist and forced it down. "Pam, quick, get a bandage, some disinfectant."

She went at once to the bathroom, her whole body shaking. Ian bent over Regina's hand and, gently, pulled the piece of glass out of her flesh. She did not even wince.

"How clumsy of me," she said. "I'm so sorry."

"Don't be silly, it . . ."

"You'd better come in here where I can clean it for you," Pamela said.

"No, please. It's perfectly all right."

"Nonsense. Pam's right. Go and wash it."

Regina stood, her thumb pressed to the wrist of her injured hand, and went into the bathroom. Ian stared at the splashed whisky, at the fragments of glass. It had shattered into four pieces. The heavy bottom was intact and the others would fit together neatly, like a jigsaw puzzle. He began to gather them up, careful not to cut himself. The glass was heavy in his hand. No one, he thought, could have crushed it.

"Well, how's that for a dramatic exit?" Regina asked, laughing. There was a gauze pad smelling faintly of disinfectant taped to the palm of her hand.

"How are you feeling?" Ian asked, standing up.

"Fine. It's only a flesh wound. I'm just terribly sorry about your glass. Oh God, and I've got blood on Appledore's sofa."

"It'll come out," Pamela said calmly. "Don't worry about it."

Ian urged her to have another drink to steady her nerves.

"No thanks. I'd like to go home now, if you don't mind."

"You drive her, Ian," Pamela said, coming to him and cupping her hands together. He tipped the pieces of glass into them.

"Yes, of course," he said.

"I'm perfectly all right," Regina protested. "Really."

"Even so, you don't want to walk along that path. You've had a shock. I'll get your coat." He draped it around her shoulders.

"Pamela, you must let me replace that glass," Regina said.

"Nonsense. There must have been a fault in it," she said. "Take her home now, Ian."

"Good-night, then."

"Good-night, Regina."

Outside, Ian helped her into the car. It was already quite dark. She sighed a little, holding her hurt hand in her lap.

"Are you sure you're all right?"

"It hurts a bit. But I'll live."

"I can't think how it could have happened."

He turned on the headlights and made a U-turn.

"I must have been gripping it too tightly."

"But even so . . ." he began to protest.

"There was probably a flaw in it, like Pam said."

"Well, it's bloody dangerous. I'll chuck the others out."

She didn't answer and Ian guessed that she was tired of all the fuss. They turned into the main drive. The lights raked the Hall, dazzled in the dark windows.

"You'd better slow down," Regina said, as they approached the dirt road. "If you care about your suspension, that is."

He slowed at once.

"I'm sorry," he apologized again. "You had a rotten evening."

"I've had worse," she said and Ian thought of the concentration camp, the dead husband, and felt completely incompetent.

"If, after tonight, you'd rather keep away from Pam, I shall understand," he said, braking as the Farm gates came in sight.

"Not at all. She interests me, more than you can ever know."

He turned toward her, surprised, but she was already getting out of the car.

"I think I can manage to stagger across the yard," she told him, openly teasing. "Good-night."

"Regina . . ."

She walked away, spotlit by the car's lights. He watched, drumming his fingers on the steering wheel, until she had gone through the gate. Then he threw the car into reverse and backed along the dirt road, onto the drive. He was angry with Pam, and angry with Regina for being so cool, so self-sufficient. And he was also, he realized, afraid.

Ian left on Sunday afternoon, shortly before the rain set in. Pamela did not question his decision or argue. She had pretended to be asleep when he returned from taking Regina home and they had not mentioned her visit. They parted with the perfunctory kiss on the cheek that was much more familiar now than the passion and genuine warmth he had displayed on arrival.

Pamela sat listening to the rain and thought that she did not regret his going. Peter was engrossed in some old film on television. Occasionally he laughed at some comic scene, and Pamela smiled automatically at him. She wondered if Ian was going back to his mistress and if they would discuss her. Still she felt nothing. She had become accustomed to living without him, without realizing it, and now she saw advantages in being entirely separate from him. He held the progress she had made with Elsa, with Peter, as insignificant. Whatever happened now, she thought, he would always have her "madness" to use against her. He even made her doubt that she had achieved anything at all.

Divorce? Well, if he really wanted this other woman, he could always provide for her and Peter. She could perhaps force him to buy this cottage for them and then she and Peter would be able to grow together, in peace. She would be stronger without Ian watching her every move, pouncing on her. She hated being watched. It sapped her confidence. There was Regina, of course, and the children, but she felt, suddenly, that she could handle that. Peter needed friends and she had nothing against the children. She could freeze Regina out easily. She felt angry when she recalled the easy intimacy she had sensed between Ian and Regina. Perhaps he was attracted to her. After all, she was competent and outspoken, everything that she, Pamela, was not.

"Why are you looking like that, Mommy?"

Her attention snapped back into the gray room. He had switched the television set off and was staring at her with puzzled blue eyes. She laughed.

"Like what, darling?"

"I don't know. Funny."

"I was just thinking, that's all." As she spoke, she felt the knotted muscles in her back and arms. She began to make herself relax, slowly, purposefully.

"Is it because Dad's gone?"

"No, of course not." She laughed again, making light of it.

"Why don't you two get along?"

"Now what kind of question is that? Isn't there anything to watch?"

"You don't make each other happy."

For a moment Pamela felt hurt, then almost triumphant. She wished Ian could hear this, could see for herself that it was not only she who put the boy under pressure.

"Sometimes people grow apart, things change. You'll understand one day."

"It used to be because of me," he said doggedly.

"Don't be ridiculous. You mustn't—"

"It *was*," he insisted. "I heard you fight."

"Would you like to play a game of Scrabble?" Pamela asked, pushing herself out of her chair. "It's still too wet to go out."

Peter's eyes followed her as she moved around the room.

"But it's not just me anymore. It's . . . what is it?"

"Peter, I really don't want to continue this conversation. There are some things you're not old enough to understand."

"That's not what Dad says," he retorted rudely. "*He* says he can talk to me like a grown-up." He bounced off the settee and went into his room, slamming the door.

Pamela looked down at the Scrabble board. Her hands were shaking, but with anger, not fear. What had he said to Peter, like a grown-up? That she was mad, sick, ill? He wanted to separate them. That's what it was. Suddenly, it all became very clear to her. He wanted to send Peter away. He knew that would kill her and then—for her own safety, of course—he could get her put away and he'd be free to do as he liked with his woman.

She hurled the board away from her, across the room. It struck the wall and fell with a clatter on the floor. She went to Peter's door and opened it.

"If you're so grown-up," she said, her voice quivering with anger, "then you'll be able to understand that he doesn't love us anymore. He has another woman. That's where he's gone now."

Peter looked at her with shock and disbelief. She walked farther into his room and sat on the edge of his bed.

"I don't know what he's been saying to you," she told him, "but I know that he wants to turn you against me."

"No," he shouted. "That's not true."

"Well . . . You certainly don't behave like my little boy anymore," she said gently. And after a pause, "But perhaps that's just because you're growing up so fast."

He hesitated a moment, then put his arms around her.

"I'm sorry, Mommy. Honest, I'm sorry."

She held him tightly, desperately against her.

"I know, darling. I know. It's all right. We'll both be all right, as long as we're together. You want that, don't you?"

"Yes." He sounded miserable, but she told herself that was imagination, was because his voice was muffled against her breast.

"Let's have that game of Scrabble," she coaxed. "Mm?"

"All right."

"That's my boy." She brushed his hair out of his eyes.

Later, she would write to Elsa, explain everything. Yes, she had used Ian, but now she no longer needed him. She was not too proud or ashamed to say so. She would make a new life for herself, with her son.

Peter retrieved then set up the board, shook the pieces in the bag. She was staring into space, with the same funny expression.

"Mommy? Come on," he said.

"What? Oh, yes. Of course."

She sat down and, in turn, they selected pieces from the bag.

"Can't do anything," she said, after a while.

"I can."

Clumsily, biting his bottom lip, he fixed the little plastic squares to the board, spelling D E A T H.

"There," he said, pushing his hand into the bag for more letters.

From the moment she hung up the telephone, having said, yes, Ian could come by, Liz could have kicked herself. She had put herself at a disadvantage. He was bound to think that she had been moping around, waiting for him to call—which wouldn't matter a damn if it wasn't true. Well, she hadn't been moping. She'd been cleaning the windows, and now it looked like rain. Her hair was tied back with a spotted kerchief. She wore an old pink T-shirt and jeans, and she wasn't going to change—not for him. It was time Ian faced the facts of life. The doorbell rang. Liz went to let him in and was furious that he seemed quite unaware of her appearance.

"You didn't do anything, then?" he asked, dropping into a comfortable chair.

"I cleaned the flat from top to bottom," she snapped, "but I don't expect that counts as 'doing anything.'"

His face tightened but he did not rise to the bait.

"Want a drink? Coffee?" Liz asked, meaning it to be a peace gesture, but sounding resentful.

"Any beer?"

"Of course."

He watched her body, snug in the tight jeans, and wondered why he had come. He despised himself a little, fleeing from one woman to another. He could easily have concealed from Liz that he had returned early, could have used the time to sort himself out.

"Your beer," she said, thrusting the cold can into his hand. "From the look of you, the long family weekend wasn't a great success."

"Right," he said, tearing open the can. She hadn't bothered to bring him a glass although she knew he disliked drinking from the can. "Want to know about it?"

"Not particularly. I seem to remember you were bored with my questions about your family."

He took a swig of beer which, though it tasted tinny, was cool and welcome.

"I'll just drink this and shove off," he said.

"Oh sure," Liz said. "And do drop by later if you

fancy a sandwich or anything. I usually stay open till midnight."

"Liz . . ." he began wearily.

"Don't 'Liz' me. I'm sick and bloody tired of being your convenience, Ian. Sick of it."

She burst into tears, which seemed to surprise her as much as it did Ian. He couldn't remember having seen her cry before. Angry, she tore the kerchief from her head and dabbed at her face. She blew her nose noisily. Ian got up and cuddled her.

"What is it? I'm sorry, love."

"It's you, you bastard," she said, nuzzling against him, sniffling. "Oh no it's not. It's me."

"I'm not sure what you're talking about."

"It's hopeless," she said, shaking her head against him. "I meant to really think things out this weekend. And all I've done is work myself up into a state. And you've had a rotten time and then . . ."

"Sh," he soothed, stroking her hair. It all seemed very clear to him then. He had wanted to tell her about Linda, not Pam. Somehow, without really considering the thought, he had felt that Liz would be able to laugh him out of Linda. But now he realized that was the last thing he could tell her. He led her to the settee, made her sit down. She rested her head against his shoulder. He reached for the beer can.

"Want some?"

She shook her head, watched him drink.

"You don't like it from the can."

"No."

"I'm a bitch."

"Yes."

"But you're a bastard."

"Yes."

"Stop agreeing with me."

"Okay."

She sighed and nestled closer to him.

"What's going to happen to us, Ian? That's what I want to know."

"I don't know. I've been wondering, too." And then he told her about Pam, the hysterics, the way she behaved toward Regina, his sudden bleak fear, and how coolly Pam had accepted his leaving early. She listened quietly until he had finished. He drained the beer and lobbed the can at the wastepaper basket, missing. Liz sat up.

"Well, you know what I think."

"That I should leave her?"

"Yes."

"And marry you."

"I didn't say that."

"I don't think I can."

"Which?"

"Leave her. Not now, anyway, because of Peter. He is my responsibility, too."

Liz twisted her hands together.

"Which leaves us where?"

"I don't know. I'm sorry. I do know it's not fair to you."

She stood up and wandered to the window. She looked at the darkening gray sky.

"It if rains, I'll scream," she said.

"It was pouring when I drove back."

"Thanks."

He stood up.

"Liz, I'd better go." She turned quickly toward him. "I can't promise you anything," he said, his voice shaking a little, "and you can't take any more. I'm too fond of you to . . ."

"Oh, get out if you're going," she shouted. Another word would have made her run to him, beg him.

He nodded, picked up his jacket, and went, without another word, to the door. As soon as it closed behind

105

him, Liz threw herself on the settee, sobbing and beating the cushions with clenched fists.

Really, Pamela had never felt better. It was hot and still again, perfect summer weather. She sat, calm and happy, fully in control. She had written it all down, carefully, explaining to Elsa. Of course, she would need Elsa's help, her support, but somehow, the moment she had dropped the letter into the village mailbox, she felt as though a great pressure had lifted from her. In the letter she had acknowledged her debt to Ian, and her bad treatment of him. Not that she excused him, but she felt she understood and could make allowances. "But I am tired of compromises," she had written. "Peter is my life, always has been, and I know that it is wrong to pretend I have the strength for two people." Yes, the sun had come out and she returned to her poppies. The painting was almost finished. And for two days there had been no sight or sound of Regina or the children. To her delight, Peter had not missed them. He was content to swim and read, to relax in the boat, to fish. She felt closer to him than ever before. Each time she looked at him, she thought of what she had written. "I will never let him be taken away from me. I don't care about anything else. It can all go. As long as I have my son, I have everything." Elsa would help her to make Ian understand. She lay down her brush and held the board away from her, squinting at the poppies. As soon as she heard from Elsa, she would begin to make plans for the future. Hers and Peter's.

"Mommy?"

"Yes, darling?" She turned to him with a ready smile.

"Can I row you around the lake?"

He was so tanned, filling out rapidly, growing strong and handsome.

"All right. If you don't feel too tired." She put the board aside and stood up. He was almost as tall as she was. She adjusted her large white hat, for the sun was in her eyes. "You must escort me down," she said, offering her arm to him. "Like a proper gentleman." He laughed and took her arm.

Pamela felt as if she was floating. Her full white skirt moved about her legs. The hat made her elegant. And he was tall and strong and handsome beside her. There were two old, stained cushions in the prow of the boat, but they looked clean and luxurious to Pamela. He bent and held the boat steady.

"Careful," he said.

She smiled, stepped in, making the boat rock. A ripple of light spread from the boat across the lake, became lost in the glare. Pamela sat down, arranged her skirt and leaned back against the cushions. He hopped in, lithe and capable. The boat rocked alarmingly, but Pamela lay back and trailed her hand in the cool water.

He rowed for a long time, hugging the banks. Pamela, peering from beneath her hat, saw the sunlight come and go, patches of shadow as they passed beneath trees, bright, white light when they moved into the middle of the lake. Peter shipped the oars and let the boat drift.

"This is lovely," Pamela said.

The voices were very far away, faint, but he turned his head sharply toward the bank. There was no one to be seen, but the voices went on, insinuating. He looked at his mother. Her eyes were closed, one hand still trailed sleepily in the water. He stood up, planting his legs wide to keep the boat steady, and strained to hear the voices. If only they wouldn't whisper so!

Pamela saw him, silhouetted against the light. His limbs were surrounded by a dazzling aura, like fire. How she loved him! No, they would never take him away from her. The light hurt her eyes. The boat began to sway. His body swayed, rocked before her. She became alarmed, struggled against the cushions, feeling dizzy. It was the heat, the rocking boat. For a moment she thought that he was deliberately shifting his weight from foot to foot. She struggled again, trying to sit up, to reach him.

Then she was tipping sideways, her mouth open to call his name. The shock of the water made her scream. But no sound came. Water rushed into her mouth.

On the other side of the upturned boat, the boy sank without a struggle. He went down, down, down. The water quickly became opaque, a sort of cold, enclosed night in which he felt entirely safe and at home.

She fought against the water. Panic made her thrash and whirl her arms against its weight, against something stronger, a kind of terror, a physical surge which seemed to suck her body along. She saw him, blue and choking, in the swimming pool, saw a face, keenly watching.

As he rose, naturally and calmly toward the surface, he glimpsed her white dress tangled round her body, which turned dreamily over and over, moving fast away from him.

The sun lit his face. He turned his neck back to welcome it. He floated, head up, bobbing, until the water became placid again and his skin adjusted to the burn of the sun. Then he kicked out with his legs, looking around him. Her hat floated on the surface of the lake, beyond the capsized, listing boat. He swam strongly toward it, trod water, and placed the wet brim of the hat between his sharp, white teeth. Like a dog, he swam for the shore, carrying her hat in his mouth.

They stood among the trees, out of sight of each other. They watched impassively until the boy reached the jetty and hauled himself, panting and dripping, from the water. Then they turned and walked silently away between the trees.

With a sigh, Regina let the tension drain from her body. She was sweating. She stood up and, with tired, dragging steps, went out into the passage, picked up the telephone receiver, and dialed Ian's number.

PART TWO

REGINA WAS ADAMANT. SHE WOULD NOT PERMIT Sergeant Benyon or anyone else to question Peter before his father arrived. Benyon, who was a kindly man, had no wish to frighten or harass the boy. He simply wanted to do his job as quickly as possible and according to the book. Regina faced him, arms folded across her breasts, face set. She had telephoned Mr. Woodford and until he got there, nobody was going to talk to the boy, who needed to be comforted, not questioned. Patiently, Benyon explained that she could be present while he talked with the boy.

"I am not *in loco parentis*, Sergeant, and I will not accept the responsibility."

He took a tougher line, hinting at the possible consequences of impeding legitimate police inquiries. Damn it all, a woman was dead.

"Is she?" Regina asked coolly, challenging him.

To that Benyon had no definite answer. The sight of his men poking ineffectually at the water with sticks, dragging the boat from the lake to the bank, made him feel even more important. He consulted them, shook his head, and admitted that it was a job for the frogmen.

113

"She must be down there somewhere," he said.

"Caught in some weeds, more like," Constable Rutter agreed. Rutter was the village policeman, to whom Regina Thomas had reported the accident.

Benyon stared at the lake as though it, too, was a hostile witness. The very least it could do was deliver up its victim.

Puffing in the heat, Benyon went up the hill, looked at the dead woman's painting things, at the sheer ordinariness of it all. Everything left, just as it would be if she had suddenly taken it into her head to go for a stroll. Maybe that's exactly what she had done. Maybe the boy was . . . ten minutes with the boy would clear it all up, enable him to write his report. He told a constable to organize the frogmen, and trudged back to Home Farm. There was a certain amount of bloody-mindedness in his insistence on questioning everyone there, but it also helped to fill in the time. At least Regina Thomas did not object to that. First she repeated her own story. She had been in the barn, had heard the boy shouting, screaming. He'd stumbled into the yard, sopping wet and hysterical. The boat had capsized. His mother was drowned.

"Could she swim at all?" Benyon asked.

"I haven't the faintest idea."

"Thank you very much," he said, adding "for nothing" under his breath.

Carl, too, had been in the barn. He could corroborate his mother's story, but beyond that he had seen and heard nothing. Reggie had been drawing and the sulky one they called Grizzle seemed half-dopy to Benyon. Nothing from either of them. Finally Linda, who had been sitting with the boy.

"Has he said anything to you, miss?"

"No."

"You haven't asked him exactly what happened?"

"No."

"I see."

Benyon was puzzled. There was something too calm, too detached about them. They all claimed the boy as their friend yet they seemed almost unperturbed by his mother's death. You'd think at least one of them would have been out in the woods, near the lake. And they weren't in shock, either. He felt they were as crafty as a wagonload of monkeys. Saw nothing, heard nothing, and said little more. He told himself he was imagining it, looking for something on which to pin his frustration. But he went back to the chalet or whatever it was the woman had rented and drew Rutter aside.

"What do you know about that lot up at Home Farm?"

"Nothing much, Sarge."

"How long have they been there?"

Rutter thought, making slow mental calculations.

"Three, four months."

"And you haven't noticed anything, not had any trouble?"

"No, Sarge. Course, there's talk."

Benyon pricked up his ears.

"What sort of talk?"

"Oh, usual stuff. Nothing, really. There's an old chap, Fred Mabey, used to be the keeper here before this American chap bought it. Anyway, afterward old Fred still did a bit of hunting round here."

"Trespassing, you mean," Benyon pounced.

"Well . . ." Rutter removed his helmet, which left a red indented line on his forehead, and mopped his brow.

"All right. So what does he say?"

"He won't come near the place, that's all. He says they give him the willies."

"Who?"

"Them up at Home Farm, the kids. But when he's had a few in the pub, old Fred'll say anything. Specially if someone else is buying. Still, people reckon they're loonies."

115

"Loonies? What sort of word's that?" Benyon snapped.

"I don't know, Sarge. Funny in the head, you know."

"More likely, Mrs. Thomas probably warned him off, and now he's getting back at her."

Rutter thought about it and decided it was better to agree with his senior officer, even though old Fred had never said anything of the sort. There wouldn't be much worth shooting on her land. It was in the woods that Fred caught rabbits and such. "I expect so," he said. "But all he's ever said is he don't like being up here, not with them around."

Benyon grunted. The woods on the far side of the lake looked a bit creepy to him. Too dark, too enclosed. Yet the sun was blazing down. And that bloody lake.

"What about the woman?" he asked suddenly. "This Mrs. Woodford?"

"Don't know, Sarge. Never set eyes on her as far as I know. They were only visitors."

"Yes," Benyon sighed. "Fine summer holiday theirs turned out to be. Mind you, I've always said that letting a kid fool around with a boat is asking for trouble."

"Yes, Sarge."

"People never learn."

"No, Sarge."

"I wish the bloody father would get here."

"Yes, Sarge. Though the traffic's bad from London. Terrible bottleneck at Potter's roundabout. It'll be all different when they finish that new overpass. Or so they say."

Benyon couldn't stand it. A routine accident with no victim, an unavailable witness, and a village constable muttering on about traffic congestion. He walked away in disgust.

Ian could not believe it. He didn't doubt it. Regina would never have telephoned him if she wasn't certain, but he could not absorb the fact of Pam's death. He could not imagine her dead. There was something stubborn and intractable in his head that made it impossible for him to accept. What had she said exactly?

"There's been an accident. You'd better come at once. Peter's here. He says his mother's drowned. Can you come at once? Yes. I'll call the police."

Pamela was a poor swimmer. She didn't like water. For a moment he thought it was not an accident, but immediately told himself not to be stupid. Such thoughts were simply morbid. There had been a time when he had feared the possibility of suicide, but that was long past. Unless he had been too hard on her over the weekend? She had seemed so indifferent when he left.

The traffic snarled at Potter's roundabout. Cars with roof racks piled with luggage, camping equipment. Three trailers. The holiday exodus to the country, the coast. The construction of the overpass meant they'd had to set up temporary traffic lights, and with a four-way flow converging on the roundabout, the delays were long. Horns honked. Children fretted, their bored faces pressed to the back and side windows, staring.

Peter.

Ian's first thought was what the hell would he do with Peter? A wave of guilt enveloped him. He tried to imagine what the boy must be feeling. What had he been through? What would he need now?

"That boy needs you every bit as much as he needs mothering."

It had been easy, then, to agree with Regina, to voice something he had always known but had never been able to practice. And perhaps it was not just because of Pam and her possessiveness. Perhaps he had not tried because he could not. He thought of his own father, but that was too long ago. He'd just been there, solid,

117

ordinary, a man who took him to football matches and told him to do as his mother said, or else. There was no help there. Ian had not been excited or even particularly pleased when Pam had found Peter. By then, the whole idea of adoption had become so clouded and fraught by Pam's attitude that he had wanted to call it off altogether. Of course it would have been different if Peter was his own child, if he had actually, biologically fathered him. Or even if Pam had wanted a baby instead of this fantasy child, this image that she had tried so hard to make Peter fit. He felt more than pity for Pam then. Barren and now dead. He could not begin to imagine it. Of all deaths, she would not have chosen water. And why couldn't he have understood sooner that the root of the trouble was that she had chosen a child to fit a fantasy? Where the fantasy came from he had no idea, but it explained her determination to find the one and only special child. Peter. He could have stopped it, somehow. He should have.

The traffic moved at last and for a while Ian's attention was entirely taken up with negotiating the roundabout.

Then it occurred to him—with much more force than the idea of Pam's death—that he had inherited that fantasy, only now it was real, flesh and blood, and his responsibility. Panic fluttered in his throat. He did not know what to do, how to behave. He forced himself to calm down. He would have to know. He could learn. After all, he liked the boy. He was a nice boy, but search as he might, Ian could not feel whatever it was fathers feel when they contemplate their sons. He could think only of the responsibility and his inadequacy. And all that was tied up with the mess of his marriage, which had ended so suddenly, out of the blue.

At last he was able to turn off the main road. He had devised this part of the route himself, by trial and error. The villages through which he must pass in order to reach Halford Hall were becoming a familiar litany in his head. He recited them, like a superstitious chant, to keep what lay ahead at bay. There was one straw of hope in all the confusion: Regina. She would know what to do. She was experienced with children, fond of Peter. Except that it wasn't her responsibility. For a moment, he felt coldly angry. Pam had wished this upon him. It was her legacy. His throat felt tight. Tears pricked his eyes, not tears of anger or self-pity, but of corrosive, frightening guilt.

He wanted to stop the car, pull over, and knew that he must not. If he stopped now, he felt that he might not be able to go on. And whatever else might await him, whatever he might feel, Peter needed him. His young life seemed, suddenly, more doomed than Pam's. He had never known his real parents and now he had lost the only person who had ever fully loved him. Loved him too much, but that seemed unimportant now. It would only make the loss greater. Ian could find no comforting comparison between the death of his own parents and what Peter must be feeling now. He had been an adult, had years of family security to lean on. All Peter had was him, and every confused and frightened instinct Ian had, told him that was not enough.

He slammed on the brakes. The car skidded a little. The gates to Halford Hall, tall and imposing, were closed. A police car was parked in the entrance and a constable, his shirt-sleeves rolled up, was leaning against its hood. Very slowly, he pushed himself away from the car and came toward Ian, who felt unreal, felt that the man was going to tick him off for some minor motoring offense.

"I'm sorry, sir, but you can't . . ."

"My name's Woodford," he said, his mouth dry. "My wife . . ."

"Oh yes, sir. Sorry. We've been expecting you. I'll open the gates. You'd best go straight to the house. Sergeant Benyon's waiting for you."

Ian could not speak. It seemed real at last. As he waited for the gates to be opened, he saw Pam stretched on the bank below the house. He saw phantom hands lifting a sheet and he did not want to look at what lay beneath it, what remained of her.

The policeman waved him through. The gravel crunched beneath his tires. The better-surfaced drive to the cottage looked abnormally dark. There were two more police cars parked on the tarmac rectangle, next to Pam's car. He felt weak and slightly dizzy. He sat, clutching the steering wheel, afraid to look down at the lake.

"Mr. Woodford?"

"Yes."

"Sergeant Benyon."

The man opened the door, silently inviting Ian to get out. He fumbled nervously with the release catch on his seat belt, climbed out stiffly. The sun dazzled him. He had to look down at the lake. Nothing. Nothing that he had feared. Two or three policemen. The boat up-turned on the bank.

"Where is she? My wife?"

"If you'd just come inside, sir . . ." Benyon touched his elbow, propelled him toward the house.

On the veranda, Ian stopped. "Sergeant, I . . ."

"I'm very sorry, sir."

He was afraid of the house. Afraid to see her there.

"Is she . . ."

"Oh no, sir. No." Benyon sounded almost as relieved as Ian felt. "I'm afraid we haven't located the body yet." Ian stared at Benyon. He didn't understand. "You'd best come and sit down, sir."

It was like a dream, as if he was onstage, playing a role, and realized too late that he didn't know the part, the lines. He barely heard what Benyon was saying. The lake was deep. Caught in weeds, probably. Frogmen, in the morning, to do a proper search. Very distressing.

"Peter? My son? I want to see him."

"Of course. He's up at the Farm, with a Mrs. Thomas. I take it you know her?" Benyon added, hoping to prove her an interfering, obstructive neighbor.

"Yes, of course. I must go to him."

"We haven't spoken to the boy yet, sir." Benyon rose on the balls of his feet, rocked, and settled back. "Mrs. Thomas insisted that we wait for you."

Ian shook his head, trying to clear it.

"I don't understand."

"She wasn't prepared to take the responsibility, him not being hers. She felt you should be present when we questioned him."

"I see."

"It's highly irregular, of course. The lad is the only witness. But under the circumstances . . . Anyway, when you feel up to it, Mr. Woodford."

Ian stood up. Benyon regarded him critically.

"We'd best go by car, I think."

Then he was outside again, dazzled, sitting in the back of a hot police car, driving back the way he had just come.

"Was your wife a good swimmer, Mr. Woodford?"

"No. She wasn't. She didn't like the water."

"Was she in the habit of going out in that boat?"

"I don't know."

"You don't know, sir?"

"I've hardly been here. I don't know how she and Peter spent their time. Yes, I expect she did, go out in the boat, I mean. I don't know."

"But the lad uses the boat a lot, by all accounts."

"Yes, and swims. He's very good at both. I was out in the boat with him only the other day. I remember thinking how competent he was. My wife would have been perfectly safe with him." His voice cracked and he had to shut his eyes tight against a rush of tears.

The gate to Home Farm stood open. The car

bounced a little on the ruts. Chickens fled, squawking. As Ian got out, Regina came slowly toward the car. She took his hand in both of hers.

"I'm sorry."

"Peter?"

"He's okay. I wouldn't let them question him."

"The sergeant told me."

"I thought you should be with him."

"I want to see him."

She led him into the house. Benyon, feeling more than ever that his authority was being flouted, followed, taking out his notebook.

"If you'll wait here, Sergeant," Regina said, "Mr. Woodford will bring Peter down in a few minutes." She did not wait for a reply but went straight up the stairs. Ian had an impression of white walls, old timber, plain, latched doors. She led him down a long passageway, opened a door.

The first person he saw—and he saw her as though she was a memory made flesh, a person from another time and world—was Linda. She sat, pale and composed, beside a narrow bed, her hands folded in her lap like some bleached, impassive madonna. For a moment Ian stared at her, speechless. Then she stood up and the huddled figure on the bed rose up toward him, calling to him. He grabbed Peter, held him tight, and rocked him gently back and forth.

It was all right until his father came. It was like bursting through a skin, a circus paper hoop from one world into another. Then his whole body felt cold and he knew that he would never see her again, except as a ghostly doll, drifting past in the water, turning over and over like the gingerbread lady. He screamed then and his body shook with sobs. Slowly, as the knowledge of her death sank into him, he became aware of his father's special smell. The arms that held him were strong but not particularly familiar. He cried for a long time and was surprised, interested even, that Ian cried with him, sniffing a lot and apologizing.

"She's dead," he said at last. "I won't ever see her again."

"You mustn't think about it." Ian did not know if that was right or wrong. Besides, he had to think about it. "Can you tell me exactly what happened?"

Peter shook his head, fighting back more tears. He did not want to remember. There were holes and gaps in his memory. It was like the games, hazy, difficult to tell what had happened and what was just imagined.

"There's a policeman downstairs. He has to ask you about it. I'll come with you, but you must tell him everything, exactly as it happened."

"Do I have to?" He wiped his nose with the back of his hand.

"I'm afraid so. And it's best to get it over with."

He nodded. Ian gave him a handkerchief and smoothed the hair out of his eyes.

"Come on, then," he said. "And don't cry. She wouldn't have wanted that. Just tell them what happened."

"You'll stay with me?" There was a hint of panic in his voice.

"Of course."

Peter seemed to have lost all his recently acquired confidence, his slightly knowing, grown-up manner. He held Ian's hand like a little boy and told himself that it would be like going to the doctor or the dentist. It was never as bad as you imagined. Only she had always been with him, worrying for him, reassuring him, promising treats. He looked nervously at Ian.

"It'll be all right," he said.

Regina watched them come down the last flight of stairs. Peter's face was pale and puffy. Ian looked gray, as though recovering from a long illness.

"In here," she said and led them into the passageway, past the telephone, to a sitting room that was still bright with sunlight. Benyon stood up, nodded at Ian, and looked diffidently at the boy. Regina went out, closing the door behind her.

"Peter's ready to talk to you now," Ian said, squeezing his hand. The sergeant cleared his throat. Ian sat down and pulled Peter close to him, holding him.

"Well now, er, Peter, I just want you to tell me exactly what happened this afternoon. Do you think you can do that?" Benyon's forced tone suggested to Ian that he did not relish the task.

"Go on," Ian urged him. "There's nothing to be afraid of."

"Well, I was out on the lake. Mommy was painting up by the house, and I thought it would be nice to row her around." He paused, swallowed, glanced at Ian, who smiled encouragement as best he could. "She said yes, because she'd finished her painting, and so we went down and got in the boat and rowed around for a bit."

"Your mother was where?" Benyon asked.

"In the boat."

"No, I mean where was she sitting in the boat?"

"Oh. In the prow, only she wasn't sitting exactly— more sort of lying, on the cushions. You know," he said to Ian.

"Yes. There are a couple of old cushions in the boat, Sergeant. Go on, Peter."

"Well, then I rowed out to the middle and just let the boat drift. Mommy was asleep. Well, I think she was. She had her eyes closed. I thought I'd do some fishing, so I stood up and—"

"Ah," the sergeant said. "You shouldn't go standing up in boats, you know."

"He often does it," Ian said. "It's perfectly safe."

"Yes, sir. Only it wasn't, was it?"

There was no answer to that. Ian tightened his grip on Peter.

"I stood up, anyway. I was very careful. I had my back to her. I don't know what happened. But the boat started to rock and . . . I don't know. I just fell into the water and when I came up, the boat was upside down and I couldn't . . . I couldn't find her." Tears trickled down his face. Ian pulled his son's head down to his shoulder.

"Isn't that enough, Sergeant?"

"Well, would you perhaps say your mother was trying to sit up?" he asked.

"Peter? Did you hear?"

"I don't know. I had my back to her."

"And you didn't see her in the water?"

"Yes." It was a broken whisper. Ian and the sergeant exchanged pained, frightened glances.

"Under the water. She sort of floated past me. I just saw her dress, really, her white dress. And now she's dead." The last word was a wail. It acted like a signal on Benyon, who closed his notebook at once and stood up.

"I'm very sorry," he said. "Don't upset yourself, son." Clumsily he squeezed Peter's shoulder. "Accidents are terrible things, but they can happen to anyone."

Peter's body shook against Ian.

"If I could just have a word with you, sir?" Benyon indicated the door with his eyes.

"I can't leave him," Ian protested.

"I'll see if I can find the lady of the house." Benyon was obviously not to be put off.

"Don't leave me," Peter said. "You promised you wouldn't leave me."

"I won't. I'm just going to speak to the sergeant. You stay with Regina, just for a few moments. Come on." He pushed the boy gently away from him. "You did very well. It's all over now. You can be brave a bit longer, I know you can."

Peter sniffed, scrubbed at his wet cheeks.

Regina came in and went straight to him.

"Oh, Peter, love. Come on. It's all right. Come on, now."

Ian stood up, avoiding Peter's stricken face. He did not think that he could bear it if the boy should ask him to stay again. But Regina was cuddling him, making soothing noises. He hurried out of the room.

"I'm sorry about that, Mr. Woodford. Poor little lad."

"It had to be done," Ian admitted.

"Well, it seems clear enough. The shock of being thrown into the water would be bound to make him a bit confused. I think probably she woke up, or opened her eyes and got alarmed, seeing him standing up—"

"What the hell does it matter?" Ian burst out. Benyon's dry, solemn voice had the power to paint pictures. "She's dead. I don't care how it happened."

Benyon suppressed the retort that sprang to his lips.

"I understand, sir. Well, I'll file my report. I don't think we'll have to trouble the lad again. However, I shall have to ask what your plans are, sir."

"Plans? I don't know. I haven't thought."

"Will you be staying on here, sir?"

Ian did not know and he could not think.

"There'll be the identification, sir. It would be best if you took care of that."

Ian saw the sheet again, draped over a formless lump. He did not want to look. Then he realized what Benyon meant. If it wasn't him, it would have to be Peter.

"I'll be here," he said.

"Thank you, sir. The frogmen'll be here first thing. It shouldn't take long, though that lake is deep. Best to keep the lad out of the way."

"Yes, of course." Ian felt sick.

"I'll leave an officer on duty throughout the night,

126

down by the lake. Just in case anything should . . .
surface."

Ian turned away. He could see that as well. The pale,
lifeless body floating on the still, black surface of the
lake.

"Well, that'll be all for now, sir. My condolences,
Mr. Woodford, on your sad bereavement."

"Thank you." The stiff, formal words sounded
hollow and stupid to Ian.

"You've got a fine boy, there," Benyon said gruffly.
"Watch out for him."

"Yes. Yes, Sergeant, I will."

He wondered if he should shake hands, but Benyon
saved him the bother. Putting his cap on he nodded
curtly and went out into the yard. Ian stood in the hall,
unable to think clearly. He heard the car start up. Then
he turned back to the room where he had left Peter and
Regina.

She had quieted the boy. He was sitting in a
high-backed winged chair, his face in shadow. Regina
was looking out of the window but she turned when Ian
came in.

"I'll make some tea," she offered, walking past him.

"Peter?" He squatted beside the chair.

"Can we go home now?" The boy sounded exhausted.

"In a little while. Let the police clear out first."

"Mm." He nodded and closed his eyes.

"Do you want anything?"

"No."

"Do you feel sleepy?"

"A bit."

"Sit quietly then. I'll be right here."

Ian sat on a large, chintz-covered sofa. His hands
were shaking and he had to grit his teeth to prevent
them from chattering. Yet he felt nothing. His body
reacted independently and he was able to observe its

spastic movements as though they were happening to
someone else.

Regina brought him a cup of tea but he was shaking
too much to hold it. She placed it on a low table in front
of him. He could smell that it was laced with brandy.

"I don't like the police," she said, sitting beside him.
"All those damn questions."

Stuttering, Ian said, "They're only doing their job.
It's necessary."

"Even so." She looked at Peter, who seemed to be
asleep. "Try to drink it," she said.

"Thanks." Ian took a long breath. "I'll be all right in
a minute." He tried hard to control the shaking.
"You've been very kind, looking after Peter." Regina
said nothing. "It wouldn't be so bad if they'd found her.
The thought of her . . ."

"Don't," she said, and laid a hand on his jerking
arm. She looked again at Peter. Ian nodded, felt
ashamed. Her touch helped him. He breathed deeply,
telling himself to be calm. At last he was able to hold
the cup without spilling any of the tea. He drank
gratefully.

"What do you want to do? You're welcome to stay
here."

"Thanks, but I think we'll go back to the cottage."
Regina frowned. "We'll have to eventually," he pointed out. "The police'll be gone soon, except for one
man. They're leaving one to watch the lake."

"Let Peter stay at least," she urged.

"No. I think he'd rather . . . We've got to face this
together," he said and knew that it sounded trite, but
trite words were the only possible ones just then.

"Well, if there's anything I can do."

"Tomorrow," he said quickly, remembering the
frogmen and Benyon's advice. "If Peter could come to
you while they look for her."

"Both of you come. Why put yourself through it?"

"They may need me, to identify her."

"Well, come for breakfast at least. You can leave Peter here and—"

"Can we go home now, Dad?" Peter was leaning forward in the chair, his eyes fixed on Ian's face.

"Yes, okay. I'm sorry," Ian said to Regina, afraid that Peter's insistence would seem rude to her.

"Don't be silly. Just remember, if you want anything, you know where I am."

"I will, thanks. Okay, Peter, let's go."

"Should I drive you?" she offered.

"No. A walk will do us both good, eh, Peter?"

"Yes. Come on."

Regina looked as though she wanted to say something else and Ian guessed that it was the boy who inhibited her. But he could not send him away.

"I'll see you tomorrow. We can talk then," he said.

She nodded, smiled.

Outside, in the yard, Peter took his hand again and held it tightly.

At the cottage, Peter sat automatically in front of the TV set. Ian was glad of its mechanical drone. The white chair and table, the fallen poppies, especially the abandoned painting and her watercolors, seemed to accuse Ian. He poured himself a stiff drink and stood in the open doorway, looking at them. It was difficult to believe that she would not suddenly appear or call to him from the kitchen, asking him to carry the furniture onto the veranda. He knew that he had to fetch her things inside. He downed his drink in one gulp and realized how easy it would be to get drunk and that he must not, for Peter's sake. He put the glass down and went to the table. He kept his back to the lake, closed her paintbox, and carried it into the house. Peter glanced at him, at what he was carrying, but said nothing.

"I'll get us something to eat in a minute," Ian said. The alcohol reminded him that he had not eaten since his hasty sandwich lunch.

"Can you cook?" Peter raised his voice above the noise of the television.

"I used to be able to." He put the box in a corner of the room, among a clutter of other painting materials. Outside again, he studied the neat, careful drawing of the poppies. The waning sun softened the bright orange-red. He would have it framed. It was sentimental and silly, he supposed, but he would do it. Then he realized that it was not sentimentality that bothered him, but that he did not know how he would remember Pam. What could he cherish from their marriage that was good? He put the drawing board down quickly on the table and carried the whole lot, jar of poppies and all, onto the veranda, then went back for the chair. At last he was able to look at the lake. It was unchanged and that surprised him. What had he expected? He knew the answer to that and it frightened him. He had expected to see her, floating facedown, her arms spread. He snatched up the drawing and carried it into the house. The room seemed larger. It took him much longer to cross from one point to another. He had an urge to draw the curtains over the windows, to shut out the lake. It was a long, long way to the kitchen door and he knew that this sensation was not caused by the alcohol alone. Everything was out of kilter, like the world of a dream.

"You hungry?" he asked, watching the kitchen stretch and become larger.

"Yes, a bit. I don't know."

"You must eat something." Ian felt that he had struck the right note, calm, competent. It was important to get on with things, ordinary things. He went to the refrigerator and checked its contents. "Fish sticks or an omelette?" he shouted.

"Fish sticks." After a moment, Peter added, "Please."

Ian began to prepare the meal. It was simple, but he was out of practice. He checked each stage over in his mind, keeping busy. He did not notice when Peter switched off the TV, did not notice him leaning in the doorway until he said, "Dad?"

"Yes? Won't be long now. You must be starving." Ian moved about the kitchen unnecessarily. He was afraid that Peter would ask the question he dreaded.

"I'm all right."

"You could set the table."

"Okay."

Methodically, Peter set two places. Then, again, he asked, "Dad?"

"Yes?"

"What are we going to do?"

Ian gripped the edge of the sink tightly, keeping his back to the boy. He wanted to be honest—he did not have the energy to invent—but was afraid that to do so would be to cast the boy even further into uncertainty.

"I am not quite sure. We'll talk about it tomorrow."

"When tomorrow?"

"We'll see."

Ian began to serve the meal: fish-and-chips, salad.

"Will I have to go back to the home?"

The plate Ian was holding clattered on the Formica table.

"Whatever gave you that idea?"

Peter would not look up. He pulled the plate toward him, stared at the food. Too late, Ian realized that he had not reassured him.

"I thought that, now that Mommy's . . . you know, that you wouldn't be able to keep me."

"Don't be silly. Of course I can." Now was the moment to reach out and touch the child, tell him that he loved him and would keep him safe. This was the

131

moment to start the relationship Ian knew they must have, but he could not do it. Fetching his own food, all he could manage was, "Of course I want you."

"Good," Peter said, and began to remove the crisp bread-crumb coating from the fish, exposing the white, moist meat. Ian made himself eat, without thinking or, as far as possible, tasting.

They ate and washed up together, in silence. The sun had set but it still was not dark. Instead there was a thick, pearly gray light, almost like a mist in which, to Ian, everything seemed to happen in slow motion. He opened a bottle of wine, thinking that it would be safer than spirits, and poured himself a glass.

"It's past your bedtime. Don't forget we're having breakfast at Home Farm."

Peter walked slowly to his bedroom door.

"You'll be all right?" Ian asked awkwardly.

"Yes."

He went into his room, leaving the door ajar. A few minutes later he reappeared wearing the bottom half of a pair of pajamas and went into the bathroom. Ian watched the strange light, listened to the gurgles and the rattles of the plumbing.

"Leave your door open, if you like, and call me if you want anything."

"All right. Good-night."

"Good-night, Peter." There had to be something else he could say, but he did not know what. Any mention of Pamela seemed fraught with danger and yet not to refer to her was surely unnatural? While Ian was considering this, Peter went back into his room, again leaving the door slightly open. Ian poured more wine into his glass and wished he had a cigarette. He had not smoked for years but suddenly wanted one. To escape the longing, to escape all feeling, he went onto the veranda. The trees were dark, shadowed into a single mass under a sky that was still somberly blue. The lake retained a sort of sheen. Ian looked at the fallen poppies, thought that he should throw them away, but did not. He began to rearrange the chairs, which before he had dumped down hastily, blocking the veranda. As he did so, one chair knocked over something leaning against the wall. It fell with a clatter on the boards. Ian bent over the chair, picked it up. At first he did not give it a thought. It was, after all, an everyday part of life at the cottage. And then something stirred in his memory. It was Peter's fishing tackle, the rod dismantled into three sections and neatly parceled in its nylon cover. Landing net, basket, and bait box, all stood against the wall. He held the rod and remembered.

Peter had stood up, in the middle of the lake, to fish. He had stood up in the boat, turning his back on Pam. That's what he'd said.

I thought I'd do some fishing.

But how could he fish if the rod was here, all the time? Ian turned toward the door, still holding the rod. Something cold and unthinkable clutched at him.

The bed smelled of Pamela's perfume. Her satin nightgown had slipped to the floor. The dressing table was littered with bottles, tissues, a screwed-up handkerchief, all of which reminded Ian of her. He concentrated on the undraped window. The long twilight had thickened into a misty dark. He could not remember the name of her perfume, but she had always worn it. Her clothes, her skin, the sheets in which she slept had always smelled of it. In a way, the scent *was* Pamela. Ian tossed and turned. He did not think a fishing rod would sink. The reel was surely too light to weight it down? So the police must have pulled it out of the water, along with the boat. Then, with unexpected care, one of them—probably an angler himself—had dismantled the rod, found its case, and placed it with the rest of the tackle. But the bait box would have sunk, unless it was empty and the lid was open. Who would bother to rescue an old box? Only an angler who knew the value of such things.

Peter had only said that he *thought* he would do some fishing. Maybe, when he stood up, he realized that he had left the rod behind.

The police had been extraordinarily thoughtful. Ian must remember to thank the sergeant tomorrow. Then he remembered that an officer was supposed to be keeping watch by the lake, but he had not noticed anyone down there. Would he have a tent or something? Ian felt that he should have at least offered him a drink. Only they weren't supposed to drink on duty, were they?

He threw off the bedclothes and thrust his feet into an old pair of sneakers. He pulled on a robe and went out onto the veranda. There was no moon. The bank lay in shadow. There could be somebody down there, somebody discreet, but he could not be sure.

The basket would float: Anyone would rescue the basket, and if they had it would be damp. He knocked against a chair, swore quietly, and picked up the basket. It was quite dry. So dry that it creaked a little in his hands. But if it had been standing there a long time, in the sun . . . The bait box was heavy, at least half-full, heavy enough to sink.

What was he trying to prove? That Peter had made a mistake? After the sort of shock he had had, would anyone remember why they had stood up in a boat, seconds before their mother drowned?

He was a strong swimmer. Why hadn't he tried to save her? He would associate the act of standing up in the boat with fishing. He was distressed and shocked when he spoke to the police.

He had not said, specifically, that he had *not* tried to save her. If he had tried, and failed, it would not be something he would want to mention. Not yet.

Ian felt that he was going mad. He, too, was in

shock, and nothing that his mind offered now should be given any credence. More than anything, he needed sleep. He went inside again, closing the glass doors behind him. Another glass of wine would make him sleepy. And if the bedroom was too full of painful associations, the sofa was comfortable enough. He turned on the lamp, poured the wine, and sat on the sofa. Pamela had not cleaned it. The whisky stain had dried a grayish-brown, but Regina's blood, three neatly defined spots, were almost black.

A sound like a pistol shot, a loud crack.

For a moment, Ian thought that he had conjured the noise, that his mind was playing tricks. Then he realized that he had jumped, spilling some of the red wine onto his robe. He had not imagined the sound. He stood up quickly, looking around the room. Everything seemed all right. His eyes settled on Peter's door. The sound had been loud enough to wake him. He pushed the door open and fumbled for the light switch.

Peter was sitting bolt upright in bed. His legs seemed rigid beneath the sheet. His arms were bent stiffly at his side, like a wooden doll's. His hands were clenched into tight fists. The light startled him. Ian only glimpsed his face. He had been staring straight ahead, his teeth bared, eyes wide open. Then, in less than a second, he was blinking, turning toward Ian.

"Peter?"

"Hello, Dad."

"What happened?"

"Happened?" He yawned sleepily, lay down at once, hitching the sheet over his bare shoulder.

"Didn't you hear a noise?"

"Don't know. I was asleep."

He went to the side of the bed and felt Peter's forehead. It was hot and dry.

"Would you like me to stay with you for a bit?"

"No. It's all right."

He was almost asleep. Ian straightened the bed-

135

clothes although they did not really need it. He looked down at the boy, feeling a mixture of pity and guilt.

"Good-night, then," he said, softly.

Peter murmured something incoherent, shifted a little. Ian turned away, then stopped in his tracks, catching his breath.

On the wall, facing Peter's bed, was a watercolor Pam had painted for the boy when they had first adopted him. He had insisted on bringing it to the cottage with him. Ian remembered clearly taking it to be framed and now he stared in shocked disbelief at it. The glass was shattered. He went closer, peering at it. It seemed rather that the glass had imploded. In the very center of the picture was a neat, round hole from which radiated, in perfect symmetry, elongated triangles of broken glass. He thought for a moment that it was curiously beautiful, like a spider's web. Then he glanced at the bed. Peter was sleeping innocently, but he had been facing the picture when Ian entered the room. Not quite sure what he was doing, Ian took the picture down and carried it into the other room, snapping off Peter's light as he went. The thing looked as though it had been subjected to an incredible force which had shattered it in this curiously geometrical way. He thought of the fragment of glass sticking into Regina's palm. That glass had been broken in a similarly ordered way. Peter had, at that time, been asleep in that very room.

Ian stood the painting on the floor with its ruined face to the wall. What he was thinking—had thought—was ridiculous. He tried to laugh at himself, but could only make an exasperated noise in his throat. First he had come close to accusing Peter of negligence over Pam and now, ludicrously, he was endowing him with the ability to shatter glass at will. The two incidents were pure coincidence. There was a flaw in Regina's glass, and the picture, which had a wooden frame, was probably shattered by the frame's contracting or ex-

"Yes, a bit."

"It'll be better now."

"Why?"

"We can play more games. Better games. And she won't worry all the time."

Peter plucked at the hay, not knowing how to answer that.

"It's different with you," he said, without thinking about it, meaning that away from Reggie and the others he would be sad and frightened without her.

"Course. With us you can be yourself."

"How? What do you mean, Reggie?"

Reggie clucked his tongue impatiently.

"Are we going to see the frogmen or not?" he asked, standing up.

"Yes. Okay."

"Keep quiet then."

They waded through the hay, brushing it off their clothes. Reggie glanced warningly toward Grizzle's hideout. Peter went down the steps first. Carl took no notice of them, and there was no one in the yard.

"Just act casual, like we're not going anywhere," Reggie advised, climbing the gate. "Then we'll slip into the trees and no one will see us at all."

Peter's heart thumped with excitement. He let Reggie take the lead and they stole into the trees, picking their way carefully toward the lake.

"Listen."

"What is it?"

"An outboard motor."

They moved on until they could look down at the bank. The policeman who had questioned Peter was there, and his father, looking unhappy. A black rubber dinghy, splashed with yellow stripes like a wasp, was puttering toward the bank. There were two frogmen in it. Peter was suddenly afraid.

"What if they do find her?" he whispered to Reggie.

"They won't—you said they won't."

"I know, but . . ."

"You know they won't," Reggie insisted. "Look, they're going to dive."

Peter edged closer to him. The sun caught the frogman's goggles as he adjusted them. A moment later, headfirst, he splashed over the side, and disappeared, flippers waving. Reggie said he looked just like a duck with its behind sticking up, and Peter had to put his hand over his mouth to stifle his giggles.

The frogmen began in the middle of the lake, surfacing at intervals to make negative reports to the officer who sat in the boat. They had begun to make wide sweeps toward either bank when Ian arrived and told Benyon what Peter had said about a gate, a subterranean stream.

"You don't think the lad could be making it up?"

"I thought of that, but I don't think so. I'm simply passing on information, Sergeant. It's up to you what you make of it."

Benyon visibly relaxed. Cooperation, acknowledgment of his authority invariably worked like a balm. Cupping his hands about his mouth, he shouted to the dinghy, signaling the men to come in.

Ian didn't care if Peter was lying or whether or not Benyon acted on the information. He felt detached from the whole process and if that was a defense mechanism against his own fear of having to identify Pam, he didn't care. He moved away as Benyon strode out onto the jetty and held a hurried consultation with the man in the boat. Ian had decided not to mention the fishing rod, not to inquire if some kindly policeman had retrieved it and returned it to the house. His motives for this were mixed. Again, he did not care. The old cliché operated with surprising force: nothing would bring Pam back. And if informed, Benyon's most likely

course of action would be to question Peter again. Ian
wanted to avoid that at all costs. He had seemed so
normal, so happy at breakfast and Ian wanted to keep it
that way. That's what Pam would have wanted.

"Mr. Woodford?"

"Yes?" He walked toward the sergeant, who was
clumping back along the jetty.

"The frogmen confirm a strong pull down there, out
in the middle. We've decided to check your information."

"Oh, fine."

"I expect you'd like to come along."

Benyon did not give him a chance to refuse, but set
off up the hill as though it was all a matter of urgency.
Ian followed automatically. If Peter was right, there
was nothing to fear, and if they found something, he
might as well get it over with, quickly.

Benyon paused on the veranda and explained,
unnecessarily, that they would take the path to Home
Farm and then drop down to the far bank. Ian nodded.

"Tell me, Mr. Woodford, what sort of woman was
your wife?"

Ian laughed, more out of surprise than anything else.

"I don't know how to answer that. Why?"

"I mean, was she in good health, for example?"

"Yes."

"Nothing worrying her?"

"What are you trying to imply, Sergeant?"

"Nothing at all, sir, but in cases like this we have to
consider all possibilities."

"Including suicide," Ian said drily.

"I wouldn't have put it as strong as that . . ."
Benyon began, sounding put out, as though Ian had
made some kind of social gaffe.

"I can put your mind at rest, Sergeant," Ian said,
refusing to play the policeman's game. "My wife
adored Peter. Had she had any reason to harm herself,

145

or any wish, the first thing she would have done would have been to make sure that Peter was a long way away and absolutely uninvolved."

"People can sometimes act on the spur of the moment," Benyon said cautiously.

"My wife was not an impulsive woman," Ian declared.

"We have to check these things, you know." Again Benyon sounded defensive. "I think we can get down there quite nicely."

Slithering down the slope, Ian saw a small khaki-colored tent on the bank. Obviously the abode of the nightwatch officer, he thought. The black dinghy was making slowly toward them, leaving a silver wake like a neat furrow. Panting, Benyon jumped the last few feet onto the bank.

"Where exactly do you reckon this gate is, then?" he asked.

"I've really no idea. Peter just said it was up here," Ian replied and walked away from the sergeant. The suggestion that Pam might have killed herself had rattled him. It was one thing to think of it himself, but to have Benyon suggest it made him angry, and a little afraid. Had somebody said something about her state of mind? Regina? No, she wouldn't. Her hostility toward the police was too strong for that. Besides, what he had said to Benyon was true. It reassured him. If Pam had been going to do anything at all, she would have sent Peter away.

What sort of woman was your wife?

She seemed now so like a woman he barely knew. Yes, ever since Peter, he had known, consciously, that they were growing apart, but it had taken her death to make him realize that she was a stranger. Then he remembered something she had said, that the only impulsive thing she had ever done was to marry him. So he had been right to say that she was not impulsive. He could see her then, sharply and clearly, as she had been

146

when they were first married, younger, of course, and pretty. She had always reminded him of a slightly startled animal. Her eyes were large and brown and had a hesitant, darting look. She disliked eye contact, tended to look off to one side or down at her hands. But with him she had overcome her shyness.

Ian sat down, his back against a tree trunk. The sergeant was squatting on the edge of the bank, talking to the frogmen.

He had met her at a party, his party. One of the first things he had done after seeing his parents off on that last holiday was to throw a party, to repay all his hosts and hostesses. She had come with somebody—he couldn't for the life of him remember who—and he had liked her at once. Her escort, boyfriend—whatever he was—had abandoned her. The party was breaking up when he found her sitting in a corner and she had admitted that she was stranded. Now he remembered. The chap who'd brought her had disappeared—into one of the bedrooms, he was fairly certain—with a large-busted girl who had an irritating giggle. It was because of that, the possible embarrassment of Pamela finding out, that he had offered to drive her home. She was a graphic-design art student and he had clumsily said that she didn't look like an art student.

"Perhaps that's because I'm older than most. I didn't decide until I was twenty that that was what I wanted to do."

But Pam had never fit in. He realized that as he got to know her better. She went through the course because she had set herself to do it. Liz had once said to him that Pamela sounded as lacking in purpose as Ian was. And now, sitting under the tree, watching and yet not really seeing the routine dive and rise of the frogmen, Ian thought that was true. Both of them had lacked purpose and yet, for a time, the idea of marriage had seemed a purpose in itself. If his parents hadn't died, he might have put all his plans into action, set up on his own, as a proper architect. They had talked of Pam working with him, handling the interior design. But somehow he had got enmeshed in Woodford and Hasell. Pam had been there, consoling, waiting. There was money enough, an easy chance to make more. They had married. Their plans were only deferred, they told themselves. But when she told him that she couldn't conceive, everything had become so . . .

"Mr. Woodford?"

The sergeant was leaning over him.

"Yes? Sorry. I was miles away."

"It seems your lad was telling the truth. There is an exit down there, and a hell of a current."

"What about the gate?" Ian asked, feeling both relieved and scared.

"A sort of grille affair, I gather. God knows why anyone should bother to put it there, but it is there all right. Rusted away, though. Lying on the bottom now."

"I see."

Benyon straightened up, assumed his official tone.

"It is my duty to warn you, Mr. Woodford, that this materially alters our search." He cleared his throat. "It seems quite possible that the late Mrs. Woodford could have been drawn into the stream down there."

Ian stood up, partly for something to do, partly because he did not like the sergeant towering over him.

"So what now?"

"We shall go on looking, of course, though I must warn you that our expectations—"

"What happens if you don't find her?"

"The coroner will have no choice but to record an open verdict, sir. However, we shall contact the local water board, the county surveyor's office and attempt to determine . . ."

Ian did not listen. Trapped down there, locked down there forever, decomposing, floating.

"If you'll excuse me, Sergeant, I'll be at the house."

Blindly, he began to pull himself up the slope, grabbing at trunks and branches.

When the policeman went over to Ian, Reggie dug Peter in the ribs and jerked his head, indicating that they should go. It had been pretty boring anyway. He followed Reggie quietly, bending low to avoid snagging branches.

"Do you know what I think?" Reggie said when they reached the path and were safely out of earshot.

"What?"

"What's the biggest and most beautiful house you know?"

"Why?"

"What is?" Reggie insisted.

Peter couldn't see the point of the question and it did not interest him very much. He picked up a stick and thwacked it against the spindly trunks of the young firs as they walked.

"Come on," Reggie said impatiently. "What?"

He thought of his own home, but that wasn't large or particularly beautiful. He thought of Buckingham Palace, but he'd only seen the outside and the soldiers had interested him much more than the building.

"Halford Hall, I suppose," he said, because his father had said it was beautiful and it *was* big.

"Right. Well, if I was you, that's what I'd think, that she was somewhere like that, in a big, beautiful house, waiting for you."

Peter stopped. He didn't like the idea. He wished Reggie hadn't said it, or that he had chosen Buckingham Palace after all.

"Why?" he said at last, chucking his stick away.

"Because that's what ladies like, isn't it? Big houses and stuff like that. And kids. Please yourself, but that's what *I'd* think." Reggie's eyes were innocently blank.

149

He suddenly pushed Peter and challenged him to a race. "Let's find the others. Bet I can beat you."

Peter regained his balance and set off after Reggie, shouting that it was unfair, they hadn't had a proper start. Reggie won and Peter continued to complain across the yard and back up into the loft. They were all there and Peter appealed to Linda for support.

"Oh shut up, Peter, and sit down," Carl said, not angrily but in a way that compelled obedience.

Normally, he would have thrown himself sulkily into the hay, but he sat quietly, tucking his legs under him. He thought that they were probably going to play one of their games, but nothing happened. They were having, he supposed, one of their quiet spells. They usually happened when Regina was in the house, and they always made him uncomfortable. It was like a game but one he could not join in. He looked at them in turn. They were quite still, absolutely silent. He could not even hear their breathing. He shifted and fidgeted, bored and a little apprehensive.

Still

The command startled him. He thought it was Carl's voice and turned his head toward him. The young man had apparently not moved or spoken. Yet Peter had heard the word, or perhaps felt it. He looked at Linda.

Concentrate

It was like something exploding at the back of his head. A sensation, not a sound. It did not hurt exactly, but it made him feel strange. He shook his head violently, as though he could shake the words out. But there were more words, more scrambled voices.

Like Linda Look Linda Like

Liquid words, sloshing in his mind. He had to keep still or these words, sounds from nowhere, would take over. He could not take his eyes off Linda, although she did not look at him. Her eyes were cast down, hooded.

You like Linda

It was Carl's voice, but Carl had not spoken. He did not need to look at him to know that. Carl's voice inside his head, like a whisper, exploding. He stopped trying to resist or understand it. He clung to the words which were more than sound.

Grizzle Grizzle Grizzle

Linda began to fade, as though the light was dimming.

Watch Watch Grizzle

He had no knowledge of moving his head, turning his gaze from one girl to the other. He saw Grizzle, indistinctly. Her face was in profile. She looked at something he couldn't see. He could not understand and wanted to.

Watch

And from somewhere on the periphery of his vision, he saw it, moving. An old-fashioned hurricane lamp, its glass clouded with dust and cobwebs. It wobbled a little, some six inches above the floor. And it moved toward him, halted, and set itself down a few feet in front of him, on the board floor.

Con cen trate

The word was three separate muffled explosions, echoing and fading one into the other. It seemed louder than any of the other words in his head. It hurt him, like a sudden too-loud shout in the ear, except that the hurting was all inside his head. Bits of broken words, chasing against his skull. He stared at the lamp, stared and stared and stared at it. A thin lick of flame danced inside the glass.

You You You You

He leaned toward it.

Now You You Nowyou youyou You

Another part of his mind, a part that was not bruised and rattling with intruding words, tried to understand what was required of him. He watched the flame, became dazzled by it and then, without his knowing

151

how or why, the glass around the flame cracked and shattered, fell in four pieces onto the floor. The flame went out.

His head was empty then, quite empty, and his thoughts were his own again.

They were all smiling at him and Linda clapped her hands together with pleasure.

There was no one about when, later that afternoon, Ian went to Home Farm. The front door, however, was open and he went into the hall, calling Regina's name. At the second attempt, he heard a faint answer and then footsteps upstairs. She looked flustered, as though he had interrupted something, but she cut his apology short.

"Peter's off with the kids somewhere. Shall I go and shout for them?"

"No," he said, relieved. "I want a private word with you, actually."

"Oh?" She pushed a lock of thick hair from her face. "Let's go into the sitting room then."

Ian nodded. The room was the one in which Benyon had interviewed Peter and now Ian was able to take a better look at it. There was some fine paneling, a large open stone grate, and an impression of rich, almost exotic color. This last came from the bold chintz upholstery and a number of cheap but colorful Indian rugs on the darkly stained boards.

"I gather they haven't found anything," she said, indicating that he should sit on the sofa.

He shook his head, told her about the stream and the possibility that Pam might never be recovered, or, if so, in some river, miles away. "But they haven't given up entirely. They're going to do a proper dredge tomorrow."

She said nothing to this but Ian felt that she was sympathetic, that she would understand his feeling that it didn't much matter anymore—except that he kept imagining Pam bobbing up to the surface while Peter was swimming or fishing.

"Anyway, that's not what I wanted to talk to you about. I really must go back to London, if only to get a few clothes." He looked apologetically at his crumpled cotton trousers. "I mentioned it to the police. If I were to go this evening, I could be back by noon tomorrow."

"You'd like Peter to stay here?" she asked at once.

"I don't know. I'd welcome your advice."

"What's the point of taking him to London, just for one night? Unless, of course, there's someone you could leave him with?"

"Not really."

"Well then." She made it sound as though everything was settled.

"It's the next few weeks I'm really bothered about, that and leaving him at all. Yesterday he seemed terrified of my going away. He even asked me if he would have to go back to the home now."

"What did you expect?" Regina asked mildly. "He's bound to be insecure."

"I know."

"Only you're not sure how to cope?"

"In a nutshell," he admitted.

"Well, if you want my advice . . ." She stood up and moved to the high mantel over the fireplace and began to straighten a row of matching copper jugs. "I'd let him stay here. I would make as few changes as possible. Could you get time off? Until the lease is up on the cottage?"

"Yes, easily, but I'd need to go to London."

"Well then . . ."

"You don't think it would be better to take him away somewhere immediately? You don't think the associations here—"

"What would you do with him?" She turned around and fixed Ian with her dark, penetrating eyes. "Look, I don't know you well, but you wouldn't know how to keep him amused, what the hell to do with him. Here he's got plenty to do, friends. Carl and Linda are old enough to understand. They'll help him. And he's got to come to terms with what's happened. Running away never works, you know. And that goes for you too," she added sharply.

Ian laughed with relief.

"I'm sorry," he said. "It's just that your directness is very refreshing."

"A lot of people think me rude." She came back to the sofa and touched his arm. "I don't mean to be," she said gently. "It's just that I speak my mind. It seems best to me. But what I've said is only my opinion. It's your decision."

He smiled. "It sounds like good advice. You're right about my—well, I wouldn't know what to do with him, whereas down here . . ."

"That's settled then. You'll go tonight?"

"It would be best. I could see my partner and make the rest of the arrangements in the morning."

"You'll want to see Peter, then," Regina said, and walked to the door.

"Regina?"

"Yes?"

"There's something else."

"What?"

"How do I . . . I mean, I don't know how to talk to him about Pam, about what's happened. Christ, I don't even know if I should."

She sighed and walked slowly back to him, shaking her head.

"Kids are natural, Ian. They take things to heart, but in a very uncomplicated way. Just be natural with him. He'll deal with it. And unless I'm very much mistaken, he'll let you know when he wants to talk, and when he doesn't."

"Thanks." Ian pressed her hand.

Voices and thundering footsteps sounded in the hall.

154

"Here they are," she said, smiling. "Shall I send him in to you?"

"No." Ian stood up. "I'll take him back to the cottage and explain. I think he might be a bit upset. I can easily drop him back here in the car."

Mention of the car reminded him of something else. "By the way, do you think somebody could take Pamela's car into Halford for me?"

Regina looked at him uncertainly. "Carl would be glad to do it, of course, but . . ."

"Pam was always hopeless about getting it serviced, and I thought, well, it would be one more thing done." He couldn't say that the sight of it, sitting there, never to be driven by her again, nagged too painfully at him.

Regina inclined her head and went out, shouting to the children to make less noise.

"Are the frogmen gone now?"

Peter was walking ahead of Ian along the path to the cottage.

"Yes, but they'll be back tomorrow. They were very glad of your tip about the stream."

He made no sign that he was pleased nor did he say, as Ian half expected, that they were wasting their time. His interest seemed almost academic, a natural boyish interest in frogmen. Ian was glad. With Regina's advice fresh in his mind, he dared to hope that Peter was already beginning to adjust.

"Look, Peter, I've got to go back to London. Only for a few hours. Would you mind staying at Home Farm, just till tomorrow?"

Peter's step faltered, but only for a moment. It could have been a bump in the path, something entirely unconnected with Ian's announcement.

"How long?"

"I should be back by noon tomorrow. Early afternoon at the latest."

"Why can't I come?"

"You can. Only it will be very dull for you."

They had reached the veranda. Peter rested his hands on the wooden balustrade and stared down at the lake.

"I've got to see Jim Hasell and collect some clothes. Sit down a minute, Peter, I want to explain."

Dragging his feet, a sulky frown on his face, Peter plonked himself down in one of the white wicker chairs.

"The reason I'm going is just to fix things at the yard so that we can stay down here, for the rest of the summer. Would you like that?"

"With you, all the time?" His face and voice brightened.

"I may have to pop up to London now and again, but on the whole, yes."

"All right."

"Unless you'd rather go back to London?"

He thought about this for a moment, then shook his head. "No."

"And you won't mind staying with Regina tonight?"

"No, if you promise to come back tomorrow."

"I'll not only do that but I'll telephone you as soon as I get to London. I've also promised the police. Would you like it in writing, as well?"

"No." He laughed, a natural, cheerful boy's laugh.

"And listen, Peter. I want you to understand something and to promise me something else."

"What?" A sort of wariness clouded his eyes.

"There is absolutely no question of me letting you down. I don't want you ever to think about going back to the home. Do you understand?"

"Yes." He looked at his feet and shuffled them.

"While I'm down here, during the rest of the summer, we'll work something out for the future together. I shall need your help, okay?"

"Yes, and what have I got to promise?"

"To stay away from the lake until further notice. I don't want you swimming, and the police have said that nobody must touch the boat. Will you promise me?"

"Yes."

"Word of honor?"

"Cut my throat and hope to die."

The familiar, childish vow embarrassed both of them.

"Well," Ian said quickly. "I'd better be making tracks." He stood up and went into the house. He collected his toothbrush and electric razor from the bathroom.

"You will be back tomorrow?"

"What did I say?"

"You said you'd ring, too."

"And I will. Peter, you must trust me. I wouldn't go now if I didn't have to, and it's only so we can stay on here. You do want that?"

"I said so." He went into his room.

In his own bedroom Ian straightened the bedclothes and looked around for anything else he should take with him. But he'd only brought the bare essentials. He was pulling on his jacket when Peter appeared in the doorway.

"Dad?"

"Yes?"

"Where's my picture? The one of the rabbits. It's gone."

The tense business of the day had driven the picture from Ian's mind. Now, he said the first thing that came into his head.

"I took it down, it needs fixing. I'm glad you mentioned it. I'll take it with me."

"Why? What's wrong with it?"

Peter followed him into the living room. Ian picked up the watercolor, keeping its shattered surface facing away from the boy.

"It needs mending. I'll get the poppies framed at the same time. Will you roll it up for me, carefully, like Mommy showed you?"

Peter stared at him and then walked across the room,

grasped the frame of the picture, and turned it around. He caught his breath sharply.

"I didn't—"

"What?" Ian asked urgently.

"Dad." He looked at him desperately, his lips quivering. "I didn't know. I . . ."

They both turned toward the door, which stood open, and on which Linda had tapped lightly. Something prompted Ian to snatch the picture from Peter, to hide its damaged face from the girl.

"I came to fetch Peter," she said, smiling gently. Carl was standing behind her, also smiling.

"Ready, Peter?" he asked.

"We thought we'd save you a journey," Linda explained, looking directly at Ian.

"That's very good of you. Go and get your pajamas, Peter. And don't forget your wash kit." He propped the painting against the sofa and went to the table. He explained, as he unclipped the drawing of the poppies from the board, that he was going to have it framed.

"Come on, Peter," Linda said to the boy, who was still standing in the room. "I'll help you." She led him into his bedroom.

"We'll take good care of him, Mr. Woodford," Carl said.

"I know you will. There. Now, I'm all set."

Peter came back, carrying his pajamas and wash kit. Linda's hand rested tenderly on his shoulder.

"Be a good boy, Peter. And don't worry, okay?" He glanced at the painting. Peter nodded. "I'll call you later."

Linda gave the boy a little push toward his father. Ian hugged his stiff, recalcitrant body briefly, then gathered up his luggage. They followed him out onto the veranda. Linda closed the doors. Ian laid the painting, glass-side down, on the back seat of his car and called good-bye.

They stood on either side of Peter, smiling. At the last minute, the boy waved. There was something sad and lonely about the gesture which made Ian feel bereft. To compensate, he sounded the horn as he entered the dark driveway, and the little group was lost to view.

Regina stood beside his bed, watching. She was almost feverish with excitement, yet she knew that calm was essential. It had to be done carefully, purposefully. But to be so near, after so long, was like a pain in her, an ache beyond yearning.

Voices roamed in his head, like insistent music. Looking down, perhaps to escape them, he saw inside his own body. It appeared as a vast and empty landscape. A great, dark sky bound it. There were limits beyond sight. Dimly perceived colors, red and brown. And voices—voices of pain and grief, of intense, racking hatred. These voices called to each other, like hunter and prey. If the voices should ever touch . . .

He stirred on the bed, fighting. Regina allowed herself to relax. She felt his resistance, the tension of the search and struggle, drain away. The night sounds of the house were suddenly loud all around her. Peter turned over in the bed, snuggling against the pillow, but still Regina could not pull herself away. Beyond the familiar sounds of the settling house, the ordinariness of the peacefully sleeping boy, she could still hear and sense something, someone. Her sigh drove the last vestiges of a presence from the little room, the house. She felt weak, exhausted, but she could not leave. So near, so close. She shuffled to the window and looked out at the humped and moonlit fields. So empty, empty. It would take all her strength, perhaps more than she had. With an expression almost of hatred, she glanced at the bed. His face was framed pale in the moonlight, the eyes moving rapidly beneath the thin lids. Evidence of dreaming. What dreams, she wondered, and smiled a little, gathering her strength together.

It was an afterthought, a suddenly remembered courtesy that prompted Ian to telephone Elsa Rath. His case was packed, the milk and newspapers canceled. He had spoken to his neighbor, Mrs. Swift, and left a spare key with her. He felt almost overwhelmed by the weight of sympathy which became embarrassed and, he thought, suspicious, when he explained that Pamela's body had not yet been recovered. It had been even worse with Jim and Edna Hasell, whom he had seen the night before. How could such a thing happen? There was no difficulty about him taking time off, as much as he wanted. The summer was a slack time anyway. People were more interested in vacations than improving their homes. And if the Grubb thing came to anything, well, Jim could get in touch. But most of all it was their shocked concern for him as a man on his own, with a young boy to bring up, that he found intolerable. Edna shook her head. Jim sighed. Mrs. Swift made offers of help they both knew she could not possibly keep. Ian felt himself labeled, but not to their satisfaction. There remained something unspoken, a doubt. Jim, he felt certain, wanted to say that now he would have to get his act together. A man on his own. They shook their heads sadly. He felt claustrophobic and angry. Until then the idea of a few weeks in the country had been for Peter, but suddenly he wanted to get away from them all, to put together a new face so that when he and Peter returned, he would be proof against their sympathy and doubts.

"Seven-three-five-two, Elsa Rath speaking."

Ian had only spoken to her once or twice before and he was taken aback by the power of her slow, deliberate speech to evoke that time when he had been desperate, desperate for Pam to see somebody, get help that he could not begin to provide. He heard himself stuttering.

"Ah, Mr. Woodford. Yes?"

"It's about Pamela," he said. "My wife." He waited, but Elsa Rath said nothing. "There's been an accident. I'm afraid she's dead. I thought that I should let you know. She was writing to you. I imagine you had another appointment to see her which, obviously, now, she won't . . ." It was her silence, her professional, studied, lying-in-wait silence that made him gabble stupidly, stumbling over his words. He shut his mouth firmly, stared at the suitcase waiting to be carried out to the car.

"I am sorry," she said at last. "So sorry."

"Thank you."

After an unusually brief pause, she said, "I should like to see you. I have had a letter from your wife. I could see you at . . ." The silence stretched. Faintly Ian heard the rustle of pages.

"I have to go straight back to the country," he said into the silence. He did not want to see her. "Peter and the police are waiting for me."

"At eleven o'clock," she said. "If you can make that in time."

"Yes," he said, glancing at his watch, "but I have to—"

"Good. I will see you then, Mr. Woodford."

The line went dead leaving Ian no choice but to hang up. Possibly she only wanted to hear the details firsthand. Psychotherapists keep notes, he thought. She would want to close the case, officially. Perhaps there was an outstanding bill which she wanted settled. It was annoying, but it need not take long. South Kensington, where she lived, was not far out of the way. He considered ringing Home Farm to explain that he might be delayed but decided against it. Probably it would only make Peter more anxious, more restless. Regina would reassure him. After all, he had said that he might not get there until early afternoon, and he had no intention of letting Elsa Rath keep him long.

He started to move away from the phone when he realized that he should call Liz. He reached for the receiver but did not pick it up. What made him hesitate? If only out of courtesy he should ring her, but suddenly Liz seemed irrelevant. He had been catapulted into a world that had no place for her, yet. The thought was shaming and he avoided prolonging it by carrying his luggage out to the car. When it was all safely loaded, he made a last check of the house. Gas and electricity turned off. Windows and doors locked. For a moment he looked at the rolled picture of the poppies, the damaged watercolor of the rabbits. He had been going to take them both to be framed, but now they would have to wait. He wished, as he locked the front door, that he had not rung Elsa Rath, but then he thought that at least it provided him with a kind of excuse for not contacting Liz.

Elsa Rath opened the door herself. She was a tall woman, with a soft, flawless skin that must once have made her a beauty. Her face remained unlined, which made it difficult to guess her age. Her hair, though, was the color of iron filings, streaked with paler gray. It was piled, teased, and lacquered into a froth of waves and curls which suggested a recent visit to the hairdresser. There was something vain, some remembrance of beauty, Ian thought, in this convoluted hairstyle. The impression was reinforced by stark blue nail varnish which looked incongruous on her large, ugly hands. She wore crimson, a sort of loose overdress, which accentuated her white and matte complexion.

Ian remembered the room into which she waved him. It ran the depth of the house, looking out onto the small, paved front garden, and the tangle of neglected weeds at the back. Elsa waited patiently while he chose one of the two almost facing chairs. Only when he had selected, sat, and crossed his legs, did Elsa sit, folding her hands together.

"Tell me, please, exactly what happened to Pamela."

Ian had repeated the details so often in the last few hours that he felt he was giving a prepared speech. The words as he spoke them lacked emotional resonance. When he had finished, adding that he must get back to Halford, that he was expected, Elsa sat for a long time, stiff and silent. Then she got up, crossed the room to a bureau, and returned, holding an envelope.

"How was she when you saw her last?"

"Not so good," he admitted. "She was very worried about Peter again. She seemed to have regressed. We had a row about it actually."

"And this fight, did it end in any conclusion?"

"No." Ian shook his head. Their rows never ended in any conclusion. They were just staging posts on a spiral of misunderstanding, fear, anger, self-pity.

"You said nothing about sending Peter away? To school perhaps?"

"No." Ian looked at her, alarmed.

Elsa held the envelope in her large right hand and tapped it lightly against her knee.

"This is a letter from her, the last I had. You had better read it." She offered it to him, then turned her attention to a corner of the room. Something in her expression, her complete withdrawal, made it impossible to ask questions. He unfolded the letter and read.

The letter hurt him on many levels. The fact that it was addressed to a paid stranger, rather than to him. That she had discussed Liz with Elsa. The sense of determination, eroded by panic. Surprisingly and most of all, the fact that she felt able to do without him.

"I didn't know," he said, folding the letter and slipping it back into the envelope.

"What?"

"Any of it."

"I do not think Pamela meant it." She leaned forward, one hand extended, asking for the letter. "I believe it was a fantasy, this idea of leaving you. But I am interested to know why she felt someone was trying to take Peter away from her, since you did not suggest anything of the kind."

"I thought about it," he admitted, not looking at her. "But I said nothing, nothing at all." It was suddenly very important to defend himself. "And she didn't mention her hysteria to you. She doesn't say how badly she upset Peter. This is an extremely biased account of what . . ." He couldn't go on.

"She does not need to. It is quite clear in every line."

"Why?" Ian asked, trying to get a grip on himself. "Why did you show it to me?"

"Because I thought, when you telephoned this morning, that it might have been a form of suicide note."

"No," he almost shouted. "You know as well as I do that—"

"Oh yes," Elsa interrupted calmly. "She would not have done anything to herself with Peter there. I know. She would always protect him. But then if her death, if she saw her death as a form of protection . . .?"

"I don't understand," he said and suddenly he was crying. He felt ashamed that the first tears he could shed for Pam could be prompted by this childish sense of rejection, but once they had begun, he could not stop them. Elsa stood up, outwardly quite unmoved by his tears. She placed a box of tissues on the arm of his chair. But then it did not seem so shameful. She had rejected him, ever since she had found Peter, and rejection always hurt. He saw that it had driven him to Liz, more than desire for her or to hurt Pamela. He had been seeking comfort, somebody to soothe him, dress his wounds, and tell him it would be all right. He blew his nose loudly.

"I'm sorry."

"Please." Elsa dismissed his apology and tears with a gentle wave of the hand. "Pamela was a very complicated woman. You are not to blame, you know."

"I could have done more."

"Perhaps."

"I had no idea she wanted to leave me."

"You did not know, did you, how much she had hurt you?"

He shook his head, feeling his throat contract against the return of his tears.

"I, too, perhaps, could have done more, if that is a comfort to you. But I have been puzzling all the time over where she got this idea that someone was trying to separate her from Peter."

"I think," Ian said with difficulty, "I can explain that."

"Please."

"He was becoming more independent. He's made friends with some other children down there. Pam tried to be pleased, she pretended, but really I knew she was afraid. I think she knew, in a way, that she could not hang on to him anymore."

Elsa considered this for a long time, while Ian mopped at his face and felt more foolish than ever.

"Or she invented it," she said at last, "invented it because she could not bear to be peaceful, to be happy. She was beginning to cope with things, to accept reality." She shrugged. "Anxiety can work like a drug, especially in a case like this. In a way, perhaps we should think of Pamela as an addict. She needed to be anxious, to atone. But now I must not delay you any longer." She stood up. A clock chimed, silvery and discreet, as though on cue.

"What do I owe you?" Ian asked, reaching for his checkbook.

"Nothing. Pamela's account was settled."

She moved silently to the door and opened it.

"If I can be of any help, on any matter, Mr. Woodford, you know where to contact me."

"Thank you."

"How is Peter?"

"Surprisingly well. He seems to be taking it in his stride."

"You are prepared, though, for a delayed reaction, no?" She shook her fantastically coiffed head. "I do not mean to alarm you, but under the circumstances . . . I have a friend who is very good with children, should you feel . . ." Suddenly a smile lit her face, transforming it. "But you have had enough of psychotherapists. I understand."

"I'll remember," he promised, and meant it.

"Good luck, Mr. Woodford. And again, I sympathize."

"Thank you."

She held out her hand brusquely. Ian clasped it and turned quickly away. The door shut behind him before he had reached the white painted metal gate.

Peter stared and stared and stared at the little square of mirror. He had found it among the clutter of bottles and things on his mother's dressing table. Now it was propped against the pillow on the big bed. He crouched over it and stared, willing it to shatter.

Nothing happened and he did not know whether to be relieved or afraid.

Outside he could hear the chug of engines. There were two boats today, but he had been so anxious not to be seen that he had barely glanced at the lake. The cottage was the only place he could think of where he could be alone. And he had to be alone to find out if he could really do it, if he was really like the others. Somebody shouted down by the lake. The sound of the boats' motors continued. They made it difficult to concentrate and maybe that was why he couldn't do it. Perhaps he should take the mirror off somewhere, by himself, away from the noise. He climbed off the bed and peeped through the window. The boats were out of sight now, but there was something trailing in their wake. He saw policemen, in their shirtsleeves, moving on the bank. He went back to the bed, screwed up his forehead, and glared into the mirror. He tensed every muscle in his body, but nothing happened.

He couldn't do it. And yet he had done it. They all said he had, and when he had seen the painting, he had known that it was possible. Maybe it was because it was a mirror. Mirrors were no good. All you saw was your reflection and that put you off. He climbed off the bed again and went back to the dressing table. His attention was attracted for a moment by a movement outside. Holding his breath, he saw a policeman start up the hill toward the house. He seized a bottle, the one nearest to hand, and tiptoed into the living room. There was no back door, but he could get out of his bedroom window and go straight into the woods. Clutching the little bottle tightly, he opened the window and climbed out. In a moment, he was hidden by the trees.

He made slow progress at first, for the trees were very densely packed, their branches tangled one with another. He had to stoop down, almost wriggle under them in places, but as the gradient behind the house became less pronounced, the going was easier. Soon he could glimpse the track to Home Farm and beyond it, sliced and cut into fragments by the trees, the solid block of Halford Hall. Nobody ever went there. That would be a good place. He would not be able to hear the boats and nobody would disturb him. He was excited, and when he cleared the trees, he began to run toward the house.

Panting, he climbed the steps onto the terrace and looked around him. The silence was extraordinary. No birdsong, no breath of wind. He looked at the gray house, at its black, forgotten windows, and felt afraid. It was not because of the house. It was because of what Reggie had said to him, about imagining her there, waiting for him. What did Reggie know? He pulled the little bottle from his pocket and inspected it. It was her perfume. A small, round bottle, half-full of amber-colored liquid. He looked at the label.

Je Reviens.

He tried to remember what it meant and could not. Resolutely turning his back on the house, he placed the bottle on the smooth flags of the terrace. It gleamed in the sun. Squatting down, he focused his entire attention on it. He narrowed his eyes until everything but the bottle became gray and diffused. The sun dazzled him, reflected back from the bottle. He shifted his position a little, so that his eyes were shielded from the glare. Again he focused entirely on the bottle. He had to know if he could do it, or, more precisely, if he could do it at will.

A long time passed, a long time of silence. The bottle seemed to waver and shimmer. His eyes slid from it and he felt cold. He felt that someone was looking at him as fiercely and totally as he was looking at the bottle. He tried to ignore it. He took a deep breath and stared at the bottle again, but the feeling would not go away. The bottle was his experiment, but somebody was looking at him in the same way, making him their experiment.

He flung himself round, losing his balance, falling on his side. The long narrow window towered above him and, just for a second, a split second, he saw something white, melting, moving away—like something glimpsed underwater. A sort of cry escaped him, but he thought perhaps it was only because he had been holding his breath. He scrambled up and went close to the window. He saw his own reflection, pale and murky from some fault in the glass. That must have been what he had seen, the reflection made even more fleeting by his fall. He put his nose to the window and placed his hands beside his face to shut out the light. It was so dark inside, dim and gray, like seeing underwater, that he could not make anything out.

Then he heard it, the sound. He did not know what it was. A sort of explosion, a booming noise which seemed to roll and swell, amplified by the house. A door closing, or someone knocking to be let in. He stepped backward quickly. The sound horrified him. It was the sound of emptiness itself.

"Peter, oh thank God. I've been looking everywhere."

He whirled around at the sound of her voice. His foot accidentally kicked the bottle. It rolled away, making a rattling sound against the flagstones. It hit the balustrade and smashed.

They stood as though frozen, both staring at the bottle. Regina sniffed, wrinkled her nose, and then walked slowly toward the bottle. She peered down at it, inhaling the perfume which was too strong, sweet and sickly.

"That's your mother's perfume. I remember it. What on earth were you . . .?" She straightened up, looked at the shivering, stricken boy.

It seemed to him that she looked beyond him, at something framed in the window. Her face was pale. Her hair, hanging loosely about her face, was damp with sweat where it touched her skin. He made himself look at the window again, but there was nothing there, nothing but its blackness and the dim, unfocused splash of their imperfect reflections.

She spoke his name softly and, although he did not want to, he went to her. She put one arm round his shoulders and led him along the terrace. He was shivering and the moment his feet touched the grass, he broke free of her and ran as fast as his legs would carry him.

The sound, the booming sound of emptiness, still reverberated in his head.

Ian got back in time to receive Benyon's negative report on the day's dredging and diving. They would pursue inquiries about the possible course of the underground stream and alert the local police should a likely exit, into some river, for example, be found. However, Benyon was not hopeful. Even if the late Mrs. Woodford was not a large woman, these underground passages tended to be narrow, too narrow for a fully grown woman to pass through. Ian willed him to shut up. The sergeant cleared his throat, tipped his cap, and told Ian that he would be informed of the time and place of the inquest—a mere formality, under the circumstances, but one which must be observed.

Ian lugged his suitcase onto the veranda feeling hopeless and very, very tired. He poured himself a drink and listened to the motorcade of police cars and jeeps crunch away down the drive. It was an ending of a kind, but irritatingly inconclusive, as though even in death Pamela eluded him, remained private and alien. His mind recalled and then shied away from her letter. It was too early to be drinking on an empty stomach, he told himself, and there was no point in brooding. He carried the suitcase into the bedroom but felt too tired, too drained to unpack. He ought to go to the Farm and fetch Peter. But instead he went to the bed. The boy was quite safe. He could take a nap, just half an hour.

The small mirror, still propped against the pillow, hurled his blurred reflection back at him. He recoiled, startled. For a moment he did not understand. He glanced over his shoulder and then, angry with himself, picked up the mirror. How had it gotten there? Who would . . .? His eyes traveled to the dressing table. A bottle was on its side. In the corner of his eye he sensed rather than saw a movement. The sliding door of the wardrobe was partly open and it seemed that Pam's clothes moved, as though touched lightly by a searching hand. Imagination, he told himself, staring at the still, protruding folds of dresses and skirts. The room felt full of her. But tiredness plays more tricks than imagination, he told himself. He set the mirror face-down on the bedside table, removed his shoes, and stretched out, hiding his face in the pillow.

It lacked the illogic, the displacement of a dream. It ran before him like a film. Blurred sunlight on the black waters of Halford Lake. The lake exactly as he knew it. No icy gray waste of water. Peter in the boat, far out. Peter standing in the boat, his body softened and fuzzed by the direct sunlight. Ian calls to him, his voice floating across the water, returning to him in echoes. Peter does not acknowledge him but before he can call again, the boy sits, takes up the oars. The boat moves sluggishly through the water. As it draws closer, he can see the boy's back bending, the play and stretch of the muscles under his shirt as he pulls hard on the oars. Deftly, he turns the boat, aligning it with the jetty. Ian leans out, grabs the gunwale to steady it. A woman in a white dress lies in the bottom of the boat. He is not really surprised. Her face is covered by a large, white sun hat. She is sleeping, her eyes shrouded from the sun. He looks questioningly at Peter. The boy smiles enigmatically and looks down at the woman. Impatient now, Ian reached out, grasps the brim of the forward-tilted hat, and lifts it.

Linda.

Her face hung over him, eyes startled. She withdrew her hand, almost guiltily, and he realized that she had been touching him. A patch of his skin, just above the breastbone, felt cold. Instinctively, he put his own hand over the spot. As she straightened up he saw, could not help but see, the soft curve of her breasts beneath a cheesecloth shirt. The sight recalled the intense, almost palpable attraction he had felt for her, and he struggled to sit up, embarrassed by the memory and her presence.

"I'm sorry I startled you. We wondered if you had come back yet." She turned her neck as though he had been undressed. "I saw the car outside," she went on, "and knocked. I couldn't seem to make you hear."

Ian's head throbbed as he bent to put on his shoes.

"I was dreaming," he said, as if that explained something. He felt disoriented.

"Of me?" She looked over her shoulder, her face lit by a teasing, excited smile. Ian was shocked, though whether at her flirtatiousness or the disturbing quiver of desire which it produced, he was not sure.

"No," he said brusquely, and stood up, tucking his shirt more securely into his jeans. "At least, I don't think so. You woke me before I had time to find out." He made himself face her. She was pouting with almost melodramatic disappointment. She was not a good actress and the role she had elected to play did not become her. Apart from anything else, Ian thought, as he watched her lean, young body move out of his bedroom, she didn't need to be coquettish.

"That wasn't very gallant of you," she said, running her hand along the back of the sofa. "But I suppose I can't blame you since I interrupted you."

Ian ignored this and, keeping well clear of her deliberately posed body, went into the kitchen. The drink had been a mistake. He needed some coffee.

"If you have the dream again, if you finish it, undisturbed," she said, following him, "will you tell me, whether it's me or not in your dream?" She smiled, one hip thrust out, breasts cleanly outlined. He stared at her small, bold nipples.

172

"Linda?" The call came from the open door.

Her whole attitude changed at once. She stood upright, shoulders slumped a little as though in apology for her breasts. Over her shoulder, Ian saw the thunderous frown on Carl's handsome face, and Peter's wide-eyed interest in the tension which had suddenly become electric between the three adults.

"Since you were so long," Carl said gruffly, "I brought Peter over."

"Hello," said Ian, looking at Peter, who grinned at him.

Linda walked toward Carl, who had already turned away.

"Thank you," Ian called. He didn't blame the boy. On the contrary, he felt sorry for him since he realized the game, the very obvious game Linda was playing. She wanted to make Carl jealous. Being young, with only one available man to admire her considerable charms, she wasn't afraid to play with fire, to use Ian to hurt Carl. But it hadn't been like that the first time, he thought. Or had it? He couldn't remember. It was as though he was a different person then. He had simply reacted to the girl, whether she had led him on or not. He became uncomfortably aware of Peter's grinning face and turned quickly back into the kitchen.

The next morning they drove into town to shop, mostly for food, although on impulse Ian bought a new bathing suit.

"Does that mean we can go swimming again?" Peter asked eagerly. The thought made Ian's stomach contract. Probably, he would never be able to swim in that lake.

"Not yet," he said, paying for the suit.

"What do you want those for then?"

"There are other sorts of bathing."

"Like what?"

173

"Ever heard of *sun*bathing," Ian said, ushering him out of the shop. For that was what he wanted to do, to soak up the sun, relax.

Peter chattered on, apparently without a care in the world, even through an enormous fish-and-chips lunch. By the time they started back to Halford, the sun had disappeared behind menacing gray clouds.

"So much for my sunbathing," Ian grumbled.

"Never mind, you can have a rainbath instead." Peter laughed hugely at his own joke.

At the last minute, unable to think of anything more original, Ian had bought a large bunch of red roses for Regina and, after they had unpacked the car and stowed the food away, he and Peter strolled over to Home Farm. The clouds were massing so thickly that beneath the trees it was already dusk. The gray light made the untidy yard seem more forlorn than ever. The hens were pecking among the weeds. One was taking a busy, flurried dustbath. Ian pointed this out to Peter to add it to his repertoire of "funny" baths.

"It looks as though they've gone out somewhere," Ian remarked.

"No." Peter shook his head.

"The car's gone," Ian argued. He went up the short brick path to the house and knocked, but there was no reply.

"I know where they are," Peter said. "Come on."

Ian saw him, walking determinedly toward the big door of the barn.

"What are you doing?" he asked, wondering if he should leave the flowers on the doorstep.

"Come on," Peter repeated.

Ian walked toward him. He could leave the roses with one of the youngsters. Then he thought of Linda and that he must make it absolutely clear that they were for Regina. He didn't want Carl getting the wrong idea.

Inside the barn it felt warm and smelled sweetly of cow dung, hay, and straw. In an improvised pen, a few

174

cows were munching contentedly. Peter ran ahead, soundlessly, into the gloom. A rough flight of wooden steps, something more than a ladder but less than a staircase, rose up to a square hole in the roof. A loft, Ian realized, remembering the upper doors he had seen outside. Peter climbed the steps, pulling himself up easily.

"It's only me," Ian heard him say. "And my dad. It's all right, isn't it? It's all right if he comes up?"

There was no reply.

Peter went on, disappearing into the loft. His feet rustled in the hay.

"Peter?" Ian called.

"It's all right, they don't mind. Come on."

He went up, climbing awkwardly because of the roses. His head and shoulders appeared through the square opening into the loft. It was darker up there, with the loading-bay doors closed, dark and dry-smelling. He saw the bales of straw, neatly stacked, the pile of hay smelling of summer and forgotten times. It was just the sort of place children would choose to make a den, he thought. Hay slides, pretend houses in the bales—a perfect place to play.

But they weren't playing. They were sitting absolutely still, not close together but disposed in a rough semicircle around the opening. And they were all staring at Ian, blankly, but with piercing concentration.

Off to Ian's left was Carl, his hands gripping his knees. Apart from him and a little below, Linda, her legs folded yogalike under her. Higher up, his head almost touching the roof, perched at the highest level of the bales, was Reggie. And almost directly below him, Grizzle, her lumpish body slumped forward, her hands dangling.

Ian tried to smile. He wanted to apologize, excuse himself, get out of there. He felt that he was intruding on something more than a private place.

"Dad, it's all right."

Peter took his free hand and drew him away from the opening in the loft floor. He led his father back behind it. Only with a considerable effort could Ian tear his eyes away from them. He stumbled a little, walking crab-fashion, until a bale of straw struck his legs. He sat down and only then realized that he was facing them and their implacable stares.

"It's all right," Peter whispered again. His hand rested for a moment on his father's shoulder. "They don't mind."

Ian twisted toward him. Peter's face was in shadow and he could not read the boy's expression. Already he was moving away. Ian heard his rustling disappearance and felt a strong, ridiculous desire to call him. He did not want to be left alone. It seemed as though Ian was the child, Peter the father. He wanted him to stay close.

It's all right

Nobody had spoken and yet he felt that it *was* all right. He felt calm, faced them again. He sat there for what must have been minutes, growing used to their uncompromising, unfaltering stares. During those long moments, absolutely nothing happened, and gradually, he began to feel embarrassed again. He felt like a man with his fly open. The situation was ludicrous and he felt a spasm of anger at Peter for having led him into it. He was a grown man sitting in a hayloft with a group of young people who wanted to be alone, whose privacy he had rudely and unnecessarily invaded.

Because he felt that he could count on her sympathy, he looked at Linda. His face felt frozen, but he was determined to smile, to say something, about the roses perhaps. He managed to clear his throat. He saw again how pretty Linda was. Her normally braided hair was hanging loose, a bright river of pale gold, falling softly about her face.

And then she was naked. He could see her small, pointed breasts. The nipples were hard. One breast wobbled, like something rubbery, under the brush of her hand. His entranced gaze followed the passage of her hand as it moved down her body, the sharp bars of her ribs showing beneath the skin below the newly developed breasts. He felt a wounding surge of desire for her, shameful, but intense. Her hand caressing, sharp little nails dragging at the skin of her thigh, resting there, waiting, beside the downy triangle of her pubic hair, darker than the hair on her head. She was lying down, her throat tilted back, its veins and sinews showing in tense relief. Ian had no memory of her moving. She was suddenly, simply there, naked, lying in an unmistakable posture of invitation. Her mouth opened. Her thighs opened. Her whole naked, glowing body opened, invited.

Ian felt sweat, sharp and bitter, on his aroused but horrified flesh.

Carl's face, its angular, Slavic bones, was etched against the gloom of the loft. His dark eyes burned, glowing with an unnatural light. His beautiful, narrow eyes bored into Ian.

I'll kill you Kill you You can depend on it

The words echoed with the exact pulse and rhythm of Ian's unsteady heart.

He stared back at Carl, and Linda was sitting where she had always been sitting, her hair loose, her legs folded yoga-fashion underneath her. And, of course, she was fully clothed. He felt the blood burning in his face. A dirty old man's fantasy made real, made flesh. He heard a whisper of laughter, a child's laughter. Peter's? He glanced around, into the shadows, looking for him. Or Reggie's? He lifted his face to look at Reggie, perched above him, grinning down. He wanted to protest, defend himself. But it was only his imagination. They could not have seen. *He* had not seen, only dreamed.

Reggie.

Something black and insidious, like a visible stench, seemed to rise from the square hole in the floor. One moment it was a harmless rectangle of deeper shadow on the floor, and the next it seemed to throb and move with a terrible, palpable blackness. Ian's left foot was close to its edge and he tried to snatch it back to some crazy idea of safety. His legs scarcely moved. Something stronger than paralysis seemed to grip him. It took all his strength, more than strength, his entire will, to move his foot an inch or so, and all the time he sensed the hole as a living entity, a darkness which drew him toward it. He found himself leaning forward, straining to see more and better of that infinite, calling blackness.

Then there was a flash of movement and light. The spell, or whatever it was, of the hole in the floor was broken by something streaking through the air. Ian threw up his hands to protect himself. A pitchfork thudded into the floor, its tines quivering with the force of impact, one on either side of his left ankle. The shock of this sudden, dangerous movement seemed to release them all. A sound like a collective sigh brushed past his ears. His eyes crept along the trembling shaft of the pitchfork, which he could have sworn glowed with a sort of silvery light, a force of energy, to meet Grizzle's baleful gaze. The girl was standing and the angle of the pitchfork was such that its rounded end pointed directly at the spot between her eyes. Ian looked into them. They were the sullen eyes of an overweight, plain, teen-age girl. Their expression was both withdrawn and angry.

"What's going on up here? What are you doing?"

Regina's head and shoulders appeared from below, framed in the now harmless hole in the floor. Everybody looked at her in surprise.

"Ian!" she said.

He tried to say something but, like a child caught in a

guilty act, he could not speak. He felt relieved, but beneath that, as common sense returned, he knew that Regina had cause to be angry.

The young people moved toward her, to the steps. As he passed by Ian, Carl easily twisted the pitchfork free of the floor.

"It's all right, Mother," he said, his voice quiet and consoling.

"It most certainly is not." Her head disappeared from sight. "I want to see you all in the kitchen, at once," she shouted, her voice trembling with anger.

Ian got up and was the last to shuffle shamefaced across the loft and down the steps. Regina stood at the barn door, watching the children file past her, one by one.

"In the kitchen, immediately," she repeated.

Ian came up to her. He was still clutching the roses, so tightly that their sharp thorns pricked his skin. To his relief, her eyes lost some of their fury when she looked at him.

"I'll explain this later," she said curtly. "Right now, I must deal with them."

Ian nodded. It was still impossible to speak or to give her the roses.

"You're all right?" she asked, a little frown of concern creasing her forehead.

"Yes." He looked at the chastened file of kids slowly crossing the yard. "Peter," he called, stepping past Regina.

"I think I'd better deal with him, too," she said, catching Ian up.

"But . . ."

"He took you there?"

"Yes."

Peter seemed not to have heard him or, if he had, to be deliberately ignoring his call.

"Please." Regina's voice took on a note of urgency.

179

"I think you trust me. Just give me a little while. I'll come to the cottage." She walked past him and hurried after the children. Then she stopped, looked anxiously back at him.

"Please."

Ian thought that his legs were going to give way. The house seemed to swallow the children. He did not want to leave Peter there and yet he was afraid to call him back. He turned toward the gate, stumbling a little, not noticing that he had dropped the roses in the dust.

The obvious explanation—that Ian had experienced, been part of or the victim of some kind of psychic phenomena produced by the children—was one he could not accept. He knew little about such things, but had always approached them with what he regarded as a healthy skepticism. Like most other people, his knowledge was confined to odd pieces in the press. He had watched Uri Geller bending spoons at a touch for the gloating TV cameras, and had found the apparent clash between a kind of science and show business slightly unpleasant. He had read some of Matthew Manning's book, which Pam had borrowed from the public library, and had been convinced that there was some other explanation, possibly neurotic. Although he was not prepared to dismiss entirely the possibility that the human brain possesses powers that the majority of mankind does not use, is unaware of, he found the automatic copying of a Dürer-style drawing or the twisting of metal curiously pointless and therefore uninteresting exercises. Such powers, if they existed at all, seemed to him unproductive and best left alone.

But nothing he had experienced in the loft compared with anything he had read or seen, with the possible exception of the hurled pitchfork—and that was just plain, bloody dangerous. He was angry and his anger carried him further from the simplest explanation. He had not been looking at Grizzle. She could, easily, have thrown the thing physically, which made her some kind of psychopathic monster. But he had seen the pitchfork glowing, quivering with a sort of inner energy, as though its very molecules had become unstable.

Nonsense, he told himself. His hand shook, clinking the whisky bottle against the side of the tumbler as, with difficulty, he poured himself a strong scotch. By then his mind had been so frazzled, he could have imagined the glowing, the sense of an inexplicable or not inexplicable force.

The whisky warmed but did not calm him. His sweating and twitching were caused by anger, he argued, not fear. If he examined the whole thing calmly, rationally . . . He sat down, gripping his glass and made himself rethink it, remember exactly.

It had begun with Linda. Okay, he fancied Linda. He wasn't particularly proud of the fact and he certainly didn't intend to do anything about it, but he had wanted her, badly, on three other, absolutely normal occasions. He believed in a sort of chemical attraction between two people. He had felt it for Pam at first, later for Liz. The girl just had more of it than most, so he had mentally undressed her. Not the first time a pretty girl had occupied his fantasies, but never as vividly before. He remembered the sniggering, dirty laughter that had followed his voyeuristic enjoyment of Linda's body.

If he had not imagined it then somebody—Linda herself?—had imagined it for him, which meant that somebody?—Carl?—could get inside his head, see inside his head.

I'll kill you Kill you You can depend on it

Could a voice get inside his head, a voice speaking without speech? Inside?

He took another deep swig of his drink and grimaced as it burned his throat.

Anyone could see that Linda was putting him on. Carl had seen it yesterday. No doubt Ian's own face had betrayed his reactions as clearly as Carl's had. There was no mystery there, or none to speak of. Even Peter has sensed it.

Peter.

Where the hell did he fit in? The broken glass, here in this room. The shattered picture, the sight of which had frightened him. He had looked that evening, before Carl and Linda arrived, like a guilty child, caught in some mischief. No, something more than mischief. Something . . . he pushed the word *sinister* out of his mind.

His vagueness about the fishing rod. How and why had that boat capsized? The certainty about the gate beneath the water.

His anger rose again. He could not sit still. He walked to the door. It was almost dark in the room. Unnoticed by him, it had begun to rain. He saw it pitting the black surface of the lake. That black hole, insidious, drawing him in.

He could hear the rain beating on the veranda roof. It had grown cooler. That was why he was trembling. He slammed the door shut, put down his glass, and went into the bedroom to find a sweater.

Pam's mirror. The overturned bottle.

He would not be spooked. He would not allow himself to be spooked. Above all, he would not spook himself.

His teeth chattered. He all but tore the sweater, putting it on in anger. He went to the window and shut it. A few drops of rain had blown in, lying among Pam's cosmetic clutter like tears or drops from the drowned hands of a . . .

"No," he said aloud. "Get a bloody grip on yourself."

Back in the main room, he put on all the lights, found

182

his glass, and drank again. It was some game. Some ridiculous, unpleasant game.

With a different kind of coldness he knew that Pam had been right to be frightened. Her letter suddenly made another sort of sense. Selfishly, he had concentrated on the parts which concerned him. But if she had discovered something about the kids, those damned kids—they were the ones who were trying to take Peter away from her.

He tried to recall Peter's explanation, that morning on the bank, but all he could remember was that it seemed now too pat, too easy. He had *wanted* to be reassured because Pam's hysterical talk of danger had been so depressingly in character.

Christ! If he had abandoned her to something inexplicable . . . If he had, he realized, then he, too, had walked right into the same trap.

Peter. If they wanted Peter. He had to get Peter. Now, at once. He should never have left him there. But if Peter had broken that glass, shattered the picture, then Peter was one of them. It was not the kids who were taking him away but something nameless, something other. Some force or power that . . .

The room seemed to tilt and whirl. He shut his eyes. Listen to the rain, the drumming of the rain.

He had done the very thing he had vowed not to do. He had spooked himself, allowed imagination to fit bits and fragments together to make a fiction, a fantasy, a madness.

He was in shock. There had been no time to absorb the reality of Pam's death. His nerves were shot to pieces. He had read that at such times the mind was easily influenced. He needed a drink, another drink. He was also tired. Prolonged tiredness, lack of sleep— he had not slept well for two nights—made the mind suggestible, lowered resistance. His hand shook so much that he spilled some whisky on the table. A sane man, a man in control of his nerves, would go into the kitchen, find a cloth, and mop up what he had spilled. Ian made himself do that and the actions calmed him a little.

The black hole was just a hole in the floor. If you stared at anything long enough, especially when you were tired, it could change shape, become liquid, become menacing. He remembered—and at this his mind clutched gladly—when he was a boy, sitting up in bed and staring at the wall because somebody, some boy at school, had said that if you did you were bound to see a ghost.

Peter, sitting up in bed, rigid. Had he seen a ghost?

Ian had not. And it was a bloody shame to rinse a decent shot of whisky down the drain. As he wrung out the cloth, something peculiar happened to the window over the sink. It seemed to glow. The spattered raindrops caught fire. He backed off, collided with the table, and then, as sweat broke out all over him and he heard his own panicked breathing, the phenomenon resolved itself into a pair of headlights emerging from the dark drive, hitting the window. They swung away and, in the wet and early dusk, he recognized Regina's car drawing to a stop outside. He slumped against the sink, trembling. He stood there a very long time, watching the water run from the tap until the sound of it became a cataract of noise in his head and he reached to switch it off.

In the sudden, rain-pattering silence, he heard her confident step on the veranda.

"Should you be drinking quite so heavily?" Regina asked. Droplets of rain clung to her untidy mass of hair. She looked tired. There were lines on her face that Ian had not noticed before. He had offered her a drink but she had refused, watching him critically as he slopped neat whisky into his glass and drained a third of it off in one gulp. She walked restlessly to the window, stood with her hands on her hips, looking out at the rain. "I always seem to bring bad weather when I come here," she said.

Ian recalled her previous visit. Then it had been Pam who had drunk too much, and now he wasn't sure that he blamed her. He could not resist saying, "Why not have a word with your precious foster children? Surely it can't be beyond them to change the weather."

Her body stiffened as though he had spat at her. She seemed to hang, undecided, between anger and something he could not name. He heard her sigh. She twisted her hands together in front of her.

"I hoped you wouldn't take that attitude," she said quietly, still looking out of the window. Then she made herself turn around. "Look, I'm sorry. What happened shouldn't have happened. For many more reasons than you begin to know. However, since it has . . ."

"What are you running up there, Regina? Some kind of freak factory?" He saw but did not heed the wince of pain which crossed her face. "And what's more to the point, where is my son?"

"Eating his supper with the others," she replied, keeping her voice level.

"Well I want him back here, away from those . . ." He searched wildly for a word strong enough to express his fear and anger, but Regina interrupted him.

"What, monsters, psychopaths, loonies? Crazy, dangerous people? Come on, take your pick. Those are the most common terms, the ones most 'normal' people use." Her voice rose and broke with anger. Her chest heaved. She looked at Ian with a mixture of loathing and bitterness. He could not bear the look. He sat down, his face turned away from her.

"I just don't want him mixed up in . . ." He did not know how to describe it. He did not know what it *was*.

"What?" she demanded.

185

"For God's sake, Regina, I don't know."

"But whatever it is, you don't want any part of it. I know, I've been through this enough times to know. And I admit that I was a bloody fool to think that you might be different." She clapped her hands together suddenly and began to pace up and down. "I really thought you had enough sensitivity to understand. I thought you might want to try to understand, but you don't. You're just like everyone else. You react out of ignorance and there's no reaching you." She stopped suddenly. "Very well, I'll fetch Peter. We'll leave it at that." She walked toward the door but did not open it.

"Regina, please, I'm sorry."

She shook her head.

"There's no need. I can't walk out anyway. I wish to God I could, but—"

"Why can't you?" he asked, watching her.

"Because of Peter. Look, can I have that drink after all?" She turned toward him, trying to smile.

"Of course."

"It's okay, I'll help myself."

He waited while she poured herself a drink. He was afraid to ask her what she meant. Besides, he felt that to show too much curiosity was somehow to give her an advantage.

"I shouldn't get angry. I ought to know better by now." She sat down wearily and sipped her drink.

"Are you going to tell me about it or . . .?" He deliberately kept his voice low, neutral.

"Of course, that's why I came here. I was going to anyway. I don't have any choice."

"But you wish you had?"

"That depends on you. Anyway, facts are facts."

"I don't understand."

"Well, to put it bluntly, in terms you can understand, Peter is one of my 'freaks,' one of the 'monsters,' or however you want to put it." Her voice was heavy with bitterness.

"I don't believe you," he said automatically, stubbornly.

"No? Then I really have misjudged you. But you don't have to take my word for it. It can easily be verified, if you dare."

"All right. What exactly are you talking about?" He moved around on the sofa so that he could see her face. She looked him straight in the eyes.

"What are commonly called paranormal abilities, psychic powers, if you like. The terms are vague, imprecise. People like you find it easy to scoff at them, and I don't really mind that. I only ask you to think what such an attitude does to a child who, through no fault of his own, happens to possess powers which, probably, everybody has latent within them."

"Just a minute," Ian interrupted. There was no mistaking that she had said this many times before, but repetition had not dulled her conviction or her passion. "You're going too fast for me."

"Lay off the scotch," she advised. "I suspect you're going to need a clear head to take most of this in."

"Okay. What is it, precisely, you maintain Peter can do?"

"You really need me to answer that? You've noticed nothing?"

Instinctively Ian wanted to deny it, but her cool, challenging stare made it impossible. He stared at the glass in his hands.

"Glass," he whispered. "I've noticed that he . . . I think he might have . . ." He looked at her, an appeal for help.

"He broke that glass the night I was sitting on that sofa. He did it again the other day. All the kids witnessed it. And only this afternoon I found him trying it again."

Ian swallowed, raised his glass to his lips, and then changed his mind. He set the glass down on the floor.

"That's not quite all," he said quietly. "A picture he

187

had, hanging in his bedroom. The glass was completely shattered, as though some incredible force had been applied to it."

"And you thought there was some other explanation," she mocked him. "You just let it go."

"What else could I do? I felt guilty, if you must know, for even thinking that he might be capable of . . ."

"I'm sorry," she said at once. "I'm so used to this sort of thing myself that I expect too much of people."

"But how did you know?" he asked.

She laughed, a scornful, humorless sound.

"What's the phrase? It takes one to know one?"

Ian stared at her. She was an ordinary, rather handsome, even attractive middle-aged woman. There was nothing odd or different about her. He could not believe that she—

"Yes, me too. I'm one of the freaks. And I recognized Peter's difference the moment I saw him, just as I recognized Linda and Reggie, poor little Grizzle."

"I . . ."

"Don't believe me or don't know what to say?"

"The latter, I think," he admitted.

"Well, that's an improvement, anyway."

"Regina," he protested, "you can't expect me just to take all this in and say 'Great, wonderful.' It's beyond my comprehension."

"No it isn't," she answered fiercely, "not if you'll stop being afraid. If you'll only open your mind a little. Peter's still Peter. He's just a boy, a nice boy. Intelligent, nice-looking. In spite of the difficulties, you and Pamela have done a good job. Don't just back off from him now because he's different."

Ian thought, I've been backing off from him ever since I met him, for one reason or another. He shook his head. She made sense.

"Can you make me understand? Please?"

"I don't know," she admitted. "For one thing, I

don't know enough about Peter. He can shatter glass, we all know that. But how?" She shrugged. "He can do it over amazing distances, too, comparatively speaking. But what else? I suspect he's telepathic. In fact, I suspect he possesses powers we can't even guess at yet. I'm experienced but I'm not an expert. He resists me. I could find out more if he weren't wary of me, but that's only to be expected. It's a means of survival. Grizzle and Reggie were just the same. You have to conceal it, if you don't want to be a monster."

"Please," Ian said miserably. "I'm beginning to get the point."

"Good, it's important. Have *you* noticed anything else about Peter?"

"No." He shook his head. He was quite definite.

"What about this home he was in, before you adopted him? There were reports? Any mention of anything unusual?"

"No. They said he was withdrawn, they'd thought he was autistic when he was a toddler, but Pam always said that was just a way of protecting himself. They labeled him in many ways, like those people always do— educationally subnormal, emotionally disturbed."

"Yes," Regina agreed. "They always do. Those are invariably the official explanations. Pamela was undoubtedly right. The symptoms of autism are a good cover. I'd be prepared to bet that Peter learned very early to conceal something which adults found unacceptable. He did something and was punished, so he withdraws. It's classic. And it's become a habit. He relaxes a bit with the children because they've not been afraid to show him how they are, but with me, you, Pamela, he's still holding back. He knows I'm on to him. That's what that business with the glass was about, I think, sort of to warn me off."

"Did you ever mention this to Pamela, what you suspected?"

Regina shook her head.

189

"I thought about it, but she scarcely seemed in a fit state of mind. Anyway, I would have needed to know her better. Like you say, it's not something people can accept just like that, and Pamela was too jumpy."

"You don't think she might have noticed something, or guessed?"

"Yes, I do. And I think she was terrified of it. Like you, she associated it with danger, blamed my kids, denied it. And that's what drove Peter to the Farm, to the kids. He'd reached a point where he needed to be himself. And fortunately—though you probably wouldn't agree—he met my kids just at the right moment. He realized he wasn't a freak, wasn't alone. But how could he tell that to his mother?"

"Christ," Ian said and, despite her advice and his resolve, picked up his glass and drank. "There seems to be no end to that child's misfortunes." Or to Pam's, he thought. Elsa had said that if Pam could see her death as a form of protection . . .

"His abilities are not necessarily a misfortune, if handled properly, accepted. That's the most important thing and, in my view, it's especially important in Peter's case. This resistance I feel, the reluctance to admit, use, accept his own powers, whatever they may be, could be dangerous."

Ian looked at her, alarmed.

"Acceptance," she went on, speaking clearly and slowly, "is crucial. To deny these things, through fear or incomprehension, is like, well, like bottling up some strong emotion. You know what happens then. Eventually something has to give. It's the same with these abilities. And if they are as great as I think—believe me, I know what I'm talking about."

Ian studied his glass, his fingernails. The question which was forming in his mind would, he knew, offend her.

"What do you recommend?" he asked, stalling.

"The first step for any child in this situation is to

190

realize that those closest to him are not afraid, can accept him as he is."

"Before I can do that, I have to know—this power, or whatever it is . . ."

"Yes?"

"Well, is it for good or evil?"

He could not look at her. He had expected her to be angry, and her laughter took him completely by surprise. He looked at her in dismay. She was genuinely laughing, her head thrown back.

"Oh Ian, Ian," she said at last. "I'm sorry. It's just that surely you don't believe in good and evil, as actual entities? Any power, anything—the power of speech, for example—is of itself neutral. It is how we, we human beings, use it that makes it good or evil. And even though I laugh, it does make me angry. You see, the moment the subject comes up, even a sympathetic, intelligent man like you falls back on quasi-religious mumbo jumbo. 'I don't understand, therefore I am afraid.'"

"I'm sorry," he said after a pause. "I had to ask. After all, that glass did cut you."

"That was nothing, a little gesture. No, I'm too tough on you. But that's because. . . . look, there's only one question you should ask yourself. Is Peter an evil child? Is he? Would you call him a malevolent kid?"

Ian did not answer at once, because the honest answer was that he did not know, was not sure. But he said, "No, of course not."

"Good." She sounded relieved, as though some difficult problem had been satisfactorily resolved. "Because you see there is nothing to be afraid of." She caught his eye and smiled. "Oh, I know that's difficult to believe after this afternoon. I *am* sorry about that, so are they. I gave them a good dressing down, I promise you. It was the very worst way for you to find out. I've told them that. And I ask you, please, to believe that I was going to tell you. As soon as you were settled in and, I hoped, when I had a little more knowledge of Peter."

"Yes," Ian said. "I believe you, of course I do."

"You see, there are flaws in my method, too, in any method. They got overconfident this afternoon. They were showing off, the very thing I try to guard against. In a way I am at fault. They're too relaxed, not enough on their guard. But you must make allowances for them. They're old enough to know better, but these kids have led such strange, cutoff lives that they are emotionally very immature. And then the thrill of being able to amaze, impress somebody. But then it wasn't just that. Peter took you there. In a curious way—can you understand this?—they did it for Peter. Peter wanted to tell you, for you to see, to share. They were helping out a friend, a colleague. These kids form very close bonds. Am I making myself clear?"

"Yes," Ian said. "Yes, I think so. I can understand, but I was . . . well, frankly, I was bloody frightened."

"It won't happen again," she promised.

"I can see that it would be impossible for him just to tell me," he said, thinking aloud.

"Right. But the others shouldn't have put on a performance for you. It only served to frighten and therefore alienate you. Beside, this whole performance idea terrifies me as much as their being made to feel like lepers. My whole job is to steer a course between repression and exploitation. Both of those frighten me. I know what it's like to feel that you don't belong, that you are unacceptably different. I also know what it's like to be used, just because you can do certain things, perhaps understand something. Can you imagine what a field day the media would have with them?"

Ian could imagine, all too clearly. And he understood Regina's anger. He felt afraid again, but not for himself—for Peter.

"If what you say about Peter is true, the last thing I'd want to happen to him would be for him to be paraded, shown off. Funny, I was thinking about that before you came. I don't know. There's something rotten about it."

"I take it all back," Regina said with a broad smile. "You *are* intelligent and sensitive."

"I don't feel it right now," he confessed.

"That's my fault. I'm sorry. I could use a little more patience."

"Will you be patient with me, help me to understand?" he said. "Can I ask you questions?"

"Of course. You're part of it all now. There are no secrets."

"I'm not sure I'm ready to be part of it but, well, you referred just now to your job. I don't really understand."

"Oh, I didn't mean in any formal sense," she said quickly. "My task—self-imposed, chosen, whatever. You see I . . . I'm sorry, Ian. But it doesn't really make sense unless I tell you my life story."

"Please," he said. "I'm interested."

"Well . . ." She did not sound enthusiastic. "Could I have another drink?" She held out her glass. Ian took it and poured her another small measure. "Let's just say that because of my own childhood and adolescence, I wanted to make sure that some children at least got a better deal, a better start."

"How many children are we talking about, all told?" Ian asked.

She shrugged.

"Who knows? Thousands? More, less, maybe. Nobody knows. Obviously, I can only help a few. You see, after the war, I met a man who accepted me for what I was. I didn't really meet him. I sought him out. I'd heard about him, read some of his articles. He was the only humane man I'd ever come across who was seriously interested in the paranormal. I met and married him, Alvar Thomas." She paused. Her expression softened, admitted that there had been something good in her life. "The name doesn't mean anything to you?

"No, sorry. I'm really not up on these things."

"It doesn't matter. He was a pioneer. That's the important thing. Oh not in any startling, scientific way, but in attitudes. He made me respect myself. Do you know what I mean? He made me, literally, able to live with myself. I loved him," she said softly. "I loved him as though I could compensate for all the hating I'd done before I met him. I'm not ashamed of that. And we decided to devote our lives to helping people like me. We wanted to understand, to investigate, to discover more about psychic and paranormal phenomena. That was important. But we wanted to do it in the right way. Most parents simply can't cope with children who have such powers—abilities, we prefer to call them. Not through any fault, they just aren't equipped."

Ian felt himself blushing, but if Regina noticed she ignored it.

"So we set up a center, a residential center, where we could educate and help these children to adjust, while trying to understand scientifically, psychologically, medically, the precise nature of the abilities, like the schools for specially gifted children."

"Yes, I've read about them. For kids with very high IQs."

"Right. Who are often regarded as emotionally disturbed, hyperactive, slow learners, etcetera, etcetera. Of course, it all became much more important to me when Carl was born. We'd always known that there was a chance that he would be able. Oh sorry, that was Alvar's term for it. To be able is to have abilities. You see? Well, when he was born, I began to see our work from the parents' point of view, too. He *was* able and I wanted him to grow up safely, with others of his kind. It was a dream, but a realizable one." She looked defiant.

"What happened?" Ian prompted.

"Oh, it went very well, but when Alvar died . . . He was older than I—much—and he was ill. I simply couldn't keep it going. Financially it was impossible and I'm no fund raiser. Anyway, there was too much distrust and suspicion. The scientific side of things continued, on a much smaller scale. My husband had a colleague, Dr. Asmussen, who understood and was sympathetic. He's done some marvelous work but I had to settle for less. I don't know. Maybe I could have done more, but when you rely so much on one person, as I had on Alvar, something goes. So, I do the best I can. I've fostered children in America and Denmark, now here. I work loosely with Dr. Asmussen. I keep up with his work and he helps me with mine." Almost casually, she added, "That's what I meant when I said that you didn't have to take my word for it. Asmussen could assess Peter. He's the only man I'd trust to do it—when the time's right, of course, when Peter has accepted, adjusted. May I tell him about Peter?"

"I don't know, it's all too much. Can I think about it?"

"Of course. I'm rushing you. I'll show you some of his articles. You must stop me when I push, Ian, and remember that all this is very exciting for me. There's such a lot to do. Peter is very, very special. I *know* it." She spoke with fervor, her eyes shining.

"You must give me time," Ian said. "Tell me how you found Reggie and the others."

"Oh, I keep my eyes open. I have contacts, credentials. Asmussen's name opens a lot of doors. Specifically, Linda I found with her parents. They were distraught, almost suicidal. Reggie, like Peter, was in a children's home, disturbed, written off. And Grizzle was in a psychiatric ward. Yes," she said harshly, seeing the shock on his face, "such things still happen. She was eleven years old when she first tried to kill herself because she believed she was unwanted, alone, mad. And of course it is mad, isn't it, for a child to try to kill herself?" Ian covered his face with his hand. "Fortunately for both of us, I had tried at seven, at thirteen, at fifteen, more times than matter—an amazing failure rate. But it enabled me to understand, and now I'm glad I failed. Can you understand? That's why I will never let any harm come to those children, to any able child."

Her voice seemed to disturb the air, long after she had spoken.

"I'm very ashamed of myself," Ian said at last. "I want to apologize."

"Don't," she said. "Half my trouble was due to the Nazis. You can't apologize for them, nobody can."

"I'm sorry." He stopped. "I just don't know what to say."

"There is nothing, though perhaps you should understand that part of it, too. I don't care to talk about it, but before the Germans invaded Denmark, I was seeing a specialist, a good man—the best my terrified parents could find. He bartered his freedom and my life with my abilities. I'm probably the only Jewess who went into the camps knowing that she would not be killed. The Nazis were very interested in people like me. Abilities would help the superrace, you see. I was a guinea pig. And, ironically I suppose, being assured of survival, I tried hard not to survive. Much as I deplore the exploitation of the media, it's nothing compared to what can be done, has been done in the name of science. Believe me, I know about good and evil. I know what I'm talking about when I say it's in the use, not the possession of abilities, that good and evil reside."

Ian felt her pain and the hardness it had forged in

her, like something tangible in the room with them, a third presence.

"What are your abilities?" he asked.

"That's a question I never answer," she snapped. "It is the first step to becoming a freak or a tool. But I will say this. Whatever abilities I have, they are nothing compared to Peter's. You must remember that."

Peter, at least in the present context, was safe ground. Ian seized on it.

"And compared to the others? Linda, for example?"

"Greater." She leaned forward, her eyes shining again. "That's why you must stand by him, Ian. You must help him. I'll do everything I can, I promise that."

"But I don't know what to do," he protested. He knew that she was right, but he was afraid to commit himself.

"If you will trust me, then between us we can help him. Really, all I'm asking is that you be a good father to him. Love him, accept him. He'll do the rest, he and I and Asmussen."

Ian leaned back on the sofa. His thoughts whirled about aimlessly.

"You will trust me, you will try?"

Slowly, he opened his eyes. "Yes," he told her.

"Good. We've made a bargain. And you don't know what a weight it is off my mind." She stood up, brisk and competent again. "Peter will be perfectly all right at Home Farm." She looked at her watch. "In fact, he jolly well ought to be in bed." She stood close to Ian. "Let him stay. You get a good night's rest."

"You don't know how tempting that sounds."

"I do, I feel just the same."

"Regina?"

"I know. You don't know how to thank me. So don't. Peter's the one who matters. We matter, you and I, because he needs us. It's really very simple."

He took her hand and squeezed it.

197

"I really must go. Would you like to come for breakfast or shall I send Peter over? The police are through here now."

"Yes. Would you mind just sending him over? I'd rather like to sleep in."

"Fine, go to bed."

He followed her to the door. It had stopped raining. Water dripped sadly from the roof.

"Good-night, Ian."

"Good-night, and thank you."

. He remained at the door until the red taillights of her car vanished along the drive. He felt so tired. It smelled fresh and damp after the rain. He took deep breaths of the night air. He would leave everything until the morning. He closed the door and carried the remainder of his drink into the bedroom and began, slowly, to undress.

What had he thought, right at the beginning? That Peter was his inheritance from Pam. He had resented the idea then. Now it took on a new meaning and seemed like a challenge. With Regina's help, he would be able to meet it and the gains would not only be Peter's, but his as well.

A series of rooms, connected by double doors. He passes from one to another. The doors close behind him with a terrible booming sound. The rooms are gray, vast and rectilinear, without furniture. The booming is absorbed, eaten up by the silence. The characteristic of these identical, interconnecting rooms is silence.

Boom.

He wonders what he is doing there.

Boom.

Looking for something? Someone?

Boom.

For Peter?

He turns back, like a rational man. Whatever it is, he knows that he will not find it.

A storm had sprung up. Half waking from the dream, he heard rain gusting against the window. The wind-lashed branches tapped and scraped and rattled like old bones against the wooden walls and roof. The house seemed to be alive with sound. He turned over, onto his back, his eyes flickering open.

She stands at the foot of the bed. Black hair plastered to her white skull, white dress clinging like a shroud to her body, hair, limbs, dress, all running with water. She could be made of tears.

He could not make out her eyes but felt them, cold, sliding over him.

He drew up his legs. Whimpering, he cowered back against the wall.

Her mouth creaks open. She raises both arms, fingers white as bone extend toward him. There is an old, ugly smell, of stagnant, brackish water. Water runs from her fingers, drips onto the bedclothes.

The wind suddenly roared. Something crashed against the window, drawing his attention for a moment. She is gone.

The house was quiet, a brief lull in the storm, in which he thought he heard retreating, squelching, wet footsteps.

Fumbling, he turned on the lamp beside the bed. The wind rose again, rattling and shaking the house. The room was empty, yet he was pressed against the wall. He had seen her so clearly. He shook himself and reached for his robe. He pulled it on, shivering. He had to go to the bathroom. He walked around the foot of the bed.

"Oh my God."

His feet recoiled from the carpet, from the icy touch of water. He stared down, his ears buzzing. He stepped back, squatted. An area of the carpet at the foot of the bed was soaked. He touched it with his fingers, shuddering. Ice-cold water, where Pamela had stood, reaching for him.

"Oh my God," he groaned again.

He stood up and went to the doorway. The glass door leading to the veranda was open, swinging in the wind.

He looked back at the carpet. Even from this distance, even in the inadequate light of the lamp, the wet patch was clearly visible, a darker stain on the carpet, where she had stood.

PART THREE

THE INQUEST ON PAMELA MARY WOODFORD took place a week later and lasted barely half an hour. The delay was due to the time needed by the local water authority to search the archives for old maps and surveys which might show the course of the subterranean stream. Its presence was noted in old records, but the apologetic representative of the authority could not enlighten the coroner as to its depth, width, or the point at which, if any, it might surface. Embarrassed, the man agreed with the coroner that it might well be time for a new and more comprehensive survey to be made.

Peter, fortunately, did not have to give verbal evidence. Ian was relieved. He had declined Regina's offer to accompany him, and sat in the court feeling oppressively lonely. Benyon presented Peter's evidence and gave his own. He looked annoyed when the coroner asked if the entrance to the stream had been sealed. To the best of his knowledge, Benyon admitted, it had not. This, however, was not a matter for the police but for the owner of the lake.

"Then advise him of his responsibilities," the coroner snapped.

203

"The gentleman appears to be out of the country, sir."

"But presumably someone's in charge of the estate?"

"Yes, sir. I believe so, sir." Benyon had a hunted look.

"Very well then, inform them."

Ian's turn came at last and it was quickly clear that the coroner thought his presence unnecessary since he had been miles away at the time of the accident. As a matter of routine, or perhaps in an attempt to justify his presence before the court at all, the coroner asked the inevitable questions about Pamela's health and state of mind. Ian lied without compunction. He saw no point in parading Pamela's difficulties now, and deep down he was afraid that any such questions might touch on Peter, on things which he desperately wanted to keep secret.

"So there were no problems?" the coroner inquired.

"None."

No problems. He felt like laughing cynically. None that need concern the court, anyway. None that he could possibly make them understand. None, presumably, to bother her now.

He stepped down and listened as an open verdict was returned. It was explained to him that the regrettable absence of a body meant that, officially, the case must remain open. This was, however, only a formality and should not prevent him making any suitable arrangements he might wish. Ian did not understand, but he kept his mouth shut. The sympathy of the court was expressed in formal, detached terms, and it was all over.

Pamela was dead, officially.

He walked quickly out of the court with a sense of anticlimax. He kept his head down, wanting to avoid Benyon, who was the only person likely to speak to him. He would have walked right past Liz had she not plucked at his sleeve and spoken his name. He stared at her as though he had completely forgotten her, which, in a way, he thought feeling guilty, he had. He wished instinctively that she had not come. If Liz read any of this in his face, she did not let it faze her.

"Buy you a drink?" she said, smiling.

People milled past them, one or two giving them a second glance of curiosity. Liz tucked her arm through Ian's.

"Are they open?"

He pulled away from her to look at his watch. "Yes, come on."

She led him down the corridor, across an echoing, tiled lobby, and out into the hazy sunshine.

"I noticed a pub just up the road, unless you know a better one?"

"No." Ian shook his head. He had never been to the town before.

"Let's try that then." She set off briskly, pulling him with her. He felt numb, though whether because of Liz's unexpected appearance or as a hangover from the inquest, he was uncertain. They walked to the pub in silence. It was virtually deserted and Liz steered him to a corner as though he was a patient, newly released from the hospital. He sat and watched her at the bar. Everything about her seemed to shine with health. She looked wholesome. Ian winced at the word. The particular shade of dusky pink she wore suited her. He searched in himself for some spark of emotion. He should be at least touched by her kindness, glad to see her. Watching her walk slowly back to the table, balancing drinks, he had to remind himself that, only a few weeks ago, he had been in love with her.

"A large scotch for you," she said brightly, setting a glass in front of him, "purely medicinal." She sat, her clothes rustling. She looked good, beautiful even. "Cheers," she said. He tried to smile, nodded, and took a sip of his drink.

"How did you find out about the inquest?" he asked,

more because he felt he had to make conversation than because he wanted to know.

"It's easy," she answered, laughing a little, "when one's father is a Queen's counsel."

"Oh yes, of course." He had forgotten. Her father was, at best, a shadowy figure, someone she mentioned from time to time, with noticeable affection. "It was good of you to come," he said.

"I thought you might need a bit of moral support."

"Thanks."

"Well . . ." She looked around the bar, appraising it, then back at Ian, expectantly.

He realized that he had never told her. That in itself did not seem so bad, but the ease with which he had been able to put her out of his mind made him feel like a heel.

"How did you know?" he said, fiddling with his glass. "I should have phoned you."

"It would have been nice," she said. "I rang the yard. Your secretary was full of it."

"Sorry."

"It's okay. I expect you've been busy. There must have been masses to do. It must have been a hell of a shock. I am sorry, you know. Truly." These were things he guessed she had told herself, excuses she made for him so that she could steel herself to come.

"Thanks."

"I mean it, Ian. I never knew her but, well, it's a terrible thing to happen, to anyone. And then not finding the body. How on earth did you cope?"

He shrugged.

"Somehow. I've decided to stay on here for a while," he said quickly. Any mention of the missing body made his scalp tingle unpleasantly. "It seemed silly to uproot Peter." Speaking the boy's name made him instantly cautious. He picked up his drink again, not knowing how to go on.

"How is he?" she asked gently. "It must have been terrible for him."

"You were in court, you heard . . .?"

"Yes." She nodded quickly. "I slipped out after the verdict. How is he?"

"Okay, better than I'd expected. Kids are very resilient, surprisingly so."

She smiled at this. He who knew nothing about children, who had talked so often about his incompetence with them, now tried to sound confident, knowledgeable.

"You didn't think it might be a good idea to bring him back to London, away from what happened?"

"Of course I did," he said, irritated, "but Regina thought—" Too late, he realized what conclusions Liz was certain to draw from this casual introduction of Regina's name. Her face set a little. He said, "It's nothing like that."

"Like what?" Her composed look of polite, innocent interest was entirely unconvincing.

"Regina Thomas lives on the farm next to the cottage Pam rented. Peter's very friendly with her children. Well, they're not really hers, only one of them. The others are fostered. Anyway, she's been a great help, that's all."

"That must be very nice for you."

"It's bloody essential," Ian snapped. He could feel himself sinking in deeper and deeper and his only defense was anger.

"All right," Liz said shakily. "You don't have to justify yourself."

"I'm not, it's just that I can read you like a book."

"And evidently you don't like the story. I'm sorry, I shouldn't have come." Angrily she drained her glass, waited a moment, then reached for her bag.

"Wait a minute," Ian said. "I'm sorry. Look, let's try again. Have another drink." He started to get up but Liz shook her head.

"No, thanks, it was stupid of me just to turn up. But I didn't know. And you're a fine one to talk about reading me like a book. Look at you. Apologizing, justifying yourself because you know damn well you feel guilty. I might have known you couldn't survive without a woman to run your life for you," she said bitterly.

"Now hang on," Ian said. "Okay, I do feel guilty, but only because I didn't make time to call or write you. I should have and I don't really have an excuse. Even if I did, ten to one you wouldn't believe it. It was the suddenness of it all, being solely responsible for Peter. You know what I'm like with him, Liz. Regina just happened to be there. She knows about kids. She's spent her life with them. So, I took her advice, but that's all."

"What about me? You could have asked me."

"You know less about kids than I do."

"Thanks a lot."

They glared at each other over the table. Liz was still clutching her bag. Ian said, "I'm sorry, I shouldn't have said that. Please have another drink."

She stared at her bag, fiddling with the clasp.

"Oh, all right, why not?" She looked sad and vulnerable when she smiled.

At the bar, he felt tired. He did not want to fight. He didn't have the energy. It was just that Liz seemed like an intruder. That was unfair of him, he knew. He hadn't realized until he saw her how radically his life had changed and how little room there was in it now for anyone but Peter. She could not know this and certainly not why. He paid for her drink and carried it back to the table.

"I didn't mean to bitch," she said at once. "I wouldn't have if you hadn't started apologizing before I'd said anything."

"And I wouldn't have apologized if I hadn't known what you were thinking."

"Which leaves us where?"

"I don't know. Perhaps we know each other too well."

"Or not well enough," she said, with a hint of bitterness. "You only think of me as a mistress. That's half the trouble. And a mistress to you isn't really a woman at all, except in the obvious way."

"Drink up," he urged, because he knew that to answer her would be to start another fight.

"You have to get back?" she said, touching her glass but not drinking.

"I shouldn't be too long," he admitted. "They'll want to know the verdict."

"They?"

"Peter, Regina and the children."

"Then I mustn't keep you. Don't mind me, I've got the car. You go ahead."

"Liz," he said despairingly.

"No. It's perfectly all right. I *did* think twice about coming, and as usual, I made the wrong decision."

She sounded close to tears and he knew that he had to tell her, that he owed her more than half truths, an explanation that sounded so pat and casual it was bound to make her feel rejected.

"Listen," he said, "let me try to explain."

"There's no need, Ian. Don't you see?"

"I think there is," he said firmly. "Besides, I want to."

She said nothing, but she looked calmer.

"I don't know how to put this—it all sounds so incredible. And you must promise me that you'll keep it entirely to yourself. I don't want anyone else to know." He waited, but Liz still said nothing. "Will you promise?"

"Who would I tell?"

"Anybody."

"But I can't promise if I . . . oh, all right. Cut my throat and hope to die."

Ian took a deep breath.

"It's Peter. He's not like other children. He's got abilities, powers." He could feel her amused scorn without looking at her and it made him flounder. He wished Regina was there to explain. For a moment he wondered if he dared take Liz back with him, introduce them, but he knew at once that it wouldn't work. Regina would be suspicious and aloof, all her protective instincts aroused. She had impressed upon him the need to be circumspect with everyone, at all times. "Regina knows a lot about this sort of thing. She could make you understand. She's psychic herself. At least, I think that's what you call it. She's spent her life working with able children. She was married to a man called Alvar Thomas, who was an expert in the field and she—"

Liz's laughter began as a chuckle, but it grew rapidly. The barman glanced over at their table. Ian felt himself becoming embarrassed. Her laughter had a hollow, derisory quality.

"It's not funny," he hissed, "and for God's sake stop making a spectacle of yourself."

"You surely don't expect me to . . ." Liz stuttered through her laughter, but looking at him she saw that he was not joking, that he believed. "Ian?" she said, and now she sounded alarmed.

"It's absolutely true, Liz. That's why—one reason why—I've got to stay down here for a bit. I've got a paranormal genius on my hands, and I need Regina's help."

"Oh come on," she said. "I mean, I was prepared for you to get a fit of the heavy father, exaggerated paternal responsibility and all that, but this is . . ."

"Ridiculous, yes. I thought so, too. I thought I was going off my head. But it's true, I swear to you."

She examined his face carefully.

"You scare me," she said. "This just isn't like you, Ian. You can't believe in . . ."

"I believe what I see."

Liz sat back in her chair.

"This woman put the idea in your head, this Regina Thomas."

"She explained, confirmed what I'd already begun to see for myself," he argued.

"What had you seen, and why now? Why didn't Pam see it?"

"I don't know, I can't explain."

"Ian," she said, elaborately reasonable, "you know as well as I do that a disturbed child, especially at puberty, can get up to all sorts of extraordinary things. But there's always a rational explanation. Ninety percent of these cases—or so I've read—are directly attributable to disturbed children, acting unconsciously."

"I know all that, but it doesn't apply," Ian said.

"Peter's not disturbed? You're trying to tell me that seeing his mother drown, after all that's gone before . . ."

"He's disturbed, yes. But there's no poltergeist. The boy is *gifted*. But he can't accept it. He's obviously been concealing it for years and now we must get him to accept who and what he is. We must."

"The royal 'we' I assume?"

"You know perfectly well what I mean."

"I know you've allowed yourself to be conned rotten by some maniacal woman. Christ, Ian, you're so weak! But I never thought you'd let someone use Peter to get at you."

"Nobody's using Peter, nobody's getting at me. We're trying to help him!"

"Okay, tell me this. Isn't it a hell of a coincidence that this Thomas woman should be around just when Peter starts acting up?"

"Yes, it is. But coincidences do happen, and I for one am very grateful for them."

"Like hell they do. And what do you get out of it?

What are you grateful for? Black Masses, orgies?"

Ian felt his arm twitch. He was within an inch of hitting her. He forced his hands down, clasped them together beneath the table.

"I shouldn't have told you," he said. "I only wanted you to understand."

"Well, you needn't worry that I'll spread *this* around. I don't want everyone to know that you've gone mad."

Ian turned away from her, trying to get his temper under control.

"Ian, I'm really worried," she said, lowering her voice. "I don't think you are coping with all this. Listen, I know you don't want my advice, but . . ."

"Well?"

"You owe it to Peter to get him set up at a good boarding school. You know it's what he needs. And you should come back to London and—"

"And marry you," he sneered, not caring how much he hurt her. "No thanks."

Liz stared at him. He had expected pain, anger, tears, but she seemed only worried. She stood up.

"Thanks for the drink, Ian."

He opened his mouth to say her name, but then admitted that it was useless. She strode across the room and let herself out of the bar. The door slammed behind her. It was only a reflex action that made him want to go after her. It could only make matters worse. He had nothing, nothing at all to offer her. He stared miserably at her untouched glass.

Liz almost ran to her car, half-blinded by tears. But she did not allow herself to cry. There would be time for that later. Now, she had to keep her head, keep cool. She found an old theater program in the glove compartment and a pen in her bag. Using a road atlas to rest on, she quickly wrote down the two names he had mentioned: Regina Thomas, Alvar Thomas. Then she put the program back in the glove compartment, fastened her seat belt, and backed out of the parking space. Whatever this woman was up to, whatever she had done to Ian's mind, Liz was not going to let her get away with it—not without a fight, anyway.

It was Peter, not Liz, who dominated Ian's thoughts as he drove back to Halford Hall. Since the night of his long talk with Regina, his conscious mind at least had been concerned with little else. His world had become centered, much more rapidly than he could have foreseen, on the boy. Had he really needed Liz to show him that? He shrugged the question, Liz herself, aside. There had been, in Regina's phrase, progress and no progress. Twice she had reported finding Peter in a sort of trance, his body rigid, eyes open, his breathing shallow—much, in fact, as Ian had glimpsed him the night the picture had shattered. On both occasions, the fit or coma had ended with the breaking of glass. Peter, however, claimed to have no memory of these happenings. Regina believed that it was in these states that Peter's abilities were manifest, but that the protective habit of years blotted all recollection of them from his conscious mind. She had asked Ian to watch for a repetition of these states, but, as far as he had been able to tell, they did not occur when Peter slept at the cottage. Puzzled, Regina had set up a sort of experiment. The next time Peter stayed over at the Farm, Ian had joined her there, late at night. Together, they had made frequent checks on the boy, but he had slept normally. Regina's conclusion was simple and, Ian could not help feel, damning. He was the inhibiting factor, the block or barrier that kept Peter from fully realizing his abilities. He had, of course, tried to talk to the boy, to reassure him, but somehow Peter managed to slide out of the conversation and Ian was afraid to lean too hard on him. To force him, Regina agreed, might be as dangerous as this apparently voluntary denial. Meanwhile, though she said little, Ian knew that Regina was becoming more and more anxious.

The idea that he inhibited Peter was one to which Ian had no answer or argument. Intellectually, he was prepared to accept the boy, whatever his abilities. Intellectually, he wanted to know what was happening and how to deal with it. But in his heart, he knew that he was still a very long way from being able to feel at ease with Peter's "difference." He was afraid of it. Similarly, his relationship with the other youngsters was guarded and strained. He felt uncertain of them and was sure that they regarded him as an outsider whom they could not trust.

But there was more, something crazy and terrifying that he had mentioned to no one. A theory had begun to form in his own mind, gradually and almost against his will. It connected Peter's abilities with Pamela. Increasingly, common sense alone made Ian feel that Pam must have noticed something. She was not an insensitive woman. In fact, where Peter was concerned, she could be called hypersensitive. It seemed impossible, therefore, that she could have died in complete ignorance. And if Peter was telepathic, or gifted in some other way that even Regina could not name, then he, too, must have known the cause of Pam's anxiety during those last weeks. Preposterous as he knew it sounded, from his theory Ian concluded that Peter's abilities were used to reach Pam, to reassure her perhaps, or to expiate some guilt. The only unpreposterous thing about this idea was that it fitted with Regina's view of the situation. If one parent, the more important, had been afraid of his powers, frightened, possibly literally to death, then Peter, who knew more than Ian could guess about being abandoned, an orphan, would not dare to risk so alarming the other, the remaining parent.

Yet when all the pieces were shuffled and fitted together Ian had to admit that the idea would never have occurred to him had it not been for Pam's appearance in the bedroom that night. He still could not think of it without appalled mental recoil, a psychological shudder. He had tried very hard to see it as a dream, unusually vivid but explicable because of shock and anxiety, the fact that her body remained missing. Yet how many dreams leave external, physical evidence behind them? No matter how much he might doubt his sanity or seek to rationalize what had happened that night, he could not deny or explain the evidence of the wet carpet. It had still been damp the next morning, had taken more than twenty-four hours to dry out completely. The bedroom window had been closed. The only liquids in the room—his glass of whisky and Pam's bottled cosmetics—were unspilled, intact. Rain had gusted into the living room through the open door, but there was no way it could have reached the bedroom, or in such a concentration. The roof did not leak. He had inspected every inch of it. And the odor of stale and brackish water had lingered.

Ian had told no one. The only person he could tell was Regina and with her, on this subject, *he* felt inhibited. He did not think that she would believe him—who would?—but it was not that alone. He feared that she would see it as a morbid fear of Peter's abilities, proof, in fact, of Ian's reluctance to accept. Probably, she was right. At this point, the circle of his thoughts closed, only to begin again, round and round. He slept badly, terrified of what he might encounter and so the nights passed in an incessant reexamination and elaboration of the theory.

Inevitably, he had frequently regretted his decision to remain at Halford. The place, which had struck him as oppressive when he first saw it, now seemed threatening. It might not be morbid for Peter to remain in daily sight of the scene of Pam's death, but Ian knew that it did not do *him* any good. So it was that he approached the gates with a sense of depression and

215

unease. On one hand, he felt that he should leave. On the other, there was the question, the problem of Peter. He had no illusion that he could cope alone. If the abilities should increase, show themselves, he would be helpless. And he shared Regina's fear that if they did not, something damaging would happen to Peter, or himself. He did not want to stay and he could not leave. And to think that something might happen to him was not to regard Peter as malevolent. What he feared, in his uninformed and imprecise way, was a sort of psychic explosion, that the powers, whatever they might be, would become too strong and so harm them all.

As the car moved along the muddy, rain-softened road to Home Farm, he tried to shake off these thoughts. They confused everything and helped no one. He drove through the yard, scattering chickens, and parked. Carl glanced up from some woodwork he was doing just outside the barn, but Ian only nodded at him. There was a strong smell of baking in the house, and he went straight into the kitchen. The Farm had become a second home to him now, as to Peter. Linda and Grizzle were working in the kitchen. The latter looked up at him briefly and then concentrated on the mixing bowl in front of her. Linda's face lit up at the sight of him, making him embarrassed and all too conscious of the resentful young man outside.

"How did it go?" Linda asked. "We expected you sooner."

"An open verdict," he said automatically. "It was all they could do. Where's Regina?"

"She's lying down. She had a bad headache."

"Oh, well, I won't disturb her then."

"She said to ask you to wait. She won't be long."

"I ought to see Peter," he said defensively. He felt nervous around Linda.

"I don't know where he is, perhaps with Reggie,"

she said, making no attempt to conceal her disappointment that he would not stay.

"Reggie's in the sitting room," Grizzle said in her gruff, resentful voice.

"I'll go and see him then," Ian said quickly, making for the door. "Tell Regina I'm here, will you, when she wakes up?"

"Of course. Would you like a cup of tea?"

"No, nothing, thanks."

As he had expected and feared, Carl was hovering at the front door, watching, listening. Ian did not acknowledge him but hurried down the dark corridor to the sitting room. Peter was not there, but Reggie sat at a table by the window, hunched over a pad of drawing paper. He did not look up or give any sign of Ian's presence. His pencil moved busily, with fierce concentration.

"Reggie?"

The pencil stopped moving and yet Ian sensed that the boy had not heard him. He waited, wondering what to do. Of all the children, he found Reggie the easiest, perhaps because he was the closest in age to Peter, and then Ian had to admit that there was something open, even charming about the boy that made his present silence unusual.

The pencil began to move again, almost feverishly, flying over the paper. Ian watched and realized that he had thought the pencil moved, not Reggie's hand. It was, in fact, impossible to tell which, but the impression remained, strongly, that the pencil was the motor force. He felt that he should leave, not interrupt the boy's trancelike concentration. Then the pencil dropped from his fingers, rattling on the table. Still Reggie did not look at him but slowly his hand moved, pushed the drawing to the edge of the table, as though inviting Ian to admire it. Ian approached the table.

"Let's have a look, then," he said, hearing a strained

217

note of heartiness in his voice. "What have you been up to?"

The boy stared vaguely out of the window, as though oblivious of Ian, who picked up the offered sheet of heavy cartridge paper and turned it toward him. At first he could not make any sense of it. The lines were scribbled, formless. It was more like a large doodle than a drawing. Ian thought that Reggie was putting him on. Just as he was about to lay the drawing down, though, he "saw" it properly. It was a drawing of the lake, a sort of aerial view, showing its distinctive kidney shape. The lines which had at first seemed random, mere scribbles, were now liquid, giving the whole picture a remarkable aqueous quality. It was good, unusual and very powerful. He lowered the drawing toward the table, intending to tell Reggie that he liked it, and saw that by tilting it slightly another picture emerged. The lake, by the simple alteration of the angle at which he looked at it, became a face. It was a portrait of Pamela.

Ian's heart tripped, then raced. It was not Pamela as she had been but the dissolving, horrible Pamela of his dream. And to make it worse, much worse, she was wearing, intact and very precisely drawn, the white sun hat that she had bought specially for the cottage. The hat sat on that terrible, drowned, and melting face like a cruel and pitiless joke.

He stared at the thing for only a moment, then dropped it on the table. He did not pause to consider how or why Reggie had drawn so accurately what only he had seen. "I don't think that's funny," he said, his voice rough with anger and fear.

Reggie looked at him then, his eyes pale and smiling, the very picture of innocence.

Peter did not know why he was in the room. He blinked and peered around him nervously. It was a long narrow room, with a steeply sloping ceiling. The window was at knee height. He had never been there before and had no knowledge of the room, which was crammed and cluttered with boxes and trunks, items of unwanted furniture.

It must have happened again, he thought. The blankness, periods he could not remember, from which he emerged, usually with a feeling of lethargy, only to be questioned, shown pieces of broken glass of which he had no recollection. He waited, listening for any sound of approach. What had he done this time? There was no sound, except a distant hammering from the yard. And he did not feel tired as he often did. Instead he felt a sort of urgency.

He began to move then, quietly. He had to find it. A picture of it began to form in his mind. He touched boxes, riffled through their contents. Old newspapers, a chest of drawers. He opened the drawers, one after another, and in the last one he found it. He clutched it tightly, feeling calmer.

There was a mirror in the room, a long, freestanding swivel mirror. As he straightened up, clutching what he had found to his stomach, he saw his own reflection. He stared at himself for a long time, remembering, listening to voices that made him feel hollow and empty. Then he seemed to exist only in the mirror. The mirror-boy made movements that Peter did not, could not, experience. The other Peter raised his arms and placed the hat on his head. A white sun hat. He stared and stared at it, every nerve and muscle tensed. The noise he heard but could not understand was his own labored breathing. It became a buzz and then a roar and finally a kind of articulate scream in his head.

The mirror shattered, glass showering in even, regular fragments about the room. And in the split second before the mirror broke, he had seen his mother standing there, dripping wet beneath her sun hat.

The sound of breaking glass was followed by a cry, at first unearthly, then easily identifiable as a child's wail of distress. It pierced the house, scattered the fog in Regina's exhausted mind. By the time she got to the door of her room, pulling a housecoat around her, she could hear Ian shouting Peter's name, his feet crashing up the stairs. She saw him, wild-eyed, blunder down the corridor, shouting. Slowly, she followed him.

Peter hurled himself into Ian's arms. His sobs drowned out the man's soothing, shaken words.

"I didn't, I didn't. Dad, I didn't."

"It's all right, Peter. It's all right. I'm here, I've got you now."

Behind them the door of the lumber room hung open on uneven hinges. For a moment the floor seemed to be dotted with tongues of fire, but then she saw the fragments of mirror catching the sun from the low window. Quickly, Regina moved forward, pushing Ian and the kicking, screaming bundle that was his son toward what they all thought of now as Peter's room. She placed her body protectively between them and the children, who came clamoring up the stairs.

"There's nothing to be alarmed about," she told them. "Go on, go downstairs. Everything's all right now."

They looked at her, eyes brimming with questions.

"Carl, for God's sake," she shouted over Peter's din, "don't stand there gaping. Get them downstairs."

He obeyed her at once, pushing Reggie, grabbing Linda's hand, ushering Grizzle away.

Somehow, Ian got the door of Peter's room open and half dragged, half carried him inside.

"Can you manage?" Regina shouted, catching his eye for a moment. He nodded. She leaned into the room, pulled the door shut and latched it. She was breathing heavily as she glanced down the corridor to make sure the others had really gone. Then she went softly into the lumber room and closed the door.

She stood looking at the mess. As she had expected, the mirror had been broken according to a geometric figure. Each fragment was a triangle, some short and squat, others long and daggerlike. If the apex of each one was placed together, the mirror would be whole again. Order in chaos. There was nothing wanton or mindless about this destruction.

Beneath the now blank frame lay the hat. Stepping carefully, holding up her housecoat, Regina snatched it up and thrust it quickly into a drawer. Then, holding her breath, she picked up the nearest fragment of glass. It would indeed fit together like a piece of marquetry, and when it did it would make a picture. She tilted the piece of mirror she held, letting the light wash over it. It was imprinted with part of an image. She placed the shard carefully on the floor and made her way cautiously back to the door. The lock was old and never used. She jiggled and coaxed the key free. Outside, she locked the room and pocketed the key. Later she would get Carl to oil the lock for her.

"Just tell me," Ian said, holding Peter tightly, "calmly and quietly what happened. There's nothing to be afraid of. No one's going to be cross with you."

"I don't know, I don't know." Peter tore free of Ian and threw himself onto the bed. "You keep on asking and asking and I tell you I don't know. I didn't do anything. I didn't touch anything. I don't bloody well know."

His anger rose and smashed itself in tears. He flung himself face downward on the bed, kicking his legs and pummeling the pillow with clenched, desperate fists. Ian watched helplessly for a moment.

"Peter, please. It's all right. There's no need for this."

"Leave me alone!" He shook Ian's hand from his shoulder and then lay shaking and trembling.

The door opened. Ian looked hopelessly at Regina.

"I can't do anything with him," he told her, shaking his head.

She looked at the boy on the bed and then back to Ian's pale, ravaged face.

"Leave him," she said quietly. "Let him have his tantrum. He'll get over it."

Ian hesitated, but the boy did seem quieter. Regina held the door for him.

"I don't like to leave him like this."

"He'll be all right," she insisted.

"Peter? I'll be downstairs, all right?"

Sniffing, the boy nodded.

"Come on," Regina said.

He walked out into the corridor and leaned one hand against the wall to steady himself.

"You look done in," Regina said. "Come downstairs."

He went slowly, dragging his feet. The children could be heard in the kitchen, talking. Regina touched his arm.

"Go into the living room. I'll join you in a minute."

He did as she asked him and sat with his head in his hands. The very thing he had been afraid of had happened, or so he thought. Peter was no longer able to control his power and the effects of it had terrified him.

Regina came rustling into the room.

"Linda's making some tea," she said. "Would you like something stronger?"

He shook his head miserably.

"You couldn't get anything out of him?"

"No." He pressed his fingers to his temples as though to clear his head. "He just kept saying he didn't know, he hadn't done anything."

"And then he got angry? It seemed like a fine old show of temper to me."

"Yes, perhaps I shouldn't have gone on at him so much. Something frightened him."

"Well," she sighed, "he's done it again. A mirror this time, a large one."

"Oh God, no." Seven years bad luck, Ian thought.

"It doesn't matter. I should have chucked it out months ago."

"I didn't mean that. My mother always said to break a mirror brought seven years bad luck."

Regina chuckled. "I should've thought the last few days would have cured you of superstition, Ian."

"I don't know, Regina, what's going to happen? He's out of control, terrified."

"Not so fast. For heaven's sake don't let your imagination run away with you. We've got enough problems as it is."

"But you saw—" he protested.

At that moment, Linda came in, carrying a tea tray.

"Thanks," Regina said, crossing the room and taking the tray from her. "Get them started on the chores," she said, looking at the girl. "Tell Reggie to help Grizzle with the milking."

Linda nodded. "Is Peter all right?"

"Yes, but leave him alone. Only don't let him go wandering off anywhere."

"All right," Linda promised, and quietly left the room.

"Will you have a drop of brandy in this?" Regina asked, pouring tea.

"No thanks."

"What happened this morning?"

For a moment, Ian did not know what she meant. The scene with Peter had emptied his mind of everything else.

"The inquest," she prompted.

"Oh, open verdict. Technically the case remains open, until she's found, but otherwise it's all over."

"Poor Ian. You didn't need a shock like this on top of that. Here."

He took the cup she offered him.

"They said something about I could make any arrangements. I didn't really understand."

"For a memorial service, I suppose. That's the form, isn't it, if there's nothing to bury?"

"I don't know."

"It's up to you."

"I don't feel much like it," he said, sipping the hot tea. "Anyway, that can wait. It's Peter."

"Before you go on, there's something I want to tell you. I got a letter this morning from Asmussen."

"The doctor? The one who's carrying on your husband's work?"

"Yes, he's coming over to England. It was a complete surprise. I promise you I haven't mentioned Peter to him. You asked me not to—"

"When?" Ian interrupted.

"Soon, I can't remember precisely. The letter's upstairs. Of course he'll be coming here. He always visits me when he's in Europe. Ian . . ." She put down her cup and leaned, imploring, toward him. "Will you let him see Peter, please? Before this all gets entirely out of hand?"

"Yes," he said. "Anything. Anything at all, because I can't take much more of this."

"Thank God," she said, her shoulders slumping with relief.

They looked at each other, not smiling, not needing to say anything. Asmussen, Ian thought, was their only hope.

"It will be all right," Regina said at last. "You must believe that. Now drink your tea."

Peter walked slowly and quietly down the stairs, looking apprehensive. From the kitchen, Linda spoke his name. He fixed his eyes on the open front door.

"I'm going home now."

"Wait a moment, wait for your father," she said.

He gave no sign, but walked slowly toward the door. Linda did not try to stop him but ran down the corridor to the sitting room.

"It's Peter," she said. "He says he's going home."

Regina and Ian exchanged a look.

"You'd better go with him," she said at once. "And take it easy."

"Yes, thanks. I'll see you later."

Peter had reached the gate. Ian decided not to call him or do anything that might precipitate another scene. He got into the car and started the engine, drove across the yard and onto the road. In a few moments he drew level with Peter, who stopped, looked at him, and then, unbidden, opened the passenger door. Ian suppressed a sigh of relief and, when the boy was seated beside him, let the car idle forward again.

"Are you mad at me?" His small hands were clasped in his lap. He stared sullenly ahead, through the windshield.

"No," Ian replied.

"You don't mind me yelling at you?"

"Well, I don't particularly . . . No. Sometimes we all need to let off steam, but don't make a habit of it."

"I'm sorry."

"That's okay."

Peter sighed heavily and slumped in his seat. Ian turned onto the main drive and then made the sharper, more difficult turn into the woods toward the cottage. Ian brought the car to a halt, and they both got out.

Peter stood beside the car, drawing on the dusty hood.

"You could wash it for me," Ian said, watching him carefully.

"All right. Dad?"

"Yes?"

"Can we go back to London?"

Ian kept his voice carefully casual.

"Why?"

"I don't know. I just thought—" He looked up then, his blue eyes troubled. He stuck his hands in his pockets. "I don't like it here anymore."

Ian knew he had to be very, very careful. He did not answer immediately, but held out his hand. Peter avoided any contact, and walked around the car and up onto the veranda.

"Do you not like it because of what happened this afternoon?" Ian asked.

"I suppose."

"That's a good reason, but I don't think going away would make any difference. Besides, there's a doctor coming here, a friend of Regina's. I want you to see him."

"I'm not ill."

"I know, he's not that kind of doctor."

Ian tried to keep his face calm and reassuring as the boy scrutinized it. After a long pause, Peter sat down in one of the wicker chairs and said, "You think I'm different. You think I'm like Reggie and Grizzle, don't you?" His head came up, in a direct challenge.

"Yes, I do," Ian said. He squatted down in front of him. "But what I think doesn't matter. What do *you* think?"

"I don't know. Sometimes I think I am, sometimes not."

"Can you tell me how it feels?"

"No." He shook his head wearily. Ian waited. Peter leaned back in the chair, rubbed his hand across his forehead. "It's all blank. There are voices, in me. I don't understand them. They want me to . . . no, I'm all empty. The voices, I don't think they're talking to me."

"To whom then?" Ian asked urgently.

He shook his head again, violently.

"You mustn't be afraid," Ian said, taking his hand and holding it. "Are you?"

"A bit, sometimes."

"Well, you must try not to be. Will you? Because it will be better if you are not. And I'll be here, and Regina. We won't let anything happen to you."

Peter pulled his hand away and turned his head toward the woods, as though he had grown tired of the conversation.

"You say you're not sure whether you're different or not. That's why I want you to see Dr. Asmussen, to find out. Will you?"

Peter tapped his foot impatiently on the boards.

"Will you?" Ian repeated.

He looked full at Ian. His eyes were blank.

"All right."

"Good."

"Only . . ."

"What?"

"Nothing."

"Please, Peter. You can tell me."

"Yes, but you wouldn't understand."

"At least let me try."

"You can't. You can't understand."

He stood up quickly and Ian had to rise too, move out of his impatient way. He felt the gulf between them then, a difference that had been acknowledged at last.

"I'll try," he promised.

Peter walked into the house as though he had not heard, as though, in any case, it was irrelevant, impossible.

"I'll try," Ian whispered.

After supper, Peter decided to wash and wax the car. The tinny sound of the transistor radio he had carried out with him drifted peacefully over the lake. He worked with gusto, soaking his clothes with the soapy water and humming along with the music. Ian watched from the veranda and was grateful for the sheer ordinariness of the scene. During the meal, he had told Peter about the inquest. Peter had asked a few questions about the open verdict but otherwise seemed uninterested. Ian had waited, thinking that perhaps now he would be ready to talk about his feelings, but he had kept them to himself. Ian had let it go. After all, they had both had enough for one day.

Ian strolled to the end of the veranda and called to him.

"I'm just going over to Home Farm. I won't be more than half an hour, okay?"

"Yes, see you."

Peter hurled cold water over the car, cleaning the detergent from the already gleaming bodywork.

"When you've finished," Ian shouted, "you'd better take a bath."

"Okay."

He felt hopeful as he walked along the path. It was difficult to hang on to such moments, but watching Peter work on the car, he could see him growing up, maturing, finding a place in the world. Surely, nothing could prevent that. And he vowed that he would try harder to remember these moments, to remind himself of what Regina had said that first night, that Peter was still Peter, an ordinary boy.

The Farm lay in late golden sunshine, peaceful and welcoming. Among other things, Ian wanted to collect Asmussen's articles from Regina. At the door, he called out and Grizzle poked her head around the kitchen door.

"Sh," she said, "Regina's resting."

"Sorry." He had forgotten her headache.

The kitchen table was littered with the remains of their evening meal. In a desultory way, Grizzle and Reggie were clearing it and preparing to wash the dishes.

"Has she still got a headache?" Ian asked.

"Yes, but it's woman trouble, too," Reggie said, and snickered.

"Shut up," Grizzle said, her cheeks burning.

Ian had never seen such a natural reaction in the girl before and he suddenly felt sorry for her. Reggie ignored her.

"Do you want to leave a message?"

"No, it doesn't matter." He turned toward the door.

"She left some stuff for you," Grizzle said, almost as an afterthought.

"Oh?"

"On the hall table."

He went to the little table and found a small stack of magazines. A note was paper-clipped to them, in Regina's bold handwriting.

Ian, he read. *Here are a few of Asmussen's articles, as promised. Hope they help.* R.

He picked up the magazines, feeling slightly guilty. Reggie and Grizzle must know what they contained and why he was reading them. They were bound to think that he was prying, an outsider who needed to be educated in order to understand them.

"Got them all right?" Reggie asked, watching from the kitchen doorway.

"Yes, thanks."

They looked at each other and, on the spur of the moment, Ian said, "That drawing you showed me this afternoon . . ."

"Yes?" He looked keen, eager to discuss it. "Did you like it?"

"Not very much. I'd like to see it again, though."

229

"Sure, I'll get it." He set off up the stairs immediately, ignoring Grizzle's protest that he was supposed to be helping her.

"Sorry," Ian told her, but she ignored him too.

He had planned to tell Regina about the picture, to ask if the boy was showing off for him again, but now it seemed better, less cowardly, to have it out directly with Reggie. He steeled himself as he heard Reggie clumping back down the stairs.

"Here," the boy said, thrusting a rolled sheet of paper at Ian, "though if you don't like it I don't see why you want to look at it."

"I want you to explain it," Ian said, putting down the magazines and unrolling the drawing. He had no difficulty in making it out now.

At his elbow, Reggie said, "It's the lake, sort of from high up. See?"

"Yes, but it's the other image that interests me." Ian tilted the drawing. "How did you know about that?"

"About what?" Reggie leaned around him, squinting at the drawing as though he was nearsighted.

"The face, the woman's face."

Only it wasn't there. He looked at the drawing. He looked at it from every angle, holding it against the light, tilting and twisting it. There was no suggestion of Pam's face nor of the sun hat. Reggie frowned at him.

"This isn't the drawing," Ian announced.

"It is. It's the only one I did today."

"No," Ian insisted.

"It is, I tell you. What are you talking about, what face?"

"Keep your voice down," Grizzle said. "You'll wake Regina."

"It isn't fair," Reggie said. "He called me a liar."

For a moment, Ian faced them both. They stood at the sink, their eyes fixed on him.

"I'm sorry," he said. "I must have made a mistake. I didn't mean to call you a liar, Reggie."

230

The boy said nothing. Grizzle turned back to the washing.

"Tell Regina I hope she feels better. Good-night."

He made himself walk at a normal pace although he wanted to get away quickly. Behind him, he heard Reggie's voice, low and complaining. He thought of the barn, the black, seeping hole, the pitchfork.

"No, Reggie," Grizzle said loudly. "You're not to."

All the time it took to cross the yard Ian expected something to happen. He had crossed them, made them angry. They would use their powers to punish him. But nothing happened. When he reached the path through the woods, he was breathing heavily and clutching the magazines in damp hands. He knew that his accusation would get back to Regina and that she would know, as Reggie and Grizzle did, that he was afraid of them. He could not deny it, though his fear was mixed with anger. The boy had played some sort of trick on him. He had deliberately scared him. And then he realized there was a much more simple explanation, one which fitted all the facts. Pam's face had never been a part of the drawing. He had imagined it, wanted to see it, was simply not in control of his own imagination. It was possible that Reggie could read his thoughts, but not his dreams. And what possible motive could he have, anyway? Ian knew that he had made a blunder. It was not only unfair to Reggie, but it revealed that his mind was playing tricks on him.

When he set off he was somewhat optimistic, but as he approached the cottage, he felt a kind of dread. Maybe everything was imagination. Maybe Liz had been right to laugh, to urge him to send Peter away and return to London. Perhaps it was he who was different, not Peter. Perhaps what Peter actually needed was protection from him.

Later that night, Ian lay in bed, trying to concentrate on one of Asmussen's articles. It was heavy going, but the real trouble was the recurrent thought that *he* needed help. Should he make a clean breast of it to Regina, get her opinion at least? He turned back to Asmussen's theory of electrical discharges from the brain.

"Dad?"

Ian lowered the magazine. Peter stood hesitantly in the doorway, looking pale and troubled.

"What is it?"

"Can I sleep in here?"

Ian was surprised. Peter had never made such a request before.

"Sure," he said, turning back the bedclothes on the other side—he couldn't help thinking of it as Pam's side—of the bed. Gratefully, Peter hopped in. He pulled the bedclothes over his shoulder and lay with his back to Ian.

"What's the matter? Did something happen?"

"No, I just couldn't sleep."

"Well, you soon will," Ian said, relieved that nothing had frightened him.

"I started thinking about Mommy. It felt so lonely."

And then, at last, he began to cry. Ian felt nothing but relief. These tears were not hysterical, not the result of fear and anxiety, but tears of love and loss, of grief. He cried quietly, his shoulders shaking. Ian patted his back but did not otherwise try to comfort him. These tears must run their own course, have their own necessary healing power. All he could do was watch and be there. He kept very still and, at last, Peter sniffed and fished in his pajama pocket for his handkerchief. He blew his nose loudly and settled down again, his hand under his damp cheek.

"All right now?"

"Mm." He nodded, his head on the pillow.

"I'm going to put the light out. Good-night, son."

"Good-night."

Ian lay in the darkness, listening to Peter's breathing.

It became more and more regular. He was sleeping, it was all right now. Carefully, in order not to disturb Peter, Ian turned on his side. The window showed as a paler square of darkness. There was no moon. The house was quiet. Ian closed his eyes and very quickly slipped into sleep.

It was still dark when the shaking woke him.

"What is it? Peter?"

He thought that Peter must be trying to wake him. He reached for the lamp and his hand lunged against it. Swearing, he grabbed it before it fell. It was the bed that was shaking. Superstitiously, he looked at the foot of the bed, but there was nothing there. Even so, the bed continued to rock and shiver, as though shaken by a strong man. Struggling, he got the light on. A fresh convulsion almost tipped him from the bed. He could hear it now, knocking and rattling on the floor, thumping the carpet, the springs protesting.

"Peter."

The boy lay on his back, completely rigid. It seemed as though he was resisting the violent motion of the bed. His body shook, but he was not thrown about as Ian was. Ian realized that if he was to do anything, he must get out of the bed. It seemed as though the thing had a life of its own, that it was determined to prevent him. As he tried to get his legs to the ground, he was thrown flat on his back and his whole body shaken. Without thinking, he flung himself over and landed with a thud on the floor. He lay there for a moment, trying to get his breath. The bed was suddenly still. But even as this fact registered, the sliding doors of the wardrobe rattled open, then closed with a crash. His startled eyes saw the dressing table rear up. The litter of Pam's bottles slid, crashing and rolling to the floor. The hinged mirror swung wildly. The sickly scent of mingled cosmetics filled the room.

Ian forced himself up from the floor and turned back to the bed. The wardrobe doors swooshed wildly again.

The lamp danced, making the light flicker eerily over Peter's face. He hurried across the room and put on the main light, just in time. The lamp was dashed to the floor and went out. He ignored it, but hurried to Peter's side of the bed.

"Peter! Peter, wake up. Stop this."

The boy's bloodless lips were drawn back from his teeth in a snarl. His eyes were closed, but a white crescent showed beneath each lid. Ian touched his forehead. It was dry and burning.

"Peter," he shouted.

The bedroom door slammed. The window rattled. Appalled, Ian watched the bedside table jiggle and tip forward, spilling the magazines onto the floor. The wardrobe doors slid back and forth erratically, as if pushed by a demented, badly coordinated child.

He leaned down, his head swimming with the noise, and shook Peter roughly. He could barely move him. It was as though rigor mortis had set in.

"Peter, for God's sake."

Then he leapt back with a startled cry. The light bulb above him exploded with a bang, raining tiny fragments of glass onto the bed. The room was plunged into darkness and with a last, final rattle, the wardrobe doors closed. Everything was still and silent.

Ian's breathing rasped in the silence. Stumbling, he felt his way to the door, threw it open, and began to switch on all the lights in the living room. Nothing there was disturbed. He went back to the bedroom, leaving the door wide open to admit as much light as possible.

He stood by the bed, smelling the pungent perfumes and powders, not knowing what to do.

A sound escaped Peter. Ian watched closely. The boy's teeth were still clenched and bared, his body stiff and hot. He made another sound, deep and guttural. Ian could not make sense of it, though it sounded as though it might have been a word, or a cry, torn from a

234

constricted throat. A tremor shook Peter and he sighed. Then, very slowly, he began to relax.

"Peter?"

Ian spoke softly, bending over the boy, who drew a long breath, sighed again, and turned over, sleeping peacefully.

"Peter?" Ian shook him gently.

"Mm?"

But he did not wake. He moistened his lips with the tip of his tongue, drew up his knees, and slept peacefully on.

Straightening up, Ian saw himself darkly reflected at a crazy angle in the tilted mirror. There were ashes in his mouth, the prickle of fear all over his body. He knew what he must do, what he should have done days ago. He should have listened to Peter earlier. He pulled on his clothes, put his wallet and keys into his pocket.

"Peter. Peter," he called, shaking the boy. His body was limp now, soft with sleep, but it was as though Ian's attempts to rouse him only drove him deeper into sleep. He was convinced that it was not, as it seemed, a natural sleep, but a form of unconsciousness. Recuperation or escape? Ian did not know and he did not stop to consider it.

He hurried out of the house, fumbling a little in the sudden darkness, and opened the back door of the car. Returning to the cottage, he snapped on the kitchen light before returning to the bedroom. He pulled the glass-littered spread from the bed and quickly folded the sheet and blanket around Peter. The boy's body was floppy and compliant as a rag doll's. Peter murmured something as, grunting with the effort, Ian lifted him, but his head lolled comfortably against Ian's shoulder. He carried him carefully out into the night. The car stood in a rectangle of light spilling from the kitchen window. Gently, Ian eased Peter onto the back seat and then lifted his legs so that he could stretch out. The boy slept on. Ian closed the car door. Something, some reflex made him return to the house and switch off all the lights. With a sense of release, he closed the door behind him and walked for the last time across the veranda, down the steps, and to the car.

It was a warm, airless night, and he was sweating. He got into the car, snapped on the lights, and turned the ignition key. The engine turned once, spluttered, and died. Ian tried again and again. The car sounded less responsive each time. He got out, opened up the hood and peered in. It was too dark to see anything. Banging his knee, grazing his knuckles, he found a flashlight in the car and shone its weak beam onto the engine. He knew next to nothing about the mechanical aspect of cars, but he checked the obvious things, spark plugs, carburetor, battery. As far as he could tell, everything was in working order. He slammed down the hood and got back behind the wheel. He turned the ignition again and was rewarded with an uncertain cough. He crossed his forearms on the steering wheel and put his head down. He could have wept then. A hopelessness more acute than any he had known overwhelmed him. If only he hadn't been so keen on having Pam's car taken into Halford for servicing, they could have used that. But he had not been able to stand the sight of it, sitting there reminding him.

He slept a little, waking from time to time, his muscles cramped. He turned toward the sleeping bundle in the back, but there was no hope or comfort there. Peter could have jinxed the car, he thought. He saw the sky lighten beyond the house, flush with pink, and he felt detached, as though watching a film. He observed the first rays creep toward the black, sleeping lake. They seemed to burn a path across its impassive surface. His eyes smarted with the reflected glare of light. Behind him, Peter stirred at last, sat up, rubbing his eyes.

"Dad?" He shivered, clutched the blanket around

him. "Dad? What are we doing here? Why are we in the car?"

"I was going to take you away," Ian answered. "I couldn't wake you."

"Why didn't you?" he asked, looking around him at the familiar landmarks.

"The car wouldn't start."

"So we just stayed here? Why?"

"Come and see," Ian invited, opening his door and getting out.

Barefoot, holding the sheet and blanket like a cumbersome cloak, Peter got out, groaning at the stiffness in his muscles. He looked, Ian thought, like a refugee as he picked his way gingerly over the tarmac, the rougher, packed earth in front of the house.

"Come on," Ian said, opening the door.

"What is it? I don't understand."

Ian led him to the bedroom. Peter caught his breath sharply, surveyed the wreckage for a long time, and then said, "What happened? It looks like a bomb went off."

The boat was on the lake again. The water erupted with sun-dazzled young bodies. Cries and shouts, laughter, reverberated all around him. He saw, as through a mist, sunlit ripples of water, a ball arcing against the dark trees. Linda rose from the water, batting the ball with the flat of her palm. He heard Peter shout, saw Carl jackknife over, disappear beneath the water.

It was like a leap in time. The day had passed as a dream. Watching them, bits of it stood out clear in his mind. Peter saying please could they swim. Oh please, could they? And Regina: "Let them, Ian. They've worked so hard."

He turned his head to the left. Regina sat beside him, wearing something loose and red, her face lifted to the sun. He felt beneath his body the familiar wicker chair, saw the remains of a picnic scattered over the white table. A boy—Reggie? Peter? Carl?—leaped shouting from the edge of the jetty. Water rose in a sun-speckled fountain, hung for a moment in the air, then fell slowly back, flashing fire. They were on the bank by the jetty. Somebody must have carried the furniture down from the veranda, but he could not remember when or who. Had he slept? He looked at Regina again, remembering.

She had arrived early with the milk, had looked at the bedroom, and instantly taken charge. It was a blur of activity. People coming, going. The house filled with their voices, hurting his head. Linda and Grizzle, little housewives, clearing up the mess, Regina presiding over it all.

He had stood beside the car, watching Carl turn the key, heard the familiar, instant response of the engine and seen the half smile on Carl's face that said he must have imagined it or been in too much of a panic to remember how to start his own car. A feeling of defeat, then. They had him running scared, round in circles.

"Everything's in order."

Regina's face, looming over him, distorted, too close.

"You think, don't you, that you're responsible? You're making it happen?"

His head hurt as though fingers were touching sore, delicate places in his mind. The lake again, bodies flashing. Hair sculpted wet to bony scalps. Cries too loud. The splash of water, hurting his head.

"It's possible that Peter's picking up your fears and using them to communicate with you. That would explain why he doesn't remember. Do you see? The need is satisfied unconsciously. There is no need for him to remember."

Regina's voice drifting in and out of the other voices.

"Here."

"Throw it, idiot."

"Grizzle, to me."

"Here, here."

"Oh you fool."

Voices drowning in the splash of water.

"If your friend, this woman, this talk of poltergeists, alarmed you, Peter might have sensed that buried in your mind. You see what this means? His abilities must be incredibly adaptable."

Had he told her about Liz? Pain, sharp as a razor, cut through his mind. He turned again to Regina, saw her quite clearly. A long, red caftan, splashed with precise, formal, patterns, in other glowing colors. Thick hair, caught back, tied at the nape of the neck, her face in repose—asleep?—lifted to the sun. He did not remember telling her, not about Liz.

"Dad, can we? Please? Say we can . . .."

"Let them, Ian. They've worked so hard."

Voices speaking to him, blurring in the wash of water. He closed his eyes. Everything became red with discs of orange, white, and black whirling against the red.

"This face you saw in Reggie's drawing, you say it resembled Pamela as you've dreamed of her. Well, since that image has stayed in your mind, maybe Reggie picked it up, just for a moment, shared it with you. But that's nothing to be afraid of, is it? It's certainly not there now. You agree, don't you?"

He remembered the taste of food then, a picnic by the lake. Linda posed against the sky, her body shining in a black bathing suit. All of them leaping into the water, laughing, dunking each other, splashing.

"I wish you hadn't told this woman, though. What did you say her name was?"

He hadn't. He hadn't.

"I hope she can be trusted."

"Oh yes," he heard himself saying, his voice echoing. "She didn't believe me. She thinks I'm mad."

"And that disturbed you. With the inquest and everything, you were upset. It's not surprising that

Peter picked up something and reacted strongly. But that's nothing to be afraid of. And what would you have achieved by going away? It won't stay here. Peter takes it with him wherever he goes."

His head ached and throbbed, a pulsing jelly, assailed by sounds, the water, the children, his drumming heartbeat.

But the car started at once for Carl.

There was quiet then, shadows moving across his eyelids, low voices. He saw towels, wrapped like winding sheets around bodies. Ice-cold water dripping from hair. He started forward with a cry of distress.

"Did you sleep well?"

He stared at Regina. She was wrapping scraps of food in foil.

"That's what you need, sleep."

She moved around the table, packing up. The sun was much lower, sinking beyond the trees on the other side of the lake. Young bodies moved past him, lifting the table, Regina's chair. A procession up the hill, calling, shouting, voices fading into a lost whisper.

"Ian?" Regina touched his arm. She was squatting beside him, her dark eyes narrow with concern. "We're going back to the Farm now. You'll go to bed? I'll ring Asmussen, as we agreed."

"I don't remember." His voice sounded thick, his speech slurred and out of time. "My head hurts."

"You're tired, too much sun perhaps."

"I don't remember. Asmussen?"

"Yes. We agreed I should call him, try to persuade him to come at once." She stood up. There was a basket hooked over her arm. "Peter can stay with us, you sleep."

He stared at the water.

"I'll sit here, just sit here for a while longer." The effort of speech was too great. He leaned his head back against the cushion, closed his eyes. Yellow now, soothing. No discs and dots to disturb him. Just yellow, infinite, still yellow.

Regina watched him for a while, then turned toward the cottage. The children stood in a row along the veranda, waiting for her. Slowly, she began to climb toward them.

Regina made the call from her bedroom. It was a dark, overcrowded room, lit with fantastic colors. She sat on the large, canopied bed, gripping the receiver, tapping the fingers of her other hand impatiently on the table. As soon as she was connected with Dr. Asmussen, she cut across his polite preliminaries.

"Look, can you come sooner, as soon as possible? Yes, yes, it's the boy. No, *the* boy." She listened for a moment, frowning. "Yes, I realize all that, but you know how important this is. I can't put it off. Yes," she admitted, "some difficulties. The father." She looked angry. "No, nothing I can't handle, but that's not the point. It has to be done now, soon. You must believe me. I shall go ahead anyway," she stated, "but naturally I'd prefer to have you here. Is it possible?" She listened again, her face intent. "Yes, all right. Do that, please. Yes. Good-bye, then."

She replaced the receiver thoughtfully. Her hand rested on it as though she might snatch it up, make another call. Then her attention was caught by Peter, standing in the doorway. She regarded him coolly, suppressing her surprise.

"Don't you know it's rude not to knock?"

"I did, you didn't hear." He was sullen, his eyes moving around the room, avoiding her.

"Were you listening?" she asked, the thought suddenly occurring to her.

His eyes moved toward her, then away again.

"You were, weren't you," she accused. "That's not very nice, either. I'm surprised at you, Peter."

"You were talking about me," he said defensively.

"And what if I was? That's no excuse. If somebody wants to make a private—"

"You were talking to that doctor, the one who's coming to see me." He looked at her at last, unsure of his rights, but determined to brazen it out.

"Ah, I see. That's what bothering you. Come here, Peter. Shut the door."

He hesitated.

"Come along," she said, patting the bed beside her.

Slowly, he closed the door and approached the bed, but he ignored her invitation to sit.

"Why is it so urgent?" he burst out. "Why have I got to see him?"

"Because," she said gently, smiling, "you're special."

"No I'm not. You know I'm not."

"Then why would I go to all this trouble? Dr. Asmussen is coming from America, you know, just to see you."

"It won't do any good. You know it won't." His lower lip trembled.

"There's nothing to be afraid of, you silly boy." She reached out to smooth his hair, but he jerked away from her. "You'll see," she said, ignoring his withdrawal.

"I'm not special. I'm not—"

"You are to me," she interrupted firmly. He stared at the floor then. "Now, what did you want?" Regina asked him calmly.

"I just came to say good-night and thank you for letting me stay," he mumbled.

"That's better. All right then. Good-night, Peter. Sleep well."

He walked, sulking, toward the door.

"Peter?"

"Yes?"

"Do you know a lady, a friend of your father's?" She concentrated, as though looking inside herself. "A blond lady," she added.

"No, why?"

"I'm just interested. Are you sure you never met a lady like that? A pretty lady, I think. Or perhaps you've heard him talk about her?"

He reached for the door handle.

"Peter."

"They used to row sometimes, about a lady."

"Your mother and father?"

He nodded.

"What was her name? Did you ever hear it?"

"Why don't you ask Dad?" he challenged her, opening the door.

"Because sometimes it is more polite to ask a third person."

"Well, I don't know. And if I did I wouldn't tell you," he said and ran out of the room, banging the door behind him.

Regina stared around the familiar room, her sanctum, and wondered how she would break down Peter's resistance. It seemed an insuperable task. She sighed heavily, stood, and tried to prepare herself mentally for the night's work. She thought she knew how Peter's resistance would manifest itself. If only Asmussen would believe, come at once. If only she could get through to him. She looked at the telephone. Maybe she had, maybe.

Although Liz had not been to the restaurant before, it was instantly recognizable as her father's kind of place. A sort of carpeted cathedral dedicated to the celebration of good food and wine, it exuded quietness and discretion. A stiffly dignified waiter led her to a corner table, partially and deliberately screened from the rest of the room by a bank of potted plants. Her father rose at once, giving her face and clothes an appraising but critical look before taking her hand and kissing her cheek. He was a handsome man from whom Liz had inherited her fair coloring. His hair was now mixed with gray, but he had the slightly shiny, scrubbed complexion of a much younger man.

"Well," Liz said, referring to his searching look, "will I pass muster?"

"Of course," he said. "You look delightful, but perhaps a touch too much lipstick. You don't need it, my dear."

There was always something. The collar of a dress did not sit quite right, or the eye makeup was smudged. A piece of jewelry did not perfectly grace the chosen gown. Something. Liz remembered that it had been so when her mother was alive. The last-minute inspection, they'd called it. Father walking round her mother, checking every detail. Liz had often wondered if all women were subjected to it, or if it was a kind of courtesy reserved exclusively for the family.

"Not that it isn't very pretty lipstick," he said. "Now, what will you have to drink?"

As though conjured by the sound of her father's voice, the waiter stepped forward. Liz ordered a gin and tonic and smiled at her father.

"And how are you?"

"I feel marvelous, if a little apprehensive. Marvelous," he went on pedantically, "because you suddenly have so much time to call me and see me, and apprehensive as to the reason."

Liz laughed. She knew that it was not a complaint. They both understood that he was as pleased as she that they did not live in each other's pockets.

"How do you know I've got the time? You insisted that I have dinner with you."

"Oh, did it sound like a command? I'm sorry. It's just this boring thing I have about parental responsibility. When my daughter telephones me and asks for advice, I feel that I should give it in style."

"Well, this is certainly in style," Liz agreed, looking around the room.

"Especially when she appears to be going into the private-investigation business. A most insalubrious trade, incidentally. Naturally, my parental alarm bells began to ring."

"You mean curiosity," Liz retorted. The waiter placed her drink before her and offered the large menu.

"Did you not say, 'Daddy, how do you go about checking on someone, anything that might have been written about them, that sort of thing?' I believe those were your exact words."

"And obviously they were taken down as evidence, to be used against me."

"Oh come now, Elizabeth," he said, giving the menu the barest glance. "I recommend the seafood. It's always fresh. And the saddle of lamb." He closed the menu with a snap, signaling the waiter.

"I'll have the vichyssoise," Liz said, "and the duck, with broccoli and peas. Thank you."

"Some people," he remarked to the waiter, looking injured, "simply will not take advice."

"Some people prefer to choose," Liz reminded him, with a slight smile.

"*Touché.*" He then ordered his own dinner in accordance with his recommendations.

"All right, Daddy. What do you want to know?"

He studied the wine list with elaborate care.

"Would you care to choose . . . ?" he asked, looking at her over its edge.

"No, thank you. That's your prerogative."

He ordered the wine, straightened his cutlery with small, carefully manicured hands, and then said, "Yes, now, talking of men . . ."

"We weren't."

"But we shall eventually, and since you gave me carte blanche we might as well start there."

"I don't understand."

"Who is the man in the case?"

"I don't believe I mentioned a man."

"No, you referred to a friend. However—"

"If I didn't know you," she said, "I'd say you were using my request for advice as an excuse to ask me unwarranted questions about my love life."

"Ah, so it is a man, and one who qualifies for a place in your love life. How *is* Ian Woodford, by the way?"

"You'd never get away with this in court," Liz said.

"I might," he told her confidently, enjoying their bantering.

"All right. It's Ian. You guessed that because I asked you to find out about the inquest."

"The two requests did follow rather hard one on the heels of the other. But you might take a trifle longer to see through my little ploys, Elizabeth."

"They're not ploys. You just put two and two together and then try to make it sound mysterious and clever. Besides, why should I pander to your vanity?"

"I do wish all those expensive schools I sent you to had taught you a little respect for your aged parent."

"No you don't. You like me just the way I am."

"Don't be too sure, Elizabeth." His eyes narrowed a little. "Now, are you going to tell me what you want, or shall we discuss something congenial?"

"I've told you what I want. I want to find out everything I can about a man called Alvar Thomas and his wife Regina."

"Yes, my dear, but why?"

"You damn well know why," she said, lowering her voice as the waiter approached.

"And you certainly wouldn't get away with that in the witness box, young lady," he said.

"But I'm not in the witness box."

"True. You must forgive the habits of a lifetime." She watched him cut his appetizer into small, neat pieces. "Why can't you tell me?"

"Because it's none of your business," Liz said.

"Oh but it is. I have a position, a reputation to protect. I can't allow myself to be a party to some sort of investigation without informing myself of why you want to conduct it. My dear, we must all learn from the example of Richard Nixon, to mention but one."

In spite of herself, Liz laughed.

"All right. I'll come clean." Briefly, she told her father what Ian had said about Regina Thomas and Peter's supposed abilities. He listened attentively, chewing his food carefully.

"I see," he said when she had finished. "And are you expecting to find something against this woman?"

"No," Liz said, too quickly. "Should I be?"

"My dear, how should I know? Thank you," he said as their plates were quietly removed. "So it's just a question of forearming yourself?"

"I'm not sure about that either. I just want to know if she's bona fide or not."

"And if she is?"

Liz shrugged.

"Whereas if she isn't, you can rush to Ian and expose her as a quack." He sipped his wine, savored it, then nodded to the waiter, who filled Liz's glass. "Not very wise."

"What do you mean?"

"If, as you fear, Ian has become—what shall we say?—infatuated with this woman, then attacking her is unlikely to put you back in his good graces."

"Who said anything about—doesn't it occur to you that I might be concerned for the boy, or for Ian's state of mind?"

"No, it doesn't. The latter, possibly . . ."

Liz made an exasperated noise, but fiddling with her

glass she had to admit that Ian had said more or less the same.

"Then he must know you very well. No"—he held up his hand, to silence her protests—"father's prerogative. I don't mind you poking around, trying to find out about this woman. Indeed, I'll help you as best I can. But I do insist that you be clear in your own mind about your motives."

"I think my motives are irrelevant," Liz grumbled.

"Not to me."

"Look, don't you think it's odd that this should suddenly come up? There's never been any suggestion before that Peter was anything but a normal kid."

"Yes, I do think it odd. And I accept that you do. But it isn't the boy you're proposing to investigate, it's the woman. A woman who appears to have suddenly begun to occupy a rather central place in Woodford's life, a woman who is possibly exercising an undue influence over him. And that, my darling, is what concerns you. Ah, the lamb . . ."

Liz remained silent while the main course was served. Because it was her father who spoke to her in this way, her anger inevitably seemed childish.

"You really should have had the lamb, that duck looks terrible. However, all I'm saying is that, whatever you discover about Mrs. Thomas and her late husband, be careful how you use it, especially if you're interested in getting Woodford back."

"Who said I'd lost him?" Liz asked, trying to sound more cheerful than she felt.

"My dear, you're dining with me, not entertaining Woodford. Besides, you've got the light of battle in your eyes. That duck is insipid, isn't it?"

"No."

"Then be so good as to eat it."

"What do you mean 'light of battle'?"

"A woman scorned and all that."

248

sense. Her hold on Ian was through Peter. She knew he would be vulnerable himself, concerned and uncertain about Peter. But what she could not believe was this mumbo jumbo about the paranormal. Such people were, in her view, either charlatans or mad. In either case they were dangerous. And Ian felt the same. She knew that. If anything, he was short on imagination, much more likely to dismiss something like that than to swallow it. The woman, therefore, must be very persuasive. She must also have a motive, unless she was simply deranged. And Pam's death, the responsibility for an adopted son he had never really wanted, on top of everything else—including, Liz ruefully admitted, her own recent behavior—could easily prove too much for him. He had come to her to escape strain and she had added her own pressures. No wonder he had withdrawn. The possibility that he had finally broken seemed more than ever likely.

So what she was doing, she was doing for him. Whatever Fairlie came up with, whatever information her father could obtain from Mr. Branscombe, she must use it to help Ian, not to attack Regina Thomas. And if they came up with nothing? She could swallow her pride and go down there herself, to discuss the situation. She could do it, but she doubted that Ian would be receptive. The more she thought about it, the more she felt that Regina Thomas was her passport back to Ian. Anything other than information, help, would make her seem like a threat, another demand on his time and energy. She recalled his face in the pub and knew that he believed. But if she could just get to him with something concrete, something that would cast at least a doubt on this conviction he had about Peter. And if she succeeded in casting that doubt, then what? She would cross her fingers and hope.

She had never meant to love him. Part of her, she knew, resented the fact that she did. She couldn't handle it. She had been too busy running her own life, making herself independent, to find it easy to adjust to this ache, this mindless need for him. She fought him when she wanted to hold him. She longed for marriage when she'd always railed against it, declared it irrelevant. But if she was a creature of contradictions, she was also a survivor.

Her father, as always, had been right. She was a big girl and the going was rough. But she could weather it. If she got nothing else out of this but proof that she could, then it would be sufficient. It would have to be.

The flickering light of three oil lamps isolated Peter's flexed body from the deep darkness. His nails bit cruelly into his palms. His eyes rolled upward beneath closed lids, pale slivers of white pupil showing. His lips twitched back from clenched teeth and sounds escaped him, grunts of effort or resistance and occasionally a half-caught word from another world.

They stood back in the darkness, watching him. Their minds roamed through him, searching, calling.

Carl crept into the room, drawing Grizzle behind him. He touched Reggie lightly on the shoulder. The boy flinched, turned his pale eyes from the body on the bed. Slowly they focused, understood. Grizzle took his place as he and Carl stole out again.

For a few moments her mind hung, lost, without direction, her body trembled a little. Then she felt the comfort of Regina and Linda close to her. She joined them. She had only to go with them, deliver up her will.

They carried her through strange caves. She saw a gate opening underwater, a body floating by. She saw fish looming, fading, dissolving. Back, farther back, beyond something. She burst into light, eyes and ears hurting with glare and noise. The smell of chlorine. Bodies jostled her in warm and steamy water. She saw, out of other eyes, a woman's terrified face. Gasping for air, arms flailing, the woman rose from her seat in the spectators' gallery, hoarse cries dying on her lips, fighting her way down. Grizzle floated peacefully in the water, watching Regina's quiet smile which suddenly switched off, blanked, and whirled into blue. Grizzle felt dizzy, felt resistance. Her mind grew smaller, comprehension left her. She peered, frightened, out of rheumy eyes. There was pain and cold and neglect all around her. Then a wizened, unknown painted face swooped toward her, a red hole of a mouth. The sudden stench of old breath as hands, warm hands, fumbled among stained and smelling pieces of cloth.

A burst of laughter startled her mind back into the room, into her own body. The light smelled of paraffin. The body on the bed shuddered.

Carl clapped his hand over Reggie's mouth, whispered fiercely in his ear. They faced the mirror, but the sounds of movement in the other room told Carl it was over. He pushed Reggie angrily aside.

Regina walked slowly down the corridor, her feet dragging.

Pamela stood in the mirror, pale and watery. Her face was uneven, crisscrossed and mismatched by cracks and fissures in the glass. Her hands were held out, open, appealing.

"It's too late," Regina said, her voice old and tired.

Carl nodded, looked accusingly at Reggie.

"I couldn't help it," he protested, shuffling his feet on the dusty floor.

She ignored him, walked forward, and took a blanket from one of the boxes. Carl moved to help his mother. Together they shook the blanket out between them and piously shrouded the picture that was not a picture, the mirror that reflected only the cracked and broken image of the dead.

Quietly, Linda extinguished the last of the lamps. Darkness inhabited the room. A long, unwinding sigh escaped the ravaged body on the bed. The door closed.

They met together in the corridor, silent, tired. Peter turned and slept on.

He was in the empty landscape again, battling against the wind. From this he deduced that he was retracing his way, for the terrain was dark and unchartable. He knew that Linda was not with him, nor other, more terrifying ghosts. This knowledge brought scant comfort. The very place he traveled was loneliness. It was in the wind and the earth beneath his feet. The darkness that pressed around him, which was all he knew of the place, was loneliness itself. This more than the wind, the tiredness, defeated him. He sank down, drew up his knees, and clasped his frozen arms around them. He made small, desolate noises, like an abandoned or wounded animal. The wind snatched them from his parched lips and wove them into its wailing, relentless song.

Sometime later he was lying in his own bed. It felt uncomfortable, as though the mattress needed turning, or he had lain too long. His throat was parched. Something brushed his face, forced his eyelids open. Light exploded. First one eye, then the other. He croaked a protest. The touch was on his arm then. A sharp medical smell. He opened his eyes, tried to snatch his arm away. Cool, strong hands held him.

"Easy, I'm a doctor."

The voice was dry, whispery. He felt a prick and had to close his eyes again.

"Dr. Asmussen. I guess you were expecting me?"

He felt himself drawn deep into the pillows. He reached for the voice, tried to hold the name in his head.

"As-muss-en . . .?"

"That'll hold him for a while," Asmussen said, dropping a swab and the disposable syringe into the bag

Regina held open for him. She did not answer, but looked at Ian. His face was leaner, gray-colored under a stubble of tawny beard. Even as she looked, it lost all expression, became vapid with unconsciousness. "Kind of like old times," Asmussen chuckled. "Remember, Regina, when you used to nurse for me and Alvar?"

Regina remembered. She twisted the neck of the bag closed.

"You can wash in there," she said, indicating the bathroom.

Asmussen nodded. Regina carried the bag into the kitchen and dropped it into the wastebasket. She wondered if it had been wise to send for Asmussen. She had not expected opposition, his niggling, paltry doubts.

"You're sore at me," he said. His bulky, rather shambling frame filled the kitchen doorway.

"Disappointed," Regina corrected him.

"I thought I'd made myself clear," he said, sighing a little. "If we could get the boy to my clinic . . . you have no idea the sort of tests we can run now, Regina."

"Machines," she said bitterly, dismissing them as beneath contempt. "This isn't a clinical experiment."

"No," Asmussen agreed. "That's partly what bothers me. But you know the value of an EEG at the very least."

"You've examined the boy. He's perfectly healthy, you said so yourself." She walked straight at him, her lips compressed with anger. Asmussen stepped aside and nervously ran his hands through the silky shock of sandy hair that was rapidly receding from his forehead. Squaring his shoulders, he ambled after Regina.

She stood on the veranda, looking at the lake. It had a grayish tint, stolen from the overcast sky.

"It's so damn humid," Asmussen commented, running a finger under his soft collar.

"Why are you against me?" Regina demanded. "You of all people."

"Now hold on, Regina. I'm not against you. I just have reservations."

"Enough to prevent me?" She turned to him then and for a moment the years rolled back. Something in the tilt of her head, the nervous clasp of her hands reminded him of the uneasy girl she had once been.

"Could anyone prevent you when your mind is set?" he asked her, smiling.

"Oh Frank." She leaned her cheek against him, clasped his arms. He patted her back gently.

"You know what bothers me most about all this?" he asked quietly.

"No, what?" Alarm lit her eyes. She pulled away from him.

"You—you're too tense, too committed, too high-strung."

"Is that all?" She tried to laugh but could only manage a cracked, uncertain sound. "What do you expect? I've waited a long time for this."

"I know. Shall we?" He touched her elbow, turned her toward the path. She glanced at the bedroom window as they passed.

"How long?"

"He's safe till dusk."

She nodded and walked on.

"Tell me something," Asmussen said, ducking his head beneath a low fir branch. "Why is it so important to have me here?"

Regina did not answer at once. Her face worked, unseen by Asmussen, as she sought the right answer from the many possible ones.

"Because I want a reliable and responsible witness when I succeed."

"*If* you succeed," he reminded her.

Her natural restraint snapped.

"You've always doubted me," she said, her voice harsh.

"That's not true. I know just how able you are. But in this, Regina. Can you tell me why? What will you gain from this?"

"Oh, Frank, really. You can't be serious."

"I mean you personally," he said, refusing to be distracted.

"You think I have some personal motive? You know my work, everything I've done. Have I ever acted from personal motives?"

"No," Asmussen said, crossing his fingers, since experience had taught him never to deceive Regina and the last thing he wanted was to make her angry. "That's why I ask you now."

Regina stopped. The path widened, giving a partial view of the lake. She waited until Asmussen drew level with her.

"We who are able," she began quickly, "have a responsibility to push ourselves as hard and as far as possible. Don't you believe that?" Her familiar look demanded an answer. Asmussen nodded. "Then what other reason do you need? Alvar taught me, taught you, if it comes to that, to value my abilities and always to extend them. This is my big push, Frank. And if there must be a personal motive, think of Alvar. Is there any better way I could serve my kind than by reaching him?"

Asmussen exhaled slowly and looked down at the lake.

"But will it be helping him? Have you thought of that?"

Regina turned impatiently away and hurried on along the path. Shaking his head Asmussen followed after her. He had begun to sweat uncomfortably.

"You never married, Frank. You couldn't understand. And of course, although I have the greatest respect for you, you aren't Alvar."

"I never claimed to be," he said, stung by her

259

reproach. God knew he valued Alvar Thomas, as a scientist and as a man, but there were limits. There had to be.

"But if you were, you could not ask such a question. *I* know."

Asmussen held his tongue. He had meant it when he said that nobody could stop her when her mind was set, but now he felt it or rediscovered it. If anything, her will had grown stronger and, he feared, more intractable over the years. At the gate, he put his hand on her shoulder.

"Regina, one last question."

"Yes?" She sounded indifferent.

"What do you want me to do?"

Her hands clenched on the top rail of the gate. When she spoke, her voice trembled a little.

"When he gets here he may need you, a doctor. I can't tell." She turned toward him, suddenly imploring. "You're the only one I can trust."

Asmussen hoped his face did not betray him. He felt revulsion, fear. He cleared his throat.

"I'll check the boy, stand by. More than that . . ."

"Nothing else is required of you," she said, swinging the gate open. "And afterward you can make your fortune writing it up."

He started visibly, looked at her to see if she was joking. Her eyes laughed at him. A nerve danced in her left cheek.

"Regina, even if you succeed, I can't write this up. You must know that."

"I don't see why." She tossed her head, flicking hair from her face. For the first time Asmussen noticed streaks of silver in it.

"You must understand."

"Because no one would believe you?"

"That, yes, and—"

"That's why there must be a witness," she said, taking his arm and leading him across the yard.

"Regina," he said carefully, "if you succeed and it were ever to get out, you'd be finished, maybe we all would be."

"No." She shook her head adamantly. "Only me, only I can do this. And it's my decision to do it. Anyway, I may not be around to suffer any consequences. So you see you must write it up. And you must make it clear that it is all my doing." She smiled at him, her eyes shining. He had thought that she had never looked more handsome, more wonderfully alive. But after her words the sight appalled him. He shook his head slowly, in disbelief. "You know, Frank," she said gaily, releasing his arm, "you've become an old fuddy-duddy."

Maybe, he thought, watching her bolt into the house, but you, Regina, are beyond reach or reason.

When he awoke, Asmussen was again sitting by his bed, or was it still sitting? He had no sense of time, nor did he recognize the man until he spoke.

"Just take it easy." He took Ian's pulse with cool, capable fingers.

It was dusk. Ian lay weakly against his pillows and studied the man. He was large with a soft, bulky body. Sandy hair spilled around his face as he bent to inspect his wristwatch. He wore light, rimless spectacles which, just then, caught the light, obscuring his eyes. The most remarkable thing about him, though, was his voice. It reminded Ian of dry, rustling leaves. It had a cracked, unhealthy sound that was more immediately obvious than his mid-Atlantic accent.

He leaned over Ian with a thermometer. Ian opened his dry mouth. The man smelled pleasantly of cologne. Then Ian became aware of another smell, delicious, spicy. His stomach gurgled with hunger.

Humming a little in his cracked voice, Asmussen stood at the window, his hands folded behind him, rocking back and forth on the balls of his feet. He smiled broadly as he took the thermometer from Ian's mouth and checked it.

"Uh-huh. Up a little, but I guess you'll live."

Ian put his hand up to his face and was surprised to find a thick growth of stubble.

"How long . . .?" His throat was still dry and he sounded worse than Asmussen. He swallowed, tried to clear his throat.

"Now just take it easy. There'll be plenty of time for talking later. First we have to get some nourishment inside you." Still smiling, Asmussen went to the door. Ian heard whispers and then, with a sudden rush of pleasure, he saw Peter come into the room, carrying a tray with studied care. Steam rose from a bowl on it, and the rich spicy smell became almost unbearable. Ian tried to sit up. At once Asmussen was by his side, helping him, deftly plumping pillows.

"Hello, Dad. I've brought you some soup. Regina made it."

His hands shook as he helped to slide the tray onto his own knees. Peter looked at him gravely.

"Try some orange juice first," Asmussen advised.

Obediently, Ian lifted the glass and drained it off.

"Better fetch some more of that, Peter," Asmussen said.

"Yes, Dr. Asmussen." Peter walked slowly across the room. Something about his movements, the set of his shoulders struck Ian. He moved like somebody exhausted. He looked at Asmussen for an explanation.

"Fine boy, really fine."

"He looks tired," Ian said with difficulty.

"Oh, maybe, but he's healthy enough. At that age they use up a lot of energy. Then I've been working him pretty hard, too."

"Is he . . .?" Ian could not find the right word.

"Try a little of the soup now. It smells good."

"I want to know, is Peter . . .?"

"Later, all right? Little boys have big ears."

His smile was so confident, so reassuring that Ian allowed his anxiety to drain away. He picked up the spoon, conscious of his weakness, and drank a little soup. Peter returned, carrying a jug of orange juice, from which he refilled Ian's glass. He could not make the boy's face out too clearly.

"Could we have some light?" he asked.

"Not yet, I think. It'll trouble your eyes," Asmussen said.

"I'm glad you're better, Dad," Peter said.

"Thanks. How are you?"

"All right."

Was it his imagination or did the boy's voice sound much deeper? I'm becoming obsessed with voices, Ian thought. And that reminded him sharply of something Peter had said, about voices. He let his spoon rest in the bowl.

"Are you really? You seem tired."

"No, I'm great."

"Your voice . . ."

"He's a growing boy," Asmussen said. "You remember. . . ." He chuckled intimately, man-to-man.

Puberty? But surely Peter's voice had broken quite smoothly, almost unnoticeably, ages ago?

"Now let's try a little more soup. We've got to build you up."

Ian needed little prompting. His stomach churned for the food. He looked at Peter as he drank it, but the boy seemed dazed, his eyes compulsively following the movement of Ian's hand but without real interest.

"I don't think he looks too well," Ian said to Asmussen.

"Now don't you worry. There's nothing wrong with that young man that a good night's sleep won't cure."

"Is that so, Peter?" Ian asked.

"What? Sorry."

"I said, are you tired?"

"Yes, a bit." His voice suddenly altered, shed its

vague quality. "We were up late last night, fooling around. Regina told us off."

Asmussen laughed his dry, unpleasant laugh.

"Well, you make sure you have an early night tonight."

"Don't keep on, Dad," Peter said, sounding irritable.

His voice was gruffer, Ian was sure of it. And his tone was that of a petulant young man bored with parental constraints. Ian finished his soup in silence and was surprised to discover how tired he felt as a result.

"More?" Asmussen asked.

"No." He shook his head.

"I'm afraid, Mr. Woodford, you're going to feel rather weak for a day or two, so remember, take it easy."

"It's weird," Ian said. "I feel completely washed out. What's been wrong with me?"

"Oh well, say, Peter, why don't you take this tray out to Regina and then come on back and say good-night?"

"Yes, Dr. Asmussen."

Peter leaned down and grasped the tray. Ian touched his bare arm. The boy seemed confused, not knowing whether to carry on with his task or respond in some way to Ian's touch. It was embarrassment, Ian supposed. He'd reached the stage where he felt too grown up for caresses and hugs. Ian removed his hand apologetically.

"I don't want to talk in front of the boy," Asmussen explained as soon as he'd left the room. "Your body just packed up on you. Delayed shock. Regina's told me . . ." He left the sentence deliberately unfinished, out of sympathy for Ian.

"It's very good of you to take such trouble, and Regina. But is Peter really—?"

"He's just fine. I'll explain in more detail later on."

"Yes, of course."

"It's only natural you should worry, but worry you

must not. I hope you'll put your trust in me, Mr. Woodford." -

Ian didn't quite know what to say and he was relieved that Peter's reappearance removed the necessity to answer at all.

"Regina says I have to go now," he said, "so I'll say good-night."

"All right." Ian stuck out his hand. Peter looked at it as though it was some foreign body, but then he drew closer and, to Ian's surprise, took hold of it and shook it formally. He had a very strong grip.

"I'm glad you're better," he said again.

Ian tried to retain his hand for a moment.

"Thanks, now you get to bed. No hanky-panky tonight. But come and see me in the morning."

"All right, Dad. Good-night, Dr. Asmussen."

"Night, Peter."

They watched him leave, Ian with a sense of loss and recurring anxiety, Asmussen with a smile of pure indulgence.

"Fine boy, Mr. Woodford, really fine."

"I wish he didn't seem so lethargic."

"Well now, I can explain that." Asmussen sat in a chair beside the bed, hitching it closer. "Like I said, I've been working him pretty hard, Mr. Woodford. And then, naturally, he's been worried about you. In addition I should tell you that the physical seizures which accompany the manifestation of Peter's abilities are in themselves pretty debilitating. Since you took sick, the rigid, comatose state, which I understand you're familiar with, has been a daily occurrence. So if Peter seems a little below par, it's really only to be expected. I assure you," Asmussen hurried on, sensing that Ian was about to interrupt, "that I've examined the boy physically, and he's as sound and healthy as any parent could wish."

Ian sighed. All the problems and fears that his period of unconsciousness had blotted from his mind came flooding back. He accepted and understood then the cause of his own illness.

"I appreciate your anxiety," Asmussen repeated, "but I want you to believe that Peter's in good hands. These symptoms of exhaustion are only temporary."

"Thank you," Ian said. "I'm afraid I've got to get used to it all again."

"You've had a bad time. Don't rush yourself. That's an order," Asmussen added, with his dry chuckle.

"Doctor, what's your assessment of Peter, as a 'gifted' boy?"

Asmussen tilted his head back, brought his hands together, and cracked his fleshy fingers loudly.

"You must understand that I'm in no position to make a definitive judgment. For one thing, we're dealing with the unknown. I would be more confident if I had the resources here to run certain clinical tests, but that's not possible. Therefore, my assessment is far from complete, but I believe you have a very gifted boy there, Mr. Woodford, and that his only problem is psychological. Now don't get me wrong—"

"I know," Ian interrupted. "He's scared to admit and accept what he is."

"Right, but you mustn't let that bother you too much. It's common in children who have had to grow up out of step with so-called normal society."

"Yes, I know. But can you help him?"

"Mr. Woodford, I'm going to be straight with you. I'm a cautious man. Mine is a cautious profession, and I learned long ago to be very careful in all investigations into the paranormal. To rush something like this is to risk alienating both the individual concerned and society. You understand?"

"Yes, I think so."

"So, I'm not holding back on you. I don't know. Without the physical resources of my clinic, I can only tackle the psychological problem. I have high hopes there and if Peter will once release and share his abilities, I feel there's a good chance we shall have the answers to all your questions."

"Thanks for being so honest, Doctor. I appreciate it."

"Well," Asmussen said, standing up and placing his chair against the wall, "I guess that's enough for now. You see, Mr. Woodford, your help is vital in getting Peter to accept, and for that you've got to get fit and well again."

"I feel better already," Ian told him.

"Sure you do, but rest is essential. Rest, no worries, and lots of good food. Now I'll tell you what I'm going to do. I know Regina wants to visit with you and I'll have her bring you a couple of sleeping tablets. All right?"

Ian nodded, though he did not feel the need for anything to help him sleep.

"You and I will talk some more," Asmussen promised.

"Thank you again, Doctor." Ian held out his hand and Asmussen, smiling, shook it.

"Glad to know you, Mr. Woodford. We'll have you up and about in no time. Now, I'll go fetch Regina."

Ian leaned toward the lamp and snapped it on. He had to close his eyes against the sudden, sharp light. Even so slight an effort taxed him. He lay back against the pillows, breathing heavily.

Regina came in a few minutes later. Ian noticed immediately that she had lost weight, almost dramatically so. Her face in particular seemed dwarfed by the mane of untidy hair which surrounded it and her long, familiar caftan no longer hinted at those full, womanly curves.

"I've brought your pills and some more orange juice. Try to drink it. How are you feeling?"

"Washed out," he told her, "but better."

"You had a good talk with Asmussen?"

"Yes. He was very kind."

"He's a good man. Here." She held out the tablets and a glass of orange juice.

Propping himself up on one elbow, he swallowed the pills and emptied the glass. Regina immediately refilled it.

"I mustn't stay long. He wants you to rest. There's some mail for you, by the way." From the pocket in her dress, she pulled out three or four envelopes and placed them on the bed. Ian touched them but without curiosity.

"Thanks for all you've done," he said.

"Don't be silly. You just get well, and above all don't worry about Peter."

"Asmussen seems to confirm your view."

"Yes." She smiled vaguely and pushed the hair out of her face.

"How long have I been . . .?"

"Four days. I was worried about you. I was going to get the village doctor, but then Frank arrived and, well, I have more faith in him."

"It was good of him to come."

"You must rest now, Ian. Linda will come over early to give you a good breakfast. Asmussen says you can probably get up for a while tomorrow and sit in the sun."

"And Peter? What do you think about Peter now?"

She hesitated a moment and when she spoke it was with barely suppressed excitement.

"I think we're nearly there. Another few days and we'll break through, you'll see."

"I hope you're right. You look tired, Regina."

"I have been rather busy." She sounded cross. "It's nothing. Now I must go or Asmussen will read me the riot act. It's good to see you better, Ian. Take care."

"Thanks. And you, Regina."

When he was alone, he lay listening to the sounds of their departure. Soon the house was still and quiet. He felt his chin experimentally and thought that the first thing he would do when he got his strength back would be to shave and have a long, hot bath. The pills, though, were already taking effect. He reached toward the lamp. As he did so, he caught sight of the letters Regina had brought him. He should look at them at least. Two were circulars, forwarded on. One was a routine letter from Jim Hasell about progress at the yard. He did not read it carefully, but noted that there were several things requiring his attention. They would have to wait. The fourth and last letter was written in an unfamiliar, gothic-style script. Opening it, he looked at once at, and was surprised by, the signature. It began—

Dear Mr. Woodford,

I have decided to write to you after long and careful thought. I have information which, I feel, I should pass on to you. It is, of course, confidential, and so I am reluctant to communicate it to you by letter or telephone. I would be grateful, therefore, if you would come and see me at your earliest convenience.

The information concerns your son. In giving it, I am in breach of the strict confidence of my profession, but I am satisfied that Pamela's sad death and your inevitably difficult relationship with Peter justify my doing so.

I shall look forward to hearing from you.

Yours sincerely,
Elsa Rath

Ian read the letter through twice. The second time the painstakingly formed characters began to swim and dance. He fumbled it back into the envelope, wondering what information Elsa Rath could possibly regard as so important that she would break professional confidence. It would make sense to go to London for a day or so, he thought, as soon as he felt up to it. He could see Jim Hasell. The effort of thinking, planning, was too much for him, though. He let his mail slip to the floor and just managed to turn the light off before sleep claimed him.

A few days later Liz met Graham Fairlie in a quiet and nondescript wine bar. He had described it on the telephone as the "rendezvous" and had given her very precise instructions about finding it. The whole meeting had a clandestine air about it, which partly amused, partly excited Liz. However, her first thought on meeting Fairlie was that only another man, perhaps only a father, could have described him as personable. Tall, lank-haired, he had a domed forehead, foxy eyes, and almost no chin at all. She did not doubt, though, that his background and prospects were impeccable. He annoyed her by making a fulsome speech about her father, how much he respected him, what a pleasure it was to help him out and, of course, to meet Liz, about whom he'd heard so much. She cut him short.

"Were you able to discover anything about these people?"

"Indeed." He patted a smart leather executive case and treated Lix to what she supposed was a conspiratorial smile. "But, first, what will you have to drink?"

Since there was an open bottle on the table, Liz replied that she would have whatever he was having, which turned out to be a slightly sweet hock. The sort of wine, she could not help thinking, that her father would have dismissed as "effete."

"The thing is," Fairlie began, after she had commented favorably on the wine, "I'm not at all clear what you are looking for. So, what I've managed to come by might be rather a disappointment."

"I'm not sure myself," Liz told him honestly. "If I could just have a look at what you've found?"

"Of course." He made no move, however, to open

270

the document case. "It's rather complicated. There's quite a lot of reading, I'm afraid. I suggest, with your permission, that I give you a sort of précis, then, when you've had time to study the documents fully, you could perhaps ask questions."

"Whatever you like," Liz said. Just as long as we get on with it, she thought impatiently.

"Very well." At last he sprang the brass locks on the case and extracted a folder. It was disappointingly slim, Liz thought. From it he pulled two sheets of paper, neatly typed and stapled together. He cleared his throat, excused himself, and then said, "I propose to begin with Mrs. Regina Thomas, née Carlesen, possibly actually Schmiessen, if that's all right with you."

Liz nodded curtly.

"She was the rather easier subject. Anyway, Mrs. Thomas, as she is known, was born a citizen of Denmark. She currently holds a British passport, granted on the grounds that her mother was English. Before that, by her marriage, she was an American citizen. Of her early life I've been unable to discover much. In 1940 she was transported to Germany and placed in what the Nazis called 'an experimental research camp.' I think one can safely regard that as a euphemism, but we'll come to that later. All records pertaining to the activities in the camp were allegedly destroyed before the Allies occupied Germany. Mrs. Thomas was officially classified a Jewess, though actually only her father is or was Jewish." He rustled the pages, cleared his throat. "After the occupation there is no trace of her until 1949 when she entered the United States. Shortly afterward, she married one Alvar Thomas, supposedly an American national. More of that anon. Are you following me so far?"

"Yes," Liz said.

"Good, because it gets rather complicated now. After their marriage, the Thomases traveled around a great deal and once again there's no substantial record of their activities. However, they finally settled in Oregon and established a clinic there for psychical research." Liz leaned forward expectantly. "The work carried out there was not widely publicized. Indeed, the Thomases appear to have shunned publicity, although Alvar Thomas published a number of articles in specialist journals during that time."

"Was this genuine stuff?" Liz interrupted. "I mean, did Thomas have any credibility?"

"Difficult to say," Fairlie replied, tugging at his ear. "It's not a field noted for reliability. However, for what it's worth, he was published in the leading journals pertaining to the field, so I suppose one may assume he was persona grata."

"Please go on," Liz said.

"Well, in Oregon in the mid-fifties, they apparently began to attract publicity willy-nilly. A number of small items began to appear in the local press. Letters from local people, a few questioning items by local reporters, that sort of thing. It appears that the clinic acted as a sort of hostel for exceptional children and young people, that is, persons claiming to have paranormal powers or whatever. Mrs. Thomas seems to have acted as a sort of housemother. Anyway, there was concern and gossip. The usual sort of stuff. The Thomases maintained that it was groundless, that people were simply mistrustful because they didn't understand. One suspects it would all have ended there had not one young woman who claimed to have escaped from the clinic, contacted a local newspaper and leveled certain accusations against the Thomases."

"What sort of accusations?" Liz asked, feeling excited.

"Sorry, I've only managed to get references to the girl's claims, not the actual stuff itself. But I think we may conclude that the gist of her complaint was that the

Thomases' work was—shall we say—less than strictly scientific?"

"But was she telling the truth?"

"Hard to say. The Thomases resisted a formal investigation on the grounds that the girl had already brought them such bad publicity that they had lost most of their clients anyway. And this seems to be true. Parents who had entrusted their children to the Thomases withdrew them, and various funding agencies and philanthropic individuals withdrew their support."

"So?" Liz prompted him.

"So, the Thomases closed down. They traveled again. Alvar Thomas appears to have lived by lecturing and writing articles. On two occasions they attempted to set up similar clinics, but the press was digging around, as you'll see in a moment. Meanwhile, Thomas began to make frequent trips to Europe, to lecture. He visited this country on two occasions, as well as France, Germany, and Scandinavia. In fact, he was on his way here when he was killed in a totally unexplained motor accident."

"I see," said Liz. "What did she do then?"

"Well there's rather more to it than that. You see, in a sense, if the press is to be believed, Alvar Thomas never existed."

"What do you mean? You've just said . . ."

"Yes, I know, and this is the bit I'm still checking on. I hope to have something a bit more concrete in a few days."

"I still don't follow."

"No, well . . ." He opened the folder and drew out a photostat of a newspaper article. "I think it would be easiest if you read this."

Liz held out her hand eagerly.

"Before you do, I should explain that this man Myerson became interested in the Thomases in Oregon and seems rather to have pursued them. I think in all

fairness one must regard this as rather dubious journal-
ism, but even so . . ." He handed the article to Liz,
who immediately began to scan it.

It was written by one Stanley Myerson and began
with a brief résumé of the Thomases' activities in
Oregon, offering no more factual evidence than Fairlie
had already given her. But it continued:

Whereas the authorities in Oregon were content
as well as relieved to see the Thomases pack their
bags and leave, I was not. Nor do I believe that the
people of California will be happy to take in the
Thomases until certain questions are answered.
That they plan to set up another research clinic
there, with the same avowed aims as those voiced
in Oregon is an open secret. Those aims are simply
stated: "To provide refuge for those exceptionally
advanced persons whose powers are not understood by society at large; to study those powers
scientifically; to aid individual adjustment to the
possession of those powers; and to educate society
at large into a proper, caring acceptance of such
persons."

It sounds good, but it does not tally with the
evidence of Marlene Tyson, who escaped from the
Oregon clinic and made serious allegations which
the Thomases have never satisfactorily answered.
Prompted by Tyson's story, which I believe, I have
been asking a few questions of my own and looking
into the background of these two philanthropic
people.

It is no secret that Regina Thomas, née Carlesen, was placed by the Germans in a so-called
special clinic in 1940. She is a Jewess. The clinic
was undoubtedly not far removed from the infa-
mous camps of Auschwitz and Buchenwald. But it
had a declared aim: "To study the mental and
paramental, psychic abilities of those especially

gifted persons and to explore ways in which these abilities may be used or learned to aid the Aryan cause." Regina Carlesen survived that clinic, disappeared, only to turn up here in the States.

I've been looking into that clinic. It was run by an honorary captain of the Hitler SS: Gunther Schmiessen. Even before he became a promising young medical student, a disciple of Freud with a special interest in the paranormal, Schmiessen was a prominent member of the Nazi League of Youth. The clinic was handsomely funded and solely under Schmiessen's direction. Unfortunately all records of the work carried out there were destroyed before the Allies got to it. Schmiessen disappeared. So did Carlesen. But photographs survive, photographs of Gunther Schmiessen at all ages, in and out of uniform. I have some of those photographs in my possession and will place them before the requisite authorities at any time.

I am certain that Gunther Schmiessen and Alvar Thomas are one and the same man. Regina Thomas has never denied her years in the clinic, or knowing Schmiessen, or that she was his star pupil. This evidence, of course, is Thomas's strongest card: his wife would never marry her persecutor, but the photographic evidence cannot be denied. Nor can the fact that there are no records, state or federal, prior to 1948, of Alvar Thomas's existence. Where did he get his passport? Where was he before 1947? We must also ask, where is Gunther Schmiessen? Vanished, off the face of the earth, a few years before Alvar Thomas is apparently "born," fully grown, an adult with no previous history. Is it mere coincidence that Thomas and Schmiessen should look alike, should have a relationship with Regina Carlesen, should share an almost identical fascination with the paranormal?

I challenge Alvar Thomas to answer these

questions publicly, and if he should fail to do so, I call for a full police inquiry into his documents and activities.

Her thoughts whirling, Liz put the article down and drank some wine. Fairlie studied her face.

"Pretty strong stuff, eh?"

"Is it true, substantially?"

"I can't answer that. Even if it is . . ." He opened the folder again and pulled out another sheet. It was a photocopy of two small items, set one above the other. Liz took it and read it. The first piece announced the suicide of Stanley Myerson, some three weeks after the publication of the article Liz had just read. The other reported the findings of a police investigation of his suicide which seemed at pains to stress that no evidence, material or otherwise, had been found in Myerson's possession to substantiate his claims against Dr. Alvar and Mrs. Regina Thomas, both of whom had cooperated fully with the investigating officers.

"It all rather peters out, I'm afraid," Fairlie said.

"What is this confirmation you hope to get?" Liz asked, returning the sheet to him.

"Well, I've been inquiring among our American friends to see if I can discover anything about Thomas or Schmiessen. He had a passport, so he must have gotten it from somewhere. I'm afraid it's the only lead left."

"Yes, of course. Thank you."

"Don't get your hopes too high."

"No, I won't. And that's it?"

"Yes, apart from the rather interesting fact that shortly after her husband's death, Mrs. Thomas left the country and has now voluntarily surrendered her American passport. Strictly between ourselves, and very much off the record, I gather the Americans weren't exactly sorry."

"And what is she doing now?"

"Nothing to attract attention," Fairlie said confidently. He collected the papers together and placed them all in the folder, which he then handed to Liz. "There you are. I hope it's of some use."

She held the folder, thinking.

"I'm not sure. It's such an extraordinary story. Anyway, I'll get in touch if there's anything I don't understand once I've read this."

"Jolly good."

Liz finished her drink and prepared to go. Her respect for Fairlie had greatly increased and she regretted her earlier reaction to him. She shook his hand warmly and, clutching the folder, left the wine bar. She felt confused, excited certainly, but there was already an undertow of fear.

The days of Ian's convalescence made Frank Asmussen more and more anxious. He had the scientist's love of knowledge for its own sake, but over the last few years he had come to believe that knowledge was useless unless it could be applied elsewhere. For the life of him, he could not see what possible application this knowledge of Regina's could have. Indeed he was not even sure that it could be called "knowledge" at all. He was facing, for the first time in his professional life, a moral dilemma. The situation was complicated by his growing regard for Ian Woodford and a nagging concern for Peter. He had satisfied himself that the boy could take it physically, but Regina's experiment, as he thought of it, was open-ended. Nobody could say where it would lead, and this fact did not bother Regina at all.

He was forced to acknowledge, too, that his attitude to Regina had changed. At first he had been a devoted follower, young and impressed by Alvar's work, her fierce determination to explore an area of human ability that most professional people ignored or scoffed at. He had been saddened by Alvar's violent death and Regina's decision to leave America, but these feelings had been countered by the honor and excitement of carrying on their work. Then, as contact with Regina had become more sporadic—the occasional letter, a biennial two- or three-day visit—the work had become truly his, although he hadn't the means to pursue some of Alvar's more ambitious schemes, nor was the climate right. In his heart of hearts, Asmussen did not regret this. A kid like Griselda now, with her kinetic powers, or Carl, with his exceptionally strong ability to transfer thought, these were worthy and delightful subjects of study.

He was fascinated too by Linda's apparent powers of astral projection. He would like to look into that, especially since—and this qualification made him feel uneasy—he only had Regina's word for it. Once he would have accepted her word without hesitation. Now he forced himself to turn away from his doubts. He had seen Reggie "in action" although he had never encountered anything like it before and there had been no time to study the boy properly on any of his visits. Yet he could not doubt that the boy had caused him to see things that were not there with the clarity and intensity of a dream—or nightmare, he thought ruefully. Asmussen had noted, too, that things Reggie conjured to a person's sight were invariably a manifestation of their deeply hidden fears. But this present scheme of Regina's was altogether something else. He shook his head. There was no avoiding it, no matter how much he might wish to do so.

It had always been there. She had spoken of it long and often, and as a theory, a possibility, of course it appealed to him. But there had been so much against it—the remote possibility of her ever getting all the necessary pieces together was only one of them—that he had never taken it seriously. He felt now that he should have because it had become an obsession with Regina. She was proof against all argument, all reason. That disturbed him and it forced him to see that, during the years of lessening contact, he had failed to give her enough consideration. Now he did not like what she had become, although he really didn't blame her. Working with the able, the gifted, he was well placed to understand the pressures they suffered, how easily they could be tipped, or could tip themselves over the edge.

Nor was he, even now, entirely against the experiment. With the full cooperation of Ian Woodford, he realized, many of his unscientific objections would be removed. And those were the ones that gave him most bother. Scientifically, he did not believe it would come off anyway. But now time was running out. Ian had told him that morning that he was planning to go to London. Of course he had business there, but Asmussen had also easily discovered that Regina had been pushing her inhibiting theory again. Besides, Asmussen knew that what Regina regarded as the most propitious day—the anniversary of Alvar's death—was approaching. Thus Asmussen tramped aimlessly and uncomfortably through the fields behind Home Farm, trying to square his conscience.

If Asmussen had a weakness, it was that he liked to please the majority of the people most of the time. He knew, with a sinking feeling, that in this case to do so would require a degree of compromise on Regina's part. And he feared that she would not compromise, which left him with two alternatives. He could simply leave, wash his hands of the whole affair. Regina might cut off the flow of cash that essentially funded his work, but he guessed a good lawyer could deal with that, under the terms of Alvar's will. He could also warn Woodford and, if asked, advise him to back out, immediately. He was a little surprised to discover that he would give such advice, but there it was. The difficulty was that, no matter how grave and strong his doubts about the whole business, he did not want to act behind Regina's back. She'd done too much, both for him personally and for the cause of all able people, for him to be able to quench his loyalty entirely. There was nothing, then, but to suggest a compromise.

He turned around, determined now, and walked toward the Farm. If she refused, he could pack his bags and get out by nightfall. He shelved the question as to whether he would speak to Woodford. That was a hurdle he would face when he came to it.

Asmussen knew that Peter was over at the cottage with his father, and that Regina had set the others to prepare the barn loft. He could hear them, talking and laughing, as he entered the yard. The big double doors of the loading bay were open.

"Hey," he called, craning his neck back, shouting up to them. "Is Regina there with you?"

A moment later she appeared in the entrance, her face flushed, with wisps of straw in her hair.

"What is it?" she asked, looking down at him.

"Can I have a word?"

Her face immediately took on a closed, cautious expression, but she nodded and withdrew into the shadows. Asmussen did not think that she had probed his mind, but then she scarcely needed to. He walked reluctantly into the shade of the barn, where everything smelled warm and comfortable, like the best bits of childhood, and watched her slowly descend the steps. She was wearing pants and a loose shirt. She had continued to lose weight and every day there seemed to be more gray in her hair. If only on the grounds of her own health . . .

"Yes?" She stopped a few feet from him. Her manner and voice made him feel hopeless. She knew what he wanted to say and had no intention of changing her mind. Asmussen knew then, as surely as he knew his own name, that all the cards were stacked against him. He felt a flicker of fear, but dismissed it at once. Of one thing he was absolutely certain: he was completely safe.

"Can we talk?"

"If it's about—"

"Regina, listen, you owe me the courtesy of hearing me out at least."

She sighed, apparently in agreement, but at the same time she managed to convey to him that it was a courtesy she found irksome. She walked past him, into the sunlight of the yard, and began to twist her loose hair into a knot.

"Very well, I'm listening."

"You know, though I haven't entirely spelled them out, that I have reservations about all this."

She nodded, but went on fixing her hair.

"I've been thinking. I've given the whole project a very great deal of careful thought, and I have a proposal to make."

"Frank, I don't think you're in a position to make proposals. You're here as an observer. True, I may need you, *he* may need you, but . . ." She shrugged, dismissing him.

"All I ask is," Asmussen went on, ignoring the fact that she had just put him very firmly in his place, "that you put Woodford completely in the picture. Tell him everything or, if you'd rather, I'll do it."

She let her hands fall from her hair and looked at him with a troubled expression. Then she went to him and linked her arm through his, leading him farther into the sunshine.

"You think I haven't considered that? Of course I have." She was suddenly all sweet, malleable reason. "I appreciate his position, but all this has nothing to do with him. He's just unfortunately caught up in it. He's an intelligent, reasonable man and I'd be happy to take him into my confidence, if it weren't for the fact that he simply couldn't take it."

"Are you so sure?" Asmussen put in quickly, before she could list the other objections he knew she had

ready and marshaled. "After all, it's the classic parental situation. You and I have handled that all our lives. I
don't believe Woodford's so very different."

"But I know him much better than you. He's only an
adoptive parent, remember. He has his own problems
with Peter, guilt, resentment. No, Frank, to tell him
would only distress him."

"But Regina, you may have to tell him. I mean, you
can't be absolutely certain what's going to happen."

"Then I'll tell him, if and when it becomes necessary.
But now, no. I'm sorry, but it would hinder everything.
It wouldn't help Ian, Peter, or me. Apart from anything
else, Frank, you seem to have forgotten how greatly he
inhibits the boy." As Asmussen stared at her, she put
her hand up to her hair again.

"Regina," he said, pitching his voice carefully, "what
is there to inhibit?"

For a split second she looked confused, but then
seemed to shake it off with a laugh.

"Oh, you know what I mean. Now, Frank, please,
there's so much to do. Let's not talk about this
anymore, okay?"

She did not wait for his reply, but hurried back to the
barn. Puzzled, Asmussen watched her go. He did not
want to believe that she had completely lost touch with
reality but he could not avoid wondering if she had
come to accept her own lies. For he knew that Peter
was not gifted, that he had no more abilities than
Asmussen himself. As he walked toward the house he
tried to imagine that her remark had been a simple slip
of the tongue, that perhaps it didn't matter anyway. He
had tried and failed, and went up to his room to pack.

A conscience, Asmussen decided later, was a trouble-
some thing. You couldn't walk away from it and it made
you deceitful. After he'd packed, he'd gone downstairs
and eaten his evening meal with Regina and the children. He had not mentioned leaving. He wouldn't allow

himself to admit that he was afraid, but it was simply a fact that he could not leave without telling Woodford. And if Regina suspected for one moment, she would try to prevent him. It would be better all round if Woodford drove him to the station, or to a hotel, just for tonight. He lingered over his coffee, smoking a cigar and trying to act as normally as possible. But he felt guilty and tense. Damn his conscience. If he could only see the whole thing as a scientific experiment. But he could not, it *was* not. He stood up and announced, as casually as possible, that he was going to stretch his legs. Nobody seemed very interested.

Outside, the barn's shadow stretched across the yard. The hens had already gone to roost.

"Hi," he said as he passed Reggie. The boy was sitting on a sawhorse, idly whittling a piece of wood. He looked up as Asmussen passed, said nothing, but he did not take his eyes off the doctor, who could feel them as he crossed the yard. He had already decided to take the long way round to the cottage, in order to allay suspicion. Once on the track, he made himself whistle tunelessly, as though he hadn't a care in the world.

Reggie stood up slowly, watched Asmussen's receding back. He dropped the piece of wood and snapped the knife shut. His legs felt weak. He could feel the beads of sweat on his forehead. The air pressed against him, impeded him as he staggered toward the farmhouse. He could see it all, and he wanted to escape it.

"Regina." He gasped out her name, hanging in the kitchen doorway. She went to him immediately, recognizing the tone. She took his pale face in her hands gently, and raised it toward her.

"What is it, Reggie? Quickly, tell me."

His shirt was soaked. His muscles clenched and trembled.

"Reggie?"

"Asmussen," he said, gasping for air. "Asmussen, he's . . . Asmussen . . . Death."

His head fell forward onto her shoulder. For a brief moment, Regina comforted him.

"Linda," she said, over the boy's head, "check his room, quickly. Carl, help me."

Linda ran out and up the stairs. Carl helped Regina guide the stumbling, sagging boy to a chair.

"He'll be all right now," she said, raising Reggie's head and holding it upright.

"All his cases are packed. He means to leave," Linda said as she hurried back into the kitchen.

Regina looked at each of them in turn. Carl blinked rapidly. Grizzle threw down the cloth she was holding. Beneath her hands, Regina felt Reggie become calm and still.

"Go along," she said quietly. "You know what you have to do."

Damn it, Asmussen thought as he saw Linda. She was standing on the terrace in front of Halford Hall, waving to him. He pinned a smile to his face and waved back, but he kept on walking. It was only then that he asked himself how she could have gotten there ahead of him, without his having seen her. She was in the kitchen when he left. He looked again. She was there all right, waving and smiling, beckoning to him. He had no intention of leaving the track or of abandoning his purpose. Then, suddenly, there was grass under his feet and he was approaching the Hall. He could hear Linda now, calling his name. He stopped and looked warily about him. The main drive seemed much farther away than he remembered.

The pain began then, at the nape of his neck. Like a clenched fist it opened, spread across the back of his head, onto the crown, like sharp fingers probing.

"Dr. Asmussen."

It was easier if he kept walking toward her, though everything seemed to tremble like a mirage.

He knew too much about it for this to be possible. He

could resist them. Besides, they wouldn't do anything to him. He was perfectly safe.

She was at the top of the steps, holding out her thin, pale hand to him. He saw the steps, every crack and fissure, every minute green organism that made up the neglected lichens. He saw as though his nose was all but pressed to the steps. He hung over the balustrade, looking down at the green grass, wanting to throw up.

"Dr. Asmussen."

Her voice was soft as a breeze brushing his ear. His head was swelling with the pain. She helped him up the steps. The shadow of the house struck him as unusually cold. He walked along the terrace, trembling. His skull was being pushed outward. He had a monstrous, large dome of a head on his shoulders. He put his hands up to his head and saw, as though it was an event entirely unconnected with him, his spectacles fall to the ground.

A door swung open. He felt a stale, cold breath. He knew that the house was evil. This beckoning, pulling house contained all that was unthinkable and terrible. He fought against it. He still had some will. Nothing would make him go in there.

"No," he said. It came out as a cracked whisper. He backed off from the house, backed right across the terrace until the sharp coping of the balustrade caught the small of his back. He stretched out his arms, tried to grip the stone.

He saw them then, coming slowly across the grass, strung out like herders or drovers. Carl, Reggie, Griselda.

"Help me," he whispered.

As though made of air, Linda was beside him, taking his arm. The pain increased. Lights flashed before his eyes. The doorway became an enormous black hole, a whirlpool sucking him in. He heard his own screams almost as if they came from outside his body. Linda released him and he pitched forward into the blackness. The house closed around him, holding him fast.

For a moment, Linda regarded his face. The features were twisted horribly out of place as though by some irresistible pressure.

At the end of the terrace, at the top of the steps, Grizzle and Carl and Reggie joined hands.

Asmussen felt his head jerk and swell. The pain increased until unconsciousness threatened. He thrashed about the dusty floor. The dark emptiness of the house clawed at him. Asmussen had never believed in evil. All his life he had scoffed at it, but it was evil that he knew in the last brief moments before his head exploded.

Linda watched the skull crack open like a ripe melon, spewing blood and gray jelly into the darkness. She closed the door quietly. The house seemed to settle as she picked up his broken glasses, smiling.

Half an hour late, gown flapping, Liz's father entered his chambers. Through the glass doors of his severely modern office, Liz watched him barking orders, distributing papers with a contained authority. Only when all the tasks had been allocated, everyone set to work, would he come into the office, find time for her. But when he did, she knew that she would have his undivided attention.

He came whirling into the room but when he closed the door it was as though all responsibility dropped from him. He leaned against the door, looking at her.

"Elizabeth, I'm so sorry. They told you?"

"That you were delayed in court, yes." She walked over to him and automatically helped him off with his gown.

"Thank you."

While she hung the gown up, he crossed the room and, bending from the waist, opened a low cupboard.

"Sherry?"

"Isn't it a bit early?" Liz queried.

"I'm calling it a day," he announced firmly. "Evening starts as of now."

"Then I'd rather have a small scotch."

"So be it." He began to pour the drinks. When they both had a glass, he settled behind his large desk, sipping sherry gratefully.

"I feel like a client," Liz said, sitting opposite him.

"In a way I suppose you are."

"You spoke to Branscombe?"

"Yes, but I got the distinct impression that I was treading on delicate ground."

"Oh, how?"

"Oh, you know—not the sort of thing a decent chap brings up. The old boy really didn't want to talk."

Smiling confidentially, Liz said, "But you persuaded him?"

"Yes, but not to much effect, although Thomas did visit this country under the aegis of Branscombe's society."

"And what did they make of him?"

"You mean professionally?"

"Yes."

"I could form no clear opinion. It appears that Thomas rather blotted his copybook. All most unfortunate, but it's the only thing that seems to have stuck in old Branscombe's mind." He leaned forward, lowered his voice and said, "The man also had an eye for the ladies—all very regrettable."

Liz laughed out loud. Her father's impersonation caught exactly a kind of gentlemanly outrage that seemed almost to characterize a certain class of old-guard Englishmen.

"How dreadful," she said, playing up to him. "Was there a scandal?"

"I think we may deduce that there was, all hushed up, of course, but Thomas was persona non grata."

"I wonder what Mrs. Thomas made of that," Liz said.

"Heaven knows. But that's all I could get. Sorry, not frightfully helpful, is it?"

"I suppose not. Did you have time to look at Fairlie's folder?" she asked.

"Briefly, a skim." He pulled the folder toward him and opened it. "This is the photograph you mentioned?" He turned a photocopied page toward her. She glanced at the washed-out, undetailed photograph of Gunther Schmiessen, aged sixteen.

"Yes, that's the one."

"Well, of course, I can't comment, but . . ."

"You think I'm imagining it? I promise you, Daddy, nothing was further from my mind. Why should I connect Peter with this man? It was just that the moment I saw it, I thought, Good God, that's Peter."

"But you've never seen the boy."

"No, I told you, just the photographs Ian carries in his wallet."

"A coincidence," he said, closing the folder. "One boy, given a certain general similarity—especially in a poor reproduction like this—"

"There are too many coincidences," Liz interrupted. "And if Thomas was a womanizer . . ."

"This is a photograph of Schmiessen," he reminded her.

"But if Schmiessen and Thomas are one and the same, as that journalist claimed . . ."

"You don't need me to tell you that none of this would stand up in a court of law. There are too many qualifications, suppositions." He pushed the folder away from him as though he found it distasteful.

"But I don't intend to bring a legal action," Liz said.

"No, which brings us to the big question." He got up and went to the cupboard. "Another?"

"No, I'm fine. Thanks."

He poured himself a second glass of sherry and stood sipping it, looking at Liz.

"Yes?" she said, raising her eyebrows.

"What are you going to do, my dear?"

"I don't know."

"Well?"

"Daddy, I'm scared. No, listen. I know it's all supposition. Not a scrap of proof, but it all adds up either to the most monumental coincidence, or something—"

"Impossible," he said dryly, moving back behind his desk.

"Improbable. Oh, I don't know. It bothers me."

"In that case there is only one thing you can do, isn't there?"

"What?" She looked at him hopefully.

"Lay the whole thing before Woodford and let him make up his mind."

"That's what I hoped you'd say." She stood up, smiling happily.

"You don't think you should wait for Fairlie's American friends to respond?"

"On the passport? No." She shook her head. "What difference would that make? This is either sufficient for Ian or I'm wasting my time."

"Very well, but one thing . . ."

"Yes?"

"Promise me you'll sleep on it."

"But surely the sooner—" She stopped, looked at his closed, rather irritated expression. "Oh, all right. Yes, I promise."

He heaved a dramatic sigh of relief.

"Thank heavens, then you'll be able to accompany me to the opera. I just happen to have two tickets for tonight."

"Honestly, you're incorrigible," she laughed.

"We'll discuss that later. Now, off you go and make yourself presentable. I have a few phone calls to make."

"All right," Liz said. She leaned over the desk and kissed him. "And thank you."

Initially, Ian felt overwhelmed by London. It was too crowded, too busy. He sensed himself becoming irritated and then slightly scared of all the noise and apparently purposeless activity. But as the day wore on and he had to give his mind to various problems, he felt himself adjusting to the faster rhythm. He began to take energy from it rather than feel daunted by it. The rhythm, the whole quality of life at Halford, was fundamentally alien to him. This was his world and he felt himself settling back into it, like putting on a pair of old, comfortable shoes.

"Well, you look better, I'll say that for you," Jim Hasell commented when their business discussions were finished. "First thing this morning I thought you looked fit to drop."

"I've just begun to get used to it all again," Ian said.

"I'm glad. I was beginning to think we'd lost you to the country for good. Not that I've anything against the country, mind."

"I know. It's just that I'm a city bloke and nothing else makes much sense. Not that I'm ungrateful for the chance to get away."

"You'll come back. And bring the boy?"

Ian paused. He wanted to say yes, without qualifications, but Peter . . .

"I hope so. I must, obviously. But I'm not sure about Peter. I may decide to send him away to school."

"Well, I never believed in that, as you know. But it's none of my business."

"It's rather complicated," Ian said, and knew that it sounded feeble.

"What you ought to do is get married again. You're young, not bad-looking. There's plenty of girls would jump at the chance."

"Thanks." Ian stood up. "Tell them for me, will you?"

"You take my word for it. Now where are you off to?"

"I want to clear up one or two things. Then I've got an appointment at six."

"With a lady friend?"

"Well, a lady, certainly. But it's not what you think. And don't you and Edna go marrying me off too soon. It's not as easy as you think."

"Marriage, easy? Come on, lad, it's a mild form of suicide, you know I've always said that."

"Thanks a lot," Ian laughed. "I'll see you tomorrow."

"All right."

In his own office he tried to push the problem of Peter out of his mind and concentrate on the stack of papers on his desk. Maybe the answer was very simple. He would have to leave Peter with Regina and the others, with his own kind. Certainly he could not stay away forever. It wasn't fair to Jim. Besides, he wanted to come back. He realized that though he had never really felt commited to his job, he had missed it. He switched on the Dictaphone machine and began answering letters which his secretary would type tomorrow. Whatever happened, he would have to make a decision soon.

The mirror stood at the foot of the bed, facing the comatose, rigid boy. From it, Pamela's frozen image seemed to appeal, to beseech in vain. Regina felt his resistance grow weaker every time. Now she was impatient with the others, who seemed to lag behind.

Grizzle felt Reggie's mind like a drag on her. She saw whirling colors, faces, back through memories which had, by now, taken on a strange familiarity. Pamela's distraught face in the gallery of the swimming pool,

Regina's smile. The old, painted face, the touch of
hands, alien and warm, lifting the small and soiled body
that was not hers. And after that a blankness, a
contentment. Warm waters washed the body that was
not her body. She felt herself lulled by them.

"Come, come now. Come!"

Regina's voice swelled and echoed, ruling Grizzle's
mind and the other questing, questioning minds that
were linked to hers. She felt Reggie pulling back, and
without knowing it, reached for him. He clasped her
fingers tightly.

"Try," Regina begged. "Try."

Grizzle felt her mind explode through to something.
She saw and did not see. Reggie cried out, threw his
arms around her. Grizzle rocked under his weight, but
her mind would not let go.

The mirror shattered.

She heard Reggie cry, "No. No. No." Over and over
until the word lost all meaning. She felt his arms, the
warmth of his body. She saw the bed through a
glistening, crystalline screen of falling glass, each
fragment no larger than a crumb. A great sigh shook
the house. Windows rattled, lamps guttered. Reggie
gripped her more tightly, moaning. The body on the
bed relaxed.

Glass crunched under Regina's feet as she moved
slowly, almost fearfully to the bed.

Grizzle put her arms round Reggie then. He made
her see faces of dead men, distorted, putrefying.

Regina leaned over the still figure. Her hands
hovered, fluttered, afraid to touch. The familiar blue
eyes flicked open, stared sightlessly out at her, at the
shadow-jumping ceiling.

She spoke his name with the breath of a dying
woman.

"*Ja.*"

The voice was a deep, echoing bass that seemed to

scrape her bones. The blond, despoiled head turned toward her.

"Regina?"

He spoke her name but with a loathing so intense that she fell back from the bed as though struck. The children watched her, shaken, appalled, amazed. Her eyes rolled in her head. Stick arms flailed the empty air.

The figure on the bed stared at her until she covered her face with her arms, and sank down, huddled against the wall. The children stared at her too, knowing that they could not help her. One by one they shuffled out of the room, leaving her alone with the thing, the boy-man she had found at last.

"No. No, I'm sorry, I simply don't believe you. I can't." Ian's voice hovered between shock and laughter.

Elsa Rath stared at her hands. Her face was chalkpale, her hair still piled and sculpted like spun sugar.

"Ask yourself, Mr. Woodford. Please." She paused, raised her hands, dropped them again into her lap. "Ask yourself what possible motive I could have in telling you such a story if it were not true? I assure you I have not the imagination to fabricate such a tale." She said this with no trace of humor in her voice.

"No," Ian burst out. "You ask yourself, Mrs. Rath, what you're asking me to believe. You're telling me in effect that everything my wife told me, the whole basis of our marriage these last few years, was a lie." He stopped, looking at her. She sat, head bowed, silent. "You're telling me that my wife, who couldn't have children, who went to the best specialists in London because she was barren, was not barren. In fact, you ask me to believe that she had a child. You ask me to believe that a woman who was neurotically concerned about being a good mother actually abandoned her own child at birth. Does that sound like Pam? It's ludicrous.

Then, like some kind of morbid fairy tale, you tell me that she found the very child she had abandoned and adopted him. I'm sorry, Mrs. Rath, but only a very active imagination could have invented such a story." Ian crossed and uncrossed his legs, shifted angrily in his chair. Elsa Rath seemed oblivious of him. Only the fact that her eyes were open indicated that she was not asleep. "Well, if that's all you have to tell me . . ." Ian prepared to stand up.

"Please, Mr. Woodford," she said in an old, tired voice. "I have a very great deal to say." She fanned out her hands, sighed and said, "To answer you point by point, your wife consulted specialists, yes, but you did not see their reports. In the opinion of two of them, her condition was psychological. She was afraid to conceive because of her guilt feelings about the child she had borne and abandoned. The third suggested a functional disorder caused by a clumsy attempt to abort the fetus." She glanced at him sharply as he impatiently moved again. "I do not speak of these things lightly, Mr. Woodford. You must believe that. As to your second argument, it is purely a matter of how you look at the facts. I suggest to you that Pamela was a neurotic mother precisely because she had been a bad mother. She was atoning to Peter and at the same time was unable to believe that she would not again be a bad mother. Finally, I cannot tell you—I do not believe that anyone can tell, one hundred percent sure—that Peter *is* Pamela's son, but she definitely believed that he was."

"How could he possibly be?" Ian demanded to know.

"All things are possible, Mr. Woodford. Did not Pamela have a very clear picture of the child, the only child she would adopt? Age, coloring. Did she not search for many months? Did she not always say to you that she would know him when she saw him? She meant the literal truth, Mr. Woodford. No more, no less."

"If—and I'm only saying 'if' because I don't for a moment believe any of this—if what you say is true, why didn't she simply claim Peter as her own?"

"She could not. She feared that she would be condemned by you, and more importantly by the adoption society. You see, she left the baby. She took a room in a cheap boardinghouse, delivered him herself and, as soon as she was able to walk, she left him. If she had admitted that, what would they have done? They would say that she had proved herself an unfit mother if they believed her and if they did not, they would disqualify her on grounds of mental unsuitability."

Ian considered this in silence for a few minutes and then a new thought occurred to him.

"I'm sorry, Mrs. Rath," he said in a steadier voice. "I believe that you are sincere, that you believe what you are saying but, well, has it occurred to you that you were taken in? This is a fantasy Pamela told you. She knew that Peter was found, as a baby, under exactly those circumstances. She just inserted herself into the truth, don't you see, to make you believe—in order to believe herself, perhaps—that she was his real mother."

She looked at him. Her eyes were cold and there were deeply etched lines of tiredness on her face.

"I am trained, Mr. Woodford, to distinguish between fantasy and reality, lies and truth. That is my job."

"With due respect, no one is infallible."

"Indeed they are not."

The silence was awful for both of them. Ian felt that he should go, leave it there, but he could not.

"Quite apart from anything else," he said, "Pamela would have told me, before we were married, if she'd had a child. . . ."

"She bitterly regretted that she did not. At that time, Mr. Woodford, she believed that she was making a new life, a new start. She believed she would have your

295

child. It was only when she failed to conceive . . . Have you never told a lie which grows and grows until it is impossible to take it back?"

"Yes, but what about her family? Surely they wouldn't . . .?"

"You never asked, Mr. Woodford, did you?"

"Of course I did. I . . . I asked."

"You asked about her family and she told you that she had none, except for an aunt she never saw. Pamela was rejected by her parents. She believed that her pregnancy killed her father. She felt responsible for his death. Her mother told her that she had killed him, and she herself died shortly afterward. Pamela believed that her mother died of a broken heart. You did not ask, Mr. Woodford. You were not interested."

"Damn it all," he said, stung by her calm, open criticism, "I wasn't marrying her bloody family."

"No, but you made it easier for Pamela to lie. And once she had begun . . ." Briefly, she closed her eyes.

"You'd better tell me the rest," Ian said tightly.

"The rest?"

"Well, presumably it wasn't an immaculate conception? Presumably there was a man involved."

"Oh yes. She met the man while doing a temporary job. It was a brief, casual affair, a few days. But Pamela was unlucky, he left the country. She appealed to him for help when her parents refused to help her. She did not know what else to do. She received no answer, and then she heard of his death."

"How very convenient!"

Elsa Rath stiffened in her chair. Her large hands became ugly fists, but her voice showed no emotion at all when she said, "Pamela always insisted that you would not understand."

"Oh, I can understand, all right. It's believing that I find impossible. I'm very sorry, Mrs. Rath, but I think Pamela made a fool of you."

"I thought," she said, unclenching her hands, "that

you would feel that. It's quite common, when one has been duped oneself, to assume that everyone else—"

"What the hell do you mean, 'duped'?"

"Doesn't it seem that way to you? You said yourself that I was asking you to believe that the whole basis of your marriage was a lie. Naturally, that pains you."

Ian stood up and walked quickly, angrily across the room. He stared out into the street where cars lined up in the softening sunlight. A young woman passed by, her face lifted toward a man, smiling gently.

"What was this man's name anyway?" he said, offhand, trying to deny that he felt duped, rejected.

Wearily, Elsa Rath said, "What does that matter now? They are both dead."

"So, he doesn't even have a name." He turned around. The gray pile of her hair was just visible over the back of her chair. "Doesn't that make you wonder? Doesn't that make you think this whole story might be a pack of lies?"

She shook her head sadly.

"His name was Thomas, Alvar Thomas. So what?"

Ian felt his heart stop. His throat contracted. He took a step toward her chair and it seemed that the whole room shifted and swung.

The world had fallen to pieces. They were unable to make sense of it, were ill equipped and lost.

Regina shuffled from his bedroom to her own room, back and forth, a series of restless journeys. They glimpsed her but could not reach her. She was an angry ghost, gone from them.

Linda and Carl stood close together, looking into each other's eyes.

"We should do something," she said in a small, frightened voice.

"What?"

"Don't you know?"

"I can't. With her . . . without her . . . Linda?"

She put up her hand and touched the sudden, broken tears which spilled from his eyes.

"I can't do it anymore. It's gone." He sounded amazed, bereft. "It was her, Regina, all along?" His voice rose, making a question of his own uncertainty.

Linda could not answer. She felt something strange in herself, too, something different, but it did not matter compared to the sudden rush of love she felt for Carl. Gently, she comforted him.

In the loft, Grizzle sat huddled, arms around her knees, on a bale of straw. There was a pain in her back, a dark, pulsing throb that made her feel sick. Cramps gripped her stomach. She felt sore and frightened.

Reggie walked around and around the loft, tracing an endless circle of movement. He could not reach anybody. His mind encountered nothing but a dreadful sense of the stranger in their midst, the dead stranger.

Elsa Rath's hand was strong and comforting on his shoulder.

"Can I . . . please I need to use your telephone. It's urgent."

"Of course, in the hall."

He crossed the room in two strides, opened the door, and picked up the receiver. For a moment his mind was blank, then he remembered the complicated sequence of figures that was Regina's number. He snatched at the dial, his finger shaking. He broke the connection and tried again. He heard the click and hum of machinery and cursed its slow, automated pace. The telephone crackled, screamed in his ear. He tried again, forcing himself to be calm, to dial each digit carefully and correctly.

"Damn," he said when the screaming sounded again, hurting his ear. He dialed the operator. There was a long wait. When at last a man answered, he asked for the number, gave Elsa's number, and waited. His hands were cold and damp.

"Sorry, but there's a fault on that line. I'll report it for you."

With a sense of defeat, he lowered the receiver into the cradle.

"Mr. Woodford?"

"I can't get through. I shall have to go now, I'm sorry."

"A moment, please."

"Look, this is urgent."

"Please." Her voice was suddenly strong, commanding. She stepped back into the room, waiting for him. "I only wanted to say"—she hesitated, closed the door behind him—"this has not been easy for me, Mr. Woodford. My training, the practice of a lifetime. It's strange, but I feel I must justify myself to you."

"There's no need, really. I'm sure your motives were—"

Speaking with evident emotion, she cut him off. "I thought this knowledge might help you. I knew that by telling you I would remove the last vestiges of the things that were good in your marriage, but I felt that was necessary, for you and Peter. Pamela's dead now. We cannot help her. I felt my duty was to the boy, to the future. I thought if you could at least accept that Pamela believed he was her own child, it would help you, help you with him and perhaps comfort you a little for the past."

Ian stared at the carpet, traced its complicated, swirling pattern with his eyes.

"I thought," he said, "right from the start, that she had left him to me—a sort of inheritance."

"Yes." She nodded her head slowly. "That is how you should think of it. That is good."

Ian looked at her pale and elderly face. She seemed frail and vulnerable. He could not find the words, any words to thank her, to tell her that it was not as simple as she believed.

"I must go to him," he said.

"Of course." She opened the door, stood back to let him out.

"I'm sorry, I'll . . ."

"No, no. Go to him. Go, he needs you. And Mr. Woodford?"

Ian looked back at her from the front door.

"Good luck."

He stopped twice on that nightmare journey of which, later, he was to remember nothing but the two vain attempts to telephone Home Farm—the line continued to be out of order—that and a curious sense of the car being stationary while the landscape flashed past in a blur. The darkness and the white glare of his own lights, the rushing passage of oncoming lights, receding, coming again, blinding him. And then the closed gates of the Hall, towering above him. He got out of the car and ran to them. Without thinking he seized them, shook them. He was not strong enough to cause any effect. He thought then, for a moment, that it was finished, but almost at once he began to reason. They were not locked. He fumbled for the bar that kept them closed. It swung out of its socket, rattling. It took all his weight to drag one gate open. It scraped in the gravel. The hinges protested. He felt that he had done this before. Panting, he leaned his shoulder against the second gate and forced it open.

He got back into the car and pressed his foot down hard. Gravel spurted from beneath his wheels. At the turnoff to Home Farm, he went into a skid. It seemed as though the car had a life of its own. The lights raked across the somber block of the Hall. It had never seemed more desolate and deserted. He spun the wheel, fought the car, but the house demanded his attention. He could not understand why. Then, more by good luck than judgment, the car straightened on the road. He saw the ruts leading inexorably to the

Farm. He remained aware of the house, on his left, but he did not look at it. He did not dare. At the last moment, he slammed on the brakes as the wooden gate rose up to meet him. The car skidded again, but stopped. The engine stalled. He threw open the door and seized the gate.

"Regina, Asmussen. Regina!" he shouted. As his fingers searched for the catch on the gate, the headlights behind him went out. He was plunged into darkness. He looked back at the car. It was just a silent, deserted shape in the darkness. "Regina. Asmussen. Help me. Help me, for God's sake," he shouted. Then his fingers connected with the cold metal of the catch and he stumbled into the yard, losing his footing.

He righted himself, hearing his own loud breathing. The house was dark, the yard silent.

"Asmussen. Regina." His voice seemed to hang in the air then fade, as though muffled.

The barn door creaked open. He turned toward it, heart leaping. Golden, dim lamplight spilled out, stretching their shadows toward him. Silhouettes. He could not see their faces. They stood a little apart, but with linked hands. He mustered all his courage and went toward them.

"Where's Asmussen?" he demanded. "I must see Asmussen at once."

"He's gone," Linda answered.

"Regina, then."

"We must talk to you."

"No, I've got to see her. I've got important information . . ."

They moved toward him as one. He stepped back instinctively.

"It's too late," Carl said.

"You must help us," Linda echoed him.

"Keep away from me, I can't help you. I have to—where's Peter?"

301

They stopped then and turned, lifted their heads. He followed the direction of their gaze. Light flickered faintly around the cracks of the loft's bay doors.

Starting forward, he said, "I'm going to take him away from here, away from all you . . ."

Carl gripped his shoulder and spun him round with surprising strength.

"Mr. Woodford, you must listen."

"Let go of me. If you think you can . . ." He bunched his fist in readiness.

"She's already done it," Carl said fiercely. "You must understand."

"Help us," Linda begged again.

"Done what? God in heaven, what has she done?" Suddenly he was shaking Carl. The boy's head wobbled on his neck. Linda clawed at Ian's arms. "What?" he shouted. His arms fell away. His chest heaving, he glared at Carl's ashen face.

"She has contacted our father," Carl said, his voice breaking, "my father and Peter's."

"It was a game," Linda said. "We thought it was just a game."

A hundred half-formed, impossible thoughts whirled in Ian's head.

"It's true then. You know?"

"Yes."

"But he's dead, whether he's Peter's father or not. Oh no, no. You're just trying to scare me."

"We're scared," Linda cried.

"You want to delay me. You want to keep me here while—"

"Peter was the vessel," Carl shouted. "Through Peter she believed that she could reach my father."

"Alvar Thomas?"

"Yes, though that is not his real name."

"You can't . . ." Ian started, but then he knew that it was possible. "Pamela . . ." he whispered, remembering the dripping, terrible thing that had stood at the foot of his bed.

"Regina has been watching you for ages," Linda said.

"She had been searching for him," Carl added, "only your wife found him first."

"She watched, followed—everywhere they went."

"When your wife rented this cottage, we came here."

"She said the time was right."

"Stop it," Ian said. "I can't make . . . I've got to see Peter."

Again Carl seized him, tugging at his sleeve.

"We don't know what will happen now. You see, we don't understand anymore."

Linda touched his arm.

"It's no use," she said gently. "You must see for yourself, Mr. Woodford."

"See what?" he almost shouted. "Peter?"

"You will be careful?"

"And help us?" Carl said. "Please help us."

"I don't know how to help you. I just want to find Peter and get out of here."

Linda started forward, into the light, into the barn.

"It's too late," she said. "Come and see for yourself."

Ian searched Carl's face anxiously. After a second of painful indecision, Ian turned and ran after Linda. Carl followed more slowly, as though exhausted.

The lamp hung from a hook set in the side of the steps to the loft. Ian saw Linda pass through the light, into the darkness. He pulled himself up behind her, blinded by the light, and then by its absence. He hauled himself through the entrance, onto the loft floor, and moved aside, to leave Carl room to climb up.

There were three hurricane lamps disposed about the loft floor, but its very size seemed to soak up and swallow the light. Ian blinked, waited for his eyes to adjust. He was aware of Linda moving softly away from him. Carl came up the steps and paused, looking around. Then he followed Linda, who had sat—taken her place, Ian felt—on a bale. The boy stood uncertainly beside her.

They were all there, ranged in a broken semicircle, each sitting on a bale. Reggie, staring at him. Grizzle. His heart pounded. The girl was hunched over, as though in pain. On top of her untidy hair, a white sun hat was perched. Pamela's hat. He took a quick step toward her.

"Grizzle, where did you get that hat?"

"I gave it to her. After all, I have no use for it now."

The voice was instantly recognizable. The timbre, inflection, the slightly breathy quality. He remembered it so clearly. But this was not a memory. He closed his eyes, afraid to turn his head in the direction of Pamela's voice. She laughed softly. He tried to tell himself that it could not be, but he felt the children, especially Carl, willing him to look.

"Peter!"

It was a game, some sort of spooky trickery. He grew calm then, calm with an icy, outraged anger.

Peter sat on the last bale, but even as Ian moved toward him, he became uncertain that it was Peter. The face, the way he sat, everything reminded him of Pam. The cupped, upturned palms in the lap, the legs neatly together. He . . . she . . . lifted her eyes to Ian's face, smiled that slight, uncertain smile.

"I don't think you really liked it anyway, did you Ian?"

"Peter?" He looked helplessly at the boy. For a moment his face went blank. It was like seeing Pam disappear, melt. There was nothing. Then the boy parted his legs, seemed to straddle the bale. He straightened his back, squared his shoulders, lifted his chin with a cold arrogance. His eyes glittered, blazed at

Ian. He jerked his head around in an almost military gesture and spoke rapidly into the darkness. He spoke in a harsh, bass voice, in German, with great rapidity. Ian saw and heard and could not believe. He did not understand German. Only one word made any sense to him: *Regina*.

There was a rustling in the darkness, a sound like a sigh and a cry. She seemed to creep into the light like a terrified nocturnal animal. Her eyes were fixed on Peter. He seemed to compel her. She spoke softly, so softly that Ian could not be sure which language she used. The blond head snapped back, the blue eyes glittered. Ian felt that those eyes could see through him, that he had ceased to exist.

Slowly, as if in pain, Regina drew herself up, one bone-spare hand grasping Peter's shoulder. Ian could barely recognize her. The tumbled, thick hair was now streaked with bands of gray. It was dull and lifeless, as though brushed by cobwebs. And her shriveled face was no larger than that of a small monkey. The skin was blotched with liver marks. Only her eyes, dark and burning, recalled Regina as he had known her. She lifted her head. Her neck was like a stalk, frail and corded. She wore some sort of old, filmy gown, the color of autumn leaves. It drifted, hung about her wasted body.

"My husband wishes to be presented to you," she said, and for a brief time a mocking, hurting smile played around her dry lips.

"No," Ian said, "stop this. Both of you, whatever you're doing . . ."

A hurl of German rattled from Peter's lips. Ian watched, appalled. The boy's features had become coarse. He had the color of a middle-aged man.

"Sprechen Sie deutsch?"

Ian understood the foreign phrase.

"Nein."

Regina leaned forward a little.

"My husband," she hissed. "Herr Gunther Schmiessen. *Hier ist Herr Woodford.*"

Ian shook his head. "No," he screamed, "this is Peter. And your husband . . ."

Her laughter cut him off. Smiling, she whispered into Peter's ear. He snarled an answer. Regina moved away from him.

"Yes, he is Peter, in a way, but he is also Gunther Schmiessen and sometimes, sometimes your dear wife. It was necessary . . ." Her voice, her expression became vague, groping. "It was necessary to change his name. You know of him as Alvar Thomas. But now, now . . ." She became confident again. Her voice took on a dark, dangerous throb. "Now he is Gunther Schmiessen, my husband. My lord and master. The man with whom I worked in Germany, during the war. The man who made me love him." She stared at Ian. "You don't believe me," she said, sounding confused once more. "That's because you don't understand. Peter, you see, was the vessel. The perfect vessel. Through him, the love child, I knew I could reach my man. I could not do it alone. He would not come for me. Oh no, not for me. No. No." Her voice sank, trembled, partly cruel, partly despairing. "He would not come back for me. *She* saw to that, your wife, the pretty little Pamela. But for his son . . ." She looked briefly at Peter, taunting him. "For the son I had deprived him of, he would come back. For his bastard!" Her voice rose, a shriek of hate and grief.

"Mother." Carl stepped forward. His body was shaking, his mouth hung open.

She faced her son, her terrible eyes fixed on Carl.

"It was for you, too. If you were man enough, agh, don't you deny me now."

Carl hung his head, broken, unable to face the thing she had become. Her frail, ridiculously overdressed body swayed a little. She seemed literally to be holding herself together, holding collapse, disintegration at bay. She began to speak in a low, rapid tone which gradually became louder and more hysterical. Her eyes darted about the loft, resting for a moment on one or another of the listening, frightened faces.

"You don't know what it's like to be betrayed. He was not a husband to me but a god, a god who reached down into the darkness and brought me light." For a moment her eyes settled on Carl. "He made me do things." She seemed lost, confounded by memories, then she forced her head up. "But he gave me dignity and hope. He gave me love, a child, and taught me that it was possible to live with this!" She banged her bony fist against the side of her head. Ian felt the blow in his own head. She began to beat her skull rhythmically, accentuating the words that were torn from her. "To live with it. To develop it, as he wanted. I had to. I would do anything for him, anything. I could not help myself. I did not want to help myself."

With a gasping sob, she let her fist drop. She staggered toward Ian. Behind her, briefly, he saw Peter's face. It was no longer human, but a twisted mask of hatred. She held out her arms, appealing. "Only to have it all taken away," she cried, "to be deprived of life itself by a stupid girl, your Pamela," she screeched, her eyes boring into Ian's. "I *felt* them making love." It was a moan, inconsolable. Her head sank onto her chest. Her thin arms were folded across her belly. "Felt it, every thrust, every movement. And when he came back she was in his eyes, her smell was on him." She made a retching noise, deep in her throat, as though the smell was still there, sickening her. "And he looked at me as if I was dead. He had shut me out of his mind." She turned unsteadily to Carl. "I begged him in your name, for your sake." She could not go on.

For a long time she was silent, swaying, her breath shaking her body. Nobody moved. Then she lifted her head again to Ian and snarled, "But she sent him such pretty, pleading little letters, and my Gunther was a man of honor, a Nazi and a German, a man who took his responsibilities seriously. He must go to her. He must help her." Gruffly she tried to imitate the voice with which Peter had spoken. Then she laughed, a bedlam sound. It seemed to give her strength. She straightened her back, lifted her ravaged head high.

"I gathered together all my strength, all my powers, all my abilities, all my being," she shouted, "and I killed him." The loft echoed with the terrible power of her voice. "On an empty road," she went on quickly, softly. "On an empty road on the way to the airport. I gathered all the lessons he had taught me and I used them against him. They said you could hear the explosion for miles. They could not piece the car together. I scattered him in little pieces on the earth."

Ian's attention shifted to Peter, who slumped forward. A moan of agony escaped him, but it was drowned in Regina's exulting voice.

"But even then I did not let him go, I vowed then that he would not rest, that I would bring him back. It was my greatest experiment, wasn't it, Gunther, to reach you beyond the grave? I knew, I swore, that one day, with the aid of his bastard, I could bring him back again. Only she got there first," she said, accusing Ian. She was swaying like a drunk, her arms sawing the air to keep some sort of balance. "She got her bastard back, but I found her out and I sent her to him, through her precious son, I sent her to join Gunther.

"But I would not, did not let her stay, did I? Reggie helped me, didn't you, Reggie?" A smile, a parody of the maternal smile twisted her features. She stumbled toward Reggie. "I sent her to him in her virginal white dress, but I kept her hat and her child, so that I could reach them and bring them back, to heap revenge on them."

She whirled around, staggering and stumbling across the floor. For a moment it seemed that she must collapse, but she managed to reach one of the bales. She sank onto it, her head drooping, her arms braced against the straw.

"Only nobody believed me," she wailed, a child wrongfully accused. "Even Asmussen, who knew what I could do, who valued my talents, even he betrayed me." Then she laughed, the sound racking her body. "But he believes now, oh yes, he knows now. You all know." Her eyes raked them all. She was panting like an animal. Her claw fingers hooked into the bale. "You all know and must believe." She lifted her head. Saliva hung like a cobweb from her mouth.

They all stared, unable to break free of her, all except Peter. With a scream that tore the air, he threw himself upon her, knocking her flat over the bale. His hands fastened viciously on her throat. Amazingly, Regina found some last store of energy. She fought him, snarling, scratching. Her fingers twined in his hair, jerking his head back. They rolled over on the floor, hissing like cats. Ian watched in horrified fascination.

"Help me, please help me."

Carl rushed forward and seized Peter's shoulders, tried to pull him off Regina. Ian's legs moved automatically. He grasped Peter's wrists. Below him, Regina appeared to be smiling, but her eyes bulged. Peter's grip was much stronger than he would have thought possible. He did not doubt as he pulled and pulled against the boy's phenomenal strength that something possessed him. Ian shouted to Carl. They took one wrist each, prying and pulling at his hands. Peter clung on, his nails tearing gouts of flesh from Regina's scrawny neck. Suddenly he ducked his head and sank his sharp teeth into Ian's hand. Somehow, Ian hung on. Carl pulled back and hit Peter hard on the side of the head. He grunted with surprise and released Regina. Ian fell back, dragging Peter with him. For a moment, the incredible strength seemed to leave his body.

"Take him, take him and go," Carl shouted.

Ian did not understand, he hesitated. Peter pulled against him, roaring.

"No," Regina shouted. She struggled to a sitting position. Blood ran down her neck. Shreds of pink flesh hung from her torn neck, exposing a vein. "Grizzle," she cried.

Suddenly, the loft became alive. A tempest gripped it. The floor shook. A bale sailed through the air and smashed onto the floor, bursting open. Another followed. It knocked over one of the lamps and flames darted up. The sharp smell of kerosene acted like a switch in Ian's mind. He pulled Peter back. The boy turned toward him, his eyes were puzzled. Ian ignored everything but the need to get him out. Using all his strength he dragged him across the bucking floor and pushed him bodily through the hole. Peter cried out. Dodging another bale, Ian heard him falling, crashing down the steps. He did not wait. His feet found the first rungs of the ladderlike steps and he descended.

In his fall, Peter had dislodged the other lamp. A pool of kerosene lay on the floor, flames trickling after it toward the far side of the barn. The boy was sitting on the ground, clutching his stomach, winded.

"Peter, you've got to get up, got to run."

Ian pulled at him so that his weight shifted, and by propping him against the steps, Ian was able to make him stand. Then he grasped Peter's wrist and began to run out of the barn, dragging his son along. As he stumbled across the yard, he felt the stinging pain in his hand where Peter had bitten it. For some reason, the pain drove him on. He slowed at the gate, pulled Peter forward, and thrust him ahead. The boy slumped on the front of the car. Ian hesitated. Dare he try and start it? Something hit him between the shoulder blades. Another missile, skimming his head, shattered the windshield of his car. Ducking low, he ran for the car, grabbed Peter and pulled him behind it.

Grizzle stood, lit by flames, just outside the barn.

She seemed quite passive, but rocks, clods of earth, even half-bricks, rose up from the littered yard and hurtled through the air, crashing onto the car. Some fell beyond it.

"We're going to make for the Hall," Ian told Peter. "Do you understand? I want you to keep down and run as fast as you can. Don't look back, don't stop. Just run."

Ian pulled the boy around, faced him toward the Hall, and gave him a push. He stumbled, righted himself, and then began to run. A stone whistled past his ear. Ian followed him. Instinct told him that it would be better if they split up, divided Grizzle's fire. Then, with a cry, he pitched forward. A rock had smashed into his left ankle. Pain shot up his leg. More rocks followed, thudding into the earth. But Peter was still running. Cautiously, Ian tried to stand. He yelped as his weight increased the pain in his ankle, but he managed to move forward. Crouched low, he limped off to the right. Peter was heading for the terrace steps, farther away. Grunting with pain, making slow progress, Ian concentrated his entire will on reaching the steps. With relief, he realized that the stones and rocks were falling short and more sporadically. He could no longer see Peter in the darkness and prayed that he had reached the safety of the terrace. He fell up the uneven steps, skinning his hand. Dimly, he made out the shape of the boy, huddled under the balustrade at the other end of the terrace.

"Peter, here, this way." He did not move.

Ian pulled himself up and clung to the balustrade. "Peter, you must try. Come on."

He reached down and tugged at the boy's arm. Peter stood up, swaying with exhaustion. Ian got an arm around him and willed him to walk back along the terrace. There had to be a way into the Hall, where, he hoped, Grizzle and the others could not, for the moment at least, reach them.

Flames lit the sky now and provided them with a rough light. The windows reflected back the orange glow. Half dragging Peter, but leaning on him to favor his hurt ankle, Ian walked along the back of the house toward the half-glass door he remembered. It seemed to him a miracle, a sign, that the door stood partly open. He did not pause to wonder why or how. He pushed Peter ahead. At once the boy's body stiffened.

"No," he said. "No."

Ian ignored him. He pushed the door open and thrust the boy through. He heard him stumbling in the darkness. Ian shut the door and leaned against it, panting with relief. His hands, on the door behind him, felt the key jutting from the lock. Thinking no further than the moment, he turned it and hurled the key away. It fell with an ordinary tinkle on the neglected parquet flooring, but the small sound seemed to be taken up, amplified by the silence in the house. The noise echoed away, moving through the house and then silence returned, enveloping them.

Reggie ran from the barn and threw himself down in the dust of the yard. His legs twitched convulsively. After a time, he rolled onto his side, drew his knees up, and covered his face with his hands. He made a soft mewling sound and rocked from side to side.

Grizzle felt the power leave her. Her stomach contracted and she gritted her teeth against the pain. Blood soaked through her underwear, trickled, then flowed down her legs. The stones were stubborn, immovable, inanimate objects. Her mind could no longer touch them. She saw the world anew; bright and crystal sharp. She stared around her, her face softened by a smile of wonder and recognition. This was how it was to be free, without abilities. She felt happy. Then the blood frightened her a little. She touched her legs with her fingers. She did not know what to do. Out of habit, she sought Regina. Her mind could not move.

"Regina?"

Linda led Carl out of the barn. Flames roared and crackled behind them. Dust and smoke billowed into the yard, spangled with bright sparks. Carl bent over, coughing. Linda held him, laid her cheek against his hair.

"You couldn't," she told him.

He twisted his head toward her. Tears streaked his smoke-smudged face.

"You tried, you couldn't get her out," Linda said urgently.

"Linda?"

"It's all right."

"I don't think, somehow—Linda, it didn't seem that she wanted to come. She didn't want me to help her. She wanted the fire." He straightened up then and turned back to the barn. The loft floor crashed down. The flames roared skyward, forcing them back from the heat, spattering sparks.

"It will be all right now," Linda told him. "It will."

He put his arms around her, tightly.

"It will be all right," she said looking into his eyes.

The smell revived Ian and almost at once sickened him. He was not sure that he had passed out. He was still leaning against the door, but he felt that time had passed. Had he closed his eyes, rested, and passed for a while into unconsciousness? The flames from the burning barn lit the room intermittently, confusing his vision.

"Peter?"

He pushed away from the door. Immediately his ankle protested, a sharp jab of pain turned into a slow, relentless throb. "Peter, where are you?" His voice sounded sepulchral in the silence. His saliva tasted bitter in his mouth. It was the smell. He looked around the large, flickering room for Peter, for the source of the smell. The fire seemed to die down and there were only shadows, gray and black, a pale orange glow on the opposite wall.

The smell was familiar and yet just out of reach. Familiar from a long way back, childhood. And then like a vision he remembered the small back garden at home and his mother's fondness for stocks. He saw her, bending to the thickly flowered blossoms. Purple, creamy white, palest pink. Stocks which filled the house with their sweetness, but that sweetness could turn rank overnight. He remembered the smell. The shut-up front parlor would be rotten with the smell of decomposing vegetable matter, the stalks slimy from the stagnant water in the vase. The smell was of stocks gone bad, but who would put stocks in an empty house?

"Peter?"

He was alarmed and it was all he could do to prevent himself gagging from the smell. He stumbled forward, wincing with pain. The house returned his voice, louder, distorted and, it seemed, mocking.

The fire outside flared up at that moment. Ian jerked his head. There must have been a fuel tank in the barn. The room grew brighter under his startled eyes. The sudden, sharp light became a cruelty, to show him the source of the smell.

It was propped against the wall, behind the open double doors.

The light was bright enough for him to see the dragged trail through the collected years of dust on the floor. He went closer, his throat clogged with bile.

Asmussen's head had been split open. A jagged fissure ran from the top of his cranium to the bridge of his nose. It was as though two giant hands had literally wrenched his skull apart. The effect was to make his face larger. The nose splayed, the eyes rolling sideways, threatening to slip off the sides of his face. And his mouth was forever contorted into a terrible, deathly oval. Looking at it, Ian could imagine the scream that must have issued from that mouth.

"Oh my God, oh no. Oh Jesus Christ, no," he murmured, clapping a hand over his mouth to control the rush of bile. He swallowed deliberately and repeatedly.

Putrefaction had set in. There was a blotched greenish fungus on the face, on the flopped-down, forgotten hands. As he stared he saw the man's thin suit also spotted with green, the fibers melting into the rotting flesh.

He had to get away from the thing. He began to cough and to fight again the almost irresistible desire to be sick. But even as he gulped the fetid, evil air through his mouth, he guessed that Peter, too, had seen it and fled into the next room.

He made for the front doors as fast as his injured ankle and heaving stomach would allow. He clung to them, pulling them closed behind him. The doors met with a hollow booming sound that rolled away through the house. He heard it over his gulping, retching noises. He swallowed and swallowed, for it felt as though his whole digestive system had been thrown into reverse. There was sweat and tears on his face. He leaned the back of his head against the doors.

Boom.

The sound brought his dream back, the dream of the gray rooms entering one into another. He opened his eyes, peered fearfully around him. The room was a gray space, fading off into infinity. It smelled of dust and of years of absolute quiet.

Twisting his head against the threatening silence, he could make out the windows. They seemed to admit a little light. Moonlight? The afterglow of the fire? He could make out a set of open doors.

"Peter?"

His voice echoed away, died in the house. He felt, with a cold shiver of fear, that the silence had become angry. And then he heard it—a shuffling, squelching noise. He could not locate it nor, at first, did he know what it was. Slowly, he understood the rhythm of slow, relentless, dragging steps. But they were liquid, oozing.

Then he saw a darting movement. A dark shape in the next room, beyond the open doors.

"Peter, Peter," he shouted.

The dark shape threw open the next pair of doors. The silence gathered itself, exploded into a deep sigh.

The rooms connected as in his dream. All the doors stood open, making a single, inevitable vista, and like all vistas this one had its focal point.

A moving puppet of light.

Afterward, he could not say where the light came from, but light there was, pallid and sickly. Against it, Peter was silhouetted while its focal point or source—Ian could not tell which—was the white, shuffling, squelching figure of Pamela.

His mind whirled in retreat.

A pillar of tears. Water ghost, fountain woman.

White, dripping, moving, her face paler than the ice-white saturated dress. Moving.

He felt a rush of cold air on his crawling skin. He smelled brackish, stagnant water which turned sweet with the hint of her perfume: *Je Reviens*. I return.

He heard the slush and squelch of her feet. He saw her pale, bloodless arms held out, offering, begging.

He saw Peter move forward, toward her.

"No, Peter. Peter, no."

He threw himself forward. Somehow he crossed the second room before his ankle turned, refused to bear him any farther. He pitched forward into the dust of the floor, jarring his shoulder.

He knew then what Regina had started and how it must finish.

Pamela had not come for him, to claim him as, in the first terrible, endless moments of her appearance, he had believed.

The silence sang. Her liquid steps oozed and slid, not toward him but Peter.

Pamela had come to claim her son.

He heard a cry escape the boy. A cry of recognition and joy, forced from his body in the voice of a man.

Pamela had come to claim her lover.

Ian raised his head from the floor. He saw her white arms encircle the boy. He saw her pale, dead face hang over his shoulder. He saw the response and clutch of passion.

In that moment he needed to believe that Regina had spoken the truth. As he saw them sink, entangled, to the floor, heard their sighs, he needed to believe that Peter's body was a vessel only, that it contained something unnameable that would be, must be exorcised by the obscene ritual that he saw and hated but could not prevent.

He closed his eyes. He covered his ears with his hands against the sounds of love or death that rose from them. He began to pray, to repeat every prayer he could recall. The silence of the house was transformed into their mingled moans and cries.

"Our Father Which art in heaven, hallowed be Thy name, Thy kingdom come . . ." His voice rose to a shout. He screamed the words, stripping them of meaning. His voice against their cries, their liquid, gurgling sighs and softly cooing moans, the sounds of love or death.

"God have mercy upon us, Christ have mercy upon us . . ."

Probably, he would never know which.

By starting out early, Liz avoided the traffic and made good time to Halford Hall. She had slept badly. Now that her mind was made up she was impatient to act. At first light she had given up the pretense that sleep would come, was wanted, and took a shower. She set off while the city still slept.

At the open gates she paused, sounded her horn, and then drove slowly up the main drive. Although Ian had described the place to her, she did not realize that she should have turned off the drive until she found herself in front of the Hall. She sounded her horn again, but only on the off chance. Ian had told her that the place was empty. She made a sweeping turn and drove back down the drive until she reached the road. The dew was still on the grass, glittering in the sunlight, and she felt optimistic. Whatever happened, she would be calm. She would not insist on the truth of anything in Fairlie's report, but she believed that it would alert Ian, make him at least ask some questions.

She recognized his car immediately. It blocked the entrance to the farmyard. The driver's door hung open, as though he had just leapt from it, and yet the vehicle had a forlorn, abandoned air. Liz got out of her car, smelling the air. The scent of burning was strong and even as she stood, one hand resting on the car door, black soot settled on her sleeve. She closed the door and walked briskly along the side of the road. The shattered windshield frightened her. She put her hand on the hood of Ian's car. It was cold.

"Ian?" she called, but only the worried cluck of chickens, scratching in the yard, answered her.

At first she could not believe her eyes. The barn had collapsed. Charred and still glowing beams rose up from a bed of ashes which covered a vast area. Flames spurted, licked, and died down. A pall of rank, bitter smoke and haze hung over the yard. But it was the presence of the silent, huddled young people that shook her most. They were like refugees, reminding her of scenes of devastation, war, famine, plague, the charnel images of international television news coverage.

Two of them, a boy and a girl, sat on the ground, close to the fire. Their arms were around each other and they could have been warming themselves at the remains of the holocaust. On the other side of the yard,

318

a red-headed boy leaned against a rusted piece of farm machinery. His knees were drawn up, his hands clasped around them. He stared at her with pale, unblinking, possibly sightless eyes. Liz approached the others.

"What happened? Are you all right?"

The girl looked at her. Her pretty face was streaked with soot.

"Who are you?" she asked, in a voice drained of all color, emotion.

"I'm a friend of Ian Woodford's. Do you know where he is?"

She turned back to the fire, as though she had not heard.

"What happened?" Liz repeated. She moved closer, careful not to alarm them.

"An accident," the girl said dully. "The barn burned down."

The boy looked at her then. His eyes were red with weeping. Tear tracks ran through the grime on his handsome face.

"Shouldn't you get the fire department?"

"It's too late," the girl said.

"Can I do anything, are you hurt? Was anyone . . .?"

"My mother," the boy said softly. He seemed to want to say more but was unable. He pointed silently at the embers, the ash, the faintly smoking timbers.

"Oh God, I'm sorry I . . . look, I'll call the police. I'll get help, okay?"

The boy and girl exchanged a look. He nodded slowly.

"There's a phone in the house," the girl said distantly, her eyes fixed on the fire.

Liz hovered near them for a moment, wanting to comfort them. She was uncertain what she should do.

"I won't be long," she said then, and began to walk quickly toward the house. They needed help. The police, somebody, must know what to do. She was halfway along the brick path when she saw the other girl, saw and heard her. She was sitting on the doorstep, her face pressed into her knees. A low keening came from her. "Oh my God," Liz said involuntarily. The girl was sitting in a pool of blood. Her legs were streaked with it. Liz ran to her, squatted beside her.

"Are you all right?" She touched the girl's shoulder. Her face was ashen, stricken. "I'm going to phone for help. How did you hurt yourself?" Slowly, Grizzle shook her head, and then it dawned on Liz what the blood was. She felt a mixture of pity and revulsion. "Don't you know what to do? Didn't anyone tell you?" Dumbly, she shook her head again. "Oh God," Liz whispered. "Look, it's all right. You mustn't be afraid." She stood up and ran back down the path. "Hey, you," she shouted to the girl by the fire. "Come here, please. You've got to help me. This girl . . ."

Like someone dazed, the fair girl stood up. Liz realized that they were all in shock and that they were completely docile and obedient. They would do anything she asked them. The girl stood for a moment, her hand resting on the boy's dark hair.

"Quickly," Liz called. "She needs help." Then she called back to the girl, "It's all right, we'll help you." She looked up anxiously at the other girl, who came slowly down the path. "She's bleeding. You understand?"

"Yes."

"She's menstruating. Have you got anything? Can't you help her?"

The girl looked puzzled.

"Grizzle?" she said.

"Is that her name?"

"Yes, Griselda. But we call her Grizzle. My name's Linda."

320

"Well, you take her inside, then, Linda. Help her. I'll telephone."

Liz pulled Grizzle to her feet. She seemed numb and probably, Liz thought, felt weak. Linda put her arms around the girl and touched her hair. Relieved, Liz went into the house. The phone was off the main hall, in a narrow passageway, beside the stairs. She snatched up the receiver, but there was no dial tone. Irritated, she jiggled the apparatus.

"Damn," she said.

Linda led Grizzle slowly across the hall.

"The phone's out of order," Liz said, going to them.

"Oh." Linda bent her head close to Grizzle's. "Grizzle, fix the phone now. Please, Grizzle? Fix the phone."

Very slowly, the girl turned her face and looked at Linda. It seemed to shine. A smile spread across it, lighting it.

"I can't," she said. "I can't anymore."

"Oh Grizzle." Impulsively, Linda hugged her. There were tears in her eyes.

Liz did not understand.

"I'll help you," she said. There was nothing else she could do.

Together, she and Linda helped the girl upstairs.

"I can manage now," Linda said, suddenly brisk. "I'll wash her and I've got everything she needs."

"All right," Liz said, feeling dismissed. "But also explain to her."

"Oh yes."

Liz turned back to the door.

"You wanted Mr. Woodford?" Linda said.

With a start, Liz realized that she had forgotten. The sight of the girl, frightened yet somehow radiant, had driven everything else from her mind.

"Yes."

Grizzle smiled at her from the bed.

"They're in the Hall," she said.

"What? Oh yes, yes I know. Thanks." She ran out of the room and down the stairs.

Peter felt them leave. He was himself again. He would never be able to describe it in any more detail than that.

He became himself again because they left. There were traces, a residue of memories. Something strange, violent, and unknown had happened to his body. He knew that and it embarrassed him. He had been torn by extremes of emotion, all muddled up. There had been joy in the grief and horror, a mindless raging horror in the pleasure and the loving. The two of them had used him. He did not want to remember that. What he would always remember was the moment when, in a fury that was also wonderful, they had burst out of him. He had felt his mind come together, lock, and he was free. He was himself again.

He would never be anyone else.

He moved. His hands brushed against something cold and sharp. He opened his eyes and stared into the bleached and empty face of a skull.

He screamed then. His scream tore through the house. He closed his eyes and pushed himself away from it. He heard bones rattle on the floor and then hands were touching him, lifting him as once, long ago, at the beginning of memory, hands had rescued him, warmed him. Hands and an old, painted face.

"Peter, Peter. Thank God."

He smelled his father, felt his warmth and strength. He clung to him, sobbing with relief.

Ian stood unsteadily, the boy's face pressed to his belly. Light filtered into the room and he had to look at the grotesque corpse.

"It's all over now. You're safe now," he said, clutching the boy's head tightly against him so that he should not see the complete, perfect skeleton on the damp floor. Should not see and understand the legs

322

drawn up. Should not recognize the tatters of a familiar white dress. The faint smell of old water lingered. How this could be, neither of them would ever know. The only important thing was that Peter should not see, should not understand. And ridiculously Ian thought that they could bury Pam now.

"It's all right," he said, turning his face from it.

"I know," Peter sobbed. "They've gone, it's stopped now. Dad?"

"Yes?"

"I'm not different, I'm not." He pulled his face away from Ian and looked up at him, imploring. "I'm not. I'm just ordinary and me. You've got to believe that."

"I know. Thank God," Ian said softly. "I know, but now you've got to help me. Stand up, help me."

Nodding, smiling against his happiness and relief which brought their own tears, Peter stood up. Ian put his arm around his shoulders, keeping him turned against the obscenity on the floor.

"I hurt my ankle. I'll have to lean on you."

"Okay, I can manage."

"Come on then."

Leaning on his son, Ian limped toward the double doors. He held Peter's head pressed against him, to prevent him from looking.

"Not this way," Peter protested.

"Yes, I threw the other key away."

He could not speak of Asmussen. He could not go into that room again except in the nightmares he knew he would carry from this house.

"I can find it." Peter tugged confidently against him.

"No." Ian raised his voice, commanding. "We must get to the front door."

Something in his voice, his fear, touched Peter. He opened the doors.

Boom.

They clutched each other. Behind them, as though blown by a wind, the other doors closed.

Boom.

The sound echoed around them. Neither of them wanted to go on. A trail of scuffed, damp dust led to the next pair of doors. It already seemed darker, as though the house, this unvisited part of the house, denied the light.

"Dad?"

"Just keep going. Hold on to me and keep moving."

They crossed the room. There was something bad in the air, in the silence. Only the fact that Ian had his teeth gritted against the shooting pain from his ankle prevented them from chattering.

Boom.

The doors slammed behind them. For a second it seemed as though they were trapped in this room, trapped in the rolling, mocking sound between two sets of closed doors. Peter looked at Ian, his eyes wide with fear. Ian nodded, urged him on.

Peter fumbled with the old brass handle. Suddenly it seemed that someone on the other side snatched the doors open for him. They faced the great foyer of the house. Chill marble floors, no windows, a staircase winding up into unspeakable darkness.

"Come on." Ian pulled his son into a diagonal path, making for the great, barred front door.

The silence thickened around them. Without knowing why, Ian felt sure that its source, the silent life of this house, was gathered at the top of the stairs. Resolutely, pulling Peter with him, he set his back against it. The hairs stood on the back of their necks.

"Dad?"

"The lock, Peter. Quickly."

The skin on Ian's back contracted, winced from some awful unwanted touch.

The lock was old and rusted. Peter could not turn the key. He tried with both hands, but it would not move.

"I can't," he said, despair and fear clotting his voice. "Dad, I can't."

Ian released the boy, leaned against the door, and took the big key in his hands. He felt as though the lock fought him.

"Oh please God," he said. "Please."

It turned. The lock snapped back. A crack shattered the silence, drove it back for a moment. But the door would not open. Behind them the silence gathered again, humming, pressing, coming closer.

"The bolt," Peter shouted. "Up there, look. I can't reach."

Ian heard the hysteria in his voice, but he looked up, instinctively reaching for the stout, vertical bolt which held the door fast. He grasped it, the sharp handle biting his palm. It squeaked and rasped.

"Dad." Peter pressed close to him.

Ian felt sweat break out on his face.

"Dad, it's coming."

He did not understand if Peter spoke of the bolt or of the other thing, the silence welling behind them. With a cry, he felt the bolt move. He used all his strength. Flakes of rust showered into his face, his hair. The bolt gave.

Peter threw one arm around him and with the other pulled the door open. Sunlight burst in where it had not entered for a long time. They both felt the house recoil behind them. It seemed to Ian that something thrust him forward. He lost contact with Peter and felt the sharp stab of gravel on his knees, his palms. Peter threw himself sideways, saw his father slumped on all fours, his head hanging down, and it seemed that a black cloud gusted from the house, over his father. It was broken by the sunlight.

It was all right then, safe. He knew it. He ran to his father, his teeth chattering.

"Ian! Ian!"

They both leapt to hear the calling voice. Peter threw his arm across his father's back, to protect him.

"Ian, thank God you're all right."

325

"Liz?"

He could not believe it. The sun tricked his eyes. She ran toward him, sunlight on her hair.

"Are you all right?"

"Liz? Yes, I . . ."

"He's hurt his ankle," Peter told her.

"Oh God, I was so worried. I . . ."

Peter stood up and walked a little way off. Even though he was still a bit dazed, he felt that it was the right thing to do. Ian knelt on the gravel, hugging the woman. She touched his face. They both spoke at once. There were tears on her cheeks. Peter looked back at the house. It was okay now. The light drove back the shadows. Drove them back, but did not banish them. He shivered. But for the first time, he saw the windows, the many windows, shine with reflected sunlight.

"Peter?"

He thought they had forgotten him. He had felt an old, remembered loneliness.

"Yes?"

"Help me, help me up."

He went to his father. The woman stood on the other side of Ian and suddenly smiled at Peter.

He ducked his head away, embarrassed.

They helped Ian up. He pulled Peter close against him, hugging him.

"This is Liz."

"Hello," he said.

"Are *you* all right?" she asked.

"Yes."

Then neither of them knew what to say.

"You wait here," Liz decided. "My car's up by the Farm. I'll bring it."

"No," Ian said, restraining her.

"But Ian, it won't take a minute."

"No, we'll come with you."

"Yes," Peter said, pleased.

He looked at Ian, who nodded.

"We don't want to stay by the house. We'll come with you."

She looked puzzled. Her eyes questioned Ian, but he simply began to limp away, leaning on Peter.

"Come with us," Peter said.

"Yes, of course," she said, putting her arm around Ian. "Here let me . . ."

They reached the grass. In the distance, they could make out a splash of blue, her car.

"Liz will stay, I hope," Ian asked and answered for her.

Tears made her eyes smart. She felt foolish, and relieved. She wanted to cry and laugh and hug them both, all at once.

"Yes, I'd love to."

"Good," Peter said, satisfied. Then, "For always?"

"You ask too many questions," Ian said, squeezing him.

"Talking of questions," Liz said quickly, for she knew that it was too soon, yet, to answer that one. "I've got hundreds. What on earth happened to you? What were you doing in that place? What happened?"

Ian felt Peter's body stiffen a little.

"Later, love," he said. "Let's just get to the car." But he knew that he would never be able to tell her. He would never know, not for certain, and what he might know was something that would remain always a secret, a bond between him and Peter. He looked at his son and felt close to him at last.

They walked on, Liz helping him as the ankle became more painful, but Peter taking most of his weight. He felt dizzy. He smelled the smoke and lifted his head, sniffing.

"There was a fire," Liz said.

"We know," Peter told her.

"It was awful. Those poor kids."

Ian felt his throat tighten.

"I came up here first, looking for you. They were shocked. The barn burned down completely. They said that the mother of one of them, a dark boy . . ."

"Regina," Ian said. He felt Peter tremble.

"God, I'd forgotten all about her," Liz said. "That's why I came, I—"

"What happened?" Ian demanded, his voice harsh with fear.

"She was burned, in the barn. She must have been trapped, I suppose."

Ian thought of her, burned, like a witch of old and could find no pity, no sorrow, only a sense of the fitting.

"It doesn't matter now," Peter said. "Does it, Dad?"

"No," he agreed. "No. It doesn't matter now."

With relief, he leaned against the side of Liz's car, raising his left foot from the ground. Liz walked on, opened the passenger door. Peter, standing by him, looked up. He reached for Ian's hand and gripped it tightly.

They were all there, standing just in front of Ian's car, Carl with his arm around Linda, Grizzle smiling, Reggie without any expression at all. Ian saw them through a mist of dizziness. They smiled, what seemed like one, intercommunicating, spreading smile. Ian pushed away from the car, hobbled to the door which Liz held open. She helped him in, bent to make sure his left foot was comfortable. She closed the door and looked from Peter to the vacant, smiling children and felt helpless. She should do something. She looked back at Peter.

"We're going home now," he told them firmly. "We're going home." He did not look at them again, but got into the car and put his hand on Ian's shoulder.

"Shouldn't we do something?" Liz said, fastening her seat belt.

Ian shook his head briefly. Peter squeezed his shoulder.

328

"They'll be all right now," Peter told her confidently. "We can go home."

Liz started the car, reversed down the road, and then headed for the main gates.

The children watched the car leave, then turned back to the dying ashes.